SWEETHEARTS

SWEETHEARTS

A NOVEL

A. M. KRICH

CROWN PUBLISHERS, INC.

NEW YORK

Copyright © 1983 by A. M. Krich

Grateful acknowledgment is made to Grove Press, Inc.,
for permission to reprint lines from *Waiting for Lefty,*
copyright 1935, © 1962 by Clifford Odets.

Published by Crown Publishers, Inc.,
One Park Avenue, New York, New York 10016, and
simultaneously in Canada by General Publishing Company Limited
Manufactured in the United States of America

Library of Congress Cataloging in Publication Data

Krich, Aron M., 1916–
Sweethearts.

I. Title.
PS3561.R47S9   1983   813'.54   82-17972
ISBN: 0-517-547449

10 9 8 7 6 5 4 3 2 1

FIRST EDITION

For J.—who knows why

Contents

SWEETHEARTS

· Prologue ·

No Sour Cream in Venice

So this is Venice! I still pinch myself. I can't believe I am living here. Not Venice, California, but the other one, where Casanova got the clap. I abide with God and Valium in a three-hundred-year-old house that looks like the set for *Rigoletto*. It tilts on a *rio*, the smallest kind of canal, whose Adriatic tides sail waterlogged dolls nestled in the springs of gutted sofas. Why are their eyes always open? And always blue?

I look down on this surrealist garbage from a terrace on which I have planted a city boy's farm. I've got a lemon tree that comes up like a slot machine with two fruit hard as stones. And an almond tree with blossoms by Fabergé. And a trough of little strawberries, *fragolini*. Every morning before breakfast I find and eat one.

"Comes the Revolution," the guy on the soapbox said, "you'll eat strawberries and sour cream!"

There is no sour cream in Venice.

Sometimes I watch a particular piece of flotsam make its way past the empty palace of the late Queen of Yugoslavia and out into the lagoon. It will end up against the battlements of the insane asylum. There are two little islands of the mad out there, one for those who have simply lived too long and one for the truly *pazzo*. They have their own waterbus, marked *Ospedale*. I can see it passing. It usually makes the trip empty except on Sunday when families bring candy and flowers to the ones who have had the *disgrazia*—the Italian word means accident, not disgrace—to be in the nuthouse. Was I knocking at its door?

· 1 ·

"Knock, knock!"

"Who's there?"

"Chester."

"Chester song at twilight."

When I lift my eyes I can see all the glories of Venice. Palladio's white *Salute,* the golden ball atop the old Customs House, the checkered facade of the Doges' palace, the pointillist dots of tourists crossing the Bridge of Sighs and the Byzantine domes of Saint Mark's itself.

When we were kids back in Jersey you were supposed to spit three times when you passed a Catholic church. Don't ask me why. And don't ask me, "What's a nice Jewish boy doing in a town where there are more churches than saloons?"

There are eight hundred other Jews in Venice. But Shylock's cousins have been here too long to know the answer. They don't speak a word of Yiddish, and my Italian isn't too good.

I could ask Kiddy, my wife of thirty years, but she's flown the coop again. This time I at least know what town she's in. As far as the neighbors are concerned, she has gone to Perugia to study Italian at the *Università per Stranieri.* The University for the Estranged, they mean! Nobody digs that I still don't have an address for her. Only this phone number, 30123, which I just got in the mail.

"If you ever . . ." her note says.

Like that, with three dots. Suspense. And no signature. Three guesses?

"All alone by the telephone, waiting patiently for yooooo!"

Knowing Kiddy the way I do, she's probably hoping I'll dash up there and tear the joint apart to find her. She'd like that.

"That's what a *real* man would do! That's *real* love. Really *real!*"

She's seen too many Bogey movies. Kiddy thinks I look like him. Something around the eyes, and my teeth are loose. "Here'sh lookin' atchoo, kid!" He got paid for busting ass and breaking up the furniture. Picture me running around Perugia, all chocolatey from the candy factory—kisses they make, *baci*— stopping people in the *strada.*

"*Mi scusi,* who was that lady I saw you with last night?"

"That was no lady, that was your wife."

For crying out loud, Kiddy, come on home! I need you to tell me how I got my ass in this sling.

You'll say you brought me here to save my life. Probably

true. Led me out of the fleshpots of Egypt, penthouses of nouveau riche psychoanalysts looking across the Hudson toward the glow of the refineries in Jersey, toward Palisades Park, from which, on a hot night, you could still hear the smacks of kisses we once stole in the Tunnel of Love.

There had been a sunset over Jersey when those Moran tugs had nudged the *Cristoforo Colombo* out of the pier at Fiftieth Street and into the Narrows. It was a beaut, the kind that's improved by dapples of smog as though Turner had touched it up. From the rail we had watched the captain and mates with bullhorns talk her out to sea. I had my last look at the Empire State Building and thought of King Kong scrambling up its tower, those goggled guys in biplanes pumping lead into his broken heart, Kong's minstrel eyes so human and lovesick, wanting Fay Wray back in his paw, a true love, platonic really, the sexy stuff being only in her screaming and kicking, her dress torn in just the right places to get us hot and bothered about girls who are the same size we are and not helpless.

We had strolled on the deck where the shuffleboard was laid out. We were in a movie. I took deep, ostentatious breaths. One lung said to the other: "This is the stuff I've been telling you about!"

We went to the first sitting for dinner, were given a table all to ourselves from where we could see the same glittering ocean my father had crossed the other way, eating all the herrings in steerage because everybody else was sick. "You can't get such herrings today! Right from the barrel!" His son was eating supreme of chicken and washing it down with Orvieto wine.

So here we were, holding hands on the white tablecloth, Kiddy wearing her wedding ring that, during our cold wars, she usually took off and left conspicuously on the bathroom shelf next to the Water-Pik. We were in the corner of the lovers, *l'angolo degli amanti* our waiter called it.

His name was Luigi. And with our pasta we learned that he had been a POW in Scottsbluff, Nebraska. That's where he had become a waiter, serving officers and himself immense American breakfasts.

"Cornflecks, em en haygs, horanche jus! So many thing! I say: 'Make my wife prigioner, make my babies prigioner!'" He had been better off as a prisoner than he had ever been in his life.

It was touching. America had everything. Even a good

heart. So why were we running away from it?

We were excited to be going by boat. The *Colombo* would be stopping in Lisbon, Palma, Majorca, Naples, and Athens before docking in Venice. I saw the voyage as a second honeymoon, classier than our first, sitting up all night on the coach to Miami. Kiddy's folks lived there. We stayed with them, used the beach where old *Arbeiter Ring* members sang Yiddish folk songs, caught a fish striped like a zebra, won a long shot on a mudder at Gulfstream, and pretended we had not been living in sin for more than a year.

I liked Kiddy's father. He had a tintype of himself as a cornet player in a tsarist army band. He still had the horn. Kiddy got her high cheekbones from him. Altogether he looked very un-Jewish in his braided uniform and Kaiser Bill moustache. I didn't get along well with my new mother-in-law. She had strong, unyielding opinions on everything. And they got stronger as the years went by. She had the look on her face of someone who has discovered the truth once and for all.

Me, I get into these terrors of indecision. I don't know what to do with myself, for myself or the people who say they love me. Including you, Kiddy.

"We were childhood sweethearts," you tell everybody.

It makes a good story. How our mothers had aired us side by side in those high-wheeled, lacquered baby carriages of the immigrant *belle epoque;* how we'd both worn a cloth locket with a clove of garlic sewn in to keep us safe from polio during the great epidemic after the War to End All Wars; how we both had been "revolutionaries"—significant pause—in high school and you got up at 5 A.M. to give out leaflets in front of the RCA plant; how I had called you flamingo in my college poems—yes, flamingo; how we'd both married other people, then met again quite by accident—fated—and how I left this Well-known Person for you; and how you typed all my poems . . . *As in a pawnshop window you will find, a hundred watches stopped at the fateful hour . . .*

I like that. My God, thirty years ago. *New American Writing.* I'm getting as bad as Kiddy. The only thing I can hang onto is the past.

"We were childhood sweethearts."

When else are people sweethearts? What were we? Boyfriend, girl friend, above-the-belt neckers, twosome, going steady, *amanti*. There probably is no word for what I think we were. If I found one, it would not be the one Kiddy wants to hear. "Sweethearts! Sweethearts!" Nelson Eddy and Jeannette MacDonald. Fifty-five candles on her cake and her sentimentality nags her. Whatever she has, she seems to want less of and nothing is enough.

"Wanting means you're still alive. Alive."

When Kiddy gets carried away, she says things twice. An excessive person. Once, she got so carried away, she said, "I pity the girl who marries you!"

Her indignation is a kind of love. And I guess I must like it. That's what *he* said, Dr. Finzi, the shrink I went to right here in Venezia. It was kind of weird, one funnydoctor talking to another one—both Jewish, too—but we were from different schools. He was Kleinian and kept hinting that Kiddy was my internalized mother. You know, the kind you swallow when you're three months old, the "bad breast" and all that. I had been sucking on Kiddy's long enough.

Same way I'm shlurping this highball. Better lay off the juice! If I don't watch out, I'll get into a crying jag. "Cahnah-diahn Cloob." Our grocer gets it especially for me. Medicine for my heart, he thinks. Doesn't know about my twelve o'clocktails. He envies the American professor who flies—poof! poof!—across the *Atlantico,* back and forth, as though he were taking a hundred-lire waterbus to San Marco. There it is, its lead roofs matching the color of the glittering dusk. A pretty sight if you didn't have anything on your mind. A fucking picture postcard.

It's one of those very still Venetian twilights, serene—that's why they call her *Serenissima*—when history hangs from the clouds and the air is so heavy with echoes you can almost taste them on your tongue and want to answer. The only real sound is the creaking of the gangplank to the waterbus.

Coming into the Giudecca Canal, a white ship is riding low and silent. She's flying the hammer and sickle and her name is *Odessa*, but it says Odecca in Cyrillic. Kiddy's mother came from there. And Mischa Elman and Jascha Heifetz. My mother-in-law had been apprenticed as a seamstress when she was twelve years old. She made this bathing suit for Kiddy.

"I had the first bikini in America."

And she's got the snapshot to prove it, making a face like Joan Crawford, all set for Central Casting. Went up for the part with her roommate Shelley, also known as Shirley. Shelley got the contract. Kiddy got me. Lucky girl!

It must be awful to be married to a man who can't make up his mind. Diagnosis: obsessive compulsive character.

"But . . . but . . ."

"But me no buts!"

How would Kiddy be with another man? I can't stand the thought. Am I going to be a two-time loser?

Oh, nuts! Keep this up, I'm going to end up on Bughouse Square. Need a refill. Give my right arm for some Jack Daniels. An arm *and* a leg at Harry's Bar. Fussy now, an A.K.—*alter kocker*. Used to have a cast-iron stomach. Gee, as a kid, drank anything—Panther's Piss at Chapel Hill, bathtub gin from Riviera Club where Kiddy was cigarette girl . . .

Suddenly, I am moved by an earthquake of love. It is a tremor of 5 on the Richter Scale, the epicenter far off but strong enough to shake me out of the bureaucracy of existence. The building that is quivering, breaking up into small pieces here and there, is me. But I am not "cracking up." In this moment, I am excruciatingly lucid, full of love, purged of shitty meanness. It comes to me that my situation with Kiddy has a meaning beyond the suffering of a broken marriage. Because of it, I have been thrown into the flow of everyday life from which I have so long felt cut off. I am many of one, a statistic as ordinary and profound as the contact of two skins.

And how many epidermises, and how many lives have touched mine in this way? Sweethearts, every single one—the mystery and the privilege and the gratitude.

And I have a sudden desire for happiness, unexpected and undeniable. A surge of tenderness is taking over, headlong and desperate and blind to everything but itself. And pity, too, which Kiddy is not here to throw back at me and couldn't because I know it is the real thing, *caritas,* and it is for both of us.

Where's that phone number? *Payroogeeah: tray, zayroh, oonoh, dooeh, tray.* Person to person. I'll have to spell Kiddy for the operator. There's no *k* in Italian. The code word is in German, for some reason, *Kursaal.* Hall of cure? I'd better just say *kappa.* Then *i,* as in *Italia.* And *d.* As in Detroit? No, Dante. And again, Dante. And *y* as in New York.

"Centralino, per piacere, la Signora Kiddy . . ."

The phone will ring. And I'll be asking Kiddy for our first date.

From Ace to Ape

· 1 ·
My First Vulva

I go to sleep to the splash of a gondola oar and wake up hearing the Oedipal trolley car rumbling down Avon Avenue. I'm back there, in kindergarten, making four-color horse reins, playing the big bass drum, doing everything you were supposed to do. What a mistake to do anything else! "Stay in your own backyard!" That's what I should have done.

Stayed in the warm demography of a row of identical six-family tenements on a street in what was, at that time, the fourteenth largest city in the United States. I hesitate to tell you its name because it was the butt of many jokes by vaudevillians, not a few of whom came from Newark themselves. Noo-uhk, they called it. Not New-ark like the one onto which Noah took the animals two by two. We only had the Newark Bears, a Yankee farm club, and the world's biggest mosquitoes, which bred around the industrial dreck in the cattail meadows between us and Powhattan's island.

Newark specialized. It manufactured pencils, condoms, jewelry, and expatriates. A great exporter of people, Newark was. Its best? Who can say? Exiled, we became cynical intellectuals who said that our hometown was "the asshole of creation."

Newark took and it gave. It stands in the shadow of New York, the Statue of Liberty at its swampy edge still holding her light as she once did for the doctor looking into the eyes of frightened immigrants on Castle Garden.

My father's eyes, thank God, were clean of the dreaded trachoma. He would have to keep them open. No sooner had he passed down the line when some Irish joker with a rubber stamp took away his God-given name. From Boris's hand he took a copy of *Taras Bulba* and into Benny's he put a shovel with which to dig for gold in the streets.

In a faded photograph, I can see that my mother, too, had clean eyes, dark and sincere, set in an oval face framed by braids of shining black hair. She walked through the gates of America into a factory where she rolled five-cent cigars with other girls from steerage. While they worked, they sang about the immigrant cousin "with cheeks like red pomegranates."

My mother, too, was given a new name, queenly, Tudor, suitable to the neighborhood where, after the usual heartbreaking greenhorn adventures, my parents came. Its street names were incongruously Shakespearean. Avon was bounded by Stratford, by Chadwick, by Belmont, by Seymour. There, upon Avon, Anne and Ben waited for me to arrive.

I came COD.

My mother's deliverer was an ageless, energetic little lady who seemed to be related to everybody on both sides of my family. There had been among its members some dangerous liaisons, cousins from one *dorf* marrying cousins from another. As though there could possibly be more than one of her, this lady was always called the *Moomeh Malkeh*. She was a professional midwife from the old country, an *accousherkeh*.

There was a doctor in attendance. But he was not trusted. Anyhow, he seems to have been drunk and asleep during the nativity. He is famous for having said to my father, who suggested I be given castor oil, "If the baby needed castor oil, he would have been born with a small bottle already!" How could such a sage physician have ended his days in an insane asylum?

They say that in her hurry to attend me, the *Moomeh Malkeh* put her high-buttoned shoes on the wrong feet. Still, with left shoe on right foot, she hopped—the trolley had already stopped running—to pull me into the world. My father watched, supervised as he has everything else in my life. To this day, I am not sure he approved.

It was the *Moomeh Malkeh* who gave me my first spanking. I hadn't done anything bad. I was only asking, "What's going on? Where am I? Who am I?" Things like that. My first blind demand of the world and the first experience of my flesh. Smack! Right on the *tuchas!*

The price of pleasure was imprinted on me. First the smack, then the soothing hand, the delicate balance that keeps us from being entirely lonesome in the world. Love, the contact of two epidermises.

From the *Moomeh Malkeh*'s initiation I might have learned not to ask too many questions. "Don't ask! Just take!" But try as I have, I have never been able to enter this paradise of the ordinary. I've done some taking, of course. And more than my share of asking. Wouldya? Couldya?

Take this. Walking down Fifth Avenue, not too long ago, I meet an old flame from the days of adolescent inexperience and slightly sullied innocence in Prohibition-time Newark. She still lives there, but at its edge, in the suburbs even beyond Wequahic Park where, in my day, the *allrightniks* lived one family to a whole house.

Selma has probably been shopping in Saks for some expensive corselet, the kind Sophia Loren and Kiddy wear. She's still statuesque, her figure's fuller, but her face is marvelously unchanged. As mine is to her.

"Imagine! After so many years!" Etc., etc. Selma goes on easily, unself-conscious, sure of herself. You can see she takes first and asks afterward. How I envy her! She knows her exact place in the world. It may be local, but it is all hers. Fame has no price for her. Let others knock their heads against its stone wall. They are doing it for her.

"I saw your name on that book, and I said to Howie . . ." I am supposed to know who Howie is. Probably owns condemned buildings in the Third Ward. "'It's him. It's got to be. Unh, huh. *Varieties of Sexual Behavior!*'" Selma gives me a special look.

She remembers! Forty years ago. That corner of the no-questions-asked saloon, gin rickeys sweating on the table, my thumb between her legs sealing her sex like a bung in a barrel of beer, she rocking against my hand, letting herself get hot in the face but still chatting, looking around the room as if she were expecting a singing telegram. What a woman!

"Would you believe I'm a grandmother? My Barbara, my oldest . . ."

The last of the red-hot grandmothers! If Selma was a virgin that night, the nick of her hymen was stretched wide enough for her Barbara to come popping out, all dressed to take tap dancing.

"You were so intellectual, so well informed. I knew you would get where you wanted. You and Leslie Fiedler."

Selma walks off. Hup! Hup! Hup!

"Get where you wanted!" I have an urge to run after her and tell her I got there, wherever it was, by accident. But she's gone, all in one Playtex piece.

Gone, too, the house in which, once upon a time, there lived Mama Bear and Papa Bear and Little Baby Bear. The very neighborhood is gone. After being half destroyed by an inner-city riot, whole blocks became an open prison for the poor, projects raised by avid mayors. In my day, the mayor was Jewish. Then he was Italian. Now he's black.

Once, six families lived in every house. Three tiers of flats faced Avon Avenue where the trolley ran, three looked out on the clotheslines attached by pulleys to high poles planted in the yard. Gone. All gone, that good life when everything was where it was supposed to be. When there was still a front and a back.

All the houses in our row were alike, built at the same time, about 1900, I guess, with stucco fronts crisscrossed by fake wood beams. I didn't know it then, but they were like the house they showed you in the real Stratford-on-Avon that was supposed to be Shakespeare's. Bigger, of course, and with an iron fire escape on the second and third floor and a weighted ladder that the big guys were always pulling down to "chin the bar."

The front faced Avon Avenue with its comings and goings. The trolley, rumbling and sparking. The milkman and his horse that was so smart, waiting at each house all by himself, going and stopping without any whoa or giddyap. And, sometimes, fire engines. The corner drugstore exploding with a boom and an orange flash and a stink of medicine and *schnapps*. Perlmutter the druggist was a bootlegger. His still had blown up. And, one morning at dawn, elephants, clank, clank, the jumbos in front and the babies behind, each holding the other by the tail. Barnum and Bailey's had unloaded in the railroad yard around the corner. Or a policeman blowing his whistle and hitting his club three times on the curb, a signal to all precincts. Or a family evicted on the sidewalk. And the umbrella man, and the knife grinder, and the peddlers. "Greps, wawdeemelons, benenehs!"

The back let out on a jungle of untended gardens shaded by six lines of wash that hung like scarecrows over the weeds and some wild sunflowers. We ate the seeds. Here grew a giant pussy willow, the first tree I knew by name. Of other flowers, we knew only the dandelion called, I don't know why, "pee in bed." Oh, yes, we also knew "poison ivory."

Savage cats roamed this antediluvian world. We hunted them with bows and arrows made from the spines of broken umbrellas. More than Freud's primal scene, their feline moans and shrieks caused us to connect mating with murder and lunacy.

The houses were separated from each other by an alley about four feet wide. This was where you found the wooden steps that took you up and down a hundred times a day, killing your feet. That's why people were always hollering out, "Ikey, throw down Mikey!"

These steps, so important to my psychosexual development, led to wooden balconies with slatted railings which joined the flats of the front to those of the back. These were called porches. From the porches we were called, as by a muezzin, to eat, to sleep, to run to the grocery and get "a half of a quarter" of belly lox. From this heaven came pennies for ices, for Jujubes, for baked sweet potatoes. From here, like patrons of the arts, we threw nickels wrapped in newspaper to wandering accordionists.

From here, we heard of unheralded deaths and unexpected births, identified only by location in the tenement.

"Who you say?"

"From the front."

"Which one the front?"

"Next door the front."

"A *zvilling!*"

"Two twins!"

"You're joking!"

"I should live so!"

"At her age!"

"Two already in high school."

"So she'll have two in kindergarten!"

"She needs like a hole in the head!"

"Another hole sewed up she needs!"

The hole! How did one baby get into the *lechel?* And how did two come out? Papa did something to Mama. But what? But why?

Many things were called down from the third floor to the first, all punctuated by beating out of pillows, but they were always endings. Nobody told you how they began.

The porches were places of denouements. From their barriers, mothers would threaten to throw themselves for a bad
mark in arithmetic. "Murderer!" they would cry out if you did
not pass. God forbid you should be held back! I always passed. I
even skipped the first grade. I had already been parked in kindergarten for two years while my mother studied English in the
Americanization classes next door.

What grade was I in when Fanny opened my eyes? Or, more
accurately, when I opened them for her? She gave me an eyeful.

I think her real name was Faygel, not inappropriate, mne-
monic enough. For Faygel, you know, means bird. "Hail to thee
blithe spirit, *faygel* thou never wert!" Fanny was more up to date,
a more American version of her given name. Like us, Fanny
lived on the top floor, desirable because nobody would be walking on your head. Fittingly, Fanny lived in the back, in the *versus,*
as Krafft-Ebing had genteelly Latinized that way of entering.
Her door was at the last turning of the steep wooden steps.

Be patient with these details of topography. Up and down
are as central as front and back to my delicious trauma. And for
the more serious reader, there will be the broader unconscious
significance of climbing stairs, *steigen,* of mounting, so brilliantly
teased out of Viennese dreams by the Old Man. *"Mein goldene
Siggy!"* his mother called him. Much dream time was spent by his
patients ascending stairs, losing their purses, unfurling umbrellas, and slipping penile feet into vaginal shoes.

Continuing in this golden vein, let me point out that in
Siggy's scheme the third floor would correspond to the Superego. It sits there like a toupee on the head of the Ego which is
the second floor. Rampant instinct should be on the first. That's
where Fanny should have lived. No! Better yet, in the cellar, in
the cellar with the diamond coals of the Id ready to burst into
flame!

Fanny was a recent immigrant, a greenie still. Her husband
was a baker, of bagels perhaps, or even of those charlotte russes,
real whipped cream with a cherry on the top, that you could get
only in winter. At any rate, Fanny's man—man and husband are
the same word in Yiddish—worked at night. Was that why he
was so pale? He could have been an example of the loss of
strength through that very excess our street gang would soon be
warned against. Maybe Fanny had sucked away his blood. Now it
occurs to me that maybe Fanny was always in her petticoat be-

cause it was the other way around. Why should she get dressed?

I was old enough to catch my mother's disapproval of Fanny. She did not go to Americanization classes. She sang too much. She was always in her petticoat. She was Lilith, round and pert and rosy with a dimpled face crowned by a fuzzy helmet, the new "boyish bob" of blond ringlets. One of those small, jazzy women on whom every part is marked with the instructions of a do-it-yourself kit: mouth to sing, boobies to bounce, legs to do the Charleston. I know that if every clock in the world were turned back, I would recognize her immediately. Peppy, always singing, Fanny was. "We got onions and scanions and all kinds of fruit; but yes, we have no benenehs."

Each tenant—in those days this meant the lady of the house—was responsible in turn for scrubbing her own flight of stairs. Would it have been once a week on the eve of the Sabbath? The steps had rather high risers. I usually ran up and down them as fast as I could, my innocent hand sliding along the bannisters rubbed smooth by other hands calloused with work and sin. What was my hurry? Where was I running?

At each landing there was a short bend before the ascent. One day, on my way up, turning one of these landings, I saw Fanny on her knees scrubbing away. She was still near her own door and the angle was steep, almost vertical. Her short petticoat was hiked up around her haunches. From where I was standing, Fanny's arm began at her buttocks. As she scrubbed away, her shift lifted and fell like a theater curtain, letting her prima donna bow and take applause.

Fanny had a merry ass, plump but not steatopygous, not one on which you could sit still. East and west went the soapy rag, swinging two pink continents back and forth. And there, between Europe and America, a blond sun was shining and a little bird fluttered, a cornsilky little thing swooped here and there but never out of sight.

What should I tell you? Nobody wants to write fiction about himself. I was too engulfed in wonder to think or say. I looked. Only looked.

Fanny stayed revealed. She twisted her head. She was, I swear, giving me a sly and mischievous, a teasing look, homing in on me with what I now know were sex-ray eyes.

"Jump! Jump over!"

I did as I was told. I always do as I am told.

My first vulva! Or was it? I suppose I had had earlier, innocent opportunities to peek. Coney Island lay close enough to Newark for us to be carted there in moving vans lined with benches. Like those antiwar demonstrators of the sixties, we laughed and sang in the Black Maria. But the tailgate was open. We were free to jump out on the Hoboken Ferry that still smelled of the piss and dung of dray horses.

These outings, organized by various immigrant societies, were an untraumatic form of sex education. You might go to the steam room with your father, but you were taken to the Ladies section to be undressed. Or to the Ladies toilet when you had to go. Somebody had to lift you up. And hold your *schmeckele*.

"A life on your belly button!" You were praised when you asked in time. *"Ah leben oif dein pupik!"*

Your *pupik* was endowed with a separate, special life. Was this Freud's displacement from below? It would be unlikely for a Jewish mother to say so tenderly, "A life on your dickie!"

What did I see in the Ladies lockers? I suppose I saw what we later called "the whole world." I was too young to be affected by the sights of the *bain Turc*. Naked we come into the world and naked we leave it. But in between hide that spot of time where, among urine and feces, we are born; worship and revile it. Cunt, D. H. Lawrence's "terrible thing of suffering, privilege and mystery."

And haven't I seen them, long and short and tall, spread-eagled on the velvet boxes of those peep-show burlesques, Candy Barr and Sugar Kane bent to the points of the compass, their pony hair touching their always silver shoes, rolling their tongues at half-crazy, unshaven old men? Me among them. "Let's see it, baby!" But I didn't pay admission to see Fanny's.

And didn't I see a powerful black woman inch up to a table's corner, lift her skirt, and pick up a folded dollar bill? The snatch! But I was drunk in the underworld of jazz where white boys don't go anymore.

And didn't I see a 16mm Marilyn teasing a Coke bottle into her crack? But that was before Joe DiMaggio, before Stanislavski, before Arthur Miller, before fame and Nembutal.

And haven't I courted them? And haven't I married them?

And didn't I sit among the sexologists in that professorial room, the shades drawn, where it was so silent, so cold all you could hear was the projector's chattering teeth? And all you saw was that jelly-red gash and the tips of two fingers, rubbing, pulling, beating that clit like dirty laundry. And Dr. Masters, so serious, pointing his pointer at that six-foot twat dripping sudate on the screen: "When those membranes turn ruby red, orgasm is inevitable."

But this has nothing to do with Fanny. Fanny wouldn't let them put a speculum into her little thing. Not for a million dollars. And Fanny would never turn it inside out and show. Not to *you!*

"What I got there? That's for me to know and you to find out!"

Well said, Fanny! Don't show it to them! It's Sabbath eve and I'll soon be running home from school. In a minute I'll be on the steps and you can start your shimmy-sha-wobble for me.

"Hello, little boy. What grade you in?"

What grade *was* I in? This wasn't *Little Half-Chick* or *Little Black Sambo!* I had never read *this* story before. We never had *this* in school! It was Recess. A long, long recess that, thank God, isn't over yet.

I was not too young not to know that babies didn't come from L. Bamberger's department store. Fanny was *schwengering,* like the lady next door. You could get pregnant in the back as well as the front. The baker had put a bagel in Fanny's oven. This knowledge may have added to my awe. Would Fanny have a *zvilling?* Later, I learned from my gang that twins come from doing it twice the same night. That would be like Fanny. Twins. Triplets. Sextuplets.

I suppose as Fanny's belly grew rounder and her petticoat was pulled up even more seductively, I was always on those wooden steps when it was her turn to scrub. And somehow I am sure that she knew I would be there. I suspect she enjoyed being the teacher of my *éducation sentimentale.* Suspect? What is there to suspect? Fanny was a natural person who loved her cunt and wanted me to love it too.

"Look, look, little boy. Look all you want."

Unlike the driven Peeping Tom who roams the streets, climbs fences, roofs, fire escapes, I have never sought these occasions for looking. All the more exciting when it just happens. It is the surprise and wonder, not so much at what one has seen, but the casualness with which the hidden is revealed, that thrills. There is a verity when the fourth wall is truly removed and the actors play themselves.

The scene need not be erotic; it need only be private. To this day the sight of a woman in a window, combing her hair or intently putting on her lipstick, touches me deeply. When they study themselves and make little flirtatious faces to test whether everything is in place and working the way it should, I am moved almost to tears. There is such a frailty in this pitiful wish to look good in the world.

You are amused? Little boys don't anticipate the future habits of their flesh, nor do grown men know where they began. You cannot command or beg for the accident in which a predilection originates. I blush to confess mine. Fanny's posture is that of the peasant woman crouched over an everyday task who so enflames Tolstoy in *The Devil.* How creamy her calves, how marble her thighs, like the arms of a caryatid holding the portal to the temple flame. Me and Lev Nikolaevitch!

I was imprinted. I now had "a centipede biting at my heart." Like Dmitri Karamazov, I would look for Fanny in "side-paths, little dark alleys behind the main road where one finds adventures and surprises and precious metal in the dust." In a small-town diner I would see Fanny leaning over to scramble two eggs. Shake, shake. I would see her washing a window with her bottom hanging out of the fifth floor, spitting on a stubborn spot and rubbing around and around, giving herself a shake shake shake. I would see her dressed as a bride in a photographer's window. She can hardly wait for the honeymoon. Shimmy and shake. And I've seen her a lot in the narrow alleys of Venice, hanging out those little black bras, singing, taking red clothespins like cherries from her mouth. I know the song. It's "Yes, we have no bananas!"

And out of the penumbra, I see Fanny at a Bar Mitzvah. Everybody is dressed in their best, but she is wearing only her petticoat, torn at the hem, ripped in impatience. Fanny wants to teach me the fox-trot.

"Come here, *boytchik.* Dance with me. Don't be scared."

I am bashful. Fanny vamps me. It is hot. I am melting. I am a little boy in a sailor suit. My hair is cut like Buster Brown.

"Oy, so big your eyes, such lashes like a girl. You know what it is already, don't you? But you don't know what to do! Should I take your little hand, let you give me a little tickle, a *kitzel* you know where! You like to look first? On the steps? I'll take my bucket. Like this is nice? She's pretty, Fanny? All over? The hand is clean? The school nurse inspected? I don't want no measles, no claps! *Ferstehst, mein* cavalier, *mein* Valentino?"

I understand! In an atomic flash I understand!

"*Nu,* hurry up! What you waiting? For Messiah?"

O Mama, O Papa! Should I? Shouldn't I? Don't listen. I am about to say yes.

But while I go to the bar for another drink, Fanny disappears.

· 2 ·

In Kinsey's Army

"Going around the block."

Where else? But you always told your mother when you picked up the cut-off broomstick that was your bat.

"Tacks in your pants," she says, *"shpilkehs."*

"For the pennant," you say. She won't ask of what league.

"Basebolshevik!" The worst of two worlds.

She didn't know you might not get into the game. Choosing sides was a ritual of balance.

"You got Looie. Gimme Noodle!"

"Okay! Then gimme Hoot!"

We all had nicknames. Noodle, naturally, was long and thin. Someone else was already called Longie. We also had Stretch and just plain Skinny. Because he had an owl's way of hoohooing in excitement, another fellow was called Hoot Gibson. Because my name begins with an *a,* I was called Ace.

But not always.

"You, *klutz!* In the outfield."

Klutz was me, butterfingers. I would be posted so deep down the street that if a ball reached me, it could be conceded as a deserved home run. Better, though, than sitting on the curb, cheering halfheartedly, hoping someone would break his neck on the cobblestones people said came from Belgium.

Around the block was where the Badgers convened. Was it beavers or badgers who built dams? Had there once been water on Badger Street? There had been Indians, the Leni Lenape. Then Quakers. And freed slaves who lived in rows of wooden houses that looked historical. Then came Krauts and Micks, Wops and Polacks and us.

Around the block was an unusual turf, rural and urban at the same time. Though it was in the heart of a residential neighborhood, Badger Street was bisected by a railroad spur which served a number of factories and a coal yard nearby. There was a sliced hill of earth still standing along the tracks. With the first snow, Flexible Flyers would take over its gradient. In summer, we dug pirate caves on its face. Sometimes we would see hoboes come off a Rock Island boxcar.

Our gang claimed one block of Badger Street from the point at which the railroad crossed Avon Avenue—there was a gateman in his own little house who cranked down the barriers to stop the traffic—to an icehouse at the other end. Here the iceman got the big blocks which he chopped down to order. "Gimme for ten cents today!" And he would climb three flights of steps and put such a piece in the economical lady's box. They were rough men, these *eizmenschen,* given to rough jokes that befitted the reputation of their trade. If you had red hair or an extra-long nose, people said the iceman was your father.

The river of our existence flowed between the two curbs of Badger Street. Its other bank was a row of tenements exactly like the one in which I lived, ending with a factory surrounded by a cyclone fence. When its whistle blew and the streetlamp went on, the Badgers gathered. Under its stanchion, cast-iron, floral, left over from the Mauve Decade, we set out for voyages to Cythera never dreamed by Baudelaire.

> *Ah! que le monde est grand à la clarté des lampes!*
> *Aux yeux du souvenir que le monde est petit!*

How big the schoolboy's world is in the lamplight! In the eyes of memory so small! Your fame was won around the block. Would you be able to stay on your feet, hunched over, your fingers hooked into the links of the cyclone fence, as one after another your peers piled on your back in a game of Johnny on a Pony? Could you piss in a high rainbow arc and put out the Church on Fire? But first, of course, you took out the potatoes, the mickies, roasting in the bonfire.

"Red Rover, Red Rover, let Izzy come over!"

And Izzy would come across the street, running like Red Grange, dodging not tacklers but a flailing stocking filled with steaming manure. The horses of the icemen gave us the base for a small ecocycle.

And would you run or stand when the Polacks raided, leaving Hoot Gibson to get pinned down and have his pants pulled off? The poor kid was left on the sidewalk with his defeat and his dick exposed to the world. He had been "cockalized."

Sex and bravery went together. Their emanations hung in the air like the mustard gas of the recent Great War. "Gas! Gas!" We were told that if you put a peach pit in a paper bag and covered your nose and mouth, you would be able to breathe safely. Goofie Looie said it worked. He had tried it out against his own farts.

Like me, Goofie Looie was one of the Juniors. We all had inquiring minds. We wanted to know everything the Seniors hinted was to be known. In school there were teachers, but they did not give these subjects. Crack wise and you'd have your mouth washed out with soap. So, the man in the moon—which gave girls the monthlies—had to preside over our lunatic seminars on the vicissitudes of humping.

"First you stick it in."

And after that?

"The gism!"

And after that?

"You lose your strength."

Or,

"You might get caught in the hole and have to have it removed by a doctor."

This last was real enough, verifiable. More than once we had seen, after the pumping frenzy to which Nature had lured him, the male dog caught, locked helplessly to the bitch, become part of a beast with six legs which staggered this way and that on the cobblestone street where we had just played a game of stickball. The dogs might even be twisted around, tail to tail, joined like Siamese twins in a pathetic tug of war.

Why go to a show? We watched in a circle with the silent fascination street theater affords. Only Goofie Looie hopped around yelling, "It's up the ass! It's up the ass!" We knew better. It was in the cunt.

But what held it there? The vagina armed with teeth was too mythic even for our tribe of wild Indians. We were, after all, in New Jersey, not New Guinea. And, at bottom, our relationships with our mothers—give or take an occasional reproach for ripping and tearing one's way out of that passage—were not schizophrenogenic.

"You almost killed me!"

"Me?"

"Nine pounds you were."

"I didn't eat *knishes.*"

"Wise guy. *Weisenheimer.*"

"I didn't ask to get born."

"Stitches they had to take."

"I didn't ask."

"Quiet! I'll give you something you didn't ask."

The mysterious and precarious cunt was a vortex, a kind of sticky cavity lined with flypaper that held you there because . . . because?

There was some powerful urge behind all this humping. On the faces of the poor mutts who had risked it we saw only pain and panic. They had humped and were paying for it. But there was more to it, price or no. Everybody did it. Only nuns were not allowed. Or else how did we get on Earth? We were only Juniors. Some day we would find out.

The Seniors already knew. One pastime, privileged only to the older guys, was to get the point of one shoe between the legs of a street pooch. Like one of Pavlov's dogs, its reflexes were already conditioned. Quickly, the dog would embrace its seducer's leg and lock its paws around it as though he were on the back of a heated bitch. You could see it had the masturbation habit. It didn't care who looked. As soon as it got going good, the dog would be chased away. It would come back again and again, fawning, pleading, risking small kicks. Its pink, pointed thing would still be twitching in and out like a piston. Would it ever ejaculate? The answer was beyond the undeclared limit of our explorations in bestiality. Who would want to get dog gism on his Thom McAns?

We also heard the Seniors talk of women who had trained dogs—police dogs were the smartest—to hump them, or something. Nymphomaniacs they were! And would the baby be a freak? Jo-Jo the Dog-faced Boy?

When he finally gave up fooling around with his gall wasps and got down to serious business, Professor Kinsey should have come to our block. He would have learned a thing or two. I met him once before he killed himself trying to prove that mammals will be mammals. He wanted to get a hundred thousand males and females into his study, be able to say, "That's the way it is, bub." I never got a chance to ask him about the police dogs.

The big debate in those days was over clitoral versus vaginal orgasm. Freud said you were fixated, a penis envier, if your bell rang when you pressed that buzzer. But sophisticated research was showing the primacy of that unique and remarkable sender/ receptor. There were no vibrators at 19 Berggasse. Dr. Masters would not take anybody's subjective impression; he wired them, took pictures with a fiber-optic plastic penis. Sex, it was turning out, was 10 percent mental and 90 percent physical.

I looked into animal behavior. I could pooh-pooh vaunted virility by pointing out that the majestic elephant took only thirty seconds to do the job while the rodent mink went at it all day long. I became unpopular with feminists who refused to believe that female orgasm had not been found in the animal world. They were as benighted as the Juniors.

I knew a lot now but I was still uncertain about the role of the educated police dog. You don't find these things in *The Psychoanalytic Review*. And I was ashamed to ask. One day, by chance, I thought I was going, finally, to see for myself.

I was between patients. Looking down out of my tenth-floor office across fallow gardens that belonged to a row of brownstones, I saw, in one of the windows, a woman stretched out on her bed, basking in the laser beams that sometimes come through the bunched clouds of an Indian summer day. This was not a morning scene. It was afternoon. The woman seemed already to have been out into her daily world. In black underthings, the kind of set that comes by mail direct from Hollywood, she was taking a Manhattan sunbath. She needed it. Her skin was too white, out of style, like a ballroom dress in a thrift shop.

Framed by the window, she was turned toward me like Goya's Duchess of Alba. No, the Duchess wears nothing but a ring on her finger on which the painter has signed his name in little diamonds. This dame rested on an elbow and she was squeezing one boob. Titian? The one in the Met where Venus squirts her own Grade A milk into Cupid's kisser? With her other hand she was giving a fluff of a dog indulgent little slaps on its muzzle. I was looking at a dirty postcard. Her toe was between its legs.

What is the opposite of *déjà vu*? I was someplace I had never been, hoping to see something I had never seen. I lit a cigarette, put on the amused grin of someone watching a blue movie in mixed company. I was not one to miss a free show.

By this time, the dog was straddled around the woman's leg. Without question, its heat was stirring her. She no longer pretended to scold the mutt. With her free hand she was steadying it, helping it to hang on with its paws and do what it could. Even if it was not what Nature had intended, the Pom's reflexes had taken over. I regretted it was not a police dog, fanged and unmanageable, that would turn the tables on phylogeny, throw the woman on all fours, and finish what she had started, *a tergo,* in the lupine way.

But I was watching a toy woman toying with a toy dog. I knew her. We had the nodding acquaintance of people who walk their dogs in the same park. I was not only a doctor now. I was a real American with an office and a dog of my own. My neighbor paraded a primped and skittish Pomeranian that matched her in size. By no accident, I suppose, its fur was the same color as its owner's hair, henna, out of a jar as in the "Does she or doesn't she?" ads. The woman was tiny, but heavy front and back. She was always elaborately dressed as though she had to go to a Bar Mitzvah every day in the week.

Not that she was Jewish. Our Irish doorman called her Frenchy. He said she was a fancy woman. She tipped him big when he got her cabs. She did all right. I understood her to be one of those semiretired call girls with her own regular clientele of older men. In the street she was snooty. She was a sex snob. When the Pomeranian sniffed my in-season terrier, she disdained to look, walked ahead with her nose in the air, disowning its behavior. Her French ass spoke without an accent. "Kiss me," it said, "where the sun don't shine!"

The sun was shining all over now. The old pro had been caught off guard by something over which she had no say. But clearly it had happened before. She knew what she was doing and the innocent beast was also playing a part it already knew by heart.

Frenchy had left off kneading her breast—always the same one and only that one—and had hooked a finger under the device that held it up like a balloon. A teat belonging to a woman twice her size fell on her chest. The black brassiere trimmed it like the apron on the maid in a French farce. Its twin stayed in its wired cage.

What would happen now? Frenchy had freed that single breast so deliberately, I felt sure I was watching a practiced auto-

erotic technique. She was stretching out that papilla like Coney
Island taffy. The gesture was out of the pages of those old case-
books on neurasthenia that recommend cold baths and walks in
the mountains for such perversions. "Thank you, thank you,
Cousin Alice/for *Psychopathia Sexualis*."

Meanwhile, the Pomeranian had worked its way up Frenchy's
thigh. The woman did not take her eyes from it. It was as though
she did not want the sadist's hand to know what the masochist's
was doing. One pinched the nipple, the other stroked the dog,
righted it when its frenzy became too much for its tiny purchase.

Frenchy was still turned on her elbow. Suddenly, she grabbed
the dog by its collar, lifted it high and let herself fall supine. In the
same movement she raised her knees and closed her thighs
around the Pompom. It let itself be held in that vise of flesh
dimpled with the cellulite of too many seafood dinners. It had
been there before. The point of its nose rooted in bitch scent.

Frenchy was arching against the dog now, making electricity
with its fur against the embroidered initial I was sure she had
sewn into her "lingerie of the stars." Beyond that, Frenchy denied the genital. Had it become excluded from intimacy? I knew
that many whores felt betrayed by any response they gave even
to those they called persistent Johns.

This one was massaging the whole of her teat now. Its au-
reola was in her palm, its nipple between her thumb and pointing finger. Was I seeing an empirical display of Freud's famous
equation: breast = penis? Frenchy was masturbating the fabled
organ. Her rhythm was slower now, calculated like the deepest
thrusts of coitus.

Then, with a last fierce tug, Frenchy finished. I was too far
away to see the heave of respiration or the twitch of contraction.
Her legs opened. The Pomeranian escaped but did not know
what to do with the body that lay there like the victim in a tabloid
photo of a bedroom murder. It watched over it, faithful to the
end. "If you want a friend, get a dog!"

How long Frenchy lay there, catalept, I do not know. I had
lost track. I was in a trance of nostalgia, whirled by a centrifuge
of titillation, riding The Whip in and out of the black hole of
time. I was happy. I had seen something no Senior had ever
seen.

"Ace! Ace! You seen?"

"Jacking off with a dog!"

"No fen?"

"A nymphomaniac!"

"What breed?"

"A Pomeramium!"

I was speaking in tongues. But they understood. Goofie Looie, Maxie, Noodle, Hoot Gibson, Yossel, Skinny, Longie, Stretch. They were calling me Ace. It was so nice to be born again in the best time and place, where you did not have to think twice about anything you said.

Frenchy came out of her little death. Her arms went up across her chest, hands on her shoulders. She could have been making a straitjacket to hold herself back from something more. Or it could have been a gesture of forgotten modesty. Either way, the point of the flagellated breast oozed out, flushed and chafed, from the crook of her elbow.

The Pomeranian watched, waited with its ears cocked like the dog on the Victrola label. Maybe it was hoping to hear the call of the wild. But it was hung up someplace in the humanoid *Lustprinzip.*

Suddenly, it invented a sadomasochism of its own. Biting its tail, it ran in circles, trying to bring its betrayed instincts to some canine conclusion. Frenchy didn't like that. Her own lapse was over. She was a lady again. She cuffed the dog, talked harshly to it. She was sitting up now, stuffing the favored tit into its sling, weighing it against the other, balancing her bosom, left and right, without prejudice.

The Pomeranian stopped its neurotic circling, begged for release, tried to lick her face. Frenchy pushed it away, slipped her Kewpie-doll legs over the side of the bed, and, walking on her toes like a ballerina, disappeared into the shadow of another room. I remember clearly how she walked, as though she did not want to dirty her feet.

I was still hearing voices and, like an idiot, I was answering.

"Did it shoot?"

"Dope! The same breed they got to be."

"Oy! One drop. Bow wow!"

"Dope! They take out the balls."

"They're cockalized by a veteran."

"No shit?"

"He grinds them up and sells them to a Chinkyman."

"Ace! Ace!"

My name was Ace again. It did not matter that we were all grown up, old guys now, Foxy Grandpas who needed an aphrodisiac worse than the Chinese laundryman and, if we were lucky enough to get it up, did not worry about getting caught in the hole. Our aim in life had changed. All we wanted was to die with a hard-on.

· 3 ·
The Lady-goer

Though for most of my life I have been carrying a quirky conscience like an albatross around my neck, I did not, until recently, know it. I used to think it was standard equipment, like having ten fingers and ten toes. I've tiptoed my way between civilization and discontent. Still, I'm not complaining. I would not want to be a sexual Eichmann doing everything and anything without a twinge.

But why didn't I take after Uncle Phil? Freud said a man is happy when he gets what he wanted as a child. Could it be that our most secret wishes are jotted down on some universal calendar—decorated with a naked lady for each month—even before we can read and write? At eighty, Freud was calling himself a "beast of burden." *He* didn't have Good Time Phil for an uncle.

Phil was easy come, easy go, jolly, foolish, and ungrasping. He was the only fat man in our family. And the only happy one. He introduced me, if anybody did, to wine, women, and song when I was barely out of diapers.

"He lives for a good time," people said about Phil.

What did *they* live for? By them, you were good when you didn't do anything.

"I'll call the policeman!"

That's what an innocent babe heard when he did something in his diapers. A few years of that and you would be calling the cops on yourself.

As between the things of milk and things of meat, as between kosher and *trayf,* the line between good and bad was clearly drawn. Bad boys went to reform school. Bad girls just went bad, like spoiled milk.

"She's on the curb," Phil might say. "On deh coib."

And he would laugh, heh, heh, heh, in a way that has taken me a lifetime to catch onto. Phil approved. The girl had taken a fling into good times, escaped from piecework sweatshops, from Woolworth's, from pushing a baby carriage, from a *finstere leben* into the bright lights of The Life, which was almost as good as being on the Pantages vaudeville circuit.

"You're a long time dead." That was Phil's philosophy.

Uncle Phil boarded with us when I was small. He didn't sing or dance or do tricks, but he was almost in vaudeville. His ambition was to be a manager. He hung around Proctor's Theater and was always bringing home, if only for a few hours, amazing trained dogs who walked, talked, and did acrobatics. It was like having your own circus.

And Phil did not wait for a wedding to take a *schnappsele*. Every day was a wedding to him. He did not punch a clock. He was a pioneer used-car dealer. He bought majestic, wooden-spoked, brass-lamped Apperson, Haines, and Fiat touring cars which he turned into racers. He did not do this himself. Somebody else stripped them down. Phil never worked with his hands. From that you could get a rupture.

Phil used the automobile to escape into the hedonistic American world. If the "heap" was clean, a "cream puff," he tried to sell it as a passenger car. He was always giving demonstrations down to the shore. That was a good destination, all flat country and downhill, with easy detours into sandy towns where Phil knew all the police chiefs. He cultivated them. He could fix a ticket anyplace in Jersey. He ran around in the brainless circles of the *goyische kopf* and was proud of it.

On Avon Avenue you did not have a good time. You went for it to other places—Asbury Park or even Atlantic City. There were just ordinary times on Avon Avenue. No lobsters. And no ladies. Uncle Phil was a lady-goer, a *ladygayer,* with lady always said in English, derogatory, fancy-shmancy, a you-know-what.

We were one of the first families on our block to have a telephone. Phil paid for it but never answered it himself. He had mysterious enemies.

"Your lady friend," my mother would tell him. "The wild Indian."

"An American goil," Phil explained. "Her *zaydeh* was a big chief in the West."

Phil came home from the barbershop all talcum and bay rum, ready to put on his silk shirt and go *shpaziering*. He had manicures by downtown manicurists who were no better than they should be, who smoked, who took your hand and put it on their pussies.

"Heh, heh, heh."

They liked it. And they got you to like it. And if you liked it too much you would become a bum, a *shmegeggy*. Nightclubs you would go. TB you would get.

Phil was a black sheep, but he was forgiven and well liked. My grandfather had ten children by two wives. My father was the oldest of the second batch. He stood on his head for the old tyrant. Feivel, also known as Phil, just went heh, heh, heh and had a good time. "If you have ten fingers and one gets hurt, that's the one you favor," Grandpa said.

Phil gave driving lessons. There were always two or three ambitious new Americans waiting in the parlor for Uncle Phil to sleep off yesterday's good time. They came up from what we called the stoop, the Avon Avenue entrance used only by special company and on Passover by *Eliahu Hanovee*, the Unseen Guest, for whom a place was always set at the Seder table. He came with the cold draft of a ghost.

That stoop was to become, for me, and my immediate peers, our university of the seamy side of life. Snug against the weather, private, watched over by six empty mailboxes, a constellation of gods whose names all ended with -sky, we sat by the hour on the stoop's brass-bound steps, our chins resting on our knees, endlessly matching pasteboard chromos of runners, swimmers, divers, pitchers, catchers, and pool sharks.

The game was simple, something like Go Fish. You put out Strangler Lewis. I put out Eddie di Palma. You put out Walter Johnson. I put out Indian Jim Thorpe. You put out Benny Leonard, the Jewish lightweight champ who never got his hair mussed. I put out Benny Leonard, too, and take in the whole pile. The man, not the picture, had to match. Your card might show the champ standing with his left out jabbing, guarding the part in his slick hair. Mine might show him wearing the championship belt over his purple trunks. Sometimes our heroes were stripped to the waist. It did not matter. They were always men.

Except hook-nosed Suzanne Lenglen and pristine Helen

Wills serving aces with their white skirts kicked up above their
knees. Could they play, we wondered, when they wore the rag?
We also speculated on what would happen if a girl got hit in the
balls. That they had them, we were sure. Only not in a sack.

We needed a teacher. And at the right time, the culture
tore—as Margaret Mead said—"the veil of reticence" from our
eyes. Like Aladdin's *jinn,* she leaped out at us from the inkwell of
pornography. Her name was Tillie the Toiler.

She came from the pen of some gifted hack who stole the
beloved profiles of comic-strip folk and, with a few quick strokes,
revealed them in the ninety-nine postures of a jocular American
Kama Sutra.

How did the little dirty comic books get into our mitts? They
were just the size of your hand, had to be, so you could hide them—
one, two, three—in the pocket of your new longies, the ones with the
hole in them through which you played "pocket pool."

The flapper-stenographer was a relatively new figure in
American life. Her predicaments and perversities were just exotic enough to keep us free from guilt at looking at them. Tillie's
goo-goo eyes were utterly insouciant. Each time the light bulb lit
up in the balloon over the Office Boy's head, we knew that the
next few squares would show some amazing feat like Tillie bent
over her desk, gobbling the Office Boy while the Boss had his
way with her from the rear. Tillie still had her pencil and dictation pad ready to take down anything he might say. It was too
funny to be dirty. What went on in an office!

Maggie and Jiggs, on the other hand, offered a conjugal
iconography. Randy little Jiggs chased the maid around the
house while Maggie took off after him with a rolling pin. Mutt
and Jeff, always inseparable, shared pranks of what would later
be labeled as latent homosexual palship.

Tillie the Toiler was more accessible to us. Some of our
aunts and sisters were taking up stenography. We could not see
them, God forbid, as Tillie, nor anybody's mother and father as
Maggie and Jiggs. We did not believe real people did these crazy
things.

We saw little of the sexual in the flesh. Kinsey brought this
out, showed "taxonomically" the inhibited behaviors of the working class—husbands who never saw their wives naked, who never
departed from the missionary position, who thought perverted
the oral-genital contacts of the middle class.

There were words for these things—muff diver, hair sandwich, going down, trip around the world—but they belonged to the vocabulary of the nymphomaniac and the slaphappy whose brains were leaking out of their dicks. And conjugal intimacy of any kind was unlikely to be seen or heard in the railroad rooms in which we lived. What grownups did was sealed from the child like those secret cattlecars of the Holocaust to come.

The only thing of interest you might see around here was the lady across the way, the *nextdoorikeh,* walking around in her corset. Her bosom, stuffed into a sack, stuck out like the brass headlights on a Pierce-Arrow. She had the kind of which, in a strange confusion of anatomy and gender, the Junior Badgers sang, "She could toss them over her shoulder like a big Russian soldier."

The peddlers, bakers, upholsterers, paper-cutters who were our fathers were not Tillie's Boss. They were nobody's boss, not even at home. Uncle Phil was his own boss. He didn't, as I was to hear many times, "listen to nobody."

"You should open a school," my father urged.

"In the Other World, I'll open."

So the greenies waited while Phil got his beauty sleep. Then he had to cure his hangover. Uncle Phil had a wonderful remedy. It was a show in itself, worth waiting for. You followed him to the corner grocery store where he would dip a cup of brine from the pickle barrel, swallow it in one gulp, burp with the force of a trombone, and be fine. This was called "giving a *greps.*" Phil could give a *greps* with anybody.

And after, he would invariably propose marriage to both of the cultured daughters of the widow who ran the grocery. These girls were a big influence on my mother. They gave her Warwick Deeping novels from the circulating library. They were as beyond Phil's reach as Tillie the Toiler was beyond mine. Phil laughed when they turned up their noses. He was only getting their goat.

"I don't need no ball and chain. I got my own *boytchik.*"

He meant me. I was his mascot, his protégé. I was three or four years old when he started to take me to Silberstein's Saloon. It seems to me this was before Prohibition. I remember Silberstein's swinging doors. Phil taught me to sing "Sally of Our Alley" and other ditties. If I sang, he let me drink beer. He also taught me conundrums which I could show off at the free-lunch counter.

"Betcha Benny's kid kin ast somethin yeh ain gonna answer!"

You could never tell what I would come out with. Phil taught me new bits all the time. He got them from vaudeville.

"*Nu*, gents? A *finnif*? A double sawbuck? I don' care how much, only American jack, no Confederal money! Yeh don wan Benny's kid to perform for nuttin? Lissen, me deh menegeh!"

Phil was drinking rye with small beer chasers.

"I'm takin woikin paypehs fuh deh Wheel, deh Keith time! Yuhz'll see dis *boytchik* by Proctor's Teeayter! Lissen! *Who takes* . . ." Phil was cueing me.

"Who takes care deh caretaker's daughter when deh caretaker's out takin care?"

Monkey sees, monkey does. Did I give a *greps*, too? Was I applauded like Uncle Phil? I was affectionately called a *momser*, a cute little bastard.

"Silberstein," Phil would say when he paid up from a big roll of singles with a couple of fives on the top, "Silberstein, you got a gold *and* a silver mine!"

Silberstein! Silverstone! Remember that alchemy. For that was the name of my first crush, my first *belle dame sans merci.*

Phyllis Silverstone! Her name alone should tell you how much class she had. Phyllis was willowy, fragile, third generation, and natural blonde. She is the one on the left in Botticelli's *Primavera,* the one in the sweater and skirt and the black-and-white shoes and the pearls and the permanent wave and already using lipstick in the Clinton High Yearbook.

"Miss Rich Bitch," Kiddy says when we reminisce. "Why didn't you pick on Janice Waldorf?" Who was runner-up for Miss New Jersey of 1932. By that time, Kiddy's father had lost all the lots and the houses he was building on them. "You always wanted an heiress."

Phyllis was. She was Silberstein's granddaughter. From the saloon, his sons had expanded and become just about the biggest bootleggers in America, with a fleet of ships bringing the stuff down from Canada under the protection of our famous Jewish gangster, "Sweets" Sugarman. Look it up! Wasn't "Dutch" Schultz gunned down in my hometown? It's history. And didn't you ever drink Silverstone's Seven Star, imported and bottled by Silverstone Ltd.?

In the small space left by the ethnic bisections of Newark, coincidence was inevitable. Kiddy later worked in the Riviera

Club, one of "Sweets" Sugarman's places—cigarette girl, as in a Jimmy Cagney movie, short skirt, net stockings, and all.

In high school, I worshiped Phyllis Silverstone from afar. She moved in different circles from me, the school poet to whom his Uncle Phil had shown love's lost face on the barroom floor. In a reversal of the Gatsby story, I yearned for the bootleg princess who was driven to school in a V-16 Cadillac.

Though both my wives turned out to be redheads, I was always, like Uncle Phil, a sucker for blondes. He liked them big, golden, and out of the Floradora chorus line. At the time I'm talking about, he had a tow-haired sweetheart who flew her great weight around in her own airplane! She was the daughter of a small-town police chief. He gave Phil a deputy sheriff's badge.

One day, two men took Uncle Phil out to a lonely country road to demonstrate one of his racers. They shot him three times through the neck and took the Buick. Uncle Phil never got to show his deputy sheriff's badge.

O Uncle Phil, why didn't I inherit your easygoing ways and your heh, heh, heh? I would have a big roll of bills and a Rolls-Roycechick and a blondie on each arm and each blondie would have a French poodle wearing a diamond collar. They would be walking on their hind legs taking up a collection for their act. I would be their "menegeh."

That was not in my cards.

· 4 ·

The Attack at Badger Gulch

Only my contemporaries will understand the *horror feminae* with which, in those misogynic days, we denied our uneasy sexuality. Yet, like a flower growing in a sidewalk crack, our sexualibus kept reaching for the sun. Rank weed? Venus's-flytrap?

Some of the Juniors were even bluffing a familiarity with the opposite sex. They sat on the milk box in front of the corner grocery store and gave judgment on the passing parade of pulchritude.

"Oy, zoftig!"

"Red hot mama!"

"McKenzie Trennen!"

Meh kenn sie trennen, she can be sewn, i.e., needle in hole, zig, zig, up and down, in and out like a Singer sewing machine doing piecework.

Gradually, repulsion was giving way to obsessive interest. The milk box became a yeshiva of psychosexuality. We pondered:

Did Fatty Arbuckle kill that girl by getting on top?

Would your voice change if your balls were bitten off by a shark?

If you swallowed gism, would you get a moustache?

If a guy was a "morphodite," would he stand or sit down to pee?

Someone without a dictionary had brought us that word. Our understanding of the homoerotic was classical, extending the "third sex" theory to include the actual hermaphrodite. One of the Juniors was having some trouble along that line. His testicles—his eggs—had not descended. We called him Lady. But as far as I know, none of the Badgers became a "morphodite." Ignorance and consensual paranoia protected us.

"One for all and all for one!"

D'Artagnan wasn't a fairy. Nor Athos, nor Porthos nor Aramis.

"Draw, villain!"

You could pull your sword out of its scabbard but once you let your cock out of your fly, you would be chasing it for the rest of your life.

We were in a war of opposites. Nice, not nice; clean, dirty; kosher, *trayf.* And on top of that, you had male, female. In Hebrew school we read on the English side of the prayerbook: "I thank Thee, O Lord, that Thou hast not made me a woman!"

"The rag every month!"

"Knocked up!"

"They can't control themselves!"

"The nuns put candles up their cracks!"

"Cockteasers!"

Look at these two walking down the street, arm in arm, singing, too.

My muddah gimme a nickel to buy a pickle.

They din have no pickle, I bought some chewngum . . .

Why do they roll their tongues around their lips?

We had barely assimilated shtupping, trenning, humping, copping cherry, jazzing, and the other vagaries of genital coupling. And here, like the false Indies Columbus had stumbled upon, was a whole, weird new geography to be mastered. And there were just so many things you could find out under the arc light supplied by the Department of Public Works of the City of Newark.

There were other places in the world, places you would never see, like Venice, Italy, where the streets are all water. How did they go to the toilet? Or the Congo where the Pygmies had *schlangs* bigger than themselves. They had to carry them in wheelbarrows. It was a disease. Or the South Sea Islands where they wear no pants when they do the hula dance. There was a whole world out there if you jumped into it. You had to start someplace.

For the Junior Badgers, there was at least the visible horizon of becoming Seniors and getting to bombard the new Juniors with rotten tomatoes and crud. We might even get to mastermind the robbery of a box of Tootsie Rolls from a delivery truck. The Seniors faced a hideous future of starting off again as nobodies. Everybody wants to be somebody. And Badger Street's braggarts were running out of brags.

And how powerful must be the wish for approval when the world is a city block, a dirty speck on the blue, yellow, green, and pink globe like the one we used in Geography.

Out of such tensions came the attack on Horseface. Did this poor *neshumah* know we called her that? Horseface was the oldest of three orphaned sisters who lived on Badger Street. The absence of a father or a protecting big brother marked these girls. In addition, their mother worked. This was not common in our crowd. Your mother was always someplace nearby. She was making the chicken soup.

Chickens were still bought live in those days. They had to be grabbed from their cages, held for the knife that drained their kosher blood. They also had to be plucked. If I am not inventing, the mother of the fatherless sisters was a chicken plucker in the market on nearby Sunshine Street. This was a lowly trade and a hard one. Each feather had to be seized between forefinger and thumb. A Yiddish poet I know told me that when he came over from the other side he had been something of a violinist. He was put to work as a chicken plucker. In a little while he could no longer play the fiddle; his fingers had taken the shape of a pair of pincers.

Horseface, the oldest sister, already grown, was tall and rawboned, strong like her mother. She had an uncompromising, equine face more suitable to a Bloomsbury intellectual. It was a face, we said, only a mother could love, and only on payday. Her middle sister had the same horsey face. But she had breasts and a glowing, rosy skin which gave her sufficient femininity to make her the target of the gang's dirty thoughts. The big question was, did she still have her cherry? And if so, who would cop it?

Nobody wanted Horseface's cherry. She had already been written out of the scenario of Eros. We could not fit this clod of a girl into our ordinary inhumanities. What strikes me is how, with the special instinct of the streets, the Badgers had sensed that girls without curves or dimples had nothing but their horse-power to sell. Horseface's was a joyless body, the kind to answer advertisements that said "Hands wanted." It was a body made to pull and haul, not like Fanny's, which was made to do the Charleston or kick up a hora at a wedding. Horseface was the same harnessed woman who had crawled naked through the steaming Midland coal seams to drag us into the Industrial Revolution. Her pretty sister was sent out on London's gaslit streets to earn the queen's shilling by quiff and quim.

On Avon Avenue, the economic motive for prostitution did not carry weight. After all, the whores charged only two bucks. No, they did it because they liked it. And they got you into their power like an opium fiend in the clutches of Anna May Wong's fingernails.

"They got slanty slits!"

"G'wan, yeh muddah's callin' yeh!"

None of us had ever seen a Chinese woman, dressed or un-dressed. We knew only the Chinese laundryman who answered in Pidgin Yiddish when his customers spoke to him in Pidgin English.

"No tickee no washee!"

"Kissee in tooshee!"

It would be for him that the powdered testes of the cas-trated police dogs would be intended. They were, in some op-posite way, as powerful as the Spanish Fly, the cantharides which the white slavers sprinkled secretly on the fancy dinners they bought innocent girls in restaurants. Why did they go? Why did they eat? Were they so hungry? No, they just wanted to eat oysters!

Of course, there were some girls you couldn't get with a blue-plate dinner or even if you slipped them a mickey. They were special. No one around here could match them.

"Gotta match?"

"My ass and your face."

These girls didn't work in no five-and-ten. Their old man owned the gold mine. They had these cows without balls, all branded, and ranches bigger than Wequahic Park and the whole Third Ward. These girls lived in Texas where everybody rode horseback; there were no trolley cars. And though they had already busted their cherries bumping up and down in the saddle, they still thought they were the Queen of Palestina.

Yessiree! Just look at them every Saturday afternoon at Fox's Cameo, running across the prairie, falling down, tearing their white dresses, getting up, hiding in a tree, putting all the furniture against the door. The bad guys got them anyhow. First they would slap the bad guys. "Ha! Ha!" It only made the bad guys laugh. Then they would hit and kick the bad guys until they had to be tied up with a lasso. They almost cried. The bad guys tickled them under the chin. The bad guys looked like they were about to eat pork chops.

"No! No!"

They had to shake their heads because they were all tied up. If you didn't understand, the word, printed in an art nouveau frame, jumped out at you.

"No! No! No!"

You'd have to give them Spanish Fly to make them say yes.

When the "No!" couldn't get any bigger, the piano played loud and they showed Tony, the Wonder Horse, using his teeth to untie Tom Mix. Tom Mix was rivers, ravines, and mesas away but he would be riding hell-bent for leather across our eyes, faster and faster, to save our Saturday innocence.

Meantime, the bad guys were breaking up the furniture, cutting up the mattress, looking for the map to the gold mine. Dopes! It's in the girl's bandeau, in her tits. We saw her hide it when no one was looking. The tootsie is tied up hands and feet. The bad guys can do anything they want. But they dassent! Instead, they get into an argument. The chief bad guy wants to give her a kiss or something. He spits out his toothpick. The other guys want to go after the gold. While these tough hombres are slapping their six-shooters, Tom Mix sends Tony to make a noise in the front of the ranch house while he busts in at the back. There's shooting and punching. The End.

It was over before you saw anything, and the unseen was making us restless. We didn't come back week after week just to see Tom Mix kiss his horse. We wanted to find out why the bad guys looked like they were about to eat pork chops. Without re-alizing it, we were identifying with the aggressors, running in our heads various cockeyed montages of censored reels. Why did everybody want to get those little sacks of gold they threw at the bartender like a beanbag? Why did Mexican girls wear black dresses and work in saloons? Why did they always have bigger tits than the girls who wore white dresses? You could hide the whole map of New Jersey in their bandeaux! And they had little rooms in the back of the saloon just like the grocery lady but they had only a bed there, no icebox or stove or nothing. And no mezuzahs on the frame of the door that closed in our faces.

So, one summer evening, the bad guys wait at Badger Gulch, spitting on their hands and talking dirty. We aren't wait-ing for the Wells Fargo Express. Ace is going to jump Horseface. They tell me I'm a rustler, an Apache, a bad hombre.

Horseface is a beast of burden, an iceman's plug, not even as smart as Tony the Wonder Horse. And if that's what she is, we will ride her, ride her in the street as publicly as the iceman's horse shows his startling hard-on. We had heard of nightclub acts between a woman and a pony—a horse was too big. Were we, in some way, playing out a deep-down penis envy, denying, as Centaurs, the intimidation of our own *schmeckeles* by that trun-cheon schmuck? Everything was all turned around cocky-locky, but we were going to do it anyway. We would jump Horseface, ride her, giddyap, giddyap, hump her in some horsey way that would tell her she should not hope to be taken down to the coal cellar even if she put a potato sack over her face.

Here is Horseface coming toward us. She is dressed in a simple cotton frock coming down below her knees. She has the look of a farm girl carrying pails of milk from the barn.

"On your mark!"

Horseface is near now. She is looking down as though she might find a lost nickel. That's about all she is going to find on Badger Street.

"Get set!"

Some instinct tells Horseface there is trouble coming. Her head goes up like that of a mustang stepping around a rattlesnake.

"Go!"

I'm on her back. I have my arms around her neck, my legs around her hips.

"Ride 'em, cowboy!"

"Put the leather to her, Ace!"

Horseface is strong. She does not fall. But she does not fight. She may be too shocked to retaliate. She bucks like a mounted mare. I fly up and down, hanging on like a bronco buster.

"Yippeeeee!"

Does Horseface cry out? Does Horseface finally throw me off? Do I come to my senses and recoil from my own bravado? I do not know. I remember nothing more than her flight into her alley. Will she tell? There is no one to tell. Most dreadful, does she take this attack as a crude flirtation, a first sign of recognition by the Seniors? The peasant proverb says, "A blow is as good as a kiss!"

André Gide says Dostoyevsky once rushed in on Turgenev, fell on his knees, and blurted out a story about molesting a child. Turgenev listened in horror. The "gentle barbarian" could find no words. Dostoyevsky, Gide claims, ran from the room, calling out, "I hate myself, but you I hate even more!"

I will not fall on my knees, but I ask you not to make me hate myself more than I did when the gang changed my name from Ace to Ape.

· 5 ·

Wild Ideas

Ironically, having gained their favor, I had cut myself off from the gang. I no longer cared about playing in the outfield. Or that Noodle could fart "The Star-Spangled Banner." Nor whether Yosel jerked off until blood came! I did not break all my ties. At World Series time I went, like the rest, downtown to Military Park and stood before the scoreboard on which tin players were jerked around the bases of a painted diamond, a minute after the news of what the real players had done was flashed over the telegraph.

Like everybody, I ran into the street to cheer for Lindy.

I saw people cry when Sacco and Vanzetti were executed.

On my Philco, I heard Jack Dempsey take the long count.

I entered a contest for sculptures carved out of Ivory soap.

I bought a tennis racket. My sister says I zipped her head into its cover.

Tennis! Did I really play tennis? Like those lonesome kids in a Ben Shahn painting, I probably played against the wall of the icehouse that separated our ghetto from the *beau monde*.

On the block, the cycle of innocence and cynicism went on like the seasons. On the milk box in front of the corner grocery store, a new crop of Juniors loafed, playing poker with the last pair of numbers on the license plates of passing cars. Now and then one ran out like a *banderillero* and dropped a penny under the trolley's iron wheels. He had to spit on Abe Lincoln's mangled face before he could pick it up. It sizzled.

Another kid who had won a penknife in the Claw at Olympic Park looked for a free inch on which to carve his name on the weatherbeaten boards I had polished with my ass, not so long ago. So many initials had been incised there that he was forced to work carefully, like a rustler burning a counterfeit brand onto the hide of a stolen steer. Biting his tongue, he put his blade to the side of the eroded *A* and carved against it a *3* that turned it into a crude *B*. It looked something like the brand

of Tom Mix's ranch. And so was obliterated the last proof of
Ace's existence on the block.

But life goes on, as they say, whether you are called Ace or
Ape. We all have more than one name. Nor are we born just
once. I found a new life in books. I read voraciously. There is, I
know, a theory that reading is a form of sexual curiosity. Folk
wisdom places it in the same class as masturbation. Too much
reading was not good for you. Out of bookworms came misfit
inventors, sissy poets, assassins of presidents.

Newark was famous for its Public Library. There one could
wander through the open stacks and pick and choose, not by
Dewey decimal number, but by quick inspection. In this period, I
read—or at least took out—as many as thirty books a month. I
was constantly being issued new cards.

I was particularly taken with the Russians. Those white
nights I spent on the bridges of the Neva! That Anna Karenina!
That Sonia with the "yellow passport!" Those Mityas, Alyoshas,
Smerdyakovs!

> "To father?"
> "Yes, to father first. Ask him for three thousand."
> "Mitya, he won't give it for anything."
> "I know he won't. I know it perfectly well. Now,
> especially. That's not all. I know something more. I know
> that for the last five days he has had three thousand
> drawn out of the bank, changed into notes of a hundred
> rubles, packed into a large envelope, sealed with five
> seals, and tied across with red tape. You see how well I
> know all about it! On the envelope is written: 'To my
> angel, Grushenka, when she will come to me.' He
> scrawled it himself in silence and in secret, and no one
> knows that the money's there except the valet
> Smerdyakov, whom he trusts like himself. So now he has
> been expecting Grushenka for the last three or four days;
> he hopes she'll come for the money. He has sent her
> word of it, and she has sent him word that perhaps she'll
> come. And if she does go to the old man, can I marry
> her after that? You understand now why I'm here in
> secret and what I'm on the watch for?"

What did Grushenka have that was worth three thousand
rubles to old man Karamazov?

My sexual world was still flat. In these books, I was beginning to search for my own Indies but, too often, passages of passion took place in an encapsulated reality so different from my own, I fell off the edge into a dizzy nothingness. Too many things were held back. The dotted lines of censorship, the blanks left to the imagination, failed me.

I was worse off than I had been on those uncomplicated afternoons at Fox's Cameo. I had skipped grades, found myself in ninth grade, junior high school, before I was thirteen. Was I doomed to spend my whole life as a Junior?

I tell you again, it's a mistake not to do what you're supposed to do when you're supposed to do it. It's a misguided accomplishment to be in high school before you've gotten your Bar Mitzvah fountain pen. You look like the other guys, pants too short, pimples, a fuzz of moustache on your lip, but precocity cripples you.

You are surrounded by flesh-and-blood blondies in white dresses with ribbons in their hair. Some of them have boobies bigger than the rancher's daughter. They get the monthlies every month. They show you their bloomers. They want to play Spin the Bottle. Some of them "lose control." You laugh when you hear one has been knocked up but you don't quite get the joke. You've gotten a head start but you never catch up. You are a Jewish Boris Karloff Frankenstein monster, clomping through a spooky tenement castle lit by lightning and frothing test tubes. You are looking for your not-yet-manufactured bride.

And you keep looking for the rest of your life. I started when I was about sixteen. Of course, I didn't have any nuts and bolts showing, and a golem doesn't have acne. My guise was anachronistic enough. From one of my uncles, I had inherited a checked, cashmere golf suit. I added a pair of Scotch-grain brogues, clocked woolen socks that came up snugly under my knickers, and a Dunhill pipe which I smoked in secret. In this getup, I made my way to New York every Saturday. I took the old Hudson Tubes that went into a hole in the Meadows around Hoboken. I guess I looked as if I'd been shooting grouse around the gas works.

I should have been wearing a beret. Wasn't I crossing the Hudson to the Left Bank of the Seine? I had a rendezvous with Kiki of Montparnasse and other pubic ladies of the museums and galleries. I went alone, always alone. As far as I know, I was the only one at Clinton High who was on speaking terms with Matisse, Derain, and the other Fauves. After I had exhausted my eyes, I went to an Automat and nursed nickels and wild ideas.

One day, I took courage from the "wild beasts" to move from representation to the raw. I went down to Forty-second Street and bought a ticket for Minsky's nonstop follies. Nobody questioned me. I was an eccentric scion on the slum.

I went often after that, until Fiorello La Guardia closed down burlesque. I loved this secret, glittering world of long-stemmed Gypsy Rose, of perfect Ann Corio, of startling Georgia Southern peeling off her arm-length gloves, finger by finger, with her teeth. I boggled at a certain Mrs. "Kingfish" Levinsky— she was married to a current heavyweight contender of that name—whose act was to strut across Minsky's boards lifting her mammae, one in each hand, aiming them like a dreadnaught's guns, challenging the baby-male in us to come out and fight. Ka-boom! She let you have it right in the breadbasket. You came out with your mouth so dry, you had to get yourself a Nedick's orange drink.

Best of all, I liked the mock-innocent foils of the baggy-pants comics: the nurses in little white caps and impossibly high heels running around the beds of imaginary invalids; the farm-er's daughters in their abbreviated gingham frocks wriggling on the traveling salesmen's knees; the gyrating widows coming back from the funeral in sexy black. Snare drum—rat-ta-ta-tat—and boom! She's throwing it right in the top banana's eye!

"Lady, your husband didn't die. He was bumped off!"

Nor did I neglect the highbrow in favor of the low. There was still a Shubert playhouse in Newark. For fifty cents, I went to matinees, sat in the balcony, and saw more sophisticated designs for living. In burlesque they chased around, in the theater they talked around. What did I do?

I was, after all, in what was to become Portnoy country. And since I was never, like some, threatened with having my hands chopped off, I must have yielded to self-abuse. Whacked off. Beat my meat. If you were under any restraint, it was only the folkways of the Badgers that told you that ipsation was some-thing like breaking training. And then, even temptation needs a familiar face. Tillie the Toiler was a paper doll. Anna Karenina was too old. And Fanny, even upended, was a spirit, a bird that was and never was.

What night pollutions I may have had belonged, by definition, to some primary person I would not meet face to face until I was on the couch. "Where Id was, let Ego be!" My daydreams I cannot disown. The introjections of the Badgers were still being digested, although the rancher's daughter was beginning to look more and more like Mrs. "Kingfish" Levinsky.

I saw her often in the disinfected corridors of Clinton High, walking with Phyllis Silverstone and other girls who were already being asked to weekends at Syracuse and Bucknell. I would be going to college soon but I would not choose frat. That was bourgeois. "Bushwaw, bushwah, bushwah."

I had already joined that growing band of -ists and -ites who were militantly opposed to whatever that word meant. We used it as much as the following generation would say pig. Fraternities were bourgeois. Shakespeare was bourgeois. Love was bourgeois unless it was free. The first ravages of the Depression were making ideologues of the haves as well as the have-nots. Except for you-know-what, I had everything money could buy. I was too innocent to think that money could buy that, too.

· 6 ·
A Lesson in Biology

Could it be that I, who had seen the famous *Nude Descending a Staircase*, had not yet kissed a girl?

In homeroom and other classes at Clinton, I sat behind Millie K. whose name put her alphabetically before me. She had them, those blessed burdens. Each was the size of a Friday-night challah. They were the kind some girls get at menarche, becoming, overnight, half nymph, half dowager. And though her starched blouse swelled, heaved like Vesuvius, there was about Millie not the slightest trace of vulgarity. She was utterly at home with herself and went through the school day smiling into space with the indifferent bliss of a wet-nurse.

One afternoon, just as my eyes had entered her shoulderblades and were swimming like isotopes in Millie's waiting milk, a messenger came to escort me directly to Mr. Capoletti, the boys' gym teacher. Me? I was not on any athletic squad. I knew I had not done anything seriously wrong unless it was to fail to clear the parallel bars in the proper dismount.

My confusion increased when I entered the gym where fifty girls were bouncing around in their sky-blue bloomers. I tried not to look.

Mr. Capoletti sat me down at the side of his desk. And now began a bewildering monologue.

"Yes," Coach Capoletti began, "we all go to the toilet."

No argument about that.

"Don't we?"

It was not a rhetorical question. I nodded my head.

"You go to the toilet, dontcha?"

My God, had I befouled something? Had my immigrant mother failed to inform me of some cloacal courtesy of the New World? I had been conscientiously potted and trained to Number One and Number Two.

"Girls go and boys go. Little babies go . . ."

I nodded yes, yes.

"And I go, too."

Why too? Were there exceptions? Over and over, there were these avuncular references to going to the toilet. Mr. Capoletti even went as far as saying "bowel movement."

"Y'know? A Crap. Dontcha?"

Then the exchange got more confidential and, to me, more lurid. Mr. Capoletti had shifted, with some logic of his own, from wastes to wastrels.

"And who goes to Burper when girls get into trouble?" Mr. Burper, honest, was the principal.

"Y'know, in the family way. Me, Cappy."

What Cappy did when he got there was a mystery. As far as I knew, pregnant girls were always expelled.

"But girls don't have the same biology."

Biology, I thought, was paramecium under the microscope.

"So we keep it on the QT, like gentlemen."

I was beginning to get Cappy's drift. The only "biology" girls did not have was the *schmeckele*. When they went to the toilet, they sat down. He was talking about something unspeakable possessed only by men.

"We don't blab about it," Cappy said.

At last, I got a glimmer about what I was doing in the office of this jockstrap Polonius. I had blabbed, violated the QT. At the time, I was in the Poetry Club, run by a white-haired old-maid English teacher named, as though by Dickens himself, Miss Wait. I had recently given her a poem that had pictured Man—capital *M*—as a half-educated ape, a kind of wounded King Kong, blundering around the hostile world with his bare face and his balls hanging out. I had actually called them genitals. Genitals! There it was. A biology and a half! A toilet thing!

"On the QT. Huh, fella?"

Cappy was calling me fella now. He was taking me into the Elks, Rotary, Shriners, and they were going to have a smoker. At midnight a couple of bims would pop out of a cake and suck your biology for five bucks a head.

The bell rang for the next class. I staggered out into the gym just as the bloomer girls were making a dash for their lockers and a quick look at their biology.

Miss Wait lost a lyric poet that day. No more Grecian urns for me. I became a proletarian poet. I may already have been one. In the seventh grade I had won a prize for a poem called "The Umbrella Man." It was a poignant slice of life, a twist on the cobbler's-children theme. An itinerant mender of umbrellas, drawn from Avon Avenue life, calls his wares in the rain that falls on his own uncovered head. "Oombrella man! Oombrella man!"

I didn't particularly choose to be a poet. The only models I had for this calling were not very attractive. They were usually strange little men, poor relatives, forty-second cousins, almost tramps, who carried torn briefcases from which they offered soiled copies of books they had had printed at their own expense. Their works were written during stays in state hospitals for tuberculosis. They were called *poyets*.

Even when you wrote prose you were called a *poyet*. For poet is not only a title earned by a few rhymes. It recognizes an obvious incompetence to deal with what is called real life. Such a person survives the real world only by his capacity to be moved by small wonders such as the way words dance in a line. So I survived Miss Wait's stab in the back. My verses became more obscure. I would never blab again.

I had made a few friends among the more radical staffers of

the school magazine who were planning to bring out a mim-
eographed underground newspaper. Because the school magazine was called *The Optimist,* ours would be called *The Pessimist.*

One of our contributors had already graduated. He, too,
had been a promising favorite of Miss Wait. But the best job he
could find in the first year of the Depression was as a plumber's
helper. He had written a rather good sketch about a poet whose
English teacher had told him to hold high the banner of pros-
ody—"truth is beauty" and vice versa. Now, because he has the
thinnest arm, the poet is elected by the boss plumber to plunge it
into a clogged WC. The poet comes up with a handful of spent
condoms. "A thing of beauty is a joy forever . . . And this is all
you need to know!"

Fresh from my experience with Coach Capoletti, I warned
the comrades that this story, rather than fiery calls to overthrow
the student government, would get us into trouble. But they all
felt safe behind clever pseudonyms. I had one too. I called myself "Michael Passos."

But even the smallest plots have their Judases. *The Pessimist*
came out and was grabbed up like hotcakes. And so were we. All
the Lenins and Trotskys, even the Lunacharskys were hauled
before Mr. Burper. Two of the ringleaders were kept from
going to college. (One became a rabbi, the other is now a movie
producer.) I, Michael Passos, was also called to judgment. But I
had contributed only a poem that made little public sense to start
with. Mr. Burper was stymied. Surrealism was not on the FBI's
list of dangerous isms. I was let go with a homily.

My role in the underground made me something of a school
hero. I even thought of asking Millie K. for a date. Now she
seemed to look back at me more often. By this time, I was having
some brushing contact with the opposite sex. When Kiddy says
we were childhood sweethearts, she is not stretching the calendar
by much. But we were neither children nor sweethearts when we
first became aware of each other. What I remember about her at
sixteen is how complete a woman she was, natively beautiful,
vibrant, driven by enthusiasm not yet dampened by history and
marriage to me.

Characteristically, Kiddy saw no contradiction in being a
cheerleader on Saturday afternoon and a naysayer the rest of
the week.

"Rackety rack, rackety rack! Give the bourgeoisie the sack!"

I admired her—all of her. She admired my mind. I had strange things to say. "The liquor of your laughter and the lacquer of your lips . . ." Like e.e. cummings, I no longer used capital letters. Kiddy knew about *poyets* and *shreibers* and *dramatistes*.

Kiddy's parents were old-time socialists. She had already begun her career with recitations at the Workmen's Circle Sholom Aleichem School. Actors like Jacob Adler and Boris Tomashevsky performed Shakespeare in Yiddish. They got more respect than millionaires.

I was still getting my share of respect from Kiddy when we received notice of the twenty-fifth reunion of our Clinton class. Kiddy wanted to go as much as I did not. Spurred by a coincidental sharp reminder of Millie, the impulse to conform won out.

Just at that time, a Mrs. G. had come to consult me—of all people!—about whether her teenage daughter should have her breasts made smaller. Yes, smaller! They had been measured and found to be beyond the plastic surgeon's fail-safe point of thirteen inches. Long? Around? And how much were they to weigh? Millie K. had carried hers lightly enough.

And so we'd gone across the Hudson and into the trees. Our tunnel of time was literal. And, as in those trick movies where divers come out of the water feet first, Kiddy and I went into the Holland, came out on top of General Pulaski's Skyway over the giant cattails of the Meadows into Newark's Broad Street, past my uncle's old used-car lot, all stainless steel, banners, and neon now, up to the best hotel in town, seedy now but once too elegant, too expensive to rent for our Senior Prom.

As a gesture to Mammon, I was wearing the semibespoke evening clothes that I had bought on Regent Street on my first trip to London. I was surprised to see how many other tuxedos there were in the ballroom. We had graduated in the cruelest days of the Depression. The proportion of success and failure had stayed fairly constant with what it had been then. Everyone looked as if they had once played themselves as a child in a historical movie. I felt I was still someplace in between. "Why be a man when you can be a success?" Kiddy's favorite quote from Brecht.

The reunion committee had hired a fast-talking professional mistress of ceremonies. She wore a circusy skirt and an "I'm only kidding" smile. She did have a good head for names. Without using a list, she called out a bunch of fellows chosen as luminaries of the class. The boy who'd had straight A's. The best shotputter the school had ever had. A small-time actor. An assistant district attorney. The school poet who had become a sexologist.

"Oooooo, a real expert!"

We all had to roll up our trousers and kick like Rockettes.

With a few snorts under my belt it wasn't too bad. I looked around for Phyllis Silverstone. She was probably in Acapulco sunning her expensive tushy. But Millie K. was there. This time I walked right up to her. I got the same old Madonna smile. Millie remembered *The Pessimist*. She even remembered that I had sat behind her. She had not strayed too far from home or her essential self. And like those Siberian mastodons preserved in the permafrost, she still was fresh enough to tempt you to take a bite.

"Your work sounds so interesting," Millie said. "And in Manhattan. Psyching people up."

Down, gentle Millie, not up. Folks furiously compliant or stubbornly oppositional, all bottled up, ready to pop their corks. And some in knotty quandaries. Like this lady, full of *Redbook* parenting lingo, who wants her daughter to have a good self-image. Thirteen inches! Like Mrs. "Kingfish" Levinsky. Maybe too much. Maybe not.

"Millie," I wanted to ask, "did you ever lay a ruler against yours?"

In her evening gown, Millie was showing more cleavage than I had ever seen in Homeroom 221. Her breasts had the same rosy glow of little veins that drunkards sometimes get on their cheeks. Between them was a valley in which yodeling cowboys rode into the sunset toward T-bones and biscuits back at Shangri-La Ranch.

In a Noel Coward play, I would have danced Millie out on the balcony, slipped her a couple of double entendres and had my milky way with her. Instead, I went home and had more than usually prolonged conjugal relations with the redheaded cheerleader of the Class of '32.

· || ·
By the Wind Grieved

· 7 ·
Look Backward, Angel

I was the first person in my family to go to college. My most affluent uncle—he had inherited the used-car business from Phil—wanted me to go to Princeton. Not that he palled around with Scott Fitzgerald or "Bunny" Wilson. Princeton was in New Jersey and he did business with the Buick dealer there. He was a self-made man, undaunted by quotas or cold shoulders. Princeton was the only college he knew.

But I was going to Carolina because I had a new friend and mentor, and that's where he had gone to school. Nick Gardenia was already something of a legend in our town. Like Chopin, of whom a thousand women claimed he had died in their arms, too many girls claimed they had gone out with Nick, at least once. Nick did break a lot of hearts. Okay for him. But why did I, who had barely dipped my toe in the sea of heterosexuality, choose to go below the Mason-Dixon line to a school attended by three thousand boys and absolutely no girls? Mistakes. That's why pencils have erasers.

Nick was a poet. Together with other students at Chapel Hill, he had started a literary broadside called *Tempo* which had brought Langston Hughes to town. Sounds innocent enough now. But in 1931, even in forward-looking Chapel Hill, there were enough Klan feelings to get a reading by a black poet banned and Nick booted out of school.

Nick had been suspended two-thirds of the way into his freshman year. The dean's letter to his father said: "Your son is too impressionable." Dean Hobble knew his job. Nick had opened his eyes too soon to the nightmare of history. He was one of those who would later be called "premature antifascists."

There was more to this suspension. I know Nick had gone AWOL to New Orleans with one of the other founders of *Tempo*. They had hitchhiked and ridden the rails. I learned this only from some fragmentary reportage Nick wrote. There was something mysterious about this adventure. The other boy was dead, and Nick would never talk about it.

For some years, that important time of becoming—at least by the calendar—an adult, my friendship with Nick would govern my life. I worshiped him. "O, lost and by the wind grieved . . ." How many times did I hear Nick say these words! Thomas Wolfe had published *Look Homeward, Angel* just two years before Nick himself had come to what Tom called "Pulpit Hill."

We had met in a class on Marxism given by an autodidact cabdriver who cracked the hard nuts of dialectical materialism like walnuts under his fist. He had the fall of capitalism ticking away like the meter in his Checker cab. Nick tended to needle him.

"And will the Pope 'wither away'? And will Mussolini just 'wither away'?"

Our class met in a hall that belonged to politically indifferent Ukrainians. They had a bar and a pool table. It was here, standing by the rack of varnished cue sticks, that I first saw Nick. He was smoothly running up a string.

"Six ball in the corner!"

He had a way of sizing up his shots that was like the pointed comments he made to the intellectual cabbie. Nick took the Ukrainians easily. He had to play with them because none of us radicals knew snooker. We were communists, not proletarians. Nick was a little of both. And an intellectual. He was as much at home in bookstores that carried avant-garde periodicals like *Contact* and *Hound and Horn* as he was in the billiard parlors and numbers joints of the part of Newark called the Ironbound. He disdained parties but revered the martyrs of the left—Mateotti, Sacco and Vanzetti. Nick looked at most things as though he were standing in an eighth circle he was adding to Dante's *Inferno*.

So Nick stood somewhat aside from the class struggle, gauging it like a carom shot for which the cue had to be well chalked.

Okay to celebrate the anniversary of the Russian Revolution, but we waited more eagerly for the next issue of *transition* than for that bannered day. There was a certain tension in this stance. You could hardly close your eyes—as some people do at a bloody scene in a movie—when you saw a man selling five-cent apples under a sign that said "Help me I am unemployed." Strangely, I can't really remember ever seeing one in Newark. But they were on every street corner in New York. And up Riverside Drive along the Hudson there was a new town still called Hooverville though Franklin Delano Roosevelt was president now.

With my kind of deluded optimism, even the Depression did not teach me Dr. Johnson's lesson that "there is more to be endured than enjoyed in the general condition of human life." It seems to me I was better off during those hard times than I have been ever since. A dollar—if you had one—went a long way and I had nobody to spend it on but Nick and myself. I even had a car, several cars, a Caddy, a Huppmobile, even a Marmon Speedster. I was working on my uncle's used-car lot that summer. I was seventeen, old enough to get my driver's license. Nick and I became the motorized column of Garibaldi's Redshirts. *"Chi va piano, va sempre sano.* Who goes slowly, goes safely. Who goes swiftly, goes to death. *Viva la Liberta!"*

Nick introduced me to speakeasies. I loved that moment when Nick knocked on the door—sometimes there were peepholes—and the guy would let us in. "Benny sent me," Nick would say even if the guy didn't ask. We always bought Booth's High & Dry. We liked the name. It would still be warm from the tub. But the label was authentic. It had a red scroll that said "By Appointment to His Majesty the King."

Nick's father ran a barbershop in the Ironbound section of town. He liked me. He had the notion I could be a good influence on Nick. I was younger, Jewish, and came from "business people." Rico knew something about the desperation behind Nick's sardonics. He never said anything to me directly, but when Nick and I left for a night on the town, Rico would signal to me with his eyes.

"My boy is weak," he would say one time. Next time he would say, "My boy is too strong." Rico always called Nick "my boy." I think he was trying to say that Nick refused to compromise in the little ways most people do.

Rico was the most dignified man I ever knew. Nick got his style from him. He could give you that feeling of personal attention you get from a concierge at a three-turret Italian hotel. I guess that's why Nick had more women than you could shake off with a stick.

"Please," Rico would say, as though you were doing him a favor by drinking his good Barbera.

Seven years later, Rico got into some kind of entanglement with the Lotto boys. He went into the neighborhood church, knelt at the altar, and blew his brains out. He picked the right place.

"Bless me, father, for you have sinned!"

But that's another story. My nostalgia is for those evenings when we would drink with Rico and listen to him play the mandolin. He had a nice tenor, tuned just right for "Come Back to Sorrento."

Warm with wine, Nick and I would go to his room with its painted plaster Madonna on the wall. Under it was a candle in a red glass, burning perpetually. Nick would use its flame to burn stuff he felt was either too private or not good enough to show anyone but me. I couldn't stop him. Nick was severe about his work. During his lifetime he published only a few poems. But he was never rejected.

At the end of that summer, just before I left for Chapel Hill, Nick got lucky with a long poem that had escaped the Madonna's flame. We walked into the magazine's bare office together, both wearing our usual dark polo shirts, ready to leave Nick's offering with a secretary. But the literary editor—a poet himself—called us into his cubbyhole. Nick pulled out the envelope with the poem and the other self-addressed one in which the rejection slips usually come.

"Let me see it," the old poet said.

And while Nick and I stood scraping our feet, he read. He had a way of nodding as though he were reading good news from home.

"That's fine, just fine." He gave Nick the return envelope. "Don't need this."

"See," I said to Nick, "you should burn money instead." Not sonnets, he knew I meant.

"Didja cock today?" Nick made it sound as if he were talking about the weather. "Hot today?" He was using a language he had invented to hide his feelings. "I beg your pock," he would say very seriously. And people would answer, "Not at all. Don't mention it."

We went to the Vesuvio, our favorite restaurant in Newark's Eleventh Ward, and had a Fantasia, a pizza with everything on it but the Bay of Naples. There was a girl along, more of a woman, really, who was obviously bohemian, a free spirit. Nick seemed to know her pretty well. We had met her on the Hudson Tube coming back from New York where she wrote "true confessions" for some magazine, under the name of Gale Storm.

"I get paid by the seduction," she said.

She kept kissing Nick on both cheeks. "I award you the Pulitzer Prize with three fig leafs," she repeated each time.

We were drinking Dago red on top of gin rickeys. Gale Storm kissed me, too. On the lips, juicy and long.

"For no goddamn good reason, kiddo," she said.

The sun also rose in Newark, N.J. We were of the Lost Generation, the three of us, Lady Brett and Mike Barnes and Jake. But I was not wounded anyplace then, above or below the belt.

· 8 ·
Sentimental Education

Newark's old Penn Station smelled of shoeshines and distances. Signal lights flashed. The locomotive came in hissing, blowing steam like a dragon. I ran toward the Pullman. It had a number and an Indian name like Lake Gitcheegoomee. My father touched me shyly, first on my shoulder and then on the lapel of my overcoat as though he were brushing away flecks of lint. I wanted to say something to him. He kissed me on the lips, Russian style.

I put up my valise and my brand-new Remington portable. I still have that machine. I've never been able to throw it out. It gathers dust in an attic and I'm afraid to open the latch on its fabricoid box. God knows what might come out. Its keys are stuck with the sticky adverbs of half a century ago.

The best minds—or bodies—of my generation were freezing in boxcars, being chased by railroad bulls. I was riding a Pullman, upper berth, would eat the best breakfast in the world: Smithfield ham, eggs over lightly, grits, and coffee poured from shining silver pots by waiters who asked you in Gospel voices whether you wanted more. I had nothing to fear but something President Roosevelt called "fear itself."

Do not think I arrived in Chapel Hill as a cynic. I was as wide-eyed as any of the frosh who came from little mill towns and tobacco farms. I was overwhelmed by the honeysuckle campus. It was bigger than Wequahic Park where the Leni Lenape Indians used to roam before Robert Treat kicked them out of Newark. A chain gang, all Nigras, as they seemed to be called, kept it manicured. The prisoners did not look unhappy. But I never heard them sing.

I loved the little town with its lazy, one-block main street, with its pecan trees and monument to the Confederate dead, a stone Johnny Reb looking down the barrel of a long rifle fixed with a bayonet. He was so real the town's hound dogs sometimes stood at point beneath his pedestal.

I moved into Aycock, one of the new red-brick dorms. My roommate was a senior from Brooklyn who always had a T-square in his hand. Breadlines were getting longer, good men were selling apples on street corners, the world was singing "Brother, can you spare a dime?" but Sy was going to be a civil engineer. A Jewish engineer, yet!

Still, he was going places. He was engaged to the daughter of a coreligionist in Tobacco City, nine miles away. I can see Sy coming down the hall after a shower, powdering his crotch, then his face, and chasing off to eat the Sabbath meal with his betrothed. He wanted to fix me up with her kid sister. I told him I was in love. At least I thought I was. With Kiddy, maybe.

"*Putz!*" he said. "At your age, you should play the field."

As Nick Gardenia's protégé I was welcomed by Eugenia and Milton Milton who were running, alone now, the broadside over which Nick had been kicked out of school. Though they were not much older than I, the Miltons treated me like a gifted child. *Tempo* had gained a national reputation, particularly for its author reviews. Few writers could resist the invitation to praise their own books. I was given a chance to report on those books which even their authors had disowned.

Milt Milton was a country boy who had worked in a textile mill when he was nine. Later, he had traveled as a kind of secretary to William Faulkner, mainly, it seemed, to keep a jug of White Mule always ready on each side of the author's typewriter. When its carriage hit the jug, Ol' Bill would know he had reached the end of a line. Stories like this made me feel I was well on my way to greatness. Had I not already begun my apprenticeship with Nick in the speakeasies of downtown Newark?

The Miltons were living behind a partition in their bookshop on lazy Franklin Street, selling the books *Tempo* received for review and renting out, at fifty cents a day, *Fanny Hill,* Frank Harris's *My Life and Loves,* and other under-the-table classics.

Where, I still wonder, had Milt gotten his Florentine edition of *Lady Chatterley's Lover?* I became a steady customer.

Through the Miltons, I began to move in a circle of congenial, even glamorous Southern intellectuals who came to the Tempo Bookshop to pass the time of day. Sometimes the president of the university himself would be there, debating "liberalism" with all comers. There was much drinking of corn whiskey and, when one could get it, grain alcohol cut with Nehi lime soda pop. People said you could go blind from the stuff. The worst that happened to me was puking over my Bam's necktie or occasionally passing out.

One afternoon, I stumbled over a dry wall in the churchyard behind the bookshop and stayed there, like Rip Van Winkle, with my nose buried in a pile of pecan leaves. But when I woke up it was morning and it was still 1933.

"Poor honey," Ginny Milton said in her stagey Southern accent, "we like to went out of our minds hunting for y'all."

It happened to be the day *Tempo* came from the printer with a little filler from an amorous alphabet I was doing. I'd gotten as far as

O is the hole in the doughnut,
The circle that surrounds the void.
Or, vocalized, runs the gamut—
Off-putting, opining, or o, boy'd!

A celebration was in order. Someone had a fruit jar of crystal-clear White Mule. I was toasted. Malcolm St. Clair, a gentleman farmer and litterateur, compared my lines favorably with "There was an old whore from Rangoon . . ."

St. Clair was said to be writing a history of the Lafayette Escadrille, in which he claimed to have flown. It was possible. The Great War was only fifteen years past. "Saint" may have been a boy pilot with or without the toothbrush moustache and the trick British accent he put on when he was sloshed. And that was often. He was tight-lipped about the Escadrille. It was too sacred to mention.

"We flew and we fucked!" was all he would say. "We flew and we fucked!"

And then he would pass out and piss down his leg.

St. Clair took me under his silver wing. He coached me for pursuits I would never pursue. What to look for in a polo pony, for example. There was a reverse anti-Semitism in his patronage.

"Be shrewd!" Saint would tell me, as though I were a failed Jew.

St. Clair had a tenant farmer called Charlie Bad Eye who kept a passel of hound dogs. They gave St. Clair the idea of the Great Hunt which began with a stirrup cup. Maybe we had two stirrup cups. The hounds were turned loose. We fanned out after them. Charlie Bad Eye had a way of hooting at his pack that seemed to keep their minds on business. They all had names.

"Yonder, Belle! Yonder, Star! Hoo! Hoo! Ya!"

We could see the rabbits streaking across the stubble of Charlie Bad Eye's fields. The dogs were smarter than Brer Rabbit. You could see them heading off the frightened cottontails, turning them in smaller and smaller circles until there was no place left for them to go. Someone would shoot and the Easter bunny would fall, kicking and convulsing in the dirt.

I walked with Milt. We raised some birds. Milt let me have his gun and I pumped away. I liked the feel of the stock against my cheek. I was a helluva long way from Badger Street. Bang! Bang! The air was full of baying and buckshot.

That night we ate a mixed bag. Milton was a country boy. He knew how to fix these things. I had never eaten game. Every so often you had to stop chewing and pluck a peppercorn of lead out of your teeth. My separation from home was complete. For when you have tasted rabbit, you can't go back to gefilte fish. But, as St. Clair assured me, "Everything is for the best, in this best of all possible worlds!" I was ready to take his word for it.

I was becoming too much of an esthete to go on living with Sy, the engineer. I moved into a single room in a small dorm,

Old South, that was the oldest building on the campus. It was like a Trappist cell. On one wall, I put up a small crucifix that Nick had given me. On the other I had a poster from a Russian movie, *Potemkin* or Gorky's *Mother*, with many bayonets pointed at the ruling class.

I was the only Yankee, certainly the only Jew, in the house. I was getting tired of being reminded of it.

"Izzy gawn Sunny school?"

The voice belonged to a farm boy with an amputated leg. When I saw his prosthesis rigged up with a shoe, leaning against the shower, I would wait another day to bathe. I was tired of feeling sorry for him.

I was counting the days until Nick's suspension would be lifted so he could come back and finish his freshman year. I was ahead of him now. In school, that is. In too many ways, I was ahead of myself. I was a romantic schoolboy traveling in fast, grownup company, some of them plagiarized from a Confederate novel of dipsomania and decay.

St. Clair, for example, was living comfortably in a ménage à trois. While I could be thrown into a turmoil by an "honest" letter from Kiddy telling me I would always be "special" but she was dating.

She gave me an excuse for drinking the gin I had made in the Miltons' bathtub. I still know the recipe: boiled water, extract of juniper, and alky.

The "flamingo" letters belong to this period, wild, intemperate, with all the endearments in all the languages I did not know. *"Chérie, mein Schatz, mi alma, dushenka . . ."* I would risk a blush to quote from them. But Kiddy's got them where I can't get my hands on them. "When I'm dead I want my son to read them. Let him see where I used to stand in your eyes." Yellowing, stained envelopes tied with Woolworth ribbon, postcards with three-cent stamps, franked with indisputable date and place. "Who killed Cock Robin?" Exhibit A.

A writer of banned books was visiting the Miltons. Like Count Dracula, he came from Transylvania. His tales were about peasant women who were always finding the Devil in their beds and being surprised by the length of his tail. He told a story about his own adolescence. He had been madly in love, talked about the girl day and night. An older friend, annoyed at his mooning, asked, "Have you ever pictured her sitting on the toilet?"

We had been drinking my gin mixed with orange juice. Count Dracula's cousin said it was—in French—*formidable*. I staggered back to Old South, tried to do the toilet trick with Kiddy. It didn't work. I fell into a crying jag. My pillow was soaked with tears.

I wanted to tell Ginny Milton about this but I was ashamed. I thought the world of her, may even have been a little in love with her. Ginny was from New York, a Hunter College intellectual who was just picking up her Southern accent. I can still see her, bright and quick, reaching for her pack of Wings cigarettes, lighting up, getting ready to recite the world's shortest poem, "Two Ahas!"

"Ahah! Ahah!"

One night, without intending to, Ginny made me painfully jealous. It must have been Milt's essences that cranked up that Schnitzler merry-go-round. Thinking he could make a little money moonshining, he had sent off for a whole apothecary of essences which could be added to alcohol—essence of rye, essence of Scotch, essence of blackberry brandy. We made up samples. They were awful but, for Prohibition, drinkable.

"I'd just as leave drink croup medicine," Milt said.

It may have been Milt's birthday. He usually abstained, but Flight Leftenant St. Clair had been plying him with various concoctions and now he was blissfully passed out in the back of the bookshop. There was something in the air, a whiff of the seraglio, perhaps the perfume of banned books. And Ginny was high and giggly. "Don't let me be alone with Saint," she was almost begging me. And then, as though she could not believe what she was saying: "Honey, did you hear me say 'Don't let me be alone with that man'?"

What to do? Tie Ginny down? And why me? Was I the court eunuch? Didn't I want to stamp my feet in that Mississippi mud? Ginny, chile, don't you suspect that I think of you as Temple in *Sanctuary*? Particularly the corncob scene. Don't I betray Milt behind his back thinking of my tongue in your Mulligatawny mouth and my hand on your tomboy *tushy*? Ginny, virginny, bathtubginny, let me light your Wings for you and y'all will teach me not to be afraid.

I was just about to jump on the carousel and try for my own

box of Cracker Jacks, when Milt came stumbling out from behind the partition. He looked suspicious. There was too much sex in the air.

"Here now," Milt said, "let's get our ducks all in a row!"

Well, I guess they lined up all by themselves. Maybe a customer came in to borrow a dirty book. Maybe the president of the university, out on one of his lonesome walks, dropped in for some debating. The other President was about to close all the banks that were still open. Prexy may have wanted to hear St. Clair's assurance that everything was for the best in this best of all possible worlds.

· 9 ·

The Depression Weekend

Maybe it was. Where else could you live without money? For about this time, FDR closed the banks. They were closing anyhow. He only made it official. For me, this disaster had a touch of irony in it. My father had given me a checkbook I had never used.

Two days before the spring break, we were all called to Chapel. Vacation was canceled, our own president told us, because he was afraid, with the banks closed and all, we would never get back. He wanted us to stay right where we were and no one was to worry about money. All the merchants were instructed to take our IOUs. The movie house would open at ten tomorrow morning and there would be a special free show. At night there would be a gala dance in the Tin Can, the big gym near the stadium. These days of license were officially designated the Depression Weekend.

Nick arrived just in time for it. He was being permitted to finish the last quarter of his freshman year. I was already a sophomore. It didn't matter. There was nothing waiting for us after graduation. He rented a room from a lady he was already calling Molly Bloom. She did have a juicy laugh. "I'll tell y'all everything but my age," I heard her say. There was a daughter, too, who looked at Nick as though he had popped out of a storybook.

Word of the Depression Weekend and the temporary end of capitalism reached as far as the bootleggers in Baltimore. They came down and took away all the real money that was left in town. No one was without one or two bottles of something. Some actually had labels. By coincidence, every bottle was eight years old.

The Depression Weekend movie was something British. The little movie house opened early Saturday morning. By noon, a hammy actor with a stock-company lisp was getting hoots and loud sound-effect smacks each time he got close to his sweetie. During a touching embrace, a bottle would go crashing toward the screen. Carolina's men laughed viciously. They had no one to kiss.

"Heeeathcliff!" They jeered for some reason lost in time.

I was spiffing up for the dance, when these yokels, Class of '36, started kicking at my door. They were just being neighborly.

"Hey, Noo Yawk, git some o' this Panther Piss, put hayah awn yo' chest!"

I pretended I wasn't there.

"Jewboy Rosfelt leave us naught but this corn-hole scrip!"

The voice was raw with White Mule and frustration. It belonged to the Gimp. He knew what poor was. Scrip was what the tenants and sharecroppers used at the company store. But there's always somebody worse off. "Nigger, don't let the sun set on you in Fayetteville." Someday all men would be brothers. Someday there would be a Soviet Mississippi.

They staggered off to the dance. The gym at the wooded end of the campus was made out of corrugated sheet metal. That's why it was called the Tin Can. They were singing the Alma Mater, harmonizing the slow part which had the same tune as "Far Above Cayuga's Waters." Then the chorus, as loudly as they could, boasting, proud of the only unchallengeable claim they had.

> I'm a Tarheel born,
> I'm a Tarheel bred,
> And when I die, hi, hi, hi,
> I'm a Tarheel dead.
> Sooooo, rah rah Ca'lina 'lina,
> Rah rah rah . . .

They were already deep into the trees of our famous Arboretum when I heard it for the first time bouncing off Chapel Hill's antebellum stones.

"Heeathcliff! Heeathcliff!"

Months after, on still, starry nights you would hear these long, sobbing wails like the keening of the insane. You began to hear it more often than the Rebel Yell. It was a woman's yearning cry. Miss Cathy on the moors. But we were not coed. These "Heathcliffs!" were without gender, a call to everything "lost and by the wind grieved."

Nick came by to get me. "The eagle screams tonight," he said. He was dressed as always in a dark suit and a navy-blue polo shirt buttoned at the neck, like a priest without a collar. Somehow he had gotten hold of what purported to be a bottle of Silverstone Seven Star.

"Utilize this on your *pupik*."

My first swig went down the wrong way. The rawness of the hooch grabbed me by the short hairs. This rotgut had never come into Port Newark and been loaded onto any of "Sweets" Sugarman's Reo trucks.

"Not used to the good stuff," Nick said. "Served exclusively at the Riviera Club." He was always reminding me of Kiddy in these roundabout ways. He liked her. "She's rambunctious," he said. "A pepperoni." It amused him the way I carried the torch for her.

"Fangoo!" I said the way we had learned to say it on Badger Street, putting the elbow of my bent right arm in the palm of my left hand. It was really *"Va fan coulo!"* and meant "Go up yours!" The arm business was to indicate the length of the member intended to penetrate.

"Nice Jewish boy," Nick said.

"You, too," I said. "When's the last time you dated a *shikse?*"

"I have been faithful to thee, Cynara Ginsberg," Nick said and rolled his eyes heavenward. "Utilize this on your circumcision."

I utilized. The second swig chased the first one like a truant officer footing after a hooky player and caught it by the pants.

"Utilize this on your rosary beads."

"Utilize this on your Bar Mitzvah."

We utilized all the way to the Tin Can, Nick saying "Let us utilize, you and I, when the evening is spread out against the sky . . ." and finishing with outrageous similes, ". . . like a dead mackerel," ". . . like a Newark whore on a bed of nails," and so on.

The Tin Can's walls were lined with hundreds of wooden dumbbells we used for calisthenics. An orchestra in sky-blue jackets was playing "Penthouse Serenade." There were girls in long gowns—where had they come from?—dancing with guys who must have owned their own tuxedos.

I had considered renting one for my high school prom. I had gone stag with some other horny stags. I didn't dance once. I didn't know how. I remember coming home later than I ever had in my young life. It was, in fact, morning. The trolleys were beginning to run on Avon Avenue. Like the people in Scott Fitzgerald's story, we had gone to New York and had pancakes at Child's.

Here, a few bumpkins, mean with rotgut, kept egging each other to cut in. No one did. They stood sheepishly on the foul lines around the edge of the gymnasium and heckled the dancers. One fellow, called High Stockings, seemed to be a special target.

"Haul ass!" he would hiss at his buddies. And this would make them happy.

Nick was doing a kind of Valentino tango all by himself. I knew he had a snootful. He was gliding up to various Tarheels and double-talking them. I got worried. These country boys didn't want you making them look like country boys.

"Didja cock today?" Nick was asking.

They looked at him as though he were a lynched nigger hanging from a tree.

"Didja punce?" He was asking very sincerely.

I got Nick under the arm.

"I beg your pock!" he said, with a little bow.

In the crowd, I lost him. Nick had this way of disappearing. I suppose he couldn't take me or anybody else for too long. In those days, he gave you the feeling he couldn't even stand himself. Ginny said he was Lucifer.

I found him passed out on top of a pile of bodies, three deep, in the men's room. Some of the guys lay in their own puke. Nick wasn't totally passed out. He was going down for the third time in a sea of gin.

I talked to him now. He got up and made it out to a tree. He pushed me away, put his finger in his throat, and threw up. It was his trick. When he did this he would turn so white I would be afraid. But he always came out of it, smooth as William Powell.

"Up the big, brown kazoo, Comrade!" he said and fell.

When I tried to help him, he looked at me so desperately with those thousand-year-old eyes I had to back off. I knew I was as close to him then as anybody ever would be. I stayed right behind him while he stumbled back to his crummy room. At the door, he put his arm around me for a minute.

"The bread I broke with you was more than bread. The wine I drank with you was more than wine."

Nick got this out and kicked the door shut. I heard him fall heavily. Maybe the widow lady picked him up.

The next I saw of Nick, he was riding up and down in front of the Tempo Bookshop in a Packard phaeton exactly like the one FDR rode in through the confetti. Malcolm St. Clair in a Panama hat was at the wheel. I don't know where they found the car. Saint had the eight-cylinder Packard lugging and stalling.

They came into the shop with two fruit jars of alky. Saint brought out a dozen eggs and a bottle of grenadine. He was going to make clover clubs. He even had a cocktail shaker. Saint separated the whites from the yolks with a palsied hand. The clover clubs went down easy and had a kick like a Georgia mule.

We drank a batch and rode down Franklin Street in the car. Then we made another batch and rode in the Packard again. Nick was standing on the back seat now, giving out blessings like the Pope. After all, it was Sunday of the Depression Weekend, and Nick had been an altar boy. He was sprinkling imaginary holy water and calling out, a little too seriously: "Bless me, father, for you have sinned!"

I think it was the same day that St. Clair did his *corrida*. He had been reading *The Sun Also Rises* and wanted to test his bravery. Milt knew a farmer who had a bull.

"Is he of a veritable size?" asked Saint. "Does he have the veritable bananas?"

The bull's bananas were big enough and his *cojones* were the size of grapefruit. Smoke was coming out of his nostrils. Saint climbed over the fence. He had somebody's old red dress in his hand. He waved it.

"Huh, *toro!*" Saint called out in his Alabama accent. "Huh, *toro! Toro!*" He thought he was in the ring at Pamplona and Lady Brett was going to throw him her nympho pussy wrapped in her famous man's felt hat.

The field was soft and Saint was up to his ankles in mud and *merda*. He was in no position to do a *veronica* or even haul his ass out of there if the bull charged.

"*Toro! Toro!*" Saint was shaking the red rag like a ship-wrecked sailor at a passing boat. The bull looked annoyed. He had no heart for the fiesta of lights.

"Fucking cow!" Saint yelled at him.

We all went back to the bookshop and drank to Saint's *cojones*. There were no more eggs so we drank alcohol poured over iced Nehi. We awarded Saint both ears and the tail of the bull who would not fight.

Again, Nick disappeared. He turned up that night with a big lip and a piece chipped off his front tooth. He had been touring in the Packard. Saint, driving on the wrong side of the highway, had plowed into a ditch. I didn't suspect that kind of death wish in the erstwhile matador. I only knew about Nick's. He drank this way sometimes, seeking oblivion. There seemed to be no ap-parent displeasure with his life. Nick simply had a strong sense of the nearness of death, a kind of yearning for the Apocalyptic. His mother, his sister, and a baby brother had died during one winter of his adolescence.

Nick finished his interrupted freshman year and went home to find a job. I had three months to go as a sophomore. We made a pact to stay out of school. College was no place for us. The campus was a kind of open city where nothing changed but the seasons and the games boys played.

Honeysuckle flooded the campus. Chapel Hill smelled like a fancy woman in an elevator. I spent a lot of time with the Miltons, who were struggling to keep *Tempo* going. The issues were irregular now. The last one had a story by Erskine Cald-well. He was living on a farm in Maine and eating apples, he wrote, three times a day. Things were winding down. The last of Milt's essences was gone.

"No use crying into a milk bottle," he said.

I was not paying much attention to school, waking up with hangovers and cutting classes and Chapel, which was com-pulsory. I was flunking French because I thought I could learn it by ear. I was flunking Geology because I couldn't stand kissing the stones. But I was writing a lot, alternating between Dada and Naturalism. *The Carolinian* had already printed some of my sketches about life "around the block." One was called "Mrs. Garlic, That Pig." Another dealt with my old playing-card hero, Benny Leonard. I was, in a small way, reversing the flow of literature from South to North.

Until one day I got a letter penned by the same dean who had given Nick the hook. He called me to his office. He wanted to know what I was doing with myself. I told him I'd been doing a lot of reading on my own.

"Reading?"

"Yes, sir. I'm into the second volume of Trotksy's *History of the Russian Revolution.*"

"Who? Tosky?"

I could see that such candor was troubling the dean. I made a quick right turn.

"I'm also writing."

"Ah, writing!"

Thomas Wolfe had written *Look Homeward, Angel.* It was the biggest thing to hit the Tarheels since Grant took Richmond. I wasn't exactly on native ground, but Dean Hobble wasn't taking any chances. He ended up showing me out of the door with a gentle caution not to skip Chapel though I was, of course, of another faith.

Prohibition was repealed. Some students got into the steeple of the Methodist church and rang its throaty bells. But for us, nothing had changed. The campus was still off limits to booze. We still went to the same filling stations and drank the same dregs.

Nick wrote to me, his *caro cugino*, that he had found a job as "night watchman in the daytime" in that huge fur-processing plant that gave its urine stink to the north end of Newark. "But neither my waistline nor my clothes was ever meant for the tempo and terror of this," he wrote.

And then, only weeks after Repeal, he added, "What America needs is a return to the speak easy, speak slowly, speak well days of our Yuletide youth. To hell with progress! Down with cocktail lounges! Up with basements!" Nick talked that way, improvising, noodling, riffing, honking, riding out a cadenza of private slogans.

In that letter, Nick went on to cheer a poem I'd published: "The world needs wit, badly, plus sentiment. Belly laugh very subversive, not the ambiguous, purchasable smile. Down with smiles! Up, up with anything catalytical!"

And he ended, as usual, with a montage of restless questions: "Where were we? Where are you? Employed? On Picket Line? Enroute? Where?"

"O, lost and by the wind grieved . . ." By the light of a torch made from your burning poems, I see you in your always mourning-black suit and the Modigliani shirts we both wore like twins, your face with its wicked smile and those moony Abruzzi eyes and me, worshiping, innocent, blundering.

Where was I? I only knew that I wanted to be with Nick.

· 10 ·
"Take It Off!"

My new window on life was through the windshield of a Chrysler 77 roadster on my family's used-car lot. Uncle Phil had broken the path to a *métier*. His place had been taken by the youngest of my grandfather's six sons who had been brought to the New World as a babe in arms. He considered himself American born and having been Yankel was, indeed, called Yank. He was a great reader of *Pluck and Luck* dime novels. It was he who had said I should go to Princeton. He was still saying it.

I tried to explain. But you did not explain to Uncle Yank. Seeing me loaf against the Chrysler's leather upholstery with a book—it was *Swann's Way* that summer—would remind him that I was still in the wrong place.

"Princeton College is good."

"Frank Merriwell went to Yale," I kidded.

"What for? Princeton College is the best."

You didn't argue with Uncle Yank. He took boxing lessons and fought secretly as an amateur welterweight.

As a kid I had worked summers on the lot. The rest of its length was used for public parking then. Even before I was old enough to get my driver's license, I became expert at lining up one jalopy next to the other with a minimum of inches and damage.

For no good ethnic reason there was a Hofbrau Haus next door to us, complete with singing waiters who yodeled and slapped out rhythms on their leather shorts. Getting out the buried cars on New Year's Eve was heroic. Once I almost backed into two women squatting and laughing at the puddles lapping at their shoes and screaming, "Don't look! Don't look!" I looked to the last drop.

In those days, all the regular parking attendants were called, interchangeably, Red and Slim and Tex. They seemed to come from the same hometown and have the same set of pocked and unwashed genes programmed for nothing but cruelty, mayhem, and hard luck. They played the ponies and owed each other disputed money. Tex borrowed from Slim on Wednesday the sawbuck he had borrowed from Red on Tuesday. The same five-dollar bill seemed to go from one hand to the other. They were always passing around a half pint of bad whiskey, cursing each other and the world. They talked of nothing but long shots and poontang.

I was about fifteen when, through them, I saw my first absolutely authentic whore. She was a dumpy blonde already this side of alcoholism. She wore, always, a flowery print dress, as though she were a bridesmaid at a perpetual wedding. She would stroll past the lot and then, making it look like a sudden whim, stop to wander among the Dodges, De Sotos, and Chrysler Airflows like a prospective buyer. I did not try to sell her. She encountered the Texans with a pathetic show of surprise.

There was a small shack of an office on the lot. In front of it, a bargain would be struck. The woman's price must have been low, but singly none of the Texans could meet it. Tex borrowed from Slim. And then, while one redneck stood guard outside the shack, the soiled bridesmaid would be on her knees in front of the other's fly. They watched each other and cursed at the angel of brute necessity.

"Goddam cocksucker!"

"Lick it, bitch!"

All one could see were two cursing country boys. The eyes of one rolled in the aura of epilepsy.

Finished, the woman would walk down the street, with her

price in her purse. Nothing marked her. She wiggled her ass like anyone else. You might have picked her out only by her aimless strolling which told you she was going no place fast.

I was considered too sheltered, I suppose, to know what was going on. But by coarse hints the rednecks let me know they would not risk more than being "sucked off" for fear of a dose. Now they all seemed to have one. For health reasons, I was warned to avoid the sacred jar into which they urinated. What did they do with that Grecian urn when it was full?

The Texans were gone now. My uncle needed the whole of the lot for his expanded dealership. The shack where Red and Slim and Tex had in turn rammed and spurted their sawbuck's worth was a proper office now with a desk and a pen on an onyx base with which deals could be closed. I was a salesman now, a man among men. But was I a real man?

I tried to be.

While Nick, in the fur factory, made his rounds punching the time clocks that said all was well among the flayed pelts and hides, I kept an eye on rows of jalopies with signs behind their wipers that said LIKE NEW or ONE OWNER or, with questionable sincerity, SACRIFICE. As far as I was concerned, they sold themselves.

The use of a roadster was a perk of the job. Having worked, or pretended to work, in it all day, I played in it at night. Nick and I would cruise around in the speedster or meet blind dates he made on the phone. Nick was very good on the phone. He enjoyed the ploys of chance encounters, made up outrageous backgrounds for us, and showed such special interest in the girls—factory workers, sometimes, even kids still in high school— that they would soon be telling Nick their wildest, secret hopes. He really was a spoiled priest, that Nick.

That summer, I had begun to see more of Kiddy. In fact, our relationship was cemented on the lot one afternoon when she passed by and my uncle's Chow Chow dog bit her. It was part of my job to watch the watchdog. The two points of its teeth showed blue on her wrist. There was a great fuss. My uncle didn't want her to get hydrophobia. He could be sued. I had to take Kiddy to a doctor. One thing led to another, and soon I began to give her my own rabid hickies.

I have a kind of déjà vu. I am embracing Kiddy in a hallway like the one in which his assassins waited for Uncle Phil. The long good-night. Will there ever be an act more anticipated and driven, more daring than the first slide of one's hand above the knee and toward the widening thigh? Higher, a little higher, half held, half pushed away until it is very close. And the girl's body twists out of your arms. And the apologies. And the pleading. And the cajoling. And the forgiveness. And beginning again. And the girl so sugar and spice and innocent and eager, doing only what she is supposed to do. This is the great thrill—to do, even badly, what everybody else does.

Kiddy wanted to be an actress. She had the looks—auburn hair and freckled white skin and legs that got her the job as a nightclub cigarette girl. Even as an adolescent, she had what are sometimes called quivering or, at any rate, dramatic nostrils.

The Revolution gave her her first break.

New York had its John Reed Club. Newark's left-wing club was named after Jack London. No matter that the old oyster pirate had said, "If fame come with cash, come cash. If cash come with fame, come fame." Or that he had overdosed on morphine when his Valley of the Moon castle had burned to the ground. Jack London had run for mayor of Oakland, California, on the Socialist ticket. And you couldn't very well name your club after Joe Stalin—even in those dreamy days.

The club boasted a drama group that specialized in "mobile agit-prop"—agitation and propaganda ready to go anyplace, anytime. It was a theater about which one bemused comrade said, "In the first act, we suffer, in the second we pass out leaflets, in the third we go on strike." There was also a dance troupe led by two sisters named Fanya and Tanya. Kiddy belonged to everything. She acted, danced barefoot in costumes made of burlap tied with diaper pins, read Lenin's *Imperialism,* and got up at five o'clock in the morning to give out leaflets at the RCA plant.

I suggested her stage name to Kiddy. In a reversal of the "injustice collecting" that has characterized our later years, she still takes it as a special sign of love that I gave her her very name. She was my creature, the sharp-tongued Bride of Frankenstein.

Kiddy looked really good in the blue work shirt that was the costume of the agit-props. With her copper hair flowing and her nostrils flaring, she would chant, "What have you done with all your gold, America? What have you calmly bought and sold, America?" Those were pretty big questions that could only be

asked with a challenging thrust of the chest. Agit-prop acting
was pretty physical and involved a good deal of raising the right
arm in the *Internationale* fist salute that, with the fall of Republic
in Spain six years later, would go down forever as a meaningful
symbol. Kiddy did it convincingly. It wasn't too far from calling
for a "locomotive" or a "rackety rack" for the Clinton High
eleven.

On the wall in the room in which we met hung a banner
which said, "Art Is a Weapon!" To hit the likes of Tex and Red
and Slim, it would have to be. A sharp one, a pointed stick or a
blunt instrument.

The talent was there but finding an audience was always a
problem. The mobile troupe performed in the streets, at factory
gates. But it got about as much attention as a Salvation Army
band. Then, some demented *Narodnik* put the *agitka* into an Amateur Nite at the Empire, Newark's only burlesque house.

Kiddy has always suffered from what Zoschenko called "zeal
beyond reason." She was, deep down, prudish, but she would
have done anything for the Revolution. Let some commissar
concoct a party line that worked a G-string into the struggle to
reach the masses, and she would be right there. "Strip for land,
bread, and peace!" Kiddy would be billed as the Titian Typhoon.
She would be a knockout. "Lady, your husband wasn't killed, he
was bored from within!" Yuck, yuck, yuck!

The Empire did extra business the night Kiddy made her
debut. A claque of Jack Londoners lent their solidarity. Wearing
the troupe's standard blue work shirt, opened an extra button or
two as a concession to the new audience, Kiddy played a social
worker ministering to The Forgotten Man. The skit was called
"Charity." The Forgotten Man, weak from hunger, fell to the
floor of the stage. Kiddy ministered, whatever that is.

Then Kiddy came to the unfortunate line: "What ails you,
my good man?"

My good man! Up came the salacious hoots and jeers and
those special tough-guy whistles made by putting two fingers
over the tongue.

"Take it off! Take it off!" the voice of the people demanded.

With her Ginger Rogers gams, Kiddy would have done better to take the hint. Before she knew what was happening, a long
metal hook caught Kiddy around the waist and pulled her into
the wings. She protested. They let her start again.

"What ails you, my good man?"

"Take it off!"

Again the hook and Kiddy pleading with the *Lumpen-proletariat.*

"But we've got something important to say!"

But they had come to see, not to hear. As the hook pulled her toward the wings again, they applauded.

"Sometimes I get the feeling," Kiddy said, "that the workers of the world are united against *us!*"

The club held discussions. It was decided to get off the streets and do a regular play with acts and costumes and tickets. Nick and I wanted to do *Gods of the Lightning,* a play about the Sacco and Vanzetti trial. We were outvoted. There were not enough speaking parts: the jury, I think, was done with twelve dummies. They chose *"Can You Hear Their Voices?"* a kind of living newspaper written by one Whittaker Chambers who was later to become the "pumpkin papers" man in the Alger Hiss case. It was about farmers protesting the dumping of milk while babies starved. Kiddy got the part of the farmer's firebrand daughter who had the final, rabble-rousing speech. On opening night, the curtain came down, uncued, right in the middle of it. Kiddy almost got conked.

I have a certain amount of confusion about the sequence of events, but somehow, between getting the hook and taking bows, my childhood sweetheart gave her cherry to the director of the fiasco. It hurt when I found out. I don't remember how much, but I tell you, it still hurts now. When you think about it, our whole story might have been different, more typical, without interruption and operatic coincidence. It was her own scenario which Kiddy so humanly betrayed. At seventeen, I did not know how, perhaps did not really want, to go beyond the adolescent intimacies we had reached. I had no claim on her. I can as little say I was rebuffed as she can say she was not courted.

Was I, even then, set apart in Kiddy's mind to represent the might-have-been? Certainly, a lifetime later, what I became was not enough for her.

In plain honesty, I was, at the time, probably too foolishly liberated for genuine jealousy. But I was conventional enough to stop seeing Kiddy. I began to look elsewhere for whatever one looks for.

Kiddy says now, "It meant nothing."

She is a feminist and pretends to be nonpossessive, but underneath the ideology she is wildly jealous. If she ever reads this, she will wonder "Who?" Who could it have been with whom I consoled myself? Like Lot's wife, let her not look back.

· 11 ·
The Queen of Sheba

Lot? Lot in Sodom.

I looked up from a passage in Proust in which a man with a woman's name was loving up a girl with a boy's name. Over the Chrysler's steering wheel, I saw Nick walking too carefully toward the lot. One look and I knew that Sebastian Pupik was on the loose. That was a name Nick sometimes used to introduce himself—or me—at parties. The other one would be Slavko Vorkapitch. We stole that name from the guy who used to do all the special effects for Warner Bros.

"Secondhand salesman, I salute you!"

Senza dubbio, he had been guzzling his old man's Strega—which meant witch, but Nick's father called it "the honeymoon drink." He was a romantic gent. His barbershop on Mulberry Street was a drop for Lotto, the Italian numbers game. On busy days, Nick worked there, giving shaves only. On himself, he used a straight razor he would sharpen like a pro on a leather strop. Right now the talcum on Nick's face made him look like a mime.

"Can you get off?" For Nick he sounded urgent.

"Something doing?"

Nick reached into his pocket and showed me a roll of bills held by a fat elastic band.

"Wow!"

"Wow! Wow!" Nick mocked. "American-Jewish Tarheel! O, lost and by the wind grieved *pupik!* Bow wow!"

It was some kind of holiday, Passover maybe, and Nick had stumbled over this bundle while making his rounds, punching time clocks in the empty plant. Even in the bowels of the Depres-

sion there were fur skinners working there who could put or
take this kind of dough playing the horses. They had a union
that put a bomb under the boss's car. Nick's idea was to spend it
all, get rid of it. There must have been a hundred bucks in the
roll.

"*Sporco,*" Nick said, "dirty Fascisti dreck!"

Filthy lucre to be spent fast. Nick didn't want me to take the
Chrysler.

"Taxis tonight!"

The last time out he had thrown up on the roadster's door.
The Dago red wouldn't come off. Nick was very mysterious
about our destination. First we would walk.

"Shank's mare!" he said. "How's your shank's mare?" He
liked the words. "And your pupik's mare? And the mare of Castelbridge? Who wrote the mare of Castelbridge?"

"Slavko Vorkapich," I said. "Where are we going?"

Nick crossed his eyes to show me we were going here or
there or two places at the same time.

"*Chi va piano, va sempre sano. Chi va forte . . .*"

"*Va la morte,*" I finished the old Garibaldi battle cry.

Neither death nor liberty was ever mentioned in my family.
Nick talked about both but never gave the impression of being
too much in a hurry to face one or the other.

"*Andiamo,*" Nick said. "*Andiamo,* friend of my youth."

I was going wherever he went and asking no questions. We
were one. Nick got a kick out of my blind allegiance. Not everyone has a puppy dog who walks on his hind legs. And reads and
writes and drinks Pernod. I would have followed Nick to the
ends of the earth. He stood, somehow without trying, for everything that I wanted for myself. Exactly what it was I still cannot
put into words, even as I still haven't given up looking for it. We
wanted something better, better for ourselves and everyone in
the world in which we lived. Right now he was giving me the Red
Front salute but holding up one "Up yours!" finger instead of a
fist.

"*Avanti, popolo!*" Nick hissed. He was leading an army of
only one.

We stopped first at the bar of the Hofbrau next door. The
Texans' whore, looking neither better nor worse for her humilia-
tions, was swallowing the last of a highball, ice and all. She paid.
As she got to the door, the bartender very pointedly broke the

glass she had used. I made a note to put that in a story someday.

We were making a tour of the old downtown speakeasies. Some of the brownstones were roominghouses again. We had a rickey here, a Tom Collins there, dropped in at the Riviera, "Sweets" Sugarman's place which had been too classy for us when Kiddy had worked there. I was surprised her mother had let her. Maybe they'd needed the money worse than I knew. Kiddy was full of surprises. She sure handed me a lalapalooza. She was the experienced one, now. I still thought the moon was made of green cheese.

Nick was full of surprises, too. He peeled off a ten-dollar bill and dropped it into the cigar box on the piano player's upright. One thing about Nick, he had a tin ear, really liked only opera, Puccini mainly. I'd seen him sit with Rico in front of the Victrola, both of them with their eyes closed, in seventh heaven, mouthing the words. Rico knew them all. *"Che gelida manina . . ."*

The piano player didn't have cold hands. He gave Nick a nod without breaking stride and then, with his left hand laying down chords, he took the sawbuck in the fingers of his right hand, folded it, and put it to his lips. He was light-skinned, looked a lot like Duke Ellington. And now he was singing softly, almost to himself as though he didn't want to let too many people in on it. "Going to Chicago, just to get my hambone boiled. . . ."

Nick was snapping his fingers out of time and looking at me like a bad angel. He was shaking up a cocktail of pity, irony, and love. The blues were rolling. "Stick out yo' can, here come de garbage man. . . ."

"Yessirree," Nick was saying, "the veritable *culo!*" He had something up his sleeve.

We found ourselves in front of the Empire Burlesque, looking at pictures of that week's spangled meat. Nick gave me one of those looks. He knew I was still carrying some kind of flickering torch for Kiddy.

"Wanna buy a duck?" he said gently. Joe Penner was the big comic around Newark then. Nick loved this kind of nonsense. "Wanna viaduct?"

I thought he wanted to go in. Instead, he took me next door into a Victorian manse with lots of gingerbread work around its windows. The little smile on Nick's bee lips got more wicked.

"We're going to repair what ails you, my good man," he said gently. He looked like a politician about to kiss a baby.

Now we were in a big parlor with a miniature bar and a flamboyant jukebox against one wall that ended at a wide bannistered staircase. We were the only white people in the place. Where did Nick find these joints? The few Negroes in the room were all well dressed. The women were large, not young, and seemed all dressed up for a ball. The men were the kind who wear a vest with an elk's tooth hanging from a couple of strands of gold chain.

Nick offered a round of drinks. "Thank you kindly. Wouldn't mind." Everybody was very polite. A record spun in the Wurlitzer. Young Ella Fitzgerald and Chick Webb were swinging "A Tisket, a Tasket." I had absolutely no idea we were in a whorehouse.

Tolstoy wrote in his *Diary,* "Horrible! But absolutely the last time. This is no longer temperament but habitual lechery. . . . Disgusting. Girls, stupid music, girls, an artificial nightingale, girls, heat, cigarette smoke, girls, vodka, cheese, wild shrieks, girls, girls, girls."

Not in this cathouse! What stays with me is the atmosphere of decorum and extreme good manners. Everybody was buying everybody drinks. And with us, drinking crème de menthe, was the tallest, straightest, most regal chocolate beauty anybody had ever seen. In today's era of black fashion models her style would still startle. Forty years ago, in or out of any house in any ward of Newark, she was the Queen of Sheba.

"I'm Pearl," she said. Nothing else.

And she was with us. No secret signs that I could see from Nick. But it was clear that Pearl was ready to be part of anything that might happen to us that night. I knew now that Nick had brought me here deliberately to lose, stylishly, exotically, my superfluous virginity.

"Truly, My Satan, thou art but a Dunce and do not know the Garment from the Man. Every Harlot was a Virgin once . . ."

Did Nick know Pearl? She would never tell. Pearl didn't even talk to the bartender, but there was another crème de menthe in front of her. She drank it through a straw. Pearl took everything in with a straw. She was not indifferent. She was professional.

Now, she was with us in a taxi and we were on our way to a

party at our friend Dave's house, little Davie with his hunchback
and the extra burden of writing the first novel that was ever, to
our knowledge, set in Newark. He was calling it *Twice Around the
Park,* at whose Leni Lenape lake after two circuits you parked to
neck.

Pearl remained perfectly impassive. What if we were taking
her to be used in some unspeakable way? We were coming from
a whorehouse and compliance was her trade. But one look at
Nick and me would have assured her that she was safe from
anything but the unexpected ways of the ofay, two white boys
who would not stay in their own skins.

They say that man is the only creature who is ashamed of
what he does. It must be because only he can think up the weird
things he will do at the drop of a hat. Nick and I were not cruel.
We did not know what we were or who we were. We were looking for ourselves in gestures. But Pearl's presence among these
good people was too challenging, and came close to insult. In
their hearts and minds they had broken the color bar, were
against what was called then "race chauvinism," but in their lives
they had had no experience of mixed company. They knew
about chain gangs and the Cotton Club and nothing in between.

The comrades were hardly prepared for Pearl. Flo, a serene
and serious young woman who was already working for the despised cloakmakers, put out her hand. Pearl just looked at it. She
was not in the needle trades. Flo was used to rebuff. People
sang: "Oh de cloakmaker's union is a no good union, it's a union
by de bosses!"

Pearl was in the world's oldest trade which had never had a
union except in Mexico during one revolution when the *putas*
had left the windows of their cribs and paraded under their own
proud banner. "What's closer than a friend," they had chanted,
"truer than a wife?"

Pearl sat in a stunned circle. They looked at her. She looked
at them, as though to ask, "Is there smut on my nose?" But she
said nothing and sipped gin from the bottle we had brought.
The others drank Passover wine and pretended Pearl was from
one of the darker biblical tribes.

Little Dave was a Trotskyite and some of the girls were
Trots but most of them were from the Young People's Socialist
League. Nowadays, when one hears nothing of the little splinter
groups, the left-wing misalliances which fought each other more

than they fought capitalism, it is hard to imagine the kind of struggle for souls that took place among them. There had been the First International and the Second and even the Second and a Half. Then the Third or Communist International. Trotsky had started the Fourth. The Socialists were for no revolution. The Communists were for revolution in one country. The Trotskyites were for something called "permanent" revolution. And then there were the groups that had split off or been kicked out—the Lovestoneites, the Cannonites, the Shachtmanites. Nick and I thought of ourselves as Anarchists. But we had never seen one of them in the "too, too solid" flesh. The Yipsels, as the girls here were called, were reformists, yes, but pretty in the old Clinton High way. We were being courted by them and vice versa. Bringing Pearl here was an act with discordant overtones.

"Try some chopped chicken liver?" Flo offered.

"People always giving us chicken," Pearl said.

Flo looked sad. The whole history of the struggle for the eight-hour day was written in her eyes.

"Wanna buy a duck?" Nick wasn't too drunk to see the way things were going. "Wanna buy a Stalinist duck?"

What happened next? I feel that I'm telling a story I heard from somebody about somebody. Pearl sat silently, the queen-slave, while the others fumbled with our thoughtlessness.

Too soon, Nick was on the floor and out like a light. Or was he? Not long ago, I ran across Edmund Wilson's description of how Scott Fitzgerald, overcome with Hemingway's greatness, lay down on a restaurant floor pretending to be unconscious but actually listening in on the conversation and from time to time needling his hero, whose weaknesses he had studied intently, with malicious little interpolations. Nick could have been doing the same. To me?

The joke was over. Dave called a cab. Nick, as always, rose like a somnambulist and walked out on his own. Pearl didn't say good night. She was ritzing all of us.

In the cab, Nick sat like a Buddha neither in this world nor the next. I sat stiffly beside Pearl. I had not even touched her hand. What did we say to each other? I cannot remember. And such dialogue would be beyond my invention.

I must have been doing one helluva interior monologue. If Pearl had been professionally seductive, it might have helped. But she did not falter an instant from aloof availability. She was available to any wish but she had none of her own.

We got back to the Victorian house. Nick pushed money at me. The carefully rolled wad looked like a paper flower now.

"Wanna buy a fuck?"

I had been thinking about it from the moment I had set eyes on Pearl, seen that corded throat rising to that totem face with its milky eyes. That Masai bride's body drove away the boop-boop-a-doop bathing beauties from the swimming pool of my private photoplay. Pearl walked through the jungle of my mind with her head shaved, her breasts high and conical with long spouts, her plucked mons only half hidden under a G-string of tiger teeth. I saw her stoop to drink sacred water in a sacred grove. Her tattoos and painted scars pointed like arrows to her own font. I wanted to enter this Eden.

But if Pearl was Masai, I didn't have enough cattle to buy her. I could not throw a spear. I carried no pouch of crushed aphrodisiac bones. How would I win her? Would she be pleased if I said to her, as I said to every girl I kissed, "April is the cruelest month . . ."? There are no months in Eden, only those days when blood flows from the sacred wound. I was Mistah Kurtz. I was Francis Macomber suffering his short, happy life.

"Will you be here tomorrow?" I asked foolishly. I puffed on my Dunhill. It was the only gesture of manhood I had left.

Pearl nodded. She took some bills that Nick held out. She did not count them. She did not even look at them.

"Nice evening," she said as deliberately as she had not said goodnight to the Yipsels.

Pearl showed no anger, no impatience, no resentment at having been taken from her true work. Whores are fussy about their time. Time is all they sell. "How about a short time, luv," a Cockney voice once asked me from a doorway in Piccadilly.

Although it had not happened to me yet, I knew with Pearl that I was one of those people who take off more than their clothes when they hop into bed. There would be nothing left of me but ignorance and awe. The sex of the situation was entirely in my head. From the neck down, I was The Invisible Man unrolled from his bandages. If Pearl's fate was to sell her body, it was real, had weight, shape, dignity. I had not arrived at the fate of a customer.

We took the taxi to the lot. Nick paid the driver with a big bill and took no change. I guess he thought he was giving a scholarship for a hackie's School of Marxist Studies. I took him home in the Chrysler and got him upstairs. His eyes were open just enough to see the child in mine and for me to see the reluctant love in his.

"Again," he mumbled, "again, again . . ."

At the time, I knew what he meant. I'm guessing now.

Was Nick trying to say we would try my defloration again? Was this the self-reproach of the somnambulist waking at the edge of a roof? Or a sadness at his heavy inebriation? It may have been. For, once we left Newark and the demons that dwelt there for him, I never saw Nick this way again.

· 12 ·

I Lose My Cherry

"He's full of shit!" Gale Storm said.

You had to laugh, hearing this out of the mouth of someone who looked like a fancy saleslady in L. Bamberger's corset department. She followed that by sticking out her tongue and making a small Bronx cheer.

"Right, kiddo?"

I laughed some more. We were already buddies.

We were listening to one of those pious glorifications of the worker as writer or the writer as worker. The topic was interchangeable at the Jack London Club.

"I write for more workers than he ever saw in his ball park. Female workers, ball-less wonders . . ."

That was true enough. She had more readers than anybody in the *New Masses* for the fake confessions she wrote under her fake name. Her real monicker was Ella Blitz. I wondered where Ella was going with this exegesis.

"Kids in Woolworth's . . ." Ella was saying. She had to stretch to whisper in my ear. Her elbow was in my lap. I sank toward her until her tongue was almost in my ear. I liked what I was hearing.

". . . and Missus Proletarian with one kid on the pot and the other on her tit . . ."

I took a closer look at my new buddy. She wasn't still water but she was running pretty deep.

"They all want the same thing. And they ain't gonna get it."

"Love?" I was helping her.

"No, kiddo," Ella said. "A new hat!"

She had me eating out of her hand. But one hand, as they say, washes the other.

"Tennis anyone?" Ella had had enough dogma for the night. She got up, very chic, all in black but not, as Chekhov says, in mourning for her life. "Okay, Mr. God. C'mon."

She was looking at me. I was in seventh heaven.

We stepped outside to the Ukrainian bar. Ella put away a couple of steins while we watched Nick shoot a rack of pool.

"A regular Willie Hoppe!" Ella mocked. "And you"—she put her finger on my belly button—"what are *you,* a regular?"

And by more little pressings and touchings Ella let me know I could come a-calling. At one point, she actually took my chin in her hand and looked into my eyes.

"Pisher!" she said affectionately. Jocasta was aiming the Oedipal pee-pee into the bull's eye of the pot.

That intimacy shocked me. I did not know how to receive it. Was it a signal to be bold? This was an "experienced woman." Somehow, I knew she meant to save me from the inevitable gaucheries of inexperience. Ella would make me be whatever and however I needed to be in this night's installment of the true confessions of herself.

Nick mentioned an Ironbound saloon he knew where the Ladies and the Gents was all one place with a swinging door.

"Like Paris!" Ella had never been there but she knew. "Romantic," she sighed. "Take me!"

Like a gent, I opened the door of the roadster for Ella. It was still stained a Picasso pink where Nick had once puked Dago red. Nothing could get it off. My uncle didn't ask any questions. Everybody was so damned good to me then.

"Let's go to hell in a wheelbarrow!" Ella said.

Kinney's saloon was next door to where Stephen Crane was born. Outside of Stephen Crane, the only literary reference to Newark we knew came from Theodore Dreiser who had described it as a quaint town with a canal running through it. Where the hell did he see a canal? He must have been plastered. But Stephen Crane was really born here. Right next door. There was a Chinese restaurant there now. The bronze plaque that told you about the author of *The Red Badge of Courage* was lit by a neon chop suey sign.

We drank to Stephen Crane. Then there were appropriate toasts to writers who were in our pantheon at the moment. They were not all famous . . . Danny Fuchs, Edward Dahlberg, Sol Funaroff, Kenneth Fearing. We liked his "One, two, three was the number he played . . ." Nick's father had something to do with Lotto, the Italian numbers game. We shared an admiration for those writers who could make poetry out of the everyday urban world in which young men dreamed of hitting the numbers and finding a perfect piece of tail, all on the same day.

We drank easily and kidded around.

"Douché!" Ella would say in a society lady's voice when Nick got to her with a barb.

Some truck driver tried to horn in. He wanted to talk about a rookie slugger on the Newark Bears, the Yankee farm club that was in the International League.

"I beg your pock!" Nick said very fast and serious.

The truck driver blinked. It always worked.

"Do you punce?" Nick went on rapidly.

He usually got away with it. I never saw anybody come back at him. But this guy had his sleeves rolled up to show a girl in a grass skirt on one arm and "Semper Fidelis" in a scroll on the other. But Nick would not quit while he was ahead. He pointed to me.

"Sebastian Pupik, Polish poet! Polish! Polish! Do ya' cock?"

"Polish, yeah." The bruiser meant he was, too. Kosciusko Street was just around the corner.

Ella saw trouble coming.

"Oooo!" she said, "who's that?" She asked if she could see the hula dancer do her stuff.

The Bears' fan had muscles like Popeye the Sailorman. He clenched his fist and, sure enough, the lady shimmied.

"Adorable," Ella said. The truck driver was tickled. He told us we could get one done in Galveston for twenty-five beans.

"Baked?" Ella asked.

The teamster laughed. We all laughed. Those goofy laughs of forty-five years ago.

Nick Leporello made sure I ended up alone with Ella. We drove him home. He put a finger to one eye and pulled on the lid. "Be smart" this meant in Italian sign language.

"*La vita breva* . . ." He began.

I knew how that ended. "*E culo luongo.*"

A short life and a long asshole.

I never planned this or any other sexual encounter in my life. Or so it seems. Somebody had plans. Ella was singing "Night and Day" with some new words she had trouble squeezing into the tune. "I've got you under my foreskin," she sang, very torchy. "But I ain't got one and you ain't got none, so what's gonna go inside of me?"

I was gunning the Chrysler toward the street on which I was born, to the house in which I was born, to find out why I was born and how I was born. My father owned the house now. We were going up in the world. "Up, up, up in my flying machine!" Flying dream. *Steigen,* mounting. *Pensées d'escalier.* We were climbing the same wooden steps where Fanny had shown me how birdies flew without leaving the ground.

Ella walked before me on those stylish legs that didn't go with her Yiddishe Mama torso. Her fine ankles seemed almost too fragile to carry her filly's weight. She exaggerated the peril by wearing shoes with heels as high as her little feet. She knew what she had.

"Men seldom make passes at girls with small asses!"

Ella pretended to be winded. She took my hands and put one on each buttock.

"Give us a lift, kiddo!"

I pushed happily like those servants in Japanese woodcuts shoving a fat master uphill.

"Who ya pushin, who?" Ella played being drunk and unwilling. "Where ya pushin, kiddo?"

Oh, she was a cutie, that Ella! She knew that I might spook. So it was all "Ooos!" and "Ahs!" and a grabbing of hands and one of mine landed on the velvet skin between her garters. I let it slip for the netherworld of her cunt. A tickly little fuzz ran from her mons down the inside of her thigh. It was all there, waiting.

"Grishkin is nice?" Ella was always putting question marks on T. S. Eliot and exclamation marks on Dorothy Parker.

At the door, Ella pulled me toward her and made little kitten sounds. I could feel the hard facade of her girdle rise and fall like Mount Etna heaving. And then Ella reached down and put her hand on me, found me and pressed. I was reachable and tingling. It was the middle of summer—I know because my folks were away at the Jersey shore—and I was wearing a linen suit.

"Ooooh!" Ella cooed as I swelled in her hand.

Oh, those prenylon suits! Oh, those pre-Pearl Harbor erections! I was Johnny-on-the-spot then. And I was a good dresser. All my suits came from L. Bamberger's. I even had a pair of black-and-white shoes, the kind Ralphie in *Awake and Sing* says he wanted all his life. And I was with a real woman, so free and easy she didn't give you a chance to worry whether your dick was big enough.

Did we drink more of the Booth's? Did we go to the icebox for a chicken leg? Or did we go right to the cubbyhole bedroom that was mine since I had gone away to school?

Ella had me in her arms and was pushing me toward the bed. She got her mouth to my ear, took a little bite, and whispered, "Do what Ella says."

I did what Ella said.

She had me on top of her. Her legs were bent and her hands were busy. I'm sure Ella put my *schmeckele* into her. How would I have found her introitus without help? She had me into her and was keeping me there. I pumped and thrust with adolescent hubris. Ella talked to me, urged me on. "Dost want her? Dost want my Lady Jane? . . . Ax 'er then!" Ella had that first good time in the gamekeeper's hut down pat. "Ax Lady Jane! . . . Cunt, that's what th'art after. Tell Lady Jane tha wants cunt, John Thomas, an' the cunt o' Lady Jane!"

Who remembers his own fall from grace? In the altered consciousness of arousal, people have sustained serious wounds, bites, burns they are surprised to discover later. Hot and cold cease to exist. Loud sounds are not heard. Couples are caught thus in *flagrante delicto*. I knew nothing except that I was losing my cherry. Bump, bump, bump.

I began to see Ella almost every night, beginning with the next. I was surprised to discover that she, whose bohemianism suggested skylit lofts, lived over her widowed mother's grocery store. (Another fatherless girl! Is there some dark meaning here?) Ella received me in what seemed to be her bedroom. There was no parlor. Stockings and garter belts were tossed around. Her bed-sitter reeked of intimacy. I was in a new ambience, half Greenwich Village, half corset store.

Ella was ready to go, but she was still in some kind of

kimono that she teasingly kept lifting aside to give me a preview of coming attractions. Again there was this high underthing rounding over her staunch backside with garters pulling silk stockings to points. Ella had good legs that could have been a few inches longer. She was built along the lines of Babe Ruth, triangular, tapering from the hips. She turned her head, looked at me looking.

"If looks could talk!" Ella rolled her eyes like Eddie Cantor.

She was dressed now but remembered a final touch. Ella went to a big flacon of cologne on her dresser. Very stagey, putting on an act like Madame de Pompadour getting herself up for the king, she dabbed some scent behind her ears and into her cleavage. She crooked her finger, commanded me to come close. With a little glass stopper she touched me on each ear.

"Prince Matchyourbelli!" she said playfully.

On very hot nights we would zip the Chrysler along the old Post Road that runs through the cattail meadows now in the shadow of the Pulaski Skyway. Was it up then? We'd go to Hoboken and take a nice cool ferry ride to New York. We'd get off and get right on again. Although Ella never seemed to want any special attention paid to her vulva, she had no objection to making the round trip with my right hand in her lap, its fingers between the panels of her girdle that was always open for business, always moist and warm and reachable.

We would go back to Hoboken, pull around the heavy timbers of the pier chipped by the shoes of the dray horses of another era, and go to a huge bar which had not changed since the Spanish-American War, famous for its clams. Women were not allowed at the long bar itself where the floor was piled with shells. But there was a Ladies Parlor to which waiters in long white aprons brought the heaps of steamers, cups of broth, and little dishes of melted butter.

If my Uncle Phil was the first, I was certainly the second man of my family to eat clams. I learned to hold the shell in my hand and take in the cherrystone, the tabasco, and horseradish sauce in one long zoop. Sometimes I would get an aphrodisiac whiff of Ella's private salty smell on my fingers. And there were pickled pigs' feet and beer sudsing over the big steins. You were back in the Gay Nineties. The Depression, like Prohibition before, stopped at those swinging doors.

By that time of night, Ella's mother would be through in the store and so we would go up to the roof. Ella would back up against a chimney and I'd have my hands under her pulling her to me. Ella had a trick of getting her girdle to roll up out of the way. A couple of quick wriggles and you were in the Tunnel of Love. She would bend back in a special way and I'd be coming with a little shiver that made her especially gay. Ella was always doing something wonderful for you. And always ready with some Dorothy Parker wisecrack.

"Tell Mr. Goldwyn I'm too fucking busy and vice versa!"

I've never been able to do it standing up with anybody else.

I don't remember touching Ella very much. She didn't seem to want it or need it. But she loved this pubic rubbing, grinding herself against me, arched and my hands under her buttocks.

"Grishkin is nice?"

"Yes!" And, oh, so *pneumatique!*

Ella never hesitated to put my round-headed little Boytchik where he belonged. She never asked: "Do you have something?"

And I never carried any "cundrums," as the Junior Badgers had called them. I was like those Trobriand Islanders who knew that "ficky ficky" made the belly big but not exactly how. The baby's uncle washed the diapers. I assume, now, that Ella wore what we used to call a pessary. None of us knew the difference between a cervical cap and a diaphragm. If that's what Ella used, she always had it on. Did that elusive little perfume between her legs come from the jelly on its rim? Ella seemed to know everything about looking after herself. She probably knew Margaret Sanger personally.

Some nights when I called for her, Ella would have the door open and be waiting for me in bed. Never naked. Perhaps she was really ashamed of that unfashionable torso whose center I adored. Those elastic sheaths, belts, slips were her badge of defiance. They excited me. Ella always wore soft, gauzy bras, transparent as a scrim. Her breasts were large in circumference but quite flat, with aureolas like targets with a surprisingly small nipple to mark the bull's eye. You could lay your head down there and rest.

"Don't be such a *fresser!*" Ella would say when I went for them. *Fressen,* to devour. She used the same word a good Jewish Mama uses when her son eats well.

But kissing her there was like kissing her cheek. Her own responses seemed all to be down there with "the boy in the boat."

Her excitement was very much like an underground spring
pouring from a leafy source.

And, looking back, where was the famous foreplay? Or
after-play? Ella's pleasure seemed to be entirely in the during-
play. I was so green, even to my own desires, that everything she
did was for me. For me? For herself as Mother Earth? No, it was
all for me! "Climb up on my knee, Sonny Boy!" Or was Ella one
of those lucky creatures who warm up fast and come even faster?
They do exist. From a case presentation:

> Mrs. V. married young and was widowed twice before she
> was thirty-five. Now she had met the man who was to
> become her third husband. But there was a problem, she
> told her therapist. She was climaxing too fast! Almost at
> once. It seemed that her first two husbands had come
> even faster. Could I help her?

Aren't we all a bunch of windup dolls? Maybe Ella didn't
come at all. With me or with anybody else. But I did. And
quickly. I was not one of those Turks who smoke a hookah of
hash while the Missus dings his dong. Or the sated Oriental of
pornography, reading the funny papers with a musical egg up
his ass.

If not my quick ardor, what did Ella see in me? I was so
simon-pure, maybe the kick of initiating me was her aphrodisiac.
I was educable. What would I not have done to pleasure her? If
I knew. And if she had shown me. I was like a willing pupil from
a foreign country, an immigrant learning a new language and a
new geography. "What is a peninsula? Describe a bay. Draw the
delta of Venus."

Out of bed, I was promising. I wrote verses, had many en-
thusiasms in the arts, knew a lot of totally unnecessary but amus-
ing things, like the patronymic of every Russian novelist or that
Guillaume Apollinaire was an illegitimate child. Photographs of
the period show me in a dark shirt looking far away with a kind
of poetic bandit look. I looked a little like Bogey playing "Duke"
Mantee. But how greedy I was! And how generous Ella was! So
easy to do business with. "A lady in the street and a prostitute in
bed." The matchmaker's dream girl.

And so, with cloven hoof and bivalve, the summer of my
manhood passed. Daytimes I would drowse against the leather of

the Chrysler parked on the shady side of the lot. The mixture of Esso and rubber that bounced off the asphalt of Broad Street was like ether. I'd take in just enough to sink without going under. And always I would fall into the same delicious moment of slipping so easily into Ella "like a sea anemone with the tide."

Sometimes Ella would come by in the afternoon, walking from Penn Station to the lot after she had done her quota of confessions for the day. She got paid by the word and had to stretch them, invent sins and situations of remorse. Her own stories were well crafted, serious, with funny and maudlin twists on the same sad but spurious confessional plights for which she got paid. She was a left-wing Fannie Hurst. Later, under that outrageous, stripteaser translation of her real name, Gale Storm became a darling of the circulating libraries.

After a day of confessing—Ella also did office work for the magazine—she would be ready for a drink. "It's so hot," she'd say, "I had to take off my nail polish!"

We would slip into the Hofbrau next door, often with Nick, who was working nights now.

"Didn't I meet you in *The Great Gatsby?*" Ella would ask him.

Ella played the *grande dame*, pretending she drank what she drank only because there was no champagne. She called the broken-nosed bartender "Sweetie." Ella was popular there. I felt proud of her and of myself. I had my own woman.

But I was bothered that our relationship, the demimondaine and the boy, was too obvious. Ella covered that as much as she could. She was a pal. But a wink is as good as a nod to a blind horse. I began to question my own motives.

I would look up from faun's *après-midi* in the Chrysler just long enough to catch a flashing leg, a jiggling flank, or the shine of damp hair falling over the shoulder bones of a girl in one of those halter dresses that were the fashion that summer. But the more perfect the vision, the stronger my troth to Ella. I suspected the lookers. They might be like those big yellow peaches that turn out to be all stringy and pulp when you take a bite. They could not be so perfect outside and have what Ella had. If Ella were turned inside out, I felt, she would light up the world.

And yet the lookers stirred a breeze as they passed. Tom, Dick, and Harry turned their heads and made the obligatory obscene remarks. There was a certain kind of woman over whom men fought. Would I fight with my bare fists over Ella? I didn't have to. Ella was available. Too easy. And she was old. Older than Nick. Old enough to vote. And I had my whole life ahead of me.

The indoctrinated eye is a saboteur. It does not see the real thing. I should have closed that eye, at least for the little time Ella and I had together, listened neither to my head nor my heart but only to the limb that refuses to walk into a lie. I should have hung around, learning—between wisecracks—about a humanity beyond my raw, youthful egotism.

Ella was busy building me up. She couldn't help it, nor could I, but the turnabout was inevitable. I came to her like all adolescents, full of hidden self-doubts. She dispelled them. I thought she was wonderful until she made me feel wonderful. Doubt makes the world go around. Couldn't a wonderful person like me do better? Ella was swell. But I was sweller. Ella had brains but—could this be?—too much ass.

My retreat from Ella was prepared. Nick and I were talking about going out to the University of New Mexico. The tuition was low. It was far away. D. H. Lawrence was buried there. There were poets in Santa Fe. There were the Pueblo and the Navajo. We would study anthropology, we told ourselves.

I said goodbye to Ella.

"Grishkin was nice? Someday you will write about Grishkin?"

I see now that those question marks were her tenderness, her exclamation marks mere braggadocio. Grishkin was nice, very nice, but I was moving on.

· III ·
Across the Divide

· 13 ·
Double Feature

Nick had laid out a route to New Mexico that took us north to Buffalo, then to Chicago, St. Louis—the Mississippi would be our Rubicon—and on across the Great Divide. This was the first of three days in a bus rolling past a world we never made. Yet nothing looked strange. We had seen it all in a Warner Bros. movie. The black-and-gray land, the big Buicks with their beer bellies spilling over the spare tire carried in a well on the running board, all the men wearing zooty hats, the fast-stepping women, the wind under those short, belted coats blowing right up their Kotex. We were in a B-movie passed by the Board of Review. And every marquee on every two-bit Ritz, Cameo, and Orpheum was offering a double feature, tragedy and comedy, plus selected short subjects and free dishes if you came in and for two hours looked at pictures of your own life.

For us, it was too late to look up, down, or back. We each had a string of tickets as long as your arm for Albuquerque, where we were going because I was going where Nick was going.

"The two of you come from the same egg," my mother said. "Leopold and Loeb."

We were not that alike. It only seemed that way because we always acted as one. Why had we chosen a part of green, wide, beautiful USA that had been Mexico not too long ago and that was mainly desert, to boot? There were anthropological Indians out there, but we were more interested in the writers of the Land of Enchantment, regionalists, expatriates in a special, *encantado* part of their own country.

There was also a John Reed Club in Santa Fe. We felt we would be welcomed with open arms. We knew a thing or two about the "classic historic objective." *The Hammer,* the proletarian magazine published in Chicago, had just printed a sketch I'd written about a starving man who had keeled over on the lot. Nick had his bushel of poems, more romantic, in the style of Edna St. Vincent Millay but urban and charged with a vaguely revolutionary restlessness.

People thought Nick was going to the Southwest because he had TB. He didn't have bad lungs but his Mediterranean skin gave him that poet's pallor of galloping consumption. That's what D. H. Lawrence had had. His grave was in Taos. On the map in my Funk & Wagnall's dictionary, Taos pueblo seemed to be just a cunt hair away from Albuquerque. We were city boys who had no idea just how much of God's country there was out there. We were beginning to find out. Our prairie schooner was dipping up and down the hilly wrinkles on its face. We were in coal country by that time. We could have been canaries in a mine.

"A *schwartz yahr!*" Nick had a little anthology of Jersey Jewish phrases for such moments.

"Nacht," I corrected. And *finster.* A dark night in what might or might not be a black year.

"Wanna bet?"

Not with that ghostly wind the six-wheeler was stirring up, ticking off the telegraph poles between wherever we had been and where we were, suddenly unfamiliar and oppressive as a movie house when the film breaks and people begin to whistle and clap. Right that minute, I had the feeling that I was making a mistake. I had run away from home and didn't know how to get back. Something like that must have been hitting Nick at the same time. He was biting his lips as he did sometimes when he forgot to be Nick Charles in *The Thin Man.* I saw a scared young Wop, an altar boy who had been caught playing pocket pool or robbing the poorbox. I didn't say anything. I didn't know anything I could say. But I didn't have to. That's why we were Leopold and Loeb.

In Cleveland, we found ourselves bending an elbow in the World's Longest Bar. It ran from one street clear through to another and was tended by a squad of beefy bartenders. One of them tipped us the nod and we picked up two girls who wanted us to take them to see *Imitation of Life*. It had just come out.

The girls were stylish. You could see they were putting most of their money on their backs. One of them, with cheekbones like a Cherokee, said she was studying to be a model. In the meantime both of them were stenos. *Average annual earnings, stenographer-bookkeeper, 1934: $926.00.*

Fannie Hurst's story dealt in a sob-sister way with the daring problem of miscegenation. The movie starred Claudette Colbert. And, as Aunt Jemima, the cook who had made everybody rich by inventing the flapjack, it was either Louise Beaver or Hattie McDaniels. They were the only mammies allowed in the kitchens of Hollywood.

The girls sat together, Nick and I on either side. They held their own hands. But they were warm and gave off a combination of ninety-nine percent Ivory soap and one percent BO, which made you feel you were floating and sinking at the same time. My date was wearing a collar of fox or some other sly beast. It was tickling me into a hard-on.

Both girls cried when Fredi Washington came home from some fancy school in the East and found out that Claudette Colbert was not her real mother. She can't believe she belongs to Aunt Jemima. You remember what she looked like. Fredi could "pass" anytime. They have to break the news to her easy. She still looks just the same in the mirror but she's Colored now and she isn't going to be a debutante. She cried and the stenos cried.

"Che cazzo e?" Nick asked. It sounded sympathetic but it meant something like "What the prick is it?"

"Huh?" his date asked.

"Isn't it?" Nick said and she gave up.

The girls took us back to their apartment. But they could not get over the movie. They were too shook up to even give us a kiss. One of them had a theory that Fredi Washington was really Claudette Colbert's illegitimate baby from her first "mistake" and Aunt Jemima was sworn not to tell.

"She's too light complected," the model said.

The other one claimed she saw a resemblance between Aunt Jemima and the daughter.

"With that figure?" the model challenged. Fredi Washington used to dance at the Cotton Club.

The other one had the monthlies and crawled into bed with her clothes on.

"I'm telling you she had her hair straightened by Madame Walker," the girl with the monthlies said. "She's a half-breed."

The girls went on and on about the picture as though we did not exist. It just wasn't true to life. That's why the picture was called imitation, see?

"Yes, indeedy!" Nick said.

They were too wrapped up in themselves to notice us take French leave. We were supposed to meet them for breakfast but we blew town. They were probably still trying to decide whose daughter Fredi Washington was.

The buses we took were beginning to feel like home. Sometimes Nick sat by himself, pretending we didn't know each other.

"Hey," he would look up and say, "didn't you go to Clinton High?"

Or,

"Didn't I see you at Tanya and Fanya's dance recital?"

And we would become friends.

We had a couple of hours in Chicago before we changed buses again. It was cold. The Loop looked like one big pawnshop. We had nothing to hock so we stayed in the station and kept warm. We bought something called a Coney Island, which turned out to be a skinny hot dog.

"Porco Americano," Nick said.

He missed the pasta of home and ate only cheese sandwiches. But mainly he missed the wine.

In St. Louis we stood on the banks of the Mississippi looking, I remember, foolishly at each other as though we had expected by that act to turn into Americans.

The land flattened out and the towns got smaller, one so much like the other that, but for the Burma Shave signs spelling out their jingles every five hundred feet, we might have been standing still. On we rolled, stopping for men uneasy to be wearing a Sunday suit on a working day and families with kids who were very quiet and sat with their mouths open because they had never before been on a bus.

In a restroom someplace in Missouri, a couple of gals flirted with us from the Ladies side of a cardboard partition that did not reach the ceiling.

"Hi there, Nick!" one called out gaily. They had heard us taking a leak and now it seemed like a good joke to let us hear them.

"O, Nnnnick, Nnnnick!" They taunted like little girls lifting their dresses. They claimed there was a secret peephole in the john.

They were going our way, and the next thing you know, we were all on the fabricoid rear bench of the bus passing a pint around. The girls were cousins from the same hometown. Like twins they had shared the same life. One was tall and one was short and they both were named Elizabeth Ann, so the shorter one had to be called Bootsie.

"Her feet's too big," the first Elizabeth Ann said. "She got all my hand-me-downs but I got her shoes."

They were both waitresses in the same beanery, a couple of sweet-faced kids trying to hang on to the last, innocent adventures of adolescence. *Average annual earnings, waitress, 1934: $520.00.*

The cousins were bright, easily amused, and only half taken in by Nick's stagey attentions. First he told them we were gangsters on the lam.

"You sound about one drink away from a tall tale," said Elizabeth Ann.

Nick admitted we were really royalty traveling incognito, making a report on how to fatten hogs and make corn whiskey. Nick introduced me as Count Culo. The girls had a ready repertoire of fast, small-town comebacks that sounded like folk songs.

"Mister, your tale is so heart-touching," Bootsie said, "it sounds just like a lie!"

Elizabeth Ann would begin to tell some tattle and Bootsie would be protesting "Shoot!" and "My foot!" They were the real thing. Their little revelations were intended to explain themselves to us. I don't think we could have explained ourselves to them. The girls could not believe where we were going or where we were coming from. When we told them the truth, they both said, "You'll be struck down for fibbing!" They had this way of saying the same thing at the same time.

Elizabeth Ann kept calling Nick "Mr. Man." She'd take a cigarette out of the common pack she shared with her cousin, hold it elaborately to her pursed lips, and say like a duchess, "Light me, Mr. Man!"

We paired off. Elizabeth Ann, the tall one, wrapped herself around Nick. She held him like a teddy bear. It was pitch-black in the coach, and cold. We used our overcoats like blankets, petting underneath them, grabbing without words for the bottle of hooch, until everything got warm and very breathy and lost to the world.

"The greatest thing since sliced bread!" Bootsie whispered.

We smooched our way clear across Kansas, sometimes half asleep, but with our legs laced under the coats, breathing mouth to mouth, mixing the harmonies of Sunday-school hymns with *The Love Song of J. Alfred Prufrock.* Holding Bootsie was like having a bunch of wild flowers in your arms. Bootsie would never need a girdle. She weighed about ninety pounds. Going over a bump or around a curve, we would be thrown hard against each other. Bootsie kissed harder then, bit my lips. Perhaps these inadvertent violences made me a proper aggressor, more like the boys she knew. *Average annual earnings, farmhand, 1934: $560.00.*

The sky was rosy when the girls got off at some flag stop in the ploughed-under wheat. It was not much of a place to be coming back to—a Phillips 66 station, a clapboard church, a row of stores, one with a plate-glass window on which an itinerant signpainter had lavished three perfect Caslon letters: EAT.

"That's us," Bootsie pointed out as though waitressing there made the cousins owners. "Best Westerns in the West!"

The girls had one cardboard valise between them. Bootsie climbed up on the seat to reach the overhead rack. I saw that her stocking had a ladder that began at the swelling of her calf and ended where it was rolled over her knee. I remembered how Ella would say "Fuck!" when she discovered a run and how she would dab nail polish on to stop it. Funny how this wisp of a country girl reminded me of Hard Hearted Hannah the Vamp of Savannah.

"Tha—tha—tha—that's all, folks!" the cousins said like Porky the Pig in the animated cartoon.

And because they said it at the same instant, they went through the ritual of locking their pinkies and pulling them apart like a wishbone. I wonder what they could have wished. They were, as I said, very real. They gave themselves entirely to every minute because there was no reason, good or bad, to hold back.

Nick was sleeping like a baby and could not say goodbye. My own lips were split, sealed with Bootsie's lipstick. The cousins blew kisses and waved as the bus went into gear.

"Thanks for the buggy ride," Bootsie called out, alone this time.

Our connection was broken as easily as you turn a page.

Nick and I slept now, opening our eyes only when the bus stopped at one-horse towns. Sometimes we passed the Joad family. They were pulled up on the shoulder. The rear wheel of their pickup, which carried all of them and theirs, was up on a jack and a young fella wearing a cap was pulling at the lugs. Tom Joad was saying how the lugs "was froze tighter'n' a bull's ass in January."

At last, we were climbing the Rockies and starting the long sweep down from Raton Pass. Neither of us had been anyplace so high and so wild. We saw our first adobes with red chilis drying on the *vegas,* the tree trunks that held up the roof. For long stretches we saw nothing at all except balls of tumbleweed rolling across the highway or a paint horse looking up, smelling the bus, trying to make up its mind which way to run. It was not a country for someone who had never sat in a saddle.

My lips still tasted of Bootsie's lipstick when I asked for a double room in Albuquerque's best hotel. The others were the kind with signs that said MEN SINGLES $1.00. Nick and I always doubled. We were honeymooners. We had eloped, run away from home.

First thing, Nick hooked his leather strop over the doorknob and gave it a few professional slaps with his straight razor. That was the only way he shaved. He always carried a brush and soap in a mug with his name on it. We were sprucing up to see the town that had once been the hacienda of the Duke of Albuquerque. And we wanted to see our new Alma Mater.

In the lobby hung with Navajo rugs we got our first look at sheepmen in fawn Stetsons with high, pinched crowns. Then, and for a long time after, we would feel like the city dudes in a Western. Everything about us said stranger. The old-timers looked us over with snake eyes. They rocked in their chairs and tipped their hats higher or lower on their heads. It seemed to be a kind of language.

The room was well supplied with spittoons. A tin sign said "Don't spit on the floor" in Spanish. *Por Favor No Escupan en el Suelo.* I guess they figured the greasers didn't know any better. Just as we passed, one old puncher let fly with a gob of tobacco juice. Bong! It made a ringing sound like hitting the bull's eye. These guys wouldn't spit on the floor. Their aim was too good.

Uphill a few minutes in a street bus, and we were looking at the watermelon shape of the Sandia Mountain that rose quickly out of the flat country. It was a great place to be an Indian. The driver stopped the bus and looked back at us. *Average annual earnings, bus driver, 1934: $2,370.00.*

"This is the university, fellas!"

That is where we wanted to go, all right. We saw a long building with a stone frieze of Greek pipers and blind bards around its entrance. It looked like Clinton High. There were other buildings, in adobe style stretching back over a treeless waste marked out by cement paths. Our hearts sank. For this we had left bed and board? If Newark was the asshole of Creation, these mudpies were the piles.

Where were the poets, the painters, the novelists? We had pictured an intimate colony of which we would be a part. There were some in Albuquerque, it turned out, isolated, cranky, lungers or hurt in other incurable ways. Sante Fe, we found out, was fifty long miles away by stagecoach, as the bus between towns was called. And Taos, where D. H. Lawrence lay under a rock at the San Cristobal Ranch, was a good moon away. Nick and I were always going to make a pilgrimage there. I never made it. Nick, at least, rests in common ground in the valley of the Rio Grande watered by the melting snow of the Taos peaks Lorenzo loved.

"This is the university, fellas!"

From now on this is what Nick would say whenever absurdity overtook expectation.

· 14 ·
The Gold Dust Twins

There were some weeks before the school term began. Nick and I rented a stucco bungalow on a dusty cactus street halfway between the university, fellas, and a billiard parlor Nick had discovered smack in the center of town. We settled in and waited for opportunity to knock on our door. But when it came, we were—like the guy in Saroyan's story—out looking for a job. Maybe it was looking for us.

One day as Count Culo and Baron Pupik were leaving the

pool parlor where the Count had just snookered the local talent, they stumbled on a dude making a speech in Spanish to a circle of listeners who looked as if they couldn't buy a cup of coffee among them. At first glance, it could have been nothing more than the Sallies beating the drum for Kingdom Come. But they didn't have a drum or a trombone or an American flag. The lost sheep huddled under a sign that said *El Consilio de los Sin Trabajo*. These sinners were just out of work. We were at a street-corner meeting of the Council of the Unemployed. Like everything else, misery in this state was bilingual.

They were listening pretty hard to a skinny squirt in an incongruous little fedora that made him look like the Mexican actor Cantinflas. *"Sí, señor!"* they were calling out when the speaker made some good point. It was like the "Amen!" from the congregation of a Holy Roller church. He was carrying on in a quavering falsetto, like a flamenco Gypsy doing a "deep song." He had the crowd eating out of his hand.

"There are two races of people," he was saying, "those who eat and those who don't."

"Sí, señor!"

I didn't get every word. But it wasn't the last time I heard Jesus Candillejo say it. Nobody was hungrier than the Spanish-Americans. Not even the Joad family, broken down and camped at the end of Central Avenue under the bridge that crossed the dry Rio Grande. These stepsons of the Conquistadors had had a long head start. They had been hungry ever since Coronado had stranded them in what was supposed to have been the Seven Golden Hills of Cibola.

There were Unemployed Councils wherever there were unemployed and, in the winter of 1935, that was just about everyplace you could go. Because the unemployed had nothing to give but themselves, they needed leaders who wanted nothing for themselves. They were a dog waiting to be wagged by its tail. Though they would have denied it fiercely then, it was the energy and sacrifice of a small band of Communists that made it wag.

The Party was everywhere then, sometimes in the shape of a single man, and here it was Jim Howard. He was tall, cadaverous—he had only one lung—and had a kind of gentle grandpa smile. His teeth had been knocked out by goons during the Imperial Valley strike. Old-timers knew what you meant when you said you had been "in the lettuce." But Jim had baby-blue eyes and was full of the joy of life he had so often put on the line. He was a Hoosier who said "you-uns" when he meant more than one person.

"The Movement needs you-uns!" Jim always spoke in the name of the Movement.

How powerful the appeal of being needed! Jim had been through the eighth grade in a one-room school and he could whip out a pretty good leaflet. He knew what to say but he didn't know how to spell it. Two students were worth a battalion to him. He immediately nicknamed us the Gold Dust Twins after the famous pickaninnies on the box of cleansing powder.

Back East, Nick and I had shied away from the Party and its followers. Even the people of our own age in the Young Communist League were too righteous, too doctrinaire for our taste. They were often obviously wrongheaded but beyond contradiction because they "were doing something about it" and you were not. I was inclined to see their point. But Nick was a lapsed Catholic who believed not in parties but in martyrs: Sacco and Vanzetti, Joe Hill, Mateotti, Isaac Babel. In a very private poem, Nick had even included among the heroes Joe Zangara, the Newark Anarchist who had fired through the noise of "Happy Days Are Here Again!" at the thirty-second President of the United States.

Everything was different here. We were almost in a foreign country, a country within a country. The people spoke another language. Invaded and oppressed, they were rising up and carrying us on the wave of their revolt. Back home there had been something called the working class. And us. The proletariat. Better than us. And the Party was the "vanguard of the proletariat" in whose name we would be redeemed. Many believed this. Some said it was a careful lie. It did seem that the Party sometimes spoke for us and acted for itself.

Here there seemed to be only the People, *el Pueblo*, to which all belonged and were equal by that fact. *Viva el Pueblo!* A man who could read and write was not better, just more useful than an *analfabetico*. Without looking for it, Nick and I had found our place. You had only to look at Jim Howard to know you were there. He had rooted himself in the soil of the Movement like a lone piñon tree at the end of a Sangre de Cristo goat trail. Jim knew that whatever Carlos Marx said, or Joe Stalin or Wm. Z.

Foster said, in this wild land the Party needed to be native to survive. After all, New Mexico had been a state only since 1912. And it was so far from the centers of theory that no one was bothering to tell us that what we would do would end up as a romantic mistake.

Nick and I had arrived on the eve of big doings.

"Crank up the ol' mimeo, you-uns," Jim said. He had a trusty Gestetner that he'd lugged from California. It was more important than a car. They had given Jim this piece of territory to organize—Utah and Wyoming, too—in his walking shoes. The organizer hitched. He knew he was welcome in any Okie flivver on Route 66 because he had true things to tell: the "contradishuns" and something he always called the "three-card Monte" of Capital.

"Tell 'em they're dumpin' milk in Minnesota an' no *leche* for the ninnies in Spanishtown."

The ninnies were *los niños,* the kids in whose name we were calling for a Hunger March.

In the summer of 1932 the veterans of the World War had gone to Washington with their Bonus March. General Douglas MacArthur, with Major Dwight D. Eisenhower at his side, had moved against their tent encampment with infantry, cavalry, machine guns, and tanks. They had burned down the vets' shacks in the Potomac swamps, driven them out with sabers. Legless veterans had dragged themselves through the tear gas. But times were changing. The veterans came again.

"Hoover sent the army," cried the second crop of marchers, "Roosevelt sent his wife."

Now there was going to be a Hunger March. First we would have one of our own in front of the Bernalillo County Courthouse. We were counting on a big turnout of the Spanish-Americans in town and the surrounding valley. These were people who ate beans three times a day. A can of sardines was a treat for them. And now they had a voice to ask for more.

Most of them were displaced sheepherders and subsistence farmers. They were Spanish-speaking hillbillies, driven from mountain villages so cut off from the mainstream of their own people south of the border they had trouble understanding the occasional drifter who turned up from Old Mexico. They spoke the king's Spanish mixed with words like *trucka* and *el Relief.*

Ironically, their leader was a Mexican, Jesus Candillejo. He had been around. He had been nailed every place except to the cross. Not to confuse him with the Other Guy, I'll call him Haysoos. He was literate, spoke English of a kind, and interpreted for us to the *compañeros*. When Haysoos did not know a word, he would improvise. Sometimes it would be a few minutes before he would turn back and let you finish. In the meantime, he had promised his audience that they would soon be riding out to meet the troops of gringo imperialism in one final battle. All they needed were the horses and the guns. The great dream was to see the Spanish-speaking northern half of New Mexico secede from the Union and become a *cucaracha* Socialist republic.

Though Haysoos was their *jefe*, the official chairman of the council was an Anglo named Stone, an ex-clerk who looked like Calvin Coolidge. He was ideologically unsound, petit bourgeois, a racist at heart, but righteously devoted to getting justice for all the clerks of the world. He was the only bureaucrat in the Movement. He became a stoolie.

But we needed Stone. Jim wanted to get more "white" people into the ranks. All we had were the Richards family. They were a small movement in themselves. Three brothers from around Ponca City had married three sisters. With a tribe of in-laws and cousins they lived in a tar-paper government camp along the Rio Grande. All the Richards boys had regal names that began with *R*. There was Rex and there was Rey and there was Royal, the baby brother. Even their car was a Willys-Knight. Rex, the oldest, had done time in the penitentiary and had a crook's idea of the Revolution, a stubborn conviction that it would be like knocking over a bank. Boom! Boom! But you would need a faster car than the old Willys for the getaway.

The day of the march arrived. I made sure to wear my argyles, my Scotch-grain brogues, and my double-breasted suit. Nothing really bad can happen to you if you are wearing a suit from L. Bamberger's Men's Shop.

At first glance it didn't look as if we would have a parade. The Richardses were there in force, all the brothers with their women and kids, looking like a troop of Cub Scouts on the Fourth of July. The Hispaños were there with their womenfolk, which was rare. They had emptied their adobes to beat on the door of El Relief. There were even a few sympathizers, lungers from the TB sanitariums who came down to give moral support. There were a few hand-painted signs asking for *trabajo* and *comidas.* But nobody was forming up. They stood quietly on the sidewalk waiting for their own parade.

Jim Howard was not going to march. He didn't want to give the doings a black eye by tarring them with a Red brush. He caught on that we didn't have a fife and a drum and a bandaged Continental soldier carrying Old Glory to get us going. Jim stepped out into the street.

"All you Richardses, fall in! Hup! Hup! Gold Dust Twins, get out there! Haysoos! Start 'er up! Vamoose!"

"Vamanos, muchachos!" Haysoos translated at the top of his voice. *"Vamanos compañeros!"*

It was a good moment for Haysoos. It was about as close as he would ever come to being a general. If Pancho Villa's sombrero was a ten-gallon job, the little snap-brim hat Haysoos wore held about a pint. It was a gringo hat he'd found someplace. He never took it off inside or out. It went with his vested suit. Haysoos never wore overalls. He was, after all, the likeliest candidate to be president of the free republic he wanted to carve out of this chunk of the United Snakes of America.

"Adelante!" Haysoos swung his hand as though he were tossing a grenade.

That's what the companions were waiting for. Hispaños and Indians think it is impolite to push yourself forward. The Gold Dust Twins took the hint. Left, right, left, right, we were actually marching.

Cops in every kind of uniform, every deputy sheriff in Bernalillo County, watched. Except for them, the sidewalks were now as empty as a one-horse town in a twister. A band of music would have been a good thing to have. Our parade was as quiet as a funeral, but it went all the way down the street and was ringing the courthouse. The county jail was on top of it. Some of the prisoners came to the windows and cheered us through the bars.

"Viva independencia!" one of them yelled.

Did they think we were coming to spring them? They were getting their three squares a day. We were a Hunger March. But their cheers broke the solemnity of our procession.

"Oiga!" someone shouted down the line and began to sing about Pancho Villa's army. The companions took up the song. It had many verses that ended, "But there's no marijuana to smoke!"

I was marching next to Royal Richards, who was stomping along on his homemade peg leg. He had lost the real one under a freight car when he was a boy. His wife, Bonnie, looking like a logger from the waist down—she was wearing high laced boots and riding pants—had a kid riding on her shoulders.

Now Bonnie was singing. She was shy and actually had to close her eyes. But out it came in a strong Sunday-school soprano.

> Oh, Herbie Hoover, the engineer, parlay voo,
> Herbie Hoover, the engineer, parlay voo,
> Herbie Hoover, the engineer,
> He engineered starvation here,
> Hinky dinky parlay voo.

All the English-speakers joined in. We had no banners, no signs, only this doughboy song to tell the oppressors what we knew. The Hispaños had Pancho Villa in their heads.

The march went once around the Courthouse. Stone and Haysoos moved up the steps and climbed out on a ledge on which a constipated limestone eagle sat and squeezed. Stone got out there and opened his mouth. But, like Silent Cal, he didn't have much to say. His Adam's apple bobbed up and down. Nothing came out.

"Friends . . . friends . . ." he kept saying, like Marc Antony at Caesar's funeral.

"Amigos, amigos . . ." Haysoos said after him.

But Stone didn't have any friends. It was too big a lie for him to tell. You couldn't blame Stone. He had been put in charge of storming the Bastille without written authorization from the Home Office.

"Brothers and sisters . . ." Stone tried and got stuck right there.

Haysoos and another *compañero* named Montoya took over. Hispaños like to orate. They educate themselves with speeches. Each orator began with a long preamble honoring the gathered guests and ended up with an urgent call to win back the land grants, huge tracts, some of them whole counties, which had been given by the king of Spain to his nobles and then taken from them by the gringos. That was only four hundred years ago. But it was expected in an oration. Our speakers carried the same noble names as the *hidalgos* but they had been, and still were, their peons. They were sharecroppers in sheep, who tended large herds but ate meat only two or three times a year and beans and chili every day.

"*El gran poder . . .*" Haysoos was telling them how much power they had. They were beginning to believe it.

"Listen to Candlestick!" Candillejo was living up to his name. He was showing them the light in their dark lives.

One after the other, now, they had their moment of glory. The WPA had built a nice wide flight of steps to the eagle. The speakers were surrounded by their audience, they looked out on a Greek amphitheater turned backward. In a photo taken from far away by one of our tubercular sympathizers, we look like amebas in a culture.

In the confusion, it took us some time to realize that as each speaker stepped down from the ledge that acted as a podium, the police were taking him right up to the jail. They let you talk and then they tossed you in the hoosegow, the *jusgado*. So now every speaker was a volunteer for the can. It was a time for poets. And Nick was up there looking good next to the sick eagle. Haysoos was giving him a flowery introduction.

"*Compañeros,* we are truly honored to have with us a descendant of that very Columbus who discovered the land where we stand and struggle. This grand poet, this grand benefactor, this grand student . . ."

What did Nick say? Because of my double-breasted suit, I was on the grievance committee getting ready to present our griefs to the commissioner of relief and did not hear him. It was customary for us to bring greetings from the students of the world. It sounded good. Then we found something to say about the present and then we got to the future. We anticipated many struggles. We never expected so many defeats.

The grievance committee was talking to the guy in charge of El Relief. He was a politician. He didn't like that parade outside his window. Every state had two Senators and New Mexico had a smaller population than the Bronx. These people voted even if they had to sign with an X. Word came to us that our speakers were being grabbed. The commissioner tossed us some bones. One of them was the immediate release of our prisoners without charges. We went to get them.

My first time in jail, I was on the outside looking in. I came with the liberators. We went through the *jusgado* and found our people in a cage. They had not been there long enough to be scared.

They were singing the Red version of "The Four Corn-fields," which I translated as:

> How much evil we pass
> Under the sinister ruling class;
> They are traitors, egotists and such,
> And their priests are just as much.

Montoya had been roughed up. He showed us some round marks on his sheepskin where he'd been poked by rifles. He wanted to stay and get a free meal from the *cabrones*.

"In the *lucha* of the classes," Haysoos told him, "to be too brave is *loco*."

Where was Nick? I was afraid for him. I knew from Jim Howard that these small-town cops were mean. "They arrest you for everything from squeezing pimples to jacking off," Jim used to say. We found Nick in solitary behind a door as thick as a safe with a little hole in it for the Evil Eye.

Nick was okay, untouched but white in the face. He got out fast. But when he passed me, he still managed to say under his breath, "Did you cock today?"

I thought he was saying it was a great day.

· 15 ·
Adventures Above the Belt

We started school. I went to classes, but my life was centered now on the Movement. I began to soapbox in scrubby parks. I was watched by a part-time cop who was also an assistant football coach at the university. In my last year there, he would play an unwitting role in my campus apotheosis.

When I recall Nick's then-recent suspension from Chapel Hill, it seems incredible that we were taken into the University of

New Mexico at all. For, by the time of registration, we were acknowledged Eastern agitators, Reds with pockets full of Moscow
gold. It did not occur to the Chamber of Commerce that if we
had it we might have chosen a better place to spend it.

I joined the campus Christian Endeavor League in order to
bore from within. The girls who belonged didn't hold a candle to
the Yipsels back home. They tried to convert me harder than I
did them. What was I doing there? Was I confusing altruism—if
that's what it could be called—with the abnegations of my Di-
aspora, my flight from the psychosexual homeland? Well, it was
only temporary. When you are nineteen, everything is only
temporary.

Academically, I had an incandescent triumph that lit a few
dark nights. On a sociology exam, I answered correctly an impossible one hundred out of one hundred true-or-falses. That I
had been racially favored by the instructor, who was also the
rabbi of Albuquerque, could not be. The questions were, after
all, "objective."

Through the rabbi of Albuquerque—he not only taught sociology, he was also the only spiritual guide of the Semites in the
Land of Enchantment, as it was called on the red-and-yellow license plates stamped out in the penitentiary—I was invited to
the Temple to speak to the men of B'nai Brith. I took as my
subject "Will Fascism Come to America?" My considered opinion—after pointing to Il Duce, the disturbing rise of a man
named Hitler in Germany, and our own Father Coughlin—was
that Americans in general and Jews in particular were too smart
and too nice to dump democracy.

I may have gone a little heavy on the party line, but the sons
of the Covenant gave me a circumcised cigar and shook my hand
anyway. They were all merchants, some of them descendants of
those itinerant peddlers who followed the covered wagons with
packs of needles on their backs. You couldn't buy one needle
from them now—it would have to be a gross. They were big
shots now. One of them said, "If the *Ahntehsemits* call Roosevelt
Rosenfeld, it's a compliment!"

The president of the B'nai Brith ran a factory that made
Navajo jewelry. For him a dozen Indians stamped out fake silver
thunderbirds and put chicken feathers on kachina dolls. His
niece Shirle was visiting from New York or, as she pointed out,
"really the Bronx." There was nothing counterfeit about the
counterfeiter's niece.

Shirle was petite, dark-haired, with dimpled skin that bounced back when you pressed it as though she had no bones. She wore lots of Saks Fifth Avenue black that set off a throat that was the color of hand-made paper from Fabriano. She was like the pasteurized sweet-cream girls I had never dated at Clinton High. Their fathers were usually certified public accountants. So was Shirle's. I guess they have to be to keep track of how much their daughters are worth.

Shirle was very well brought up, as obedient to her date as she was to her parents. She did everything just so. When you kissed her she opened her mouth just so and put her tongue on yours just so. She closed her eyes just so and let you go into that expensive lingerie just at the right time and just so far. With Shirle you could be sure that your whole life would be just so. In Shirle's trousseau there would be a set of silver and many table-cloths to be graced by the candles of the menorah. And, tucked neatly between the folds of a crêpe de chine nightgown, there would be a brand-new diaphragm.

I liked Shirle. She liked me.

"You're different!" She was complimenting the combination of ardor and awe she stirred in me.

But I wasn't really different to her nor was she to me. "The acorn does not fall far from the tree." We both had the same roots. Wasn't I born with a kosher spoon in my mouth? We both missed lox and bagels. We both agreed that the West made us nervous. We both understood the hundred and one nuances of saying, this way or that way, that someone or something was *meshuggah.*

Being with Shirle, out here and at this moment, completed me. I felt rich. Without her I had, as we used to say, "nothing to lose but my brains." Without her I was nothing more than a *schlepper,* a striver, not much better off than an Okie. No, worse off! They had the reality of themselves. I had only my cryptic fantasies.

After our first meeting, I looked forward to seeing Shirle again. I even thought of "getting serious."

I knew immediately that something was wrong when Shirle picked up the phone. The banter of dating was gone.

"What's wrong?" I had to ask.

"I can't," she said in an ambiguous way that meant we had overnight become star-crossed.

"Can't what? I can take it."

"I can't . . . I can't see you again." Her pain was honest. "My uncle won't let me go out with you because you're a Communist."

Good-bye trousseau! Good-bye bagels! Good-bye American Jewish Congress!

"I know it's bigoted. It's awful. But he says I'm in his house and all. . . ."

Baal Shem Tov! The Master of the Good Name. Now I had a real, personal grievance against the ruling class. I took it hard. I became a nihilist, a wildman of the arts and politics.

I had by that time a newcomer's small reputation both as a poet and an activist of the Movement, which gave me access to the circle of people in Albuquerque who read and wrote books, who weaved on looms, acted in the Community Theater and collected the black Zuñi pots of Maria. They knew they "were not doing enough." They needed a Bazarov. They got me.

And I got the indulgences of Dorothy. Dorothy ran a gallery for regional arts and crafts. She was the widow of a rich man who had come to the Southwest to die of TB. Dorothy had weak lungs and strong opinions. She was a great defender of all "the nice things" I said had to be smashed. Our quarrels became an undercover courtship.

"You're so young, so young. . . ."

Dorothy called attention to the difference in our ages too often. She was a dainty forty, a box of bonbons of which only the ribbon had been untied.

"Too young my ass!" Tough guy.

"Guttersnipe!"

Dorothy used words like that, but she said them with a little sigh that let me know she was happy I didn't think she was too old for me to be too young. I don't know how much of this I actually saw at the time. I did see that she was manicured and pedicured and nicely preserved. She was a mature version of that forbidden Shirle so recently taken from me by avuncular veto.

Dorothy pretended that "all of this"—with a little wave of the hand—was over for her. If Dorothy wore black she wore it because she knew the unsullied woman was aphrodisiac and the color became her. She encouraged me to appreciate "the better things." At the little dinners she made for me, I read my verses to her while she plied me with that golden tequila that has a worm sunken at the bottom of the bottle. I had my own can of worms.

My hostess sighed, my hostess sipped. Her tastings were so small, the woman stayed half empty and half full. Sip, sip. Dorothy sipped at life. And after our little dinners became cozier she let me sip at her. Lightly, like a hummingbird.

Dorothy smelled a little different every day, but always of some garden of delights. Her bathroom had a rainbow shelf of lotions, unguents, and perfumes.

"A bad smell in here would have about as much chance as the proverbial fart in a windstorm," I told her.

"Really! Really! What am I going to do with you!"

What was she going to do with me and vice versa? We had no scenario. But my occasional scatologies let Dorothy play the lady swept from respectability. Her pretended shock at each four-letter word was already an intimacy. Her teasing hesitations about letting things go any place, let alone too far, were heady.

We met only in Dorothy's world. I had never taken her into mine. What would she say to Jim Howard? And vice versa? What would she make of brave Bonnie and Royal Richards' pegleg? Or of Haysoos with his dreams of machine guns? Or the Old Man who never let you forget he had shaken hands with Eugene V. Debs?

The Harlem Globetrotters came to town. I asked Dorothy to see them with me. It would be our first time "in public" together. Dorothy said she shouldn't but she did. When I called for her, she was just stepping out of her bath. She called out to me to let myself in and pour myself a drink. I did. Dorothy had the door to the bathroom open a crack so we could talk.

"Is my gigolo properly dressed? White tie and tails?"

"Are you?"

I pushed the door open and found Dorothy in something I have always thought was a peignoir. She let me look on as she put on those little touches of powder and paint without which she would not be caught dead. The peignoir opened when she raised her arms and showed me a lot of roundness with nice little puckers such as the Old Masters liked to put into a woman's flesh. Dorothy's skin was very white. It dazzled my eyes like sun on snow. Her demure striptease put wild ideas into my head.

After Meadowlark and the Trotters dribbled through "Sweet Georgia Brown," they trounced the varsity five, hiding the ball in their shirts, dropping shots with their backs turned to the hoop. They made the white boys look bad. But it was jes' clowning. They were still playing in their own segregated backyard.

Being away from her own refined milieu had excited Dorothy. When the Globetrotters got on each others' shoulders and made themselves twelve feet tall, she forgot she was a lady and actually pointed. She nudged me, cackled. Maybe there was something to Sherwood Anderson's idea of "dark laughter."

When I brought Dorothy home, I pressed my suit with an insistence that amused her.

"Silly, silly . . ."

I didn't stop. Dorothy scolded less, yielded a little more with each demurrer. There was no difference in our ages now. There were no more quips from Dorothy. Her silence was like a nakedness. I buried my face in the milky valley inside her black bodice. Using my nose to push aside the yielding stuff, I got my lips against the first rising of softness. I wanted to bite. Dorothy lifted my head and gave my teeth her lips instead. As we held there she sighed. I thought it meant surrender.

Dorothy had curled up on the couch. One knee rested in the crook of the other and her dress was hiked up to the portal where I assumed no man had entered since she had begun to wear the black that, on her, spoke more of seduction than sorrow. I do not believe she was aware of her exposure.

I slid my hand first on silk, then flesh.

"Behave!" She was whispering to me but warning somebody else.

I was engorged. Boytchik beat against the buttons of my fly. Until now, he had only known Ella's hoyden cunt. I told myself he must want to brag he had known more. This one! This one, almost virginal, that had been locked in the convent of early widowhood.

This place became Dorothy. I should not have forgotten the rest of her. She reminded me.

"No!"

She was not talking to me. She was in a kind of trance of indecision. I think she saw she had crossed the line of flirtation. In a moment we would be intimate. I would become an unplanned, untamed part of a life that was as ordered as that little glass shelf of scents. I'm sure Dorothy had no lover. If I had moved to her without words, taken her by the hand, and led her to bed, I would have been with Dorothy that night and many others of my *Wanderjahre,* wined, dined, bathed in bubbles by Chanel.

But when all this was happening, I did not know those things.

Dorothy was standing now, half turned from me, as though she still might turn back. She was not entirely her old self or a new one. Her little spit curls were undone. Her mouth was open. She had stopped thinking. I had to do the thinking now. I had wanted her to take me. Now I had to take her. It did not occur to me that we were, in the immediacy, equals. I had waited for her to become the naughty widow again. I had waited too long, long enough to see myself in the mirror of her new face. Suddenly she was my sixth-grade teacher at Avon Avenue School.

Dorothy would send me home with "a note." My mother would have to come to the principal's office.

No! Please! I'm a good boy! I'll fold my hands and keep them on top of the desk where you're supposed to. When I want to "leave the room" I'll raise my hand and say, "May I? May I?" Even if I'm pissing in my pants. I won't be rough. I won't hit girls. I'll pledge allegiance to my flag and to the Republic for which it stands. I won't climb fire escapes. I won't. I won't. I promise!

Dorothy was Dorothy again, "sophisticated," patting her permanent, putting on her pearl earrings.

"That was silly," she said, telling me we would never be silly together again.

O, Jewish Superego! O, Ego super Jewish!

· 16 ·
The Workers' Flag

"To look at a woman's finger," the Talmud says, "is to see her naked."

I looked at many fingers and, still not sated, at the multiplied toes of Busby Berkeley's hoofers tapping out "Remember My Forgotten Man" in *The Golddiggers* of that year. Nick sat a few rows behind in the Thunderbird Theater, pretending he did not know me.

I continued to write and publish verse, rough, loaded with urban imagery. The wide-open spaces of New Mexico were lost on me. I would always be of the "one-armed coffee joint" school. My little poems earned me a certain amount of respect. I hung out with other free-spirited students at the Casa Grande Saloon, drank concoctions of rum and grenadine sold as Planter's Punch, and listened to the new Benny Goodman quartet on the nickel jukebox.

I still had that unquestioning readiness to jump on any handy soapbox, to turn up at some Godforsaken village, to orate, to sleep on the floor of a mud-brick *casa* cold as a refrigerator, to wake up to be treated to tuna fish stirred in chili or, sometimes, *huevos rancheros,* sunny-side eggs fried in deep bacon fat, with green chilis on the side and thick hot chocolate for a chaser. *"Muy bueno!"* The daughters of the house, innocent of all but the unchanging cycle of seasons, would look at me as though I were a movie star. I came from far away and my name was not Chavez or Vigil.

My act drew big crowds in the dancehalls of the mountain villages where Haysoos was now organizing the League of Workers and Farmers. The *salon de baille* was always the biggest room we could find. *La Liga* was spreading like wildfire. If the village elder joined, you had everybody, man, woman, and child. Sometimes they all had the same last name. In the village of Vigil, for example, everybody was named Vigil.

"Compañeros, I greet you in the name of the revolutionary students of the East!" Absolutely nobody had elected me. But it made everybody, including me, feel less alone in the job of changing the world.

Shy señoritas listened, standing along the wall. Spanish-American women never sat with their menfolk. When we were fed chili at trestle tables, the older women served. The chili came in grades of hotness to the tongue, which made a contest of eating. The girls stood in the corners waiting to see when *el estudiante* would quit to put the fire out. When they laughed, they covered their mouths with their aprons.

"Ahyeee! *Mucho calor!"*

"It's hot. It's cold." That's about all I ever said to any village girl. Some of them were beautiful. Mexicali Rose. Dolores del Rio. Lupe Velez.

Celibacy is secret. If my tongue was hanging out, I still looked aloof. The smile of approach was twisted into the frown of rejection. Was I not Count Culo, scion of vast Transylvanian estates? Or was I Pupik, the court jester?

Suddenly it was a bad time. Nick took a powder. Went AWOL from the class war. Worse, he may even have gone over to the enemy.

"White wine is poison for the Red soldier!"

I'd see him riding around in this Pennsylvania Wasp's roadster, Nick looking very out of place, with two Irish setters plunked in the rumble seat snubbing the hoi polloi. She drove, of course. She, who had broken up the Gold Dust Twins! I envied Nick and I despised him. Jim was tolerant, dismissing Nick's decampment with a frontier toast.

"A whiskey glass and a woman's ass made a horse's ass out of him!"

It almost made one out of me.

I had the pining blues and I hung them on Bonnie Richards. Bonnie was on the executive of the council now. Jim had made her treasurer. I'd be sitting next to Bonnie, taking in her woman-smell, watching how she bit her tongue when she wrote in her notebook. My heart went out to her.

"My God," I thought, "we're the same age. And she's got kids and all." It was the "and all" that was so mysterious.

Jim would tell Bonnie how much one of his contacts—a lunger or a rich liberal in Santa Fe—had given him and how much he had spent on stamps and how much on grub. Jim also told Bonnie how much he had laid out for whiskey. He wanted that down in case anybody should ask.

I reminded Jim of how President Lincoln had sent a barrel of whiskey to General Grant.

"Why doesn't the Ninth Floor send us'ns a few jugs?" Jim said.

The Ninth Floor was the code name for the leadership of the Movement. They met on the ninth floor of the *Daily Worker* building on Thirteenth Street in New York. Jim did not pay much attention to the Ninth Floor.

"I entertain a motion to adjourn to the back parlor of Clancy's Saloon," Jim would say at the end of a meeting.

"I second the motion!" Bonnie would say in a happy way that made everybody feel good.

And we'd have a drink out of the bottle Jim always carried

in a leather briefcase some contact had given him. It contained the office of the Movement. He'd reach for the pint and say, "All present and accounted for!"

We were all present but not exactly accounted for, the night our unit got plastered. No special reason, it just happened. We were in the parlor of the Old Man's house where Jim lived. It was also headquarters. The house belonged to an old railroad fireman, a Socialist who had known Gene Debs. He had buried a wife someplace out there near the old Atchison, Topeka spur at Lamy. Now he slept on the back porch, which had tent flaps. The Old Man disapproved of both Russia and drinking. But he loved Jim. Jim called him Dad and hid the bottles.

There were just a few of us around. There was Jim and maybe Haysoos, who couldn't drink. He was like a Navajo. One big gulp and he was in a trance, dreaming of a gringo printing press that could do leaflets and newspapers and counterfeit money for the *Movimiento* to buy machine guns, *ametralladoras* for the secession.

And Bonnie and Royal Richards were there. Royal was good-natured and not too bright. Bonnie took care of things. All the Richards women were very competent. They had to be, living on surplus food in a tar-paper shack. Bonnie was a vegetarian—at least it looked that way. She took the government rice and beans and flour and made the best meals in town. When the Richardses sat down to say grace, it looked like a restaurant.

Bonnie was good at everything. Jim asked her for a song. He had been out in the field, rustling up contacts, and he was tired. He was nodding in the rocking chair that had probably come over the Pass in a covered wagon when the Old Man still had a wife.

"The Workers' Flag," Jim said.

Bonnie did it like a hymn, head thrown back, looking at the ceiling, telling somebody up there what it was like down here.

> The workers' flag is deepest red;
> It shrouded oft our martyred dead;
> With heads uncovered, swear we all
> To bear it onward 'til we fall.

I saw how pretty Bonnie was. She was a big girl with honey-colored hair brushed back like a boy's. In those britches and logger's boots that laced up to her knees she looked like an androgyne lumberjack. She was wearing the same working stiff's shirt I saw her in at the Hunger March. Come to think of it, I don't suppose she had another. Under it were those hard little breasts that had nursed two babies. But she was still a teenager. I couldn't get over that.

"We're both the same age!" I thought again. I had never looked at Bonnie so closely or so openly. She knew I was looking. And we both knew we were old enough to know better.

The stuff we were drinking tasted like kerosene. It and the heat had everybody snoozing. The Old Man had the iron parlor stove banked to burn day and night. We looked like Act One, Scene One of *The Lower Depths*. Royal was sleeping with his peg leg up on a chair. Jim was nodding. He had hitched from Santa Fe where a lady sympathizer was going to get him a car. Haysoos was passed out. Bonnie unbuttoned the neck of her shirt. She looked at me. We were both thinking a lot of maybes.

"Cup of java be good?" Bonnie asked.

We both got up at the same time, bumped, but didn't make a sound. We knew why. I followed Bonnie into the kitchen, watched her throw some coffee and eggshells into a pot. The sleeves of her lumberjack shirt were rolled. Her arm had the muscles of many chores. But her belly would be soft from the babies and a "beans, bacon, and gravy" life.

"Doesn't it percolate?" I'd never seen coffee made the hobo way.

"Best way," Bonnie said. "Gets all the goodness."

I came closer to her. I wanted to ask her about the eggshells but I was afraid to cut the connection that was holding us in tow. Bonnie was feeling it. Her woman-smell was steaming up, bubbling like the mocha java on the lid of the coal stove where the Old Man kept it cooking hot.

"Lonesome, ain't it?" Bonnie said.

"Ain't it, though!" Just then, I was so much a part of her, I was talking like her, like an Okie from Fenokee.

Bonnie looked at me as if she were ready to unbutton that old blue shirt and give me titty. I wanted it bad enough to go up against Rex Richards. He would have killed me sure, messing with Royal's woman. And maybe Bonnie, too. I don't think that would have stopped her. She was twice the man he was and knew her own mind. She knew we were just breaking the ice of pining, nothing more.

We stayed that way, just looking at each other, more intimate than if we had touched, until we heard Royal's peg leg hit the floor.

"Bonnie! Bonnie!" Royal sounded more helpless than her three-year-old.

Bonnie turned from me, took the coffee and a couple of cups like rings on the fingers of her left hand.

"We could have some ham and eggs if we had some ham and eggs," she said cheerfully.

The others stirred. Jim Howard stretched, opened his eyes. He had the situation sized up pretty quick. He adjusted his choppers and said, "All present and accounted for!"

I came in behind Bonnie. I don't know what Royal or anyone thought. I didn't care. We hadn't done anything wrong. We had only done what every Comrade should be doing for every other Comrade in the world.

· 17 ·
Gypsy

I went home for the summer. Without Nick the trip was eremitic, three days and nights inside a rolling sausage. I got off one bus only to get on another. In Kansas we came up against a black sky that looked like rain ahead. We rode into a wall of dust. The land had been plowed under and was blowing against us, going to California with the Okies trying to catch up. The cracks around the windows filled with anthills of fine powder. The highway disappeared.

We pulled into a town where everybody was walking around with bandana masks, kind of like Jesse James and his gang going up against the Wells Fargo Bank. The town was called Liberal. Liberal, Kansas. We were laid up for some hours looking for daylight and I had a long think that ended up, as usual, with uneasiness and no particular conclusion.

Newark was strange now, like a face repaired by surgery from which one wants to turn away but is constrained not to notice. I was glad to put distance between us again. I got back on the bus, closed my eyes, and didn't open them until I was back in *la terra encantada,* the Land of Enchantment.

Meanwhile, back at the *rancho,* Jim had organized a weekly newspaper. It was going to be the organ of the Farmer-Labor Party. As I have said before, Jim wasn't too good at spelling, so I dropped out of school to become the managing editor of *The Voice of the People.*

I moved down to Oldtown, the original Spanish settlement. I had a room there with Erich von Braun, a mysterious German architect who was the chief backer of the *Voice.* His studio was in a long U of adobe that was called the Palace of the Governors. People said General Lew Wallace had headquartered there when he'd taken the territory from the Mexicans.

Erich had turned up after doing a ranch-with-polo-field for a New York stockbroker. He was very aristocratic, lonely and ascetic, an exile, not an expatriate. It was assumed he was married to wealth. Though I was to live side by side with him for some months, I never saw hide nor hair of a wife, rich or poor. I had a hunch the heiress was no more and that Erich had given all he had to start the paper. He had a drafting table, lots of sharp pencils and graph paper, but as far as I could see he had no clients. The polo field had been his last chukkah. He spent a lot of time playing the flute.

The Movement had such good and brave sympathizers. Erich was not a citizen, and I knew that he was worried about being deported. What happened to Erich? He was too stubborn to escape whatever it was the Nazis did to Red aristocrats who played the flute.

In each week's issue of the *Voice* we found some battle to which we called to arms anyone who would listen. We did it in all the languages of the land. The Spanish pages—two, since the whole paper had only four—were handled by a new Comrade. Percy Riley had been a lawyer for the striking farm workers of Imperial Valley. Before "the lettuce," he had been the youngest member ever to sit in the State Legislature of Montana. He was a drunk now. The story was that he had married a beautiful Mexican girl, she had had a child, and both had died. *Pobrecito!* Drunk or sober, Percy was a brilliant lawyer. Not the kind you could stick in front of a jury. Sober, he had a tendency to giggle when he made a point. Drunk, he had a tendency to nod off with a Bull Durham burning between his fingers. His suit was always scorched. In a new one, though, he was better than a *habeas corpus*. In any condition, Percy's Spanish was perfect. He could put WALL ST. LAYS AN EGG! into Castilian.

Our reporters were the unemployed, the sheepherders, the villagers, who told their stories to Haysoos who gave them to Percy to write down. I did my writing under several names, the fanciest of which, suggested by Jim Howard, was Forrest Mac-Kaye. There had been a real Forrest MacKaye. Jim remembered him as an itinerant IWW bard.

"He wrote poetries," Jim said.

As Forrest MacKaye, I covered a story about a shoot-out between deputy sheriffs and strikers in a metal mine at the end of a hairpin gorge nine thousand feet up the Sangre de Cristo where the Pecos River had its start. There was lead and silver in them thar hills and it all belonged to William Randolph Hearst. It was an impossible place for a strike. The ore came down the mountain on a bucket conveyor that snaked through the piñon trees. The sheriff tried to run in scabs. The union men blocked the road with boulders and there was some real Wild West lead flying around. Torerro was a good place to be brave but a hard place to be a man. The miners had to give up when they got down to their last can of beans.

The story had a Jack London twist. The despoilers against the toilers, the bullets pointed with the lead they had dug from the earth by the sweat of their brows. The piece was widely reprinted. It was the first and last time the labor press would run a story under the banner GUNPLAY ON THE PECOS.

It was as Forrest MacKaye, too, that I took up the cudgels against the banning of a touring company that came to town with *Tobacco Road*. How innocent the Thirties! It was a popular cause. Copies of the *Voice* were being hawked on the campus. I went up and ran into Nick at the Sweet Shoppe. He was in a booth with two girls. I knew Consuela. She was a local girl from an old Spanish family, Homecoming Queen, Sigma Chi sorority, and all that, who was defying everybody by going with Nick.

The other girl was curled up in the corner of the booth. I'd never seen her before. She was titian-haired like my childhood sweetheart, with a pretty face but a kind of beat-up look that didn't go with Sigma Chi. She had the eyes of a little girl who knew too much. I thought she might have had one beer too many. Consuela and Nick were handling her with care. Nick was giving me eyebrow signals. I couldn't tell whether he was saying Stop or Go.

Nick introduced me, laying it on, putting me in charge of the Comintern. Nick called her Lucy. But she said her name was Gypsy.

"Robbers and gypsies never return whence they have been!" she recited. Maybe she had had two beers too many. I should have been warned.

Lucy—or Gypsy—got on me right away about being a Red. She admired them. She wanted to be one, too.

"Make me a member!" Maybe she had had three beers too many.

"If you want to be one," I said sagely, "you already are one."

But that wouldn't do for Lucy. She was either very political or very nutty. It wasn't easy to tell.

"Are you Jewish?" she asked me in a way I had never been asked before.

"I guess so," I said. I hoped she wasn't going to ask me to make her Jewish.

"The Jewish are the greatest people in the world," Lucy said. "They are the peacemakers. They are the only ones who give a fuck."

Lucy put her hand over her mouth. "Oh, excuse me," she said. "I shouldn't say that. Whores give a fuck."

She laughed a little at her own sad joke. Lucy looked like Sunday school but she used a lot of four-letter words, unusual for those days, a vocabulary too strong for what she was trying to say.

"Piss and corruption!" Lucy said. "Are you really a Communist?"

Was I? I called myself one.

"I want to be one, too!"

Lucy was pretty and her excitement heightened this hint of not-so-lost innocence. I imagined her as one of those Russian revolutionaries, a Decembrist, a desperate girl who would walk up to the Tsar, pull a little pistol out of her ermine muff, and let him have it right between the eyes. Did these girls not come from provincial towns? Were they not "insulted and injured," ruined by a false lover, sold into marriage with a vile landowner?

"I'd be a good one. What's a good one?"

What was a good Communist after the Russian Revolution but before Spain? In 1935, Lucy's question was innocent enough to be confronting. Moscow didn't give out merit badges. Like an Indian, the best Communist was supposed to be a dead one. You were supposed to be ready to give your life.

"It's like an Indian . . ." I began to say.

"Don't shit me!" In what world could Lucy speak this way? I don't think I had ever used a four-letter word in mixed company.

"No shit!" I wanted to say but didn't.

"Listen, *amigo,* listen here. . . ." Lucy hinted a little incoherently at secrets she could give me for the *Voice.* I wondered what she might know. Maybe she *was* a gypsy. Maybe she could tell fortunes.

"You'll see, you'll see . . ." Lucy was trying another tack, putting her head on my shoulder. "C'mon, *amigo!*"

Close up, Lucy looked younger than I had thought she was at first and now, cajoling, like one of those "depraved" child prostitutes of Victorian pornography.

"Yes? Yes?"

She had really latched onto me, snuggling, rubbing those copper curls under my nose. You'd think she was asking me to take her to the circus.

"C'mon now, *amigo!*"

She wanted to go down to headquarters right now and become a Communist. I looked at Nick. Was he giving me the green, red, or yellow light?

Would it have mattered? It had been a long time since I had done anything truly personal with anybody. One is none, as the saying goes. I was hungry with the curiosity that feeds self-love and makes it possible to give even a morsel of that hoard of egotism to somebody else. Today, I cannot imagine myself doing what I did back then. But when it happened the emotions were real. It's just a story now. The difficulty is in telling it in a way that will not make it seem that I betrayed the girl. That was not the way it was. There were no deliberate dissemblements, no agonizing crises, no intentions other than those one can hardly hide in a state of sexual excitement.

We were already on the way to my room in Oldtown. The bus driver was the same guy who had said, "This is the university, fellas!"

I thought of Nick, how cryptic he had been about this girl,

and what he might still say. It was too late. I had already done everything about which I might be ashamed.

"I'll show the bastards!" Lucy was saying.

Right now I didn't want to know who the bastards were. Or what she was going to show them. Lucy reminded me—not in looks, of course—of Eugene O'Neill's Hairy Ape who walks into IWW headquarters and asks for a bomb. They throw him out. I was not going to throw out this sexy revolutionaire who wanted to overthrow the fucking government. And vice versa, I thought.

Lucy was calmer now, full of serious, little-girl questions.

"How much does it cost?"

"Nothing," I said. "Or whatever you want." I was double-talking, feeling pretty pleased with myself and scared at the same time.

"What do I have to do?"

Our dialogue was becoming Aesopian.

Lucy rested her head on my shoulder. I was too horny to realize how weary she was.

We got off at Oldtown where the bus made its turn around the crumbling church of San Felipe de Neri and the little plaza with its broken bench and the flagstaff without a flag. The Stars and Stripes would have looked wrong here. The place looked like a set for a South of the Border musical. Before the bald eagle had swallowed the plumed serpent it had been real. You could see that from the size of the old Palacio del Gobernadores. Its mud walls were three, four feet thick. The arch into the patio was eroded but still showed the way into a corral big enough to hold the mounts of a troop of cavalry. The long building was surrounded by a covered wooden walk along which the Governor's guests had gone to dance the Varsoviana in its *salon de baille*. This may have been the very room in which General Wallace had written *Ben Hur*. It was empty now. Its wide-planked floor was covered with crumbled adobe and the ordure of birds.

"Bitte!" Erich said when we came to the door. He had his flute in his hand. Lucy was impressed. So was I. He might have thrown us out. But he turned *ganz* gallant. "Please!" He said it as though we were doing him a favor.

"Hot beer and horse piss!" Lucy said. And reached into her purse and pulled out a pint of booze. She offered it to Erich who said *"Bitte!"* again. It was the same word but sometimes it meant yes and sometimes it meant no.

Lucy didn't wait for a glass. She just tipped the bottle and took a tiny drink. She did it very carefully as though she knew to the drop just how much she wanted. Or needed. She could have taken it in a teaspoon—or a syringe.

Only then did I realize where Lucy's one-track persistence was coming from. She was at the tailend of a binge. I had watched Percy nurse like that, sometimes doctoring the booze with water to make it stretch. When Percy got to this stage he dreamed dreams within dreams. *"La vida es un sueño, y los sueños, sueños son . . ."*

Lucy was another story. She craved action. She may have been driven by that desperate boredom failed suicides talk about. Right now she wanted to hear Erich play his flute as hard as she wanted to become a Communist just one swig ago.

"Will you? Will you, please?"

The combination of little girl and dipsomaniac was hard to resist. Erich started "Girl with the Flaxen Hair." Lucy was very still. She was in Erich's armchair sitting on her legs with her skirt tucked modestly under her knees. You would think she didn't even know how to spell *f-u-c-k*. That was the thing about Lucy. She was always somebody else. In the middle of "Pavanne for a Dead Infanta" she jumped up.

"Where's the can?" Lucy was hopping up and down.

Ours was in the starry patio. When I led her outside, Lucy simply squatted and peed in the dust ground by the wheels of Ben Hur's chariot. She didn't have to take anything down. Her panties were in her purse. God knows how long they had been there, snuggled up against that pint of Old Guckenheimer.

Lucy staggered a little. She wouldn't let me help her.

"I take care of myself," she said.

But when Lucy got hardboiled like this, the punches always seemed to be thrown at herself.

I know it is fashionable to treat events of one's past with irony. Not this one. I was in way over my head. Lucy may have been a victim. But not mine. She knew before I did that she was going to give me what I wanted. She knew what it was I wanted more clearly and before I did. Behind everything that happened between us, sordid as it seems, there was, I am sure, a cockeyed, romantic motive on both our parts.

There was no question of taking her home. I didn't know if she had a home. I tried to ask about her parents.

"I put them out for adoption," Lucy said.

My room had a door off the patio. We moved toward it. Lucy stopped, put her arms around me, and gave me a long kiss. It was a lovers' kiss, without art, full of yearning and surrender. I did not want it to end.

"I never kissed anybody Jewish," she said when we came up for air.

Whatever Lucy was thinking, she still had this funny, one-track lucidity.

"Got to say good night to Uncle Luddy," she said. "Got to give Luddy von Beethoven a kiss!"

Erich actually blushed. I could see Lucy's presence was painful to him. He offered her a pair of his starched pajamas. Lucy hugged them to her and almost fell through the French door to my room. She did fall on the bed. But she knew just where she was and just what I wanted.

Out of that Alice in Wonderland kisser I heard loud and clear: "Many waters cannot quench love, neither can the flood drown it."

Indian stuff? This mountain country did strange things to people. I had to undress the gypsy. There wasn't much to take off. Under her dress there was only a bra. And when I got that unhooked, pendant breasts fell out and lay on her thin chest. They looked like two creatures from outer space.

Lucy was slight, with fine bones and trim legs, but her hips, like those long mammaries, came as a shock. I got the crazy idea that she had borne children, not one but two, and like a fallen woman in de Maupassant had "farmed them out." My head was full of short stories, novels, misquoted lines. "Women with half hours for rent between their legs . . ."

Lucy was inert. I could have done anything I knew or did not know. To her. Not with her. She was compliant but only that, offered everything but nothing. She was like those women one heard about who are able to lend themselves to the cruelest perversities because in their heads it is not happening to them but to somebody else. Sex for them must be the ultimate indifference.

How unlike Ella with her stroking and *kibbitzing* and reaching out and putting the *schmeckele* where you wanted it and she wanted it. Yet Lucy was friendly enough. She did not make me feel I was forcing anything on her. It was as though an arrangement had been made without my knowledge. She was just there waiting for you to do whatever you were going to do because you were going to do it.

I had barely touched her when she raised her knees and opened her legs wide. It seemed a very practiced act, unexpectedly soon for me.

"Okay," Lucy said.

What was okay?

The light was on. To turn it off I would have to leave Lucy, pull at a beaded chain hanging from the ceiling. I was aware of Erich in the other room. And, for a moment, I lost the sense of jubilation that had carried me this far. Lucy's head was turned. I was not sure she was awake. But the part of herself that was still participating took her fingers to her mons and roughly pulled apart the labia. Again I was startled by a kind of largeness there that, like her breasts and her hips, did not conform to Lucy's schoolgirl frame. The separate parts of her portal, all glistening with mucosa, were laid out like an anatomical chart, almost like an affront.

"Okay!" Lucy said again as though she had been reading my mind, knowing with some instinct that I needed to hear her permission even as another part of me was deciding I did not.

I felt a surge of gratitude. In her own gypsy way she was being as good to me as Ella had been. What a trial those inexperienced years can be! You will think it mawkish if I say that I had, until then, thought there was a difference between love and lust.

I entered her easily. As a key clicks into a lock, Graham Greene would say. Again I had the thought that she had borne children. She was wet and open. Lucy lay back, never moved. But after my months of imaginings, I lost myself in this one-sided fulfillment.

Until we become—through familiarity or indifference—distanced from the act, sex is something about which we know little or nothing. Everything has to be learned, down to the most trivial response. That is why whores call it "turning a trick." This lost girl was honest. She did nothing more than let me learn upon herself. Or this is what I now imagine Lucy did. One misunderstands the past unless one remembers that when it is happening, its nature is to be unknown.

In the morning, Lucy awoke, showed neither anger nor affection. I had never awakened with a naked woman next to me. I was afraid she would feel tricked. She was chummy, even gay. She had no hangover. She remembered more than I did.

"Don't forget your promise," she said.

I was afraid to ask what it was.

She dressed quickly, lifting those startling mammaries one by one and dropping them into the cups of her bra. She found her panties in her purse and slipped them on. I thought Lucy was strange and marvelous. For breakfast, Lucy had a couple of small sips of Old Guckenheimer. And she ran off.

· 18 ·
The Red Wedding

The Voice of the People rented a one-room office in a wooden frontier building downtown. Our neighbors were all, for some reason, patent attorneys. I'd had no idea there were so many inventors in the world. The office had a frosted glass door with VOICE printed on it. The sign painter must have charged by the word. With that invitation, the Movement might have gotten in a stray soprano.

I was alone in the office getting the paper ready for press, pasting up my dummy, when Lucy poked in her head. She had washed her hair. It spilled over her face like a cornucopia of pennies from a bubble-gum machine.

"Good morning, sunshine!" It was more in the P.M. and it was clear she did not know my name.

"Cutting out paper dolls?"

With the scissors in one hand, laying out the banner lead for our first page, I felt like changing it to a jazzy epithalamium: FORREST MACKAYE GETS ASHES HAULED.

Lucy was smiling like a pregnant Cheshire cat. She was wearing a little coat that bulged in front. Her hands were crossed over her belly. Though I had had no condoms last night, I knew I could not be the father. Lucy must have had the same idea.

"Look, I've brought the baby!" She was enjoying herself.

She opened her coat and showed me what looked like a half-gallon bottle of bourbon.

"It's a great day for the race!" Lucy said.

I bit. Cowboys have horses, don't they? "What race?"

"The human, silly!"

We had one from the jug to celebrate.

"Oh, shit!" Lucy said, sounding like last night's gypsy again. "Tell me your name. Nick called you so many things, I got confused."

I was happy Lucy had found me. I realized I did not know where to find her. I still had no idea who this gypsy was. I had not had a chance to see Nick.

Lucy was very nice. I thought she would give me a kiss, but she didn't come near me. I wanted to give her one. You were supposed to. We had, after all, made love, made sex. Lucy didn't. So I didn't.

Lucy wanted to see how the Communist paper was printed. I tried to explain that the *Voice* was the organ of the new Farmer-Labor Party.

"What's the dif?" she said smartly. "You're all as red as my Granddaddy's long johns."

She wasn't wrong.

Lucy tucked the "baby" under her coat and we walked around to the printer. She was all scrubbed and shiny, could have been on her way to Sunday school. In bed last night, her sunny, adolescent face, half covered with her fine, straight rusty hair, looked as though it were attached to one of those carnival photos in which you poke your head through a hole in a crudely painted figure in an 1890's bathing suit. It did not belong to that jaded torso—if one can speak of the body's separate morality—already worn and stretched with dispassionate, slavish surrender.

Our four-page sheet was made up fast, locked tight in a chase. The English side came up first from the flatbed press. The sheets were turned to the Spanish side and were being folded by a machine that picked them up with rubber tips like a cardsharp giving a sucker a fast shuffle. Lucy was fascinated.

I explained to her about the giant Hoes the big-city papers used, how the *Times* fed a roll of newsprint into one end and "All the News That's Fit to Print" came out of the other.

We had snuck the baby out a few times and were buddies with the International Typographical Union.

"And it comes out here!" Lucy sang. She was tone deaf but loud.

She conducted the pressman and me like a choir.

"You push the first valve down, the music goes 'round and 'round, and it comes out here!"

Lucy wanted to sing some more but our run was over. Lucy carried away a wet copy of the *Voice*. She behaved as though she had printed it with her own inky hands.

"We did 'er, allrighty!" she said.

That seemed very important to her. She was not a spoiled child. She was a deprived child. It was a special day for her. An ordinary day would not have gotten so out of control.

On the street, Lucy waved the paper around, calling out "Extry! Extry! Read all about it!" About what? Last night she had said she would give me "dirt" to put in the paper. Whatever it was, she had forgotten about it now.

She had not forgotten about becoming a Communist. Back at the office, she asked Jim Howard, "Are you the big cheese around here?"

Jim took to her right away. He hesitated about taking a drink. "We got someone sworn off, Sis."

Percy got on his high horse about that, about as high as he ever got. "A calumny," he said, "a seditious and dastardly calumny!"

You could not stay mad at Percy. He was so rummy Jim wouldn't let him carry money. Instead he gave him a daily ration of Bull Durham and he ate off a punched meal ticket Jim bought him once a week. Lucy knew his story from me. She was speaking Spanish to him, very fluently and fast. She seemed to know a lot about the state legislature.

"You should be in there," Lucy was telling him. "Even higher!"

"Nada y pues nada," Percy said. Jim had let him have a drink from the emptying baby.

The next thing you knew, we were having a big spread at the best Greek restaurant in town. You could get brook trout there or a KC steak as big as a frying pan for a dollar. We'd picked up a pretty big crowd of our people, plus Lucy's friend, Ruthie, a roly-poly servitor, utterly devoted to her. You could have cast her for the role of madame in a French brothel. Who else was there? I know Nick wasn't, or none of the rest would ever have happened.

Our check was never presented. Lucy seemed to have con-
nections. The Greek who ran the place knew her. Jim stuck a
toothpick between his too perfect choppers.

"Nothing too good for the working class!" Jim said.

We piled into the Model A Ford a liberal lady from Santa Fe
had given him. Lucy sat on my lap. Her breasts clubbed my arm
as the little sedan left the paved streets of the gringos and
bounced into Oldtown and history. We pulled up at the palace of
mud, a pack of boozehounds. Erich came to the door.

"Bitte!" he said again.

Lucy kissed him again and he blushed again. He got more
kisses from Lucy than I did.

Who was it who got the idea that Lucy and I should have a
Red wedding? Lucy would not have known about such doctrinaire doings. Red weddings were the latest thing among the
Comrades, as popular as rent strikes. Instead of going before a
minister or to City Hall, you were spliced by an organizer of the
CP. You were thumbing your nose at church, state, and family
all at the same time. And then, as in the Motherland, all you had
to do was send your better half a postcard and you were free to
do it all over again. In a roundabout, boozy way, maybe it was
romantic. It's incredible, but we really went through with it!

Erich played "Here Comes the Bride" on his flute and then
Lucy and I were standing in front of Jim Howard who looked
like a small-town justice of the peace happy to be collecting his
two bucks for the hitching. Jim raised his hands in a remembered gesture and began:

"Brothers and Sisters! I'm no sky pilot, esatly. My Maw had
a Bible but my Paw used most of the pages o' Genesis fer rollin'.
'At's when he had the makin's. So's all I kin say is how male-uns
and female he created to cuddle and kitchycoo . . ."

Jim stopped to take a swallow of Devil's brew. He shivered a
little when it went down. He was not used to bourbon.

". . . Seein' as how between the haves and the have-nots
there can be no peace. What wif all the strivin' to keep up with
the Co-hens and the Kellys an' the private ownership o' the
means o' production, there's bound to be exploytayshun 'n ex-
propreeayshun. A piss-poor sityooayshun all aroun'."

Jim had us listening with our mouths open. I looked at
Lucy. All she lacked was a white dress and a bunch of orange
blossoms. Big Ruthie stood next to her like a bridesmaid.

". . . An 'en comes the little fellers 'n the nappies 'n pearl-divin'. So's while Johnnie Doe is out diggin' in some nice cool sewer, the Missus is sweatin' over those hot pots 'n pans o' corn beef 'n cabbitch. An' when the Ol' Man comes home from Clancy's Saloon wif half his paycheck down his craw, he beats the daylights out'n her 'cause she din't vote fer him fer dog-catcher. . . ."

Jim was going good. His choppers were clicking. He looked like Popeye chewing spinach.

". . . But unner Socialism the Missus is out 'n got the job o' dogcatcher an' they get their three squares in the collective caf-eteria—meat 'n two vegetables, coffee 'n apple pie, so as there's more pay for less work an' Daylight Savin's Time for billy and coo. So raise your banner high unto the generayshuns and make one outen two and outen the many One Big Union fer all!"

Jim stopped to wet his whistle. When we were in a meet-ing he could sound like the *Daily Worker,* but sermonizing he sounded very rural and "down home." Jim knew it. He was a smart old coot. Maybe he didn't want to make what he was doing too real.

"Forrest MacKaye, do you take Sis here to be your Comrade through thick 'n thin, on the picket line and the breadline, and promise not to stop at Clancy's Saloon, or down to the red lights . . . ?"

"Kiss the bride!" somebody called out.

I realized with a shock that I had only kissed Lucy once. I still remembered how it tasted and how surprised I had been at its sweetness.

"The ring! The ring!"

Did I actually make responses? Did Lucy? There were too many uninvited guests at this ceremony, too many people who would not "forever hold their peace."

There was lots of uncomfortable joking. Someone told Jim not to leave out the part about "love, honor, and obey." Lucy was looking at me in a way that should have told me the joke had already gone too far. Jim had another drink and another bout of sputtering.

"An' so by the power devested in me by . . ."

Jim stopped. He was shaky about finishing this thing that was beginning to be, even in caricature, too close to a solemn rite. He was beginning to sense this. Or maybe he was wondering who had "devested" him in the first place.

Jim never did get to pronounce us anything.

I could feel Lucy dropping out of the game. The Ninth Floor was not her God. The *Internationale* was not "Oh, Promise Me." Those gathered here were not her dearly beloved. The problem of pretending to be happy was becoming too much for her. Lucy pulled her hand from mine. A babble of profanity ran from her mouth like spoiled milk thrown up by a child.

"Fuck you fuck you fuck you fuck you. . . ."

The bride was running wild. The glass in her hand hit the adobe wall, took a chip out of it, rained whiskey on the dried mud and straw. She ran from one part of the room to the other looking for more jelly jars to throw. The wedding guests were trying to dodge the barrage.

Jim got hold of her. She was kicking and scratching, babbling a lot of crazy stuff. Then she stopped, turned her face to the wall. She shook as if she were sobbing but no sound came out of her. Ruth tried to wrap her in two hundred pounds of comfort.

"Oh, baby, don't take on! Don't take on!" She was crying herself.

I was helpless. I was as much of a stranger to Lucy as anybody in the room. I was like the Talmudic student who sees his bride's face for the first time under the wedding canopy.

Jim talked to her like a jockey with a nervous horse. "It's all right, Sis," he said. "It's all right."

It's funny how Lucy listened to Jim. He thought a ride out in the country would be good for her. She probably would have gone anyplace he said. He was her Dad and he would always take up for her. Jim led her out to the Model A. I tagged along. She walked between us like a thief between two cops.

I was holding Lucy by the hand. Just as Jim was backing out the Ford, she broke away from me. Jim bumped into her, not hard, just enough to push her down into Ben Hur's race track. But the spill knocked out of her that rage I was beginning to feel should have been directed only at me. Lucy was drained out, did not even bother to knock the dust off her dress. I tried. I was ashamed when I touched her. It reminded me of the night before.

I suppose I tried to console Lucy, telling her all the wrong things—if she was really listening. I could not say that our marriage had been a rigmarole. Nor could I say it had been anything less. Maybe I told her she could be a Communist now. Jim would make her one. He probably would have done that. Jim believed in the Movement and everyone who came near it. Even the finks. Why would they be here if there was not some good in them that might be readied and released to make One Big Union?

Lucy sat between us, beautiful and damned, very quiet now, looking like a kid half asleep, coming out of an unexplainable dream. We rode out as far as Bernalillo, along the dry trickle of the Rio Grande. There were a lot of farmers here who belonged to the *Liga*. They had all been married in the name of the Trinity. They raised chili and pinto beans and kids named Jesus.

What more can I say of this wedding night? There was no honeymoon. The groom never saw the bride again. Not long after, Lucy climbed out on the ledge of the top floor of Albuquerque's new hotel, hung there between two eternities until she was roped like a calf and dragged to the abattoir.

If I had only known the double mockery of our false nuptials! From Consuela, with whom she had gone through the grades, I learned that Lucy was a kind of party girl for a corrupt rich man, a politician. He had kept Lucy's mother. And now . . . a chapter from a blockbuster paperback by an author who owns two Rolls-Royces.

What can I say for myself? The words straggle on the page like surrendered soldiers. From a long distance, looking back, you can see where you have been as a terrain of forests, cliffs, plains, mountains. You boast of a trek. But when you were there, slogging along a muddy path, you did not know you were coming here. You barely knew where you were.

"Feeling better, Sis?"

Lucy answered Jim with the look you see in an animal's eyes, trying to express something and not being able to do so. Jim was driving crookedly. He always did. His mind was usually on what he called "oriental rug philosophy" or he was fishing for his courage among the old leaflets and the monstrous .45 in his briefcase. We were in a safe country now among many *miembres* who would tell you, "My house is your house."

The moon was so bright you didn't need headlights. In spots you could see the Big Ditch, the moon dancing on the racing water that came down from the Sangre de Cristo range. There were trout in the concrete chute of the irrigation canal. You had to be fast and hungry to hit them with a pitchfork when they flashed through your legs turning blue from the water that was melted ice. They were big brownies and sometimes there would be two swimming side by side, pierced by the tines. They thrashed and threw spray that made rainbows when you held the fork up to the sun.

We passed a wall on which someone had painted VIVA LA LIGA OBREROS Y CAMPESINOS.

"See that, Sis?"

Lucy sat blind and far away. You could see she did not care about any workers and peasants. Neither did I. Jim still did. The world was out there to be organized. He talked. He told stories about being a boy on the farm in Indiana. One was about a cow that wouldn't milk unless you rubbed her nose.

Finally, he drove silently, sucking at his choppers and breathing Lucy's boozy perfume into his one good lung. And I was taking it in, trying not to think of Lucy pulling her sex open and lifting her legs, trying not to think of my own seed thrown someplace high in there, in the harbor of life, everybody in the world coming from there, remarkable beauties and twisted monsters made there, all accident and suffering, and my own loathing hitting me over and over, smack, smack, smack, like the bad piston on this jalopy that Jim Howard had been given to organize Utah and Wyoming, too, when he got a tankful of gas. Everybody would get to be a Communist. Everybody but Gypsy.

· 19 ·
Cowboys Without Horses

"They've broke the back of the Movement," Jim Howard said.

If the farmers and sheepherders of the *Liga* were its arms, the miners in the soft-coal fields at the edge of the Navajo Reservation on the Arizona border were its sinews. They had a dollar in the pocket. They paid dues. They were class-conscious proletarians with a union of their own. And now, the town's sheriff was dead and three hundred of our people were charged under an old frontier law with murder in the first degree. The jail couldn't hold them. They were being guarded by vigilantes in the high-school gymnasium and in the hall of the Benevolent and Protective Order of Elks.

"*Ay, que lastima!*" Haysoos knew how bad it was. A wound. Somebody had to go to the coal town.

It couldn't be Jim—he would be picked up on the spot. Maybe worse. For joining up with the Spics, the Welsh pump-man Griffiths had been beaten so badly he never spoke again.

Percy could not go even if he could be straightened out. You couldn't have your own lawyer in jail.

Nor could it be Haysoos. He had been vagged too many times. The tinhorns would polish their boots on his skinny ass.

And so the Gold Dust Twins were elected.

Jim had it all worked out. Forrest MacKaye would take the stage—that's what they called the Greyhound bus out here—and be in the coal town by morning. Being a city dude, he would go to the barbershop for a shave. The barber was a contact, a black-listed Slovak miner who would send him to the treasurer, another Bohunk, who would turn over the miners' Defense Fund. If he didn't get back, Nick would be in reserve. Like a good soldier, Nick had reported for duty. Nobody asked where he had been.

"They should have sent Nick," Forrest MacKaye, or whoever he was, thought. "He's the one who knows about barbershops."

But there are times when you can't say no without shaming forever that live-or-die part of yourself you're sure is there, just as you assume the goodness and intelligence behind an ordinary face.

The bus driver grabbed the handle, a kind of iron phallus on a rod, and pulled the bus door shut. It closed with a sigh as though an argument had been ended and lost. The six-wheel rig croaked into gear and bucked.

Through the window, Forrest MacKaye could see Jim looking like a bindlestiff who needed a square meal. And Percy trying to put a kitchen match to a brown, spittle-sealed cigarette. The hand that held the match shook so hard he had to steady it with the other. At the same time he was shaking his head from side to side like someone breaking a piece of bad news. Haysoos was, as always, wearing his Cantinflas hat and looking like an Indian who had seen the worst. Nick would never blend in. He looked just what he was, a spaghetti-eater, a pool-hall Wop poet. He raised his hand as though he wanted to wave.

The stage was humming along now, chewing up the miles to the Arizona border. Forrest MacKaye lit a cigarette, being careful to take it out of the correct pack. He was carrying two. Jim, thinking some identification was required, had written a message on a cigarette paper. Working like a surgeon, he had rolled it into a pellet and tamped it into another cigarette. The secret one was tucked into a pack with nineteen other Camels. Forrest MacKaye—or whoever he might be—touched it hidden in his breast pocket. Otherwise he was unarmed. He had disdained the capsule of cyanide in the untested belief that he would not break under torture.

He wondered what Jim had written. And wondered why he was not afraid. Perhaps it was because the thing he had to do was not immediate. Maybe it was because he was doing something that had no connection to the prior history of his life. This risk was as unknown to him as the long stretches of flatland broken only by an occasional mesa that stuck out like the fist of a man already sunken in quicksand.

Where were the trolley cars? Where were the six-family houses with kids inside taking piano lessons or doing their homework or reading Nick Carter and chewing on a peanut butter and banana sandwich on a seeded Vienna roll? In the blue light he saw some white horses standing fixed, painted as on a billboard.

"Do horses sleep standing up?" he wondered.

And thinking about that, he thought of the Conquistadors who had brought the horse here and how their sharp-ribbed ponies had carried the conquerors toward the mirage of the Seven Golden Hills of Cibola. The gringos who followed had iron horses that needed more than grass for their bellies. This fuel was to be found in the seams of crushed fossils that ran under the land of those who called themselves, simply, The People. With strong drink and forked tongue, the palefaces had taken the land where the thunderbird flew, above and below, blasting, digging, not caring that the Spirits would never again sleep in those defiled graves.

The ways of The People were finished. Their braided braves

drowned in the forbidden firewater, pitched forward, fell some-times on the very tracks of the switching yard where the hitched gondolas filled with bituminous coal waited for a locomotive.

There was blood on those black diamonds now. This was to be expected. That was why the workers' flag was "deepest red." Blood was a word in a song. And sheriff was a man in the movies. This one lay face up in the alley by his hoosegow with a hole in his back as big as your fist. A .38 will do that. That's why the sheriff carried one himself. He was a bad sheriff. He lay there in his blood looking up at God who had cursed his soul. He had arrested a saint.

Like a real saint, little Juan Olvedo did not think his deeds were unusual. He was the leader of the *mineros* and everything he did lit up their lives. He was barely five feet tall. But he was strong like those Latin scrappers who are always pounding away at the flyweight boxing title and a busy workman in the ring.

It was Juan who got the *trompetas* for the union band that played "The Four Red Cornfields." It was Juan who held the classes of Marxismo. It was Juan who sent to Mexico for Lenin's *Que Necessitan?* run off on newsprint like the leaflets that had been smuggled to the sailors of Kronstadt.

It was Juan who tore the padlocks from the doors when the deputies came to evict the miners from their houses built on the company's land. It had been given to the miners twenty years before, during the Great War when they had unwittingly been scabs, brought from Old Mexico to break a strike of the Indus-trial Workers of the World. Now they had their own union, inde-pendent of the finks and sweetheart contracts of John L. Lewis's United Mine Workers, which the company wanted them to join.

Juan had been jailed two days before. He was being led be-tween deputies through an alley from jail to courthouse. It was a strange way to go. The union men ran to see. There was tear gas, shooting. When the smoke cleared, the sheriff was dead and Juan Olvedo was gone. The mass arrests of miners and their wives followed.

"*Que necessitan?* What must be done?"

Forrest MacKaye's task seemed simple. He took a Camel out of his working pack, lit it, and tried not to think too much about what he had to do. It was not something that he had ever studied and there was no way to cram for the test. In the smoky half light, he saw a girl across the aisle, curled up in sleep, her hands

making a pillow, her hair falling over the wooden arm of the
seat. She was one of those children of the people to whom he
was always drawn. Beautiful without artifice. They were like wild
flowers that grow in a crack in the sidewalk alongside a factory
site. A drunkard leans on the wall and empties his bladder on
them but they do not die. They wait for the eye of a poet. They
open up. They make their own sun and rain. They are usually
the poorest girl in the class, Irish or Polish or the daughter of a
tubercular Jewish tailor.

The bus slowed, rolled past the Fairgrounds where the
Navajo held their annual powwow, and pulled up at a cafe. The
passengers stretched out of sleep. This was a rest stop for them
and as long as he was with them, Forrest MacKaye would be safe,
just passing through. Abie's Irish Rose never opened her eyes.
He squeezed around her and moved down the aisle, stepped out
of the bus, and looked around. It was early, much too early even
for a traveling salesman to need a shave. Jim had thought of
everything but this. He would be as conspicuous as a pimple on a
debutante's nose.

He went into the cafe and ordered ham and eggs. He was
still playing with them when the other passengers followed the
driver back into the bus. He heard it grind its gears and pull
away, carrying his Christian maiden into the mouth of the
M-G-M lion. He gave her a gladiator's farewell.

Now he saw that the end of the counter was lined with rifles
stacked as neatly as in an armory. He looked at their owners.
The Good Citizen's Club, these vigilantes were called. They were
a posse, all properly deputized. They all look like relatives, he
thought. Were they so alike because they all did the same things
in a country in which there were not many things to do? Tough
hombres. Cowboys without horses. They were looking at him,
too, getting curious. He ordered more coffee he didn't want.

"What's up?" he asked the waitress.

"I don't bother in other people's business," she replied.

Shouldn't changing the world be her business? She had forgotten she was a daughter of the people. "We want bread! And
roses, too!" The girls in the Paterson silk mills knew their business. The unshaven one's head was full of battle cries.

He picked up the town's newspaper. He learned that the
miners' women had been released to look after the kids who had
been running around wild and unfed. The treasurer's wife

would be out, too. He could go to her. But it was too early. He'd be too conspicuous. Forrest MacKaye had a feeling his mission had already gone wrong and whatever happened now would be out of his hands.

Killing time, he read slowly every item in the small-town newspaper. The story of the shooting. The miners had been arrested under a territorial law that said all in "the mob" were responsible when a lawman was killed. The company had stretched it to include any union man. An editorial about law and order. Cattle prices. Marriages and engagements. High-school prizes. Visits to the East. East went as far as Kansas City and stopped dead, like the edge of the flat world.

With the movie gossip he stopped at the name of each famous star, slowing himself, picturing the face of each actor, sometimes picturing two faces, Kay Frances and George Brent, Dick Powell and Joan Blondell in a closeup.

A spot as small as a dime began to burn between his shoulderblades. He could sit there no longer. He paid his check and walked out.

A man with a rifle was coming toward him. In the doorway, he saw a scale that promised to tell your fortune and your weight. He got on it and turned the knob that brought into place answers to questions everybody would like to know. He dropped his penny in at "When will I marry?" No answer card came out. He stood on the scale with another penny in his hand. The man with the rifle brushed his back as he came into the cafe.

"Mawnin'!" the man with the rifle said. He didn't say if it was good or bad.

The unshaven one walked down the main street of the coal town trying to look like a man looking for a tonsorial parlor. All he could see were tin stars and Winchester repeaters.

Forrest MacKaye was near the railroad station. He sat down on a bench in the Mission-style waiting room of the Atchison, Topeka & Santa Fe. He was all by his lonesome. Usually there were squaws selling trinkets. They had had the good sense to stay on the reservation this morning. There were too many trigger-happy riflemen in Gallup, New Mexico, and no room left in the hoosegow. He suddenly wished he had a book to read, a library book that wasn't due for at least thirty days.

By now it was the time when people should be out and going to their work, if they had any. But half this burg was busy arresting the other half. Jim's barbershop trick was unworkable. He realized he would have to get the defense money before the whole Coxey's army knew he was in town. He headed across some railroad tracks, stopped in front of the treasurer's house. While he was making up his mind to knock, a gray-haired woman came out. She was looking at him with the bewildered appeal of a mom with a sick kid waiting to hear the doctor's verdict. He made up his mind. "I have a message from the Comrades," he said, "from Jim."

The woman did not say a word. Maybe she doesn't speak English, he thought. He had to take chances. He could not start fishing for that foolish, false cigarette. Just being here was enough to identify him.

"I've come for the defense money."

"Go quick inside!" She was Mrs. Tomac, all right.

They stood in the dark parlor near a polished potbelly stove. He did not know what to do next. The woman helped him.

"Jim good boy," the woman said.

Picking each word like a number from a hat, she told him about a collective good person known as Union Man and a great badness called Company Man.

He pieced the story together. The wounded miners had been hit head-on. The sheriff had been shot through the back. Jim had suspected this. There had been bad blood between this sheriff and one of the deputies who had been sheriff before. It would take much money and many lawyers to sort this out.

"*Abogado* bring!" Mrs. Tomac did not know the word in English. Bohunks didn't need lawyers.

She reached into the flue of the parlor stove and brought out a soiled envelope. He wondered if he should show her Jim's message now. It would be insulting the woman's trust. She gave him the envelope—it was a small one, the size in which death notices come. He put it in his second breast pocket. L. Bamberger suits always had two.

"You good boy," Mrs. Tomac said. "Jim he good boy. Juan good boy."

"Thank you, Mrs. Tomac." He should call her Comrade, he remembered. "Good-bye, Comrade," he said. It was like calling your grandmother Comrade.

"Oh, bad, bad, bad!" The woman was beating her hands together, with a kind of peasant applause for each woe. "How

miner kill sheriff? With shovel? All union man go for murder
charge! Company man take kids by night, tell God kill Papa you
no say Papa having gun in house . . ."

Mrs. Tomac looked like one of those women carrying a
child's coffin in a Kaethe Kollwitz woodcut.

"How you go away?" Comrade Grandmother asked. "You
look across street."

Out of the window he could see a deputy propped back in a
chair against the wall of a Phillips 66 gas station. He had a rifle
across his knees.

"Oh, bad, bad, bad!" the woman said. "Take care, boy!"

She was right. He was a boy and he should take care. But
there was nothing for him to do except to start walking back into
town. He had taken only a few steps when a pickup truck pulled
alongside. A fellow got out and blocked his way.

"Get in is all!"

He was just a high-school kid but he was wearing a buckskin
jacket with a tin star over his heart. He looked like the guys who
played football for UNM. The real players were Polacks and
Hunkies like Mrs. Tomac, sons of coal miners who got paid to
play. The local boys were not very good. They played a few
games and went back to Tucumcari and became cops.

"Get in the truck is all!" said the second-string quarterback.

Is all? Wasn't that enough? He was polite, though. He had
this shooting iron hanging in a holster on the belt that held his
pants up.

The pickup belonged to the electric light company. It was
being used as a pie wagon. That showed who was running this
town. It pulled up at a brick building that looked the way a jail
should look when it stands next to a Baptist church.

Forrest MacKaye walked in front of The Laramie Kid into a
dark room lined with rifles on racks.

"What you doing in town?" A man who looked the way a
sheriff should look was asking him questions that were nobody's
business but his own.

"Just passing through." He had already made up his mind
to dummy up. And then, quickly, as though that would give him
a margin of safety, "I'm a student at the university."

"Heading where?"

"Flagstaff." He named the first town he could think of
across the state line.

"You come on the stage. Let's see your ticket."

The lawman had the wallet in his hand and was going through it, violating several amendments to the Constitution, but nobody was telling him which ones.

"This ticket don't go nowhere but back from here, Mister. What you doing down to old Tomac's place? We know you's there."

"I stopped by to say hello. My folks knew her in the old country." He was surprised that he was able to make it all up so quickly and say it out loud.

"What kind of name is this?" The lawman was holding a Jersey license in his hand. *Eyes: Brn. Hair: Blk. Height: 5' 10".*

"Slavish," he lied.

"You know old Tomac?"

"No. I stopped over to say hello for my folks. I'm a student at the university." It was a weak story. But the student part was true.

"You a born citizen?"

"I was born and raised in New Jersey." And I went to Clinton High and joined the Jack London Club and went picketing with Kiddy in front of RCA and saw her dance in Fanya and Tanya's dance troupe.

"One of them lungers?"

"Yes, weak lungs. That's why I chose the university." His story was improving. Lying well was bravery. This was no worse than being called down to Mr. Capoletti, the boys' gym teacher, or Dean Hobble at Chapel Hill.

"What kind of name you say that was?"

"Slavish."

He could see his story was too much for the lawman to handle as truth and too little to handle as a lie. He could be thrown in the slammer. But he was a student at the university and the law already had three hundred prisoners on its hands.

"We've had a little noggin' here, Mister. So I recommend you to get on the first stage out. I don't care which way it goes."

The unshaven one, Forrest MacKaye, Sebastian Pupik, the last of the Gold Dust Twins, thought that was a good recommendation. He nearly said "Thanks!"

Outside, the sun hit his eyes hard. The first puff on a cigarette from his safe pack made the sidewalk spin. He was between two deputies. They walked him like Pat O'Brien and Jack La Rue taking Jimmy Cagney down the last mile. They stopped at the cafe where the waitress had forgotten she was a daughter of the people. There was a bench in front with the name of the bus line painted on it. He sat down. The deputies stood and smoked.

"Them Jew agitators should be strung up," he heard one say.

He couldn't believe his ears. If someone had written that dialogue in a play for the Jack London Club, it would have been discussed all night. A stereotype. Where was the real thing, the original? Here they were, big as life. Would you believe it? And here he was, pissing in the pants of his L. Bamberger suit.

The stage came in and he got on. He was tired but still too much on guard to close his eyes. He sat, looking straight ahead, trying to find himself. And now that it was over he felt a finger tapping at the edge of his heart. It was inside and going like a telegrapher's sending code. Tap, tap, tap, dash. The tapping stopped and changed to a very light, quick flutter like a moth beating against a window. This acting up was getting to be a habit of that organ.

He remembered the envelope in his breast pocket. In it he found six five-dollar bills. Just enough to buy Percy a new suit! Oh, shit! The Movement was pathetic sometimes. Well, one way or the other, he had done what he was supposed to do.

He smiled to himself but bit it off as soon as he realized what he was doing. He was smiling too much. He knew that, for him, this was a bad thing, goofy, being a "good boy" but not in the way Mrs. Tomac had meant good boy.

And why should he be smiling with all this tapping and fluttering and sometimes thumping and whomping like the tuba in a New Orleans marching band? "Soldier's heart," the doctor had called it. What did that mean? Was it like shellshock or your hair turning white overnight or losing the power of speech the way some doughboys in the trenches did? Or was it what soldiers felt when they went over the top? And did they all have it? It was important for him to know.

Fighting had broken out in Spain. An International Brigade was forming. The Center had asked him to go. They had hinted that Forrest MacKaye would be more than a foot soldier. He told himself he was thinking seriously about it. But he couldn't picture himself going to Spain without asking his parents for permission first. They would say no, of course. *Tatteleh* can't be a soldier. *Tatteleh* had diphtheria and scarlet fever when he was a kid and now he had an enlarged heart—a "soldier's heart," which means he can't be a soldier.

Forrest MacKaye knew that he was pitying himself. That was sadder than being afraid. He had finished the first pack of Camels, so he took a cigarette out of his "spy" pack. The one with Jim's message was in the corner under the tax tab. He took it out and split it with his nail. The pellet fell on his lap. He unwrinkled it. The penciled words were smudged, hard to make out. "Comrades," Jim had written, "keep your Solidarity this Comrade is O.K. J. Howard Org."

Jim would never learn about commas but Jim was more than okay. He would take this lousy thirty bucks and send telegrams to the Ninth Floor. Then he would make Forrest MacKaye write up the whole thing, putting in more than he knew and more than he had really seen, and this would become a famous case in labor history. Jim knew the organizing business. That was what he was good at. But that was like saying Jesus Christ was good at being a carpenter. Jim was good at making other people do what they were good at.

Suddenly, his heart lifted as though a surgeon had picked it up in his hands. It stayed up there, stopped for an instant, fell, and started again. This had never happened to him before. He did not know about these things and he did not know what it meant or whether it would happen again. But Forrest Mac-Kaye—or whomever he was—knew that he would not be going with the Brigade. He would not be good at it. *"Madrid que bien resistes!"* And, though he did not know then that he was giving up his share of the last great hope of his times, he already felt the secret shame that he would bear for the rest of his life.

· 20 ·

The Kayo

There was something about the Frontier Case, as it came to be called, that frustrated heroics. Perhaps it was because Juan

Olvedo, the real hero of these events, had vanished. Long after, we learned that he was safe in Mexico and running a workers' school.

For me—as myself again—there were some wild trips in the Model A, chauffering Jim who sat with his schoolboy satchel between his knees, whistling "The Workers' Flag" through his false teeth. It was set to the tune of "Oh, Tannenbaum." But it wasn't Christmas.

The .45 automatic was still unloaded, but its presence next to a pint of whiskey was some kind of comfort. There had been some rough stuff in Gallup. The important lawyers who had come to the coal town—one from each coast and one from each faction of the civil liberties groups—were seized one night by masked men, slugged, and dumped on a Godforsaken stretch of the Navajo reservation. An Indian tracker—he could read tire treads, too—picked up the abductors' trail and found the two mouthpieces shivering in a deserted hogan. They were both bald and the white cross of bandage in the center of their tonsures made them look like friars from some medieval order.

The kidnapping made headlines for a day. The attorneys weren't much missed. Percy wrote all their briefs, anyhow. He had a new suit now, with a vest. It had not yet been scorched or otherwise sullied. Percy stayed sober. He was too good to throw away any life but his own. And the charge was murder in the first degree. The case itself dragged on. Eventually, seventeen miners were tried. Three men spent a decade in the penitentiary. And I do not even remember their names.

By an irony of history they had been martyred for naught. John L. Lewis had formed the CIO. The Red trade unions were disbanded. The miners had no place to go but the fink union into which the company had been trying to drive them when Juan was arrested. Their cause had become a political embarrassment. The Movement had shifted its base. There was great hope for the new Congress of Industrial Organizations to organize the millions of the unorganized. The struggle would be fierce—men would be shot, heads would be cracked by Henry Ford's goon squad—but labor's political direction would be reformist.

"They're selling the Revolution out for a paycheck," Jim said.

The shift had been swift. It changed many lives. Mine, too.

The *Voice* lost its angel, the people lost their *Voice*. One day, Erich just disappeared. He was probably broke and ashamed to admit it. We scrounged a few issues and folded. RIP Forrest MacKaye.

And then we lost Jesus Candillejo. The G-men grabbed him and dumped him south of the border down El Paso way. Without him, the *Liga* floundered. The Movement had run drier than the Rio Grande where it passes under the Oldtown bridge.

We had entered the period of strange bedfellows. Broad alliances became the order of the day. The middle class was being wooed into political action, if only against Fascism. There was no question that, worldwide, Fascism—which Jim pronounced Fassism—was the main enemy. But Jim was uncomfortable with the shift. He had his own definitions.

"Fassism," Jim said, "is the American Legion bustin' pickers' heads fer the growers."

Jim's main concern was always "you-uns"—the people around him or within the radius of a tank of gas for the Model A. You couldn't make "theoretical mistakes" that way.

Not too long after, under the kleig lights in Madison Square Garden, Comrade Browder would be telling the world that "Communism is twentieth-century Americanism!" What had happened to the nineteenth? The children of the garment workers cheered. They liked the idea of being Americans. Jim already was one, had been for so long he didn't celebrate George Washingmachine's birthday.

"I don't hold with it," he said.

Because Jim didn't "hold with it," he was expelled from the Movement. A hatchet man came all the way from Thirteenth Street to give him the axe. He tried to talk Jim around. Jim could use a rest. A guy with one lung, and all. There was a carrot-and-stick hint of a trip to the Soviet Union.

"If I want to see smokestacks," Jim told the *apparatchik*, "I can always go to Gary, Indiana."

It was hard to see what Jim was guilty of except talking like that. Let's say he just went out of style. Jim did not fight back. It was "for the good of the Revolution." I could understand why, later, the purged Bolsheviks would confess in open court to crimes they had not committed.

The hatchet man had the nerve to ask me to take Jim's place.

"*Pro tem,*" he said. That was the way he talked.

Naturally, I refused. I moved into what used to be the ball-room of the old Palace of the Governors with Jim. Where else would I go? I was out of my job, out of school, and, for me, the Movement would always be wherever Jim parked his high-laced shoes.

All at once I was on my ass practicing a bum's life on a dialectical Skid Row. There were three brass beds in the ballroom. The third one was for Percy but most of the time he was lost in the *cantinas* reciting Lope de Vega and Calderon for drinks. "*La vida es un sueño, y los sueños, sueños son.*"

My dreams were also dreams but I don't remember being unhappy during that Tortilla Flat time. Maybe it was because I was never alone.

The hammer and sickle over the three brass beds had flaked from the wall, leaving something that looked vaguely like a cross. The joint could have been a monastery. And we did live something like monks, pooling whatever money we had, taking turns peeling spuds, hanging out the wash that Jim did in a galvanized tub, making Irish music on a washboard with Percy's only pair of long johns. There was always a big pot of something Jim called Mulligan's stew simmering on the kerosene stove. Sometimes Jim fried sardines in bacon fat. Hobo stuff.

We passed many a day doing nothing. Like going to the Albuquerque zoo. There was a cage there of what looked like ordinary chickens with Latin names. I dont know whether it's true but Jim said they stopped laying in captivity. We sympathized with its bachelor lion. Once he lifted his leg and leg fly a stream that almost got us. I think he did it deliberately. He was mean and mangy and no good to himself anymore.

"It is better to die on your feet than live on your knees!"

I heard La Pasionaria from afar. The jackals of democracy were standing by while Spain bled to death. I gave a pint of plasma in a "bloodmobile" that came across the country from Hollywood. It was driven by an unsuccessful screenwriter, and the nurse was a starlet whose option had not been picked up. Her heart was in the right place. So was mine. It was my body that was in the wrong latitude.

Nick and I did not talk much about Spain when we met in the campus Sweet Shoppe. The news from there was mainly bad but camouflaged by what Malraux later called "the lyric illusion."

We both felt guilty in our own ways. Nick was involved with school. He had caught up to me, made up the lost semesters of his suspension from Chapel Hill, and was getting his degree. He was going to marry Consuela who had defied everybody and stuck by him. I did not know what I was going to do.

As usual, Cupid gave me the fateful shove.

Sally was from Milwaukee and doing something in the summer session that had to do with Indians. We found each other quickly, would have even if Sally had not worn a Star of David on a chain around her neck. She was the only Jewish girl on campus.

Sally wondered at the way I was living, worried about how I would get back to normal.

"It looks like the picture book of *The Three Bears*," Sally said the first time she came down to Spanishtown and saw our three brass beds.

She wasn't stuffy, though. She just thought you could be bohemian without going that far. She was liberal, wanted things to be fair for everybody regardless of race, color, or creed. But she was equally convinced that you had to look out for yourself.

"If you don't, who will?"

I didn't have the answer but I was beginning to think it was a good question.

The self, Pablo Neruda wrote, survives by having two skins. One meets life, the other shies from it. But even the toughest hide turns like a plant toward the heat of the sun. Sally brought the sunshine to my alley, turned me around.

When Sally left, I shivered in the enormous room built to cool the flesh of dancers long dead. The flickering fire of revolt had gone out. Two naked bulbs lit what so recently seemed to be appropriate squalor. The paint on the emblem of our cause had chipped, leaving us with a sickle and a hammer without a head. A pair of Jim's long johns sat in a chair like a Halloween ghost. I began to look at my surroundings through Sally's *balabusteh* eyes. I saw I was in a hobo jungle, an Okie camp.

Jim was at home there. I was not. Among the migrants I had had that sad yearning for hard work that Chekhov's intellectuals are always talking about—the salvation of belonging, of being neither better nor worse than your neighbor, of having your struggles defined by them, of having a fixed, useful place and the same ambitions as everybody in that place. "By the sweat of thy brow . . ." I could not change a sparkplug. But I could read and write without moving my lips. I resolved to center myself again between others like myself. I rented a room in a campus roominghouse, threw off the hairshirt of dissent, and went back to living in the imperfect normal world.

I found a pair of black-and-white shoes still new—they had not been designed to wear while soapboxing—added a V-neck sweater, and took my place among the collegians. I can document the costume with a Brownie snapshot that shows Nick and me in an arm-around-the-shoulder pose in front of a rusty Moxie sign on an eroding adobe wall. We both look out of place, me with hair piled in a pompadour, cigarette held negligently, both of us looking like two not yet liquidated Futurists, friends of Mayakovsky when he was writing "A Cloud in Trousers."

On a good day, the campus looked pretty much like the one that had hired Groucho Marx to be its president. Of course, our girls jiggled less and the football captain did not sing duets with the sweetheart of Sigma Chi. I was not Joe College but neither was I Rip Van Winkle awakening to a changed world. I ate melts and drank floats. I took a course in linguistics. There were only three of us in the class, me, Nick, and an unusual Indian named Tony Shorty. Tony Shorty did these clicks in his throat that were Athabascan, the Navajo language. The professor took notes. He gave us all an A.

Saturday nights I went to the Casa Grande Saloon and danced the *Varsoviana*. I went to all the varsity games. The cheerleaders still went up into the air in the same pleated skirts that caught the air like parachutes. I never saw them without thinking of Kiddy.

She had had her heart set on going to Cornell, had already arranged for a loan. To her lifelong regret, Mr. Burper, the principal of Clinton High, had given her a bum rap. She had to study Stanislavsky instead.

I had never gone too far from these playing fields. If I was not wearing the maroon letter of my college, neither was I wearing the beret and bandolier of the Lincoln Brigade, holding the line in the rubble at the University of Madrid. I cheered them as I did the helmeted boys running a ball downfield. Were they not all being, at that responsible moment, something finer than themselves?

In my own small way I became a campus somebody. I pub-

lished poems in the *Quarterly,* wrote an attack on the Taos escapists who found enchantment in a burned-out, overgrazed land
plundered from its historical owners. I was refuted by Mabel
Dodge Luhan, John Reed's old girl friend who had recently married an Indian. Gossipers said she had paid cash to the Taos
tribe for stout Tony Luhan.

Of these last months at school, there remains with me the
proud memory and the sweet taste of a momentary manliness
when a misfired vengeance coated me with an illusory *machismo.*

It came about because as a freshman I had neglected the
required education of my body. Now, as a senior, I had to make
up for all those pushups, chinnings, and dumbbell knockings I
had avoided at Chapel Hill. I trotted around dogged laps, tried
to touch my elusive toes, and played an inept outfield until I
would achieve enough *corpore sano* to get my sheepskin.

Usually our *gymnopaedia* took place on a sun-baked diamond. It could get hot in Albuquerque. There were days when
you could sell tickets to Hell. You shagged a few fly balls, ran
comically along the grooved base path if you got a hit, and that
was that. There weren't any hot-doggers. You didn't want to be
too fit in those days or somebody might think you were healthy
enough to work.

One day, inside the gym, we were all given boxing gloves
and paired off with the nearest guy who was more or less the
same size and weight. Where did the Romans get all those pairs
of jumbo Everlasts? I found myself facing another gladiator who
had to take off his glasses before he could put up his dukes.

Now, it happened that the uncle who used to pay me to read
Proust while guarding his used-car lot had, during that time,
taken it into his head to become an amateur boxer. Interesting
fellow. So many of us want one thing and do another. I had
watched him spar with an old heavyweight who had fought the
best when a black man was told when to win. He had managed to
lose twice to Georges Carpentier. He, too, was called George. He
was a Senegalese who dressed like an ambassador, walked like a
tiger, and talked like Charles Boyer.

I had studied George's moves. My uncle had taken me to
some club fights. I also had seen him stopped in the first round
of his welterweight career.

So that day in the gym, I bobbed and weaved and danced
around my partner. My left under his nose added to his myopia.
He himself was flailing wildly, making me look even better. My

opponent never laid a glove on me. I peppered him with phantom jabs. My right hand was cocked, lethal, but never fired.

I had never hit anybody in my life. In fact, I still cannot see how anybody can bring himself to strike, with his bare hand, flesh and bone like his own. Would I, I wonder, even defend myself if attacked? Once, goaded by Kiddy, exasperated, no longer myself, I slapped my son across his face. I could have cut off my arm.

So here I was surprising both my classmates and myself. They stopped to watch. I flicked my left. I feinted, I shuffled. Nobody was getting hurt. I was feeling good. I had just downed a few *marcs* at La Coupole. I was walking down the Place Contrescarpe with Ernie Hemingway. We were going to meet Scotty Fitzgerald and spar a few rounds. True, I was Jewish, but I was not that unworthy Robert Cohn who had gone to Princeton and chased to Pamplona and lost his head over Lady Brett. I was of the found generation.

I did not know I was preparing my own apotheosis.

The next time we put on the gloves, I was looking for my four-eyed partner when the Phys Ed teacher singled me out.

"Let's even it up," he said.

This was the same guy who had been a cop at the Courthouse and watched our Hunger March. Was it less than three years since Nick, ducking out from behind the concrete door of his cell, had thrown at me the dialectical conundrum: "Did you cock today?" The cop was an assistant football coach now. He was so tickled at the chance to give me a dusting, he forgot to look like a cop. He had his arm around his scrapper like Howard Cosell doing a post-fight interview.

"Yeah, let's even it up." How quick the brute mentality when given sanction!

"Three minutes!" the coach said.

In less than a minute of the first round of their second fight, Joe Louis had paid Max Schmeling back for every Nazi slur.

Before I knew it, I was surrounded by a circle of jocks and looking at a hunk of body that was cut out of one piece of granite. I used to see physiques like that on the picture cards we matched on the stoop on Avon Avenue. They belonged to Tommy Loughran, Mickey Walker, Harry Grebs. This one belonged to the light-heavyweight champion of the Southwestern Collegiate Conference.

I knew the Champ, only to say hello to. He was one of those

clean-cut fellows who get three or four athletic letters and straight A's. He was smiling at me politely. He was just too polite to say no to anything, including knocking my block off.

Don't let anybody tell you a fighter goes down from one punch. He's lucky if he does. The Champ let me jab and cover. He was feeling me out, just wiping away my token jabs, taking the occasional right I risked on the laces of his gloves. I was doing everything I had learned from the Senegalese Smasher. But I was horribly out of shape. I had been to the Casa Grande the night before. I was nursing a hangover. I was seeing my own stars.

The Champ was keeping his punches short, holding back. He was trying hard not to hurt me. But he was an athlete. His fists came up from some tightly coiled spring that started down in his toes. Wherever they landed I turned into mush. I wasn't dancing anymore. My feet were anchored like steamboats. I was puffing hard. I wiped my nose with the back of my right glove and snorted as I had seen club fighters do. I never knew why. Maybe if you did you became Luis Firpo the Wild Bull of the Pampas.

The left that I had been holding out so classically, the left the Champ would at least have to walk into when he came to me, would no longer stay up. My right was hanging like a broken wing. The Marquis of Queensbury was already holding the smelling salts under my nose.

I was helpless. But the ex-cop wasn't going to stop this fight until I went down. Was anybody keeping time? Tradition permitted throwing in the towel if you could not answer the gong for what sportswriters cleverly call the next stanza. I was barely making it to the next paragraph.

I was breathing so hard my trunks were slipping off my deflated rubber tire. I hitched them up with the laces of both gloves like Jimmy Cagney saying, "Yuh rat! Yuh doity rat!" I should have pulled my trunks up around my neck. The Champ was too much of a gentleman to hit me below the belt. He was smiling sadly. You could see he didn't like being used as a bully boy. He would make it happen with the least damage possible.

I got my gloves up high enough to cover my eyes. I didn't want to see the end of this movie. The Champ uncorked a short right about six inches below my décolletage. My solar plexus exploded like a box of Fourth of July firecrackers. My trunks

started to fall before I did. I followed them like a sack of
potatoes.

I was not out. I was in some higher state of consciousness.
All eight wheels of the Avon Avenue trolley car had run over my
stomach, emptying myself from myself. But I was alive. The red
circle of the free-throw line on the gymnasium floor was making
a Byzantine halo around my head and I knew there were no
Jewish saints. The Champ bent and lifted me, like Lazarus, back
into the life of ordinary men.

That uppercut brought me grace. No wonder Hemingway
said, "My writing is nothing. My boxing is everything." Though I
walked the campus with aching ribs and Cyrano nose, I basked
in popularity. People to whom I had previously been invisible
sought me out to touch me, to say "Hi, y'all!" At the Casa
Grande they bought me Singapore slings. I even considered dating an Osage oil princess. She looked like Dorothy Lamour and
drove a white Cadillac convertible. But my schooldays were running out and the rebel girls of Newark were waiting for me. At
least I thought they were.

· IV ·
Broken Blossoms

· 21 ·
Once in a Sedan

I finished school in midterm. A chance came up for a ride East in the rumble seat of a '36 Chevy coupe. I took it and headed back to my own backyard. We hit out on route 66 toward Tucumcari and the northward swing. New Deal or not, the country seemed to be about where it had been when Nick and I had come through three years before. Over a dinky bridge at Santa Rosa we crossed the Pecos River. I was immediately carried up to its source in the Sangre de Cristo range and the hairpin road that ended at the Torerro mine from where I had filed GUNPLAY ON THE PECOS. Forrest MacKaye had scooped the world.

My former heroics, though, were becoming a soldier's tale impossible to tell to anybody who had not been there. And besides, those battles had been fought pseudonymously under names I was beginning to forget as the occasions for their use were being withdrawn. Paradoxically, now that I was only myself, I was beginning to feel that life was elsewhere. I had a pretty good idea, even then, that after the Movement I would be acting on my beliefs only in intimacy.

Once home, I immediately tried to get on the Federal Writers Project. They wanted me. I had published as much as most of the scribblers in Stephen Crane's hometown, but we were at the tail end of the Depression and the freeloading days were over. To be taken on you had to actually be on relief. How could I pretend to be destitute? There was too much neon around my name. My family had a spiffy showroom now that had belonged to the Huppmobile people before the Crash. And, next door, the old lot boasted a stainless-steel arch like a denture at its mouth, announcing the year of the firm's establishment pushed back two decades to the racing days of Uncle Phil. I had tribal rights. I began to work on the lot.

I had taken one step forward and two steps back. There I was, rereading those Proustian reminiscences, alien, androgynous, which had been written in a cork-lined room. They did not travel well in a four-door De Soto sedan. Where were the roadsters of yesteryear? And the wild ideas that went with their rumble seats? The cars had changed but I had not. Whatever I had been, I had only become more so.

What was I? I could not call myself a writer. At the university, I had been offered a fellowship in English. But one-third of a nation was "ill housed, ill clothed, ill nourished." I had taken a degree in sociology. But I had given myself and my pen to a cause. I had been "plowing the sea of the Revolution." Now I was treading water. During this life of a salesman, I wrote nothing. Like Mayakovsky, I "stepped on the throat of my own song."

It never occurred to me to set out to be a writer on my own. I regarded the future as an awesome mystery, not so much dangerous but an endless maze, into which it would be safer not to go alone. With Nick I would happily have gone to live in a garret. "Come, my friends, let us pity those who are better off than we are. For, remember, the rich have butlers and no friends. . . ." I could have sponged. All I needed to do was declare, "I am a poet!" and then stick to it. But I came from a family that let you know that "showing off" in front of the world is not the same as jumping into it feet first and coming up with a gold watch.

"You'll see, Tati will become a doctor!"

Tati was what they had called me back then, diminutive for *Tattaleh*, little father. That is to say, little future father. Sometimes my mother called me *Tattaleh Sonneleh*, little son, future father. "The child is father to the man." But I didn't go for a doctor. I began to write little poems. In the seventh grade, I had won a prize, a trip to New York—all the way from Newark, New Jersey.

"A *poyet* you can always be on the side," my grandfather said.

That had been the story of my life so far.

Two or three nights a week, I took the Hudson Tubes and the IRT up to Columbia. When in doubt, educate. All my courses were in Philosophy Hall before which sat a cast of Rodin's *Thinker*. "Here I sit brokenhearted, paid a nickel and only farted!" I held my wind and earned an MA. My thesis was on "Village Organization Among the Spanish-Americans of New Mexico." That and a nickel, as we used to say, will get you a ride on the subway.

I sold cars—more likely, they sold themselves. The lot was never closed. That is, it had no gate, no chain, and ran the length of a football field between two brick walls, ending in a cul-de-sac at the backs of decaying brownstone houses like the one in which Stephen Crane was born. In the summer it became a kind of wind tunnel of fumes and swamp air from the nearby fens where the world's first international airport was being built on piles of Newark's own garbage. The soil of the lot was soaked down with the drained oil from a thousand lube jobs. Even so, tall grasses and wild flowers grew at its edges. Nature lay there like the undiscovered body of a violated girl.

Though we were only a couple of blocks from Broad and Market, an intersection that our deluded Chamber of Commerce claimed to be the Busiest Four Corners in the World, the lot, at night, was a convenient lovers' lane. Here I pursued a few serendipitous and anonymous adventures above the belt.

Among the Badgers, incomplete coitus had been held to be the cause of "blue balls," a dangerous genital ailment that called for prompt first aid. Blue balls was the only legitimate and manly excuse for jerking off. My memories are not of such infirmities. My partners in such sex without sex—their names and faces and little cries of dismay homogenized by time—are sentimentally recalled.

Had they not been really more unselfish, more giving than those with whom I lay naked and priapic? In intercourse, the outcome is predetermined, conclusive—at least for the male. It is a performance with a beginning, a middle, and an end, a play whose dialogue, if sometimes incoherent, is regulated, fixed, and limited.

"Now? Now?"

"Didja? Didja?"

If coitus is dialogue, this other is soliloquy, mime, white-faced, existential, obsessed.

"Once in a sedan, twice standing up . . ." Here is endless yearning.

Is it not smug to call complete only that love which concludes in the genito-urinary tract? And incomplete that which, by restraint of circumstance, stays in a higher realm, above the belt, closer to the heart? Whether my partner was merely dutifully obliging the folkways of courtship in withholding all, or was herself tied to Cupid's chariot, pulling hard away from her own surrender, she was doing it with me. And that was enough.

Much is made about who is doing what to whom, but in sex we are, as some cynic has said, "in business for ourselves." Granted, there are extremes. Take the instance of the British gentleman, recorded by Dr. Glover, who would walk for a moment alongside a strolling woman until she turned to look at him. At that instant he would tip his hat and ejaculate! He needs Madame; but for her there is nothing more than a moment of perplexity.

Yes, we are all soldiers in Kinsey's army. Knowing myself better now, I would say that I had a predilection for the preliminaries. I was probably enjoying myself so thoroughly that I took what was offered without letting it occur to me to seize what was, at least ostensibly, withheld. Was I the loser?

Like Lorenz's ducklings who follow the first moving object they see immediately after they hatch, I had probably been imprinted by my first touch of Kiddy. No perfume can replace the musky suspiration from her nostrils during a long kiss. During this time of waiting for nothing, I saw her once, but from afar. As far, that is, as the balcony of the Broad Street Unitarian Church was from its lectern. Don't be misled. The Titian Typhoon had not become Aimee Semple McPherson. She was in a theater collective in New York. They came to Newark to perform *Waiting for Lefty*. For some reason peculiar to the times, the Odets play, which had been scheduled to be done in a school auditorium, was banned. The Unitarian minister took in stray cats. His church was down the street. Did Kiddy think on her childhood sweetheart as she passed? Constantly he thought on her.

The church became the cab drivers' meeting hall menaced by goons. Kiddy played Edna, the brave wife who urges her Joe to stick by the union. She hints that an old boyfriend is offering her a cushier life. Joe wants to hear more. She wants to talk about the union.

JOE: . . . He's probably been coming here every morning
and laying you while I hacked my guts out!
EDNA: You're crawling like a worm!
JOE: You'll be crawling in a minute.
EDNA: You don't scare me that much! *(Indicates a half inch
on her finger.)*
JOE: This is what I slaved for!
EDNA: Tell it to your boss!
JOE: He don't give a damn for you or me!
EDNA: That's what I say.
JOE: Don't change the subject!
EDNA: This is the subject, the *exact subject!* Your boss
makes the subject. I never saw him in my life, but
he's putting ideas in my head a mile a minute. . . .

The part was perfect for Kiddy. She brought to it her natural visionary vehemence. It was exciting. The episodes unfolded, the church became the union hall, the audience became the embattled hackies, "stormbirds of the working class."

MAN: Boys, they just found Lefty!
AGATE: Where?
MAN: Behind the car barn with a bullet in his head!
ALL: STRIKE, STRIKE, STRIKE!!!
Curtain

From every pew it came, louder than any call to Jesus. It echoed within me. The proletarian revolution was a leap from necessity into freedom. But first I had to free myself. I was hogtied by confused class allegiances. My uncle threatened to fire me for reading the *Daily Worker* on his stinking *muzhik* lot. Something had to be done. I was running the risk of becoming a member of my own family.

· 22 ·
A Madonna of the Tenements

Armed with my degree in sociology, I came out *numero uno* in a Civil Service examination for a job giving to others the relief I could not get myself. The position was a political plum. Half of my co-workers were barely literate wardheelers; on Election Day they carted their caseloads to the polls. Bread and ballots. I played hooky. They could not fire me.

We were titled Family Visitors. My families, almost a hundred, lived in a single block in Little Italy where Nick and I used to go for *pasta e fagole*. In the first days of the Great Depression, whole families on home relief were receiving an average of $2.39 a week to cover food, rent, and clothing. The allowance was more now and welfare was better organized and investigated. Each jot and tittle was entered into the budget. And I was paid $40 each week to be its keeper.

How I hated to climb those tenement stairs to knock on the doors of other lives!

"Who is?"

"Investigator!" You could hardly call yourself the Visitor.

"Da check! Da check!"

From month to month, I carried their alphabetized lives in my hands. The checks did not come from the city. They came from me, St. Francis of Assistance. Bread came from me. Wine came from me. Communion dresses came from me. And something called layettes—diapers and tiny shirts for babies—came from me.

Christmas is coming. *Natale*. And a star will shine over City Hall and Three Investigators will bring him gifts—Jesu, son of Maria and Giuseppe Pozzuoli, third floor rear, 135 Bloomfield Avenue, Newark, N.J.—gifts from the Department of Public Welfare. And Mrs. P., as she will be described in departmental records, will open the door for me with the *bambino* pulling at a peasant teat fuller than any on which the Child rests his head in any museum. And I will turn my eyes to my book of allowables and find nothing for the candle burning perpetually in a red glass under a picture that looks like her, three, four, or five conceptions before.

"Da shoes, da shoes!"

Scarpe. That was one Italian word I didn't learn from Nick. They wore out faster than the Budget allowed. And children grew faster than the Budget allowed.

"Look da shoes!"

They hold them under my nose, little first walkers that would never be bronzed, and silly, pointed things with broken heels, turned and twisted, paper soles worn through in the halls of Barringer High, where daughters took the futile Commerical Course. And, sometimes, work shoes spattered with cement and plaster. Papa had stolen a day's work as a *muratore.* There were finks among the Visitors who pursued such clues.

My visitations were always on women. Except for the infirm, the masculine of Italy disappeared during the day. Some of the women wept. Some raged. Sometimes, one recently released from Greystone, the state mental hospital, went for the Visitor with a kitchen knife. I was bitten by one who had syphilis.

If Mama wanted shoes, the divorced or deserted woman wanted stockings. They would come to the door half-dressed, barefoot. They joked, they offered wine, flattery, themselves.

"Are you sure you ain't Eyetalian? I could've sworn."

The others showed doctors' prescriptions, notices of eviction. These showed their legs.

"Whadayahsay?"

On that Grand Rapids bed with the lace dolls on its lumpy pillows, in that tenement room with the smell of Lysol and *Parmigiano* climbing up the wallpaper, under a tinted photo of a man in a soldier suit wearing the brimmed hat and puttees of the Great War, for a pair of stockings her quick tongue. Why not? Disgust is a powerful attraction. But you are a plaster saint. You stretch the allowables, give her like a suitor something the budget calls Hosiery, which she will roll around an elastic, leaving purple bracelets around her pasta thighs.

In the midst of life, my own was postponed. I made my miserable rounds, had some nondescript but unpurchased amours, and waited for the shoe to drop on the ceiling of my sensibilities. I knew I had to free myself from this quicksand of quotidian suffering to which—though mired myself—I had been assigned as watcher, given a rope to throw first to this one, then that, and even as the slime reached their mouths, tear it from their hands.

At the office, we Visitors dictated the banal tales of our daily rounds directly to secretaries. They were cheaper than Dictaphones. They were a kind of harem sequestered in a corner called the Bull Pen. The witty, the pretty, and the obliging were in demand. I liked best a little pony who trotted around tossing, like a mane, her unconscious sexuality. Her name was Anna Bonano. Inevitably it became Anna Banana.

To ward off the absurdity of putting down the weekly *comédie humaine* of diapers, macaroni, shoes, and tears into paragraphs that were already prescribed by a fixed outline, and to impress her, I sometimes used words from the back of my head, two-bit words, literary and sometimes psychiatric. Most of the other investigators just gave the raw data—births, deaths, desertions—and let the secretaries fill in the rest.

"I like to take from you," Anna told me. "You've got a large vocabulary."

We were both escaping into language. Anna never asked what a strange word meant or how it was spelled. I would see her looking up the phonetic strokes of her shorthand in a *Webster's* she kept under her machine.

Walking away, Anna's slightly unfashionable behind shimmered like the sun setting in the Bay of Napoli. Coming toward you, two tenors with mandolins sang *"O, sole mio!"* and it was hard to make up your mind which one was hitting the higher C. When Anna Banana sat down next to my desk, hair all ringlets, with an extra Eberhard-Faber #2 stuck like a hibiscus behind her ear, her little teeth kneading a stick of Spearmint, I had my own private Tillie the Toiler.

To hide my secret lust, I pedestalized her. I called her Miss B. She called me You. Her pencil would speed along so fast, I could not keep up with her and show my vocabulary. While I thought, Anna Banana would make little adjustments in her curls and crack her Spearmint. She knew her effect on me.

When I paused to light my pipe, Anna looked at me in an indulgent way.

"I hate those stogies!" She meant those twists of dark tobacco the *paisanos* smoked.

What Anna liked was defined by what she hated. These moments of hauteur were our intimacy. Anna stepped out of herself. She became Bette Davis in some Anglo-Saxon movie world.

Anna showed no pity for the disasters she set down. She was all business, making those mysterious glyphs, filling a page and flipping it over like a bank teller counting cash.

"Client taken to St. Michael's Hospital with hemor-
rhages . . ."

"Son, Pasquale, taken to Rahway Reformatory . . ."

Perhaps these laments were stale to her. She had recorded
them too many times before. And she was writing about her own
people.

"Ise regusted!" she would say about an arrest for a revealed
incest.

Sex, like the name of Yahweh, was never spoken out loud.
Never desire, only its accidents, the inevitable price paid. A girl
sent home from high school, sitting in a corner of the kitchen,
belly swollen, condemned. Beatings. Police. Ambulances.

"She shoulda listened to the priest!" Anna said.

We spoke in an arcane code in which dress stood for undress, stockings were black but not for mourning, and shoes—
"Scarpe, Mister Gentleman, scarpe!"—all had high spikes that
ground into the fetishist's skin. And always there were the
layettes, sometimes two in a single year.

"Adjust budget for new family member . . ."

"Guinees!"

"The rich get richer and the poor get children."

"Thanks for nothing!"

So it went, Faust dictating to Marguerite. Or was it Mephisto
moving that sharp point of graphite with its rubber tip?

"Mistakes," Anna said, "that's why pencils have erasers."

Anna became engaged and the girls in the Bull Pen threw a
party for her. They brought a zuppa Inglese and a jug of wine.
Anna brought me a cup. Bacchante.

"Dago red," she said.

She showed me her ring. Its diamond was impressive. Her
guy was in the produce business, ostensibly, but he was well connected, a "friend of a friend." He could get a woman on Relief
the same day her husband went to jail.

The wine was purple, heavy with sugar, sacramental.

"It's homemade," she said. "That's what Guinees are good
at!"

They were also good at singing. Anna Banana put herself
between two other stenographers and they became the Andrews
Sisters. They were groovy; should have signed up for Amateur
Nite at the Empire Burlesque.

There was a portable phonograph going and Anna danced.

Very seriously, without improvisation, each step perfect and precise. She did the Shag, the Suzy-Q, and the Big Apple, ending by leaning back, her arms heavenward. This movement was called "Praise Allah!" Anna was very reverent. And a little drunk.

"Wooo, I'm *u'briacco!*" she said, forgetting she was not a Guinee.

Anna was evidently famous for her dancing. The whole Bull Pen clapped hands and she stepped out alone, kicking her little feet, lifting her skirt, fannying, and waving a handkerchief over her head. *"Mezza luna, mezza mare . . ."* Half moon, half sea, and the children of the heel of Italy's boot in between.

Anna tugged at me once or twice to join the dancing, but I didn't know how. I was no jitterbug. The dips and bends of the Varsoviana were about all I could manage. An aunt had tried to teach me. And Uncle Phil had, long ago, let me stand on his feet and moved me around in whatever steps they were doing on the Pantages circuit in 1919. Think how different my life might have been, with God knows what outcome, if I had been able to follow the printed footsteps that tracked the floor like the fossils of paleoliths!

While the hungry at the office door—they were always there—cried out for bread, Anna Banana gave out cake.

"Manga, manga," she called out to me, "and you'll be married next!"

In the meantime, I was like the hero—if that's what you can call him—in one of those Isaac Singer stories, a corpse who does not know he is dead.

The Wehrmacht was goose-stepping over Europe. Perfidious Albion waved a furled umbrella at its bayonets. Jan Masaryk leaped from the window through which he saw his country's end. France buried itself behind a wall of venality. The local Bolshies were occupied with the hagiography of the Nazi-Soviet Pact. None of us knew to what extent that expedient would mark the end of our faith in any history but our own ups and downs. I hung around, waiting for Lefty.

But chance is the fool's name for fate. With my idiot's luck, I was saved by Hitler. I had a cause. And my pen was working for me again. Not much for Forrest MacKaye, but I was putting out the *Newsletter* of the Anti-Nazi League. The idea behind the league was to get everybody to boycott sauerkraut and bratwurst. There were no Volkswagens yet to stretch the moral dilemma.

Refugees were few, and even they did not yet suspect what they had escaped.

My father said, "If Hitler don't need the Jews, the Jews don't need Hitler!"

In the woods of northern New Jersey, Fritz Kuhn was drilling his Brownshirts. They were disguised as nudists. When they took off their swastikas, they played volleyball in the buff. I went to see. But I was stopped at the gates of the Nature Friends Camp by Hermann Goering. He was wearing a pair of *lederhosen* and a Brooklyn Dodgers cap.

BUND DRILLS IN SECRET. REPORTER BANNED.

The league held a big meeting in what had not long ago been the Yiddish Theater. I had seen my first plays there, scary and fascinating. They were usually about immigrant girls who were misled by false promises of marriage, *farfiert*. Or they were about adultery between brother- and sister-in-law. Someone had synopsized these plays: "He wants. She doesn't. She wants. He doesn't. Both want. The curtain comes down." All the actors wore lipstick and their cheeks were passionate with rouge. When not engrossed by hints of incest between cousins, I ran up and down the aisles with my own. Cries of "*Schweig, momzehrim!* Quiet, little bastards!" drowned out the broken confessions of the betrayed.

I understood few of the words I heard and less about the situations. But Tatteleh Sonneleh was very smart. Using the same word for chopped, *gehackteh*, as in chopped liver, he had named all the plays "Chopped Husbands."

Now Tatteleh himself was speaking from that same stage about real husbands being chopped up by a madman named Hitler. Some joke! First, Tati introduced the mayor. Then the head of the kosher butchers union. Then a pediatrician and an undertaker. Then the same Unitarian minister who had given sanctuary to Lefty, and an Orthodox rabbi who called everybody "My dear ladies and gents!" Two of each, just like Noah in the Ark! The meeting was guarded conspicuously by strong-arm boys supplied by "Sweets" Sugarman. For them, this was a sequel to their war against "Dutch" Schultz. Soon enough, Uncle Sam would be giving them their gats, free for nothing.

Everybody applauded and signed up to boycott.

Tati's mother wished him a life on his *pupik!*

Tati felt he was back on the track again. You see? I told you so! Life was laid out like the grades in Avon Avenue School. First you went to 1B and if you were not "held back" you got promoted to 1A. In Newark, everything was bass ackwards. There, for some reason, B came before A. *Ish gebibbel!* When you got through 8A, you went to high school and then, knock wood, you went to college. And you became a *poyet*. And you got married. And so on and so forth.

Step by step. And Tati would always be there, right on the job, safe and sound, surrounded by everybody who had attended his placental graduation from "you know where." Tati did not realize that the grades never stopped and that he would be graduating from something all his life and the same people would be there even if they were not invited. You couldn't chase them away with a stick!

"Guinees marry Guinees!"

That was how it should be. There were too many outsiders hanging around at the edge of the dance of life. And, though I did not know it then, I would soon be standing under the bridal canopy and breaking under my heel the glass by which our tribe symbolized a troth. It had something to do with the destruction of the Great Temple in Jerusalem. Perhaps it meant that as long as there would be man and wife, they would beget and multiply and be a temple unto themselves.

· 23 ·

The Invasion from Mars

So here I was sitting on the floor next to a girl with startling red hair falling to her shoulders and lighting her face as though she were standing before footlights on a stage. She was not conventionally pretty. Her nose was perceptibly too long for her face, yet it seemed perfectly suited to the Nefertiti look, which, I learned later, she deliberately cultivated. I wondered who she was.

It was one of those crowded parties to which nobody wants to go but everybody does. The sour cream of Newark's intelligentsia were there. Levé was Jersey's most successful artist. That *accent aigu,* a flick of a sable-tipped brush over his name in the lower right-hand corner of each oil, hinted at Paris. Levé did well selling his pastiches in "museum frames" lit from below by a forty-watt bulb shaped like a little boy's unabashed erection.

Levé also played the violin, better, I thought, than he painted. If you could copy Heifetz, more power to your elbow! Right now he was rendering the chicken fat out of *"Zigeunerweise."* I listened with one ear and looked at the girl with the red hair. I could not take my eyes off her.

Levé finished with a gypsy flourish. The girl with the red hair touched her palms together twice to make polite applause. She was not crazy about our *peintre-violiniste.* It was a period in which people thought a lot about class. "They draw nude ladies for *The Masses.* How does that help the working classes?" The girl with the red hair—to call her a redhead would be like calling "Girl With the Flaxen Hair" a serenade to a peroxide blonde— had the other kind of class. In spades!

When she stood up, I could see she was a couple of inches too short to be statuesque. If she had been, I might have been intimidated. But this was a "bring your own" party. I had mine on my hip in a silver flask I had inherited from my grandfather. It was an affectation of the Jazz Age I had missed and would not give up. I decanted some hooch into a paper cup and held it out to the girl. The bourbon was the same color as her hair.

"No two cents plain?" She wanted to show me she was not accustomed to the straight gargle.

I spritzed some seltzer from a siphon. The bottle was marked Garber Bros. One of the Garber boys was married to a cousin of mine.

"Distant relatives," I said.

"Small world," she said.

Our host had set out the usual slices of salami and some plates of what looked like Raisinets. The girl with the red hair looked at them dubiously. I offered her a cigarette.

"'Reach for a Lucky instead of a sweet!'"

If you're old enough to remember that ad you're old enough to read this book.

It was a Camel but she reached, lit up, took a deep drag. In contrast to her elegance, the girl with the red hair cupped the cigarette like a guy grabbing a smoke on the boss's time. In a minute she was balancing an inch of ash between fingers that were manicured but stained with nicotine. She waved in the direction of a wall of assorted Levés.

"Next week the ear!" She said it very deadpan.

I was supposed to get it without any hints and I did. One canvas was loaded with ribbons and squiggles of color, peas and carrots and mashed potatoes. Van Gogh without pain.

"They say he ended up at Dr. Guichet's eating cadmium white out of the tube."

Anything to make an impression. It seemed to be working.

"White," I said, "the milk of the schizophrenic."

The girl with the red hair did not shoot me down.

We walked around Levé's one-man show, finding a Gauguin here, a Picasso there.

"Next week Tahiti!" I said.

"Next week the Blue Period!" she said.

I was falling fast.

Her name was Mirra. She was a painter herself and had modeled her way through the Art Students League, posing for Brackman, Dehn, Kuniyoshi. Raphael Soyer had given her a lithograph, a self-portrait in a little hat, with a stub of cigarette hanging from the corner of his mouth, on which he had written: "Mirra, Mirra, on the wall whose (sic!) the fairest one of all?"

At once, I imagined and adored those startling curves pushing off that petite frame, famous at the League and the studios of the Fourteenth Street realists. Not that I had seen anything yet!

Forty years have passed but I can tell you with absolute certainty that she was wearing, that night, a demure dress of transparent voile that heightened her almost albino skin as the black gloves on Lautrec's poster do the powdered arms of Yvette Guilbert.

A model! Yet there was nothing about Mirra that suggested bohemianism. She was what my mother called "refined, a society girl." Mirra even owned an alligator bag and shoes of the same hide. These were bought, somehow, out of her WPA stipend. She shopped at Bergdorf's, but only when the clothes for the elegant kept women were reduced for clearance. Looking for bargains of that kind was for her almost a hobby. I knew this, of course, only after we were married.

But I run ahead of myself. I had to court Mirra first, and win her. It did not happen overnight.

There were times when Mirra would be inaccessible to me.

Some melodrama was being played offstage. With Lilly, another model at the League, we planned a weekend at Woodstock. I ended up going alone. Drunk with rancor and gin, I tooled Lilly and her Latin lover from tavern to tavern in an old Caddy borrowed from the lot. Some place in Saugerties, I backed into a tree. The Caddy almost knocked it over. I had my head out of the window and got a boxer's cut over my eyebrow. It bled obligingly. A country doctor took stitches.

"You poor mutt," Lilly said, "I'm gonna tell Mirraleh Shmirraleh."

Lilly told Mirra. Mirra told Lilly. Lilly told me. The "other thing" was over and done. I could come calling again.

I had caught Mirra on the rebound and I could only guess at the circumstances. I could not tell whether she was warding off or being repudiated by someone she called only That Bastard. She was suffering and could not hide it.

"I'm sorry," I said once. I didn't know anything else to say.

"You and who else?" Mirra said.

I wouldn't have given a nickel for my chances then.

"It's crazy," Mirra said, "the whole business! I guess I'm the type who's attracted to older men!"

We never spoke of it again. I did not want to know. Losing Mirra would have been, if not the end of my world, the end of my naiveté. And the problem she raised seemed extraneous, like the last cigarette offered at an execution.

I was seeing Mirra night and day now. We were luckier than most Depression lovers in that we had a place to go. Mirra was on the Art Project and had turned a second-floor loft into an immense studio. Before that it had been a sweatshop. Mirra had calcimined the space Arctic white and set herself up, like an Eskimo, in one corner. There was also a monstrous easel of which she was very proud.

"Little girl, big cunt!" Mirra used to say in the rough way she affected.

Mirra's paints and her brushes, arranged by size, were kept in a collection of Victorian chamberpots. A permanent still life of dried flowers and wax fruit was set out on a marble-topped commode of the same period. Mirra spent a lot of time in the Salvation Army warehouse. While she committed genocide on somebody's proud ancestors to get at turn-of-the-century picture frames, I looked for collector's items on extinct record labels. If you kept looking you might find Ma Rainey or Ida Cox on Black Swan.

We were both devoted to jazz. Mirra had an old oaken Victrola that she had stripped of its top, sawed off the Queen Anne legs, and painted stark white. Electric players were already available but this was the Bugatti of gramophones. On the floor next to it was a stack of shellac 78s. To play them, we kept a supply of bamboo needles that mellowed the rasp in their eroded grooves. Some of them, like Louis Armstrong's "West End Blues," were already so worn you could make out only the thump of the tuba under that heartbreaking horn cry no groove could hold.

Every day, as soon as I had added the name of another dentist or new delicatessen to the Anti-Nazi League's list of boycotters, I ran to Mirra's studio. The Wehrmacht had half of Europe under its heel. My work was becoming absurd. Hitler was making enough enemies without my help and I was not feeling particularly political. I had always been more of an esthete than a functionary. And going with Mirra, my hours were charged by Apollo and Eros. I began to realize that I was more at home in the soft easy chair of Matisse than in the steely councils of the vanguard of the proletariat. I even found a small block of marble and chiseled a Brancusi head that Mirra admired. One day I hit it too hard and it split open like those medical models that show the mental plumbing of that noble work called, always, Man.

I would arrive with a new find in my hand—let's say, Bix's "In a Mist" with him on piano, playing Chopin backward—and while Mirra worked I would crank the machine, never letting the riffs wind down. She was an artist of great sensibility who would spend a week glazing a blush on the cheek of a mesmerized girl with invisible touches of her palette knife. When Mirra painted she became an artisan. Sometimes she wore overalls and a bandana around her head in the style of that Rosie the Riveter who would work in the defense plants during the war that was soon to come. When you kissed her, Mirra smelled of turpentine and My Sin. Her easel would be turned to the north light and, sooner or later, I would come up behind her and take her round loaves in my hands. She would go on painting, pretend not to notice, until her nipples rose into my fingers.

"I'm gonna tell yo' Momma!"

And we would be rolling on the mattress on the floor and dealing with the problem of getting her overalls off.

As a lover, Mirra was free and inventive, hampered—or should I say spurred on?—by a sporadic inability to come to climax. She would reach it, now and then, very quickly, rising at once to a high place from which she plunged, holding her breath like those divers at Acapulco who drop like birds from cliff to sea. Her ecstacy was quiet. During these quick orgasms she would hum through bitten lips until, like the noise of an invisible airplane, it would fade away and she would open her eyes as I closed mine to take her quick, butterfly kisses on my lids.

Still, she talked tough. "Make love, make sex," she said. "It's all banana oil!"

She had hardened herself, I thought, in self-protection. Against *him!* I was sure there was a soft tenderness in her of which we were not allowed to speak. I idolized her and believed that was the way she wanted things to stand. That she would mistake my idolatry for foolish devotion was unthinkable. That I would cause her pain was unimaginable.

As unimaginable as the transformation of Mirra's small fear of confined places into a raging claustrophobia. That would come later. But coming events, as they say, cast their shadows before.

There were plenty of shadows that night. The studio was lit by a harvest moon that followed Mirra like a blue spot on a stripper in a smoky club. She was transfigured and I was watching her from a little distance with a hundred eyes. She had asked me to come into her as soon as she opened. She wanted the Boytchik and he, pleased and proud, let neither of us down.

Mirra usually chose to be on top. Tonight her pale torso was being lifted by my hands, pulled into me from below as I pushed into it from above. Supine, Mirra still tried to ride me. Her legs were locked around me, her calloused heels spurred my flanks, she was giving herself over to the race, going to the front like a fast filly.

I caught some signal, too, and went beyond my usual entranced strokes. I was concentrating on the act, saving a part of myself to admire, even to wonder in quick flashes if this aloofness, this small sadism, was the secret of mastery one reads about in tawdry novels in which a woman becomes enslaved by a mere glance from the man who shows the brute in his eyes.

When I think of Mirra's studio, I always think of that streamlined Victrola and somebody like Ida Cox singing, "The sun's gonna shine in your backyard someday!" It's strange that I do not remember the radio through which I half-heard that the Martians had arrived.

But there was one. Dance music was interrupted and there were some disjointed reports of some unusual event that seemed at the same time fearsome and false. The horror in the voice of the announcer was real enough but there was something counterfeit in his being there to tell about it. Meteorites or some flaming object had fallen out of the night someplace near Princeton. Now there was mention of Newark itself. Poisonous smoke was pouring in from the Jersey marshes, reaching as deep as South Street. Whatever it was, it was happening practically around the corner from where we were.

Mirra did not hear.

She was clinging to me, setting the rhythm, telling me with her nails, harder, harder. And I raised my hammer high. We were both grunting the way chain-gang prisoners do as they lift their sledges to break rock. "Huh!" As I swung. "Huh!" As she received the steel. I was aware that I wanted to hurt her as much as I was aware that I could not. I was driving into rock that melted as the iron struck sparks.

I pulled Mirra's legs apart. I wanted to disappear into her. She bent herself to me, lifted like a *saltimbanque* by her own paroxysm, and I went in deep, deeper than I had ever been into that silk pocket. There was a slap, a kind of pelvic applause, each time we joined. Now the sounds of our coupling were quicker, like bare feet running across a floor. Mirra's shoulder blades lay against my biceps. Her head had fallen back and her throat was stretched taut, her mouth was open, showing her teeth like those heaped, violated women in a *Slaughter of the Innocents* by Poussin.

She cried out. Perhaps she had heard of the end of our foolish world. I put my hand over her mouth. Her hosanna of release pierced my palm. My own meteorite exploded, fell in fragments over all the lands of the earth.

I fell on her. She took my weight easily. She held me, arms locked around me, eyes open, looking both safe and frightened. We lay entwined that way until, with a thrill, I slipped from her.

While we rested—we were, I know, both surprised with each other—someone came to the door, knocked, rattled, and went away. Mirra was sure it was her father. We dressed quickly in the dark. I, who had been so forceful moments before, listened to Mirra like an obedient child. I followed the sound of her heels downstairs.

Out in the street, there was no whiff of poisonous gas, only the usual stale, terrestrial smell of roominghouse lives. If the Martians wanted this part of town they could have it cheap. The Department of Public Works had let a streetlamp go out but it was lighter than usual, with a harvest moon bouncing off the oily scum of Port Newark. A scared knot of natives stood in front of the corner saloon looking over their shoulders and up at the sky. The bartender, still in his apron, hesitated in the swinging doors, half in and half out. He was trying to make up his mind whether what might be his customers' last drinks on earth shouldn't be "on the house."

"Jesus, Joseph, and Mary," a woman said as we passed, "don't yez go by yezzelfs. They'll take yez for sure!"

"Who'z'll take us?" Mirra asked.

I told Mirra what I had heard on the radio.

"And you didn't stop?" she joked. "My hero!"

· 24 ·
A Wireless to Bix

Unlike those catastrophes filmed by Fox Movietone News— the explosion of the Graf Zeppelin at Lakehurst, for example— the one that hit Mirra and me was unphotographable. Its cause was too small. In fact, if you put your finger on it, you would already be covering many millions of guiltless others.

Mirra missed a period. Her breasts felt fuller. Her rabbit test was positive. Was there a pinprick in the diaphragm that Mirra, like many liberated girls of the day, carried in her alligator purse? A fertilized ova was clinging to her uterus. We figured, counting back, it must have collided with an unidentified wriggling object about the same instant the Flying Saucer had smacked New Jersey on the night we had been invaded from Mars. The date, I have determined, was October 28, 1938.

What was the price of an abortion then? Whatever it was, I didn't have it. I borrowed from another, more benign uncle. Not the boxer-president. He would have forced a shotgun wedding.

Not that I was unwilling. I wanted nothing more than to be married to Mirra. If she would have me.

I didn't have two bucks for the marriage license either. However, I was—still am?—a *Luftmensch,* an air person, carried forward by a boundless, unthinking enthusiasm. I was like Sholom Aleichem's village teacher who says, "If I had Rothschild's money, I would be richer than Rothschild! Why? Because I would give Hebrew lessons on the side!"

I would write poems on the side. I wanted Mirra to take me, if not for what I was then, for what I might become. What, when, or where, I did not know. Just put me on the right trolley car. I'd find my stop when I arrived! My recent voyages of mercy into these Eleventh Ward Tenements, my errant life as Forrest Mac-Kaye, my pimpled days on the lot—I saw these as a kind of informal apprenticeship bringing me nearer to my real trade, closer to Everyman to whom I would some day address a poetry he could understand. I was too preoccupied with Mirra, right now, for verse. My little job with the Anti-Nazi League satisfied my wish to be, whatever else, identified with the fight against Fascism.

I was happy, and I wanted Mirra to be happy. One word from her and I would gladly give myself over to changing diapers. But Mirra got the name of an easygoing doctor from Lilly who knew about these things. Mirra told her mother she was spending the weekend in Woodstock. Mirra was aborted on Friday. She recuperated in Lilly's flat, which was located, ironically, just across the street from the Margaret Sanger Clinic.

Try telling yourself that a child is nothing more than a fertilized egg! Mirra was awfully blue. I took her in my arms and we both cried. Boytchik heard us and he began to cry. It was all his fault! Would he be shut out forever from the home he had desecrated? Mirra forgave him, comforted him, let him rest in her hand.

A hazy interim followed, a period of disquiet and hesitations on Mirra's part in which she let herself turn, again, to the man I was beginning to think of as a kind of Svengali. What power did he have over her? I was innocent of the motives of Mirra's masochism, could not imagine what triumph she sought in her predestined defeat at his hands. There was mystery here. But in those days Mirra's turmoil was easily interpreted—or misinterpreted—as romantic. Outwardly, she was unmarked by any sign of neurosis other than a distaste for close places.

Mirra's claustrophobia had been apparent when we first met. I saw it, at first, as an understandable distrust of precipitous elevator rides. She would take one but not if it went above the fifth or sixth floor. Now, she would not ride one at all. Sometimes she would leave a party, suddenly and without reason that one could see, except that it had become crowded beyond some count of her own. It would happen according to some inner alert, come on so fast she would be running for the door, unable even to signal me. I learned to watch and follow. I would find her shaking, in a trance. Sympathy was useless, logic insulting. Wild horses would not drag her back.

But since Mirra was otherwise cheerful, sturdy, and independent, this strange flaw made her fragile and more precious. She played down her phobia. And, I suppose, we thought that love would conquer all.

Then Mirra became "involved" again. Mirra rebounded again. I caught her again.

Nothing was said. The flurry of reinvolvement had been brief. I treated it as a storm that had passed. And before our illegitimate child would have pushed its way into the world, its unwed parents became man and wife.

Mirra and I stood under the canopy. She was veiled, looked exotic, Turkish. I was wearing a borrowed fedora, looked like my own relatives. I had the ring in my hand.

"Haray aht mekoodesheth lee bay tahbahs . . ." I had rehearsed this. "With this ring," I was saying, "hurry up, hurry up and sanctify. . . ."

After a couple of tries, I broke the glass wrapped in a white napkin under my heel. Mirra lifted her veil. I kissed the bride. It was a *simchah,* a joy to both families.

We found an apartment, near Clinton High, as it happened, but also near enough to the Hudson Tubes and New York. I thought we had the best of all possible worlds. Mirra painted at her own pace, fastidious, unambitious. My own work was taking on a new shape. Indeed, events in Europe were growing too ominous for the Anti-Nazi League's original purpose. More and more we were being absorbed into a manipulated "united front" which oscillated with the wind that blew like a vodka breath across the steppes from Moscow to Union Square. Our name on a letterhead looked impressive. This was a period in which a great deal of explaining had to be done. I did my share. Stalin's pact with Hitler had raised explanation into an ideology. Historically, it marked the end of political innocence.

My first differences with Mirra were political. She was more Trotskyite and balked at expediencies. We agreed that it was okay. We were separate people, were we not?

Hah! I did not want us to be *too* separate. I had tasted separation during her "involvement." Was I still playing second fiddle? I tried to look dispassionately at my situation. But there are secrets we keep even from ourselves. To me, Mirra represented more than herself. Without thinking about it, I was seeing my connection with Mirra and the Leopold family as bettering myself. Though I had wandered deeper into the native scene than most first-generation Americans, I had the feeling, in those days less than now, that I would always be traveling in that steerage where my father had relished, straight from the barrel, the herrings the seasick had refused. I was not ashamed. I told myself I would not have it any other way.

Mirra's parents had been born here—as though all men are not born *here* in that womanplace where the dam between blood and feces breaks. The Leopolds had been here long enough to live in a house, pillared like a Mississippi manse, which they had all to themselves. There was no "Yoo hoo!" from top floor front to first floor back. No Fanny on the steps scrubbing away, swooping you up, zoop, zoop, with that fuzzy vacuum cleaner under her petticoat. No Yossel climbing the clothes pole and announcing like Columbus, "I see the whole world!"

Mirra's father had not stood before a judge pleading for citizenship in a land for which he had not borne arms. Mine had asked to be let out of soldiering against the Kaiser because I was already swimming toward Jersey's shore in the waters of my mother's belly. Mirra's mother was a fluttery Billie Burke type who was shocked when her daughter said "Shit!" She knew not a word of Yiddish. Yet she lit candles on the Sabbath. Mine, fluent in Hebrew, was reading *The New Republic*. Mirra's father was an entrepreneur lawyer who had gone bankrupt. Mine was solvent. For his new in-law, he found on the used-car lot the last of the Packards, black, long, with wire wheels, so that when Mr. Leopold drove about collecting rents, he would have the illusion that the foreclosed properties were still his and not the bank's.

Then there was Willie, the menopause baby. She was twenty years younger than Mirra. Mrs. Leopold worried that the child would hear somebody say she was an accident. "Love child, if you please!" Her grandfather had been William—in my family it would have been Velvel—and so she was called Wilhelmina. She was a Shirley Temple sort of a kid and I got a kick out of the idea of having her for a sister-in-law.

My parents admired Mirra. They were, I think, a little afraid of her and the Leopolds. There was about them an air of faded grandeur. I admired all the Leopolds, felt a little sorry for them. Memories. Mrs. Leopold in a Spanish mantilla lighting Friday-night candles. Mirra telling her about a Renaissance headdress on a portrait of Beatrice Sforza. "The Schwartzes were in Italy, too?" Mirra's kid sister still in high school, already engaged, diamond ring and all. Mr. Leopold's fierce migraines. The punch line of one of his jokes, some confusion between Carnegie Hall and pinochle: "Horowitz is playing tonight!"

I used to know the rest of it. I remember telling it to Julie, my fiddler friend from Muskrat Street days, with whom I used to have an occasional musical night out. He was playing in a suburban dance band from which he tore away for wild jamming with black musicians who had gigs in Newark.

Julie sometimes brought us reefers. They were already rolled in preshaped tubes like real cigarettes. One Sunday Lilly came over and she ended up in the shower with Julie. Lilly had something, a good-natured wildness, which men pursued. She hinted at orgies.

"You're only young once!" she said.

"You're giving it away!" Mirra said with too much seriousness.

There was more than one Mirra. There were Dybbuks who spoke for her and sometimes spoke out of turn. She could be the fine lady, genteel, like her mother who would say, when she wanted something done, "Forgive me my little foils."

And then she could be curiously hardboiled. Like her father? "Take the air!" she would say when she was annoyed. Or, "You bet your ass!"

I wondered sometimes whether we were really so comfortable and safe in the cocoon Mirra was spinning for us, building a mixture of Salvation Army and Bauhaus. The sawed-off Victrola of the studio was replaced by a turntable hidden in a cabinet with seven layers of Japanese lacquer all hand-rubbed to milky whiteness by Mirra. She was Madame Butterfly's sister. Some of the pieces she designed were massive, using whole panels of plywood, with legs of plumber's pipe, flanged and dipped in chrome.

This was an idea we borrowed from Wim Shilling. Wim had been a highly paid designer before he chose to starve as a painter. His hair was not white then, and he was not famous and his studio was in the wholesale flower district in New York. We called him Wimpy. When we were married he gave us a gouache of Mirra's choosing. Not long ago, in the Appendix of an immense book on Wim Shilling's work, I saw a photograph of that gouache. "Project for a Mural," it was labeled. "Whereabouts unknown." My heart sank. My life with Mirra was twice gone.

We used to see Wimpy almost every Saturday night. We would leave Newark in the morning. Mirra was still able to tolerate the Hudson Tubes by closing her eyes as soon as we went into the tunnel under the river and holding tight to my hand until we came out under Gimbel's. We would do the stores and galleries, Mirra always using the stairs. Then we would buy a jug and fall by Jonah's place in back of a violin maker's in a brownstone on Fifty-second Street. "Stuff" Smith or Frankie Newton would be playing at the Onyx Club.

Jonah was our medicine man—for jazz, for esthetics, for politics. He was a great evaluator.

"The symbol transcends its model," he would say.

"Yonah," Wimpy would answer, "shtick your finger in the mustard pot!" Being Dutch, he could not pronounce *j*. None of us knew what kind of mustard Wimpy was talking about.

Jonah had nervous tics and phobias. He agonized over his neuroses, so discordant with the ideal of proletarian health. He freely acknowledged that under socialism he would be shot. He was an incurable Don Juan. He was still carrying a torch for Lilly, who seemed to be the only girl he could not have.

We saw him with a different tootsie each week. They were all models or dancers who never opened their mouths. They sat in Jonah's bed-sitter like expensive bouquets stuck in the neck of a pickle jar. In contrast to them, Mirra pounded away at Jonah's dogmas.

"On the one hand . . ." Jonah would be saying.

"What we want to know is which hand!" Mirra would jump him.

So we would drink and kick the Marxist gong around and

make small bets on who was on clarinet when you put the needle on a record and let it spin for one groove.

"Benny? The Austin High Gang?"

"Jimmy Noone?"

"Pee Wee!"

"Johnny Dodds?"

We give up. It's Frank Teschmaker leaning his ear against a telegraph pole sending a wireless to Bix. Only Jonah knows the answer. It is his record, isn't it?

Jonah's girl would go off to a rehearsal—Jonah never took these girls out—and we would go out to eat at an Armenian restaurant. Around ten, we would drop in on Wimpy, still painting, wearing a bookkeeper's green celluloid visor to keep the fluorescent light out of his eyes. Sometimes I'd lend him a ten-spot to keep the electric on. He had not been discovered yet. He was already using the big housepainter's brushes which later became the tool of the New York School. His pictures were all gorgeous pink and orange and baby *kaka* and slashes of black Duco enamel, sandpapered and scraped with a razor blade so flecks of accidental color would break through. They would never be finished. Wimpy believed that a painting should never end.

He admired Mirra's skill and taste but felt she was too constrained, was holding back in her work. He urged her to let herself fall into the painting "like a man shlipping on a banana peel."

"Stop focking around," he told her. "Shtick your finger in the mustard pot. Go out und buy a gallon of house paint, gottammit. Catch dot glimpse, dot focking frozen glimpse."

It was good advice. Mirra spent whole days putting a rosy ripening on the cheek of a green apple. Her delicate glazes were put on with a series of flexible palette knives that were as clean as Dr. Kildare's forceps. There was some tension here that Mirra was trying to shut out behind a curtain of perfection. She was afraid to "shlip" or even make a misstep.

Mirra's episodes of claustrophobic panic were becoming more frequent. She made an appointment to see Karen Horney. When she got to the Central Park South address, she discovered that the doctor's office was on the twentieth floor. Mirra considered walking up the Alps of those stairs, but that would have used up her fifty minutes. She called on the house phone. The bigger they are, the nicer they come! The author of *The Neurotic Personality of Our Time* came down and talked to Mirra in the lobby. Dr. Horney found a colleague with an office on the first floor. Mirra began analysis.

To help pay for her sessions, I was working weekends on the old car lot. It was here that I heard about the attack on Pearl Harbor. FDR cut in on Toscanini and told us that the day would "live in infamy."

By now, Uncle Sam was breathing down my neck. I had two arms, two legs, and, to the naked eye, only one head. I could read and write. And, as far as I knew, I was not homosexual. Except for the unreliable rhythm of my heart—more poetic doctors called it a murmur—I was eminently draftable.

Mirra did not want me to go to war. "Not the least bit, buddy." She had never asked anything of me so vehemently. I had become part of her and she would envision the army as an endless claustrophobia. Whatever her reasons, she was a pacifist. "The bastards set Hitler up in the first place."

I had been brought up on stories of Jewish boys of military age chopping off a finger or rubbing lye into their eyes to get out of soldiering for the Tsar. I was ready to try a less drastic alternative.

Nick and Connie were living in San Francisco where he had a draft-exempt job in a federal program that brought farm laborers from Mexico. They were not *braceros* then, wetbacks who waded the Rio Grande at night or were carried over like sacks of potatoes in the back of a truck. Nick thought he could get me taken on.

But we had not counted on the miles between coasts. I would have gotten the black-market gas for our snub-nosed Plymouth. But for Mirra, the idea of crossing America became an agoraphobic nightmare, three thousand claustrophobias turned inside out. We stayed put.

My greetings came. Stripped to my shorts, I stood in line with my fellows. Boytchik got so scared, I had trouble finding him when it was his turn to be squeezed. I was sent to the funnydoctor. We talked about Mirra's claustrophobia and he stamped me 4-F. When I got back from the Armory, everybody was so happy we all had a good cry.

How could one guy miss so many wars?

· 25 ·
Arabesque

Mirra was driving into Manhattan twice a week now, always by way of the George Washington Bridge. Over the Hudson there was sky, blue or gray, and you always had the option of doing a Steve Brodie. What a mystery this fear of confinement! The Holland Tunnel—womb? labyrinth? grave?—was out of the question. Only my dynastic connection with the automotive industry got Mirra enough octane to make her roundabout way through the circle of her private hell.

I wanted to get to the Big Apple, too. Exempt from the draft, stay-at-homes got their chance. Through a contact that went back to Albuquerque and *The Voice of the People,* I got a job with a chain of trade-union weeklies and we moved to New York.

Mirra found us an apartment near the East River and Bellevue's gray wards. There was a row of stables down the block and when the wind was right you could hear Old Dobbin neigh. Or were we hearing echoes from bedlam? I thought, now and then, of those ranting creatures with their arms laced into straitjackets to keep them from tearing out their own eyes. "If thine eye offend thee . . ." I never thought that I would want to punish mine.

I was a tuppenny hack, hired to keep my eyes open and my mouth shut. All of us at the Union Press were either too old or too peculiar to fight for Uncle Sam. But it did not keep us from beating the drums for more tanks, more ships, more bombs, and more bagels for the boys over there.

Bagels? Let me explain. We put out half a dozen papers for the AFL crafts—butcher, baker, candlestick maker. They were really the same six-page tabloid, but page one was tailored to each of the various trades. The masthead of *The Baker* showed two hands clasped around what certainly looked like a bagel. "What's round like a doughnut, has a hole in the middle, and hair all around?"

My editor was Charlie. He was a big-hearted guy with a

stomach that hung over his belt, an overgrown baby type, with marks of an adolescent acne on his face and a dreamy look in his eyes. He chewed pencils and was given to outrageous puns. He had been a classics scholar and, like me, he had been classified 4-F in the Draft. When we put an issue to bed, we would improvise a tap dance, shake our hands like end men in a minstrel show, and harmonize "I Got Arrhythmia!"

Charlie was a political masochist caught in the high purpose of infiltrating what were called the crafts—those cushy, protected jobs which were passed down from father to son through an elaborate system of nepotism and apprenticeship. The object was to get these yahoos off their asses and marching, if not in step, at least in the same parade as the more "progressive" industrial unions of the CIO.

Instead of deciphering papyri at Harvard, which was where he belonged, Charlie was assigning me to do a few inches every time one of these plug-uglies forgot to say the wrong thing. There really was not much news of an immediate nature on the bakery front or the war. We were waiting for the opening of the Second Front. In the meanwhile, like Rapunzel, we had to weave gold out of straw.

I had been hired as a reporter and to keep track of the assorted clippings and reusable mug shots of local unionists which we called our morgue. But you can't keep a good man down. I began to do rewrite and layout. I was good at that, came up with catchy, precisely counted, staggered headlines like those of the *Daily News,* the paper most of our readers read and admired. For *The Baker,* I could give Charlie leads like PREZ PREDICTS PERFECT PRETZELS.

I was beginning to get a reputation for a funny feature I wrote under the name of Eastbrook Wigler. In a little indent at the top of the column we used an actual picture of Westbrook Pegler. The guy could have sued us, but we took our chances. Pegler was Labor Enemy Number One. He worked for Hearst. We would beat the devil at his own game.

I began to hot up our pages. Every week we got handouts of boilerplate pinups. Some tootsie in one of those sexy one-piece bathing suits of the time was always being elected Miss Nuts and Bolts or Miss Tool of the Week. The bathing beauties were embossed on matrices of pink cardboard, which would be flooded with hot lead and curled into a plate for the press. It took about six inches of a single column to take care of the long gams of these fake riveters. They all looked happy to be making a little extra money standing up.

I kept a harem of them in my drawer. I chose them more carefully than a sultan. He could pinch and tickle. I could only turn the 120 stamped dots per inch this way and that in the light, seeing one instant a promise of flesh and the next, a disappointing mirage. Perhaps I looked at them too long.

Each week I chose a new favorite. I built the page around her. At the printer's, she would be laid on a leaden bed, locked in a chase between columns of Aesopian drivel. Reading proof directly from type, I always saw her upside down, laid out in the St. James Infirmary "so sweet, so cold, so bare." Then she would be rolled out, feet first, still mine alone, to the rotary press which turned her public. Like unfulfilled desires, her replicas tumbled into piles. She would always land on her feet, smiling her come-on smile. There she would be, snuggled into a banner head like BAKERS BATTER BEACHES—a member of the local had landed on a Pacific beach—hinting that she, as well as Mom and apple pie, was what our boys were fighting for.

Charlie would marvel at these patriotic teases. We had reports that the fellows in the shops were actually looking at our newspapers now! Like me, he would be seeing the particularities of a girl for the first time, black on white. Like me, he would be surprised at the sensuality she sent out.

"They make you," Charlie said, "want to believe in God. As the fellow said."

Charlie always said "As the fellow said."

There were rumors he was having wife trouble. He had married an early, unpitiable refugee, a *Mittel Europa* version of the Jewish American Princess. She was pretty in the way of the Meissen porcelain figures she had rescued from Vienna. They were kept in a glass ark like the Torah and were not to be touched without prayer. Magda was snooty, narcissistic, and hard as nails. She had Charlie, as the fellow said, eating out of her hand.

Mirra hated Magda and her shepherdesses at first sight. She liked Charlie. Except for him she had little contact with labor's Fourth Estate.

"Squaresville!" Mirra said.

She preferred Martha Graham in a rented hall to Earl

Browder in Madison Square Garden. On the QT, so did I. We went faithfully to all of her dance recitals. Martha Graham had been one of the artists who had found inspiration in the enchanted landscape of New Mexico. I had thought of them as escapists. But Graham had brought back a "letter to the world." Watching her do *El Penitente,* I was flooded by memories and misgivings. I knew these flagellants. I had been in their mountain villages, had harangued them. They had listened politely enough. Revolution was one way to get to heaven. But at Easter, one of them would be elected to carry the Cross and be nailed to it like Him. They possessed an elemental way of being I had envied and sought in that little *mondo* of sacrifice and belief. Had I been less dislocated as Forrest MacKaye than I was as Eastbrook Wigler?

What was Jim Howard up to? He was probably holed up in some one-horse town mimeographing leaflets which announced a new utopia of whiskey for Johnny and Kotex for Sis. That gringo was *loco!* I had more actual contact now with what Jim used to call the Center. We journalists were called in, from time to time, and briefed on the changing strategies for politicalizing these AFL "aristocrats of labor." It never occurred to anybody that they should, like the Tsar, have been taken out and shot. Didn't we see that they would reproduce themselves and that their sins would multiply? They would in time become the hard-hats swinging lead pipes against our own flesh and blood. "Hey, hey, LBJ! How many kids didja kill today?"

My own son would issue from the womb of another wife and would take his place in another Movement demanding another kind of devotion. "America! Love it or leave it!" I could always go back to Newark. My son's generation would have no other place to go.

Mirra and I had had our chance at progeny. It was the last. Mirra herself was being born—or reborn—twice a week in those fifty-minute *accouchements* uptown. Always, now, the faint perfume of spermicidal jelly surrounded the unmasked Boytchik like the smell of cordite over no-man's-land. It did not matter whether he came in war or peace. Our couplings were becoming less frequent and less abandoned. Too often, Mirra was giving herself to me without wanting to take more for herself than my gratitude. Mirra ritualized with whimsy the one-sidedness of these encounters.

"Thank you, kind sir, the maiden said, as she buttoned up her drawers and fled!"

Just as often, Mirra would reach a plateau from which she could not rise or fall. Then she would become desperate, furious with herself like an athlete who fails to do in an important contest what he has done many times and better in casual practice. I soon learned that if I entered her early, I would be finished and turning back to myself, unable to pursue or even keep up in a marathon whose finish line appeared and disappeared before the tape could be breasted. There was no reproach to me for this quickness. Mirra knew that at certain times no effort or means could bring her to the nullity of biology. "Roosters and men are sad after sex!"

Mirra was not left "high and dry," as that condition is described. Rather, she rested at a plane of arousal that was its own terminus. And were it not for the dictates of certain influential followers of Freud in the circles in which she moved, Mirra might have accepted that this voyage did not always end at the same destination.

I did not know, then, of the length to which Freud had gone to escape from the noose of theory that saw arousal as unpleasurable, something to be avoided. Discharge was an escape from pain. That left the Death Wish for his disciples to bend to American optimism. And then there was "penis envy" and the castigation of the "frigid" woman as infantile, fixated, and, no matter how loving, not quite a woman. It was all too heady.

Mirra could not resign herself to these "failures." I certainly never reproached her. If anything, I felt we were more tightly bound together by the difficulties attached to our pleasures. Neither of us connected Mirra's growing claustrophobia with that unease. Looking back with more age and experience, I realize that there was within her tenderness but not trust. Even in abandon there was control which made Mirra both steed and rider, pulling at the bit, reining in, whipping, rearing, but never breaking into a free gallop.

Later, in my therapy with couples of all sorts, I saw that orgasm is not given from outside but rather, as the word implies, is organic, comes from lying down in that small hollow of innocence within us, male and female, that is the cradle which was once our whole world. But that cradle is a small place, barred, a place to wait, trusting for the best. Is that what Mirra feared?

Cradle to grave. That winter, Mirra's mother died of a mercifully quick cancer. The gravesite was frozen, glazed with ice. As the coffin was being lowered Mirra seemed to slip, fell toward the pit, slid to its edge. Everybody assumed she had fainted. She had been in a trance of fright. And I, holding her arm, had felt the pull of her involuntary leap.

Am I exaggerating the depth of Mirra's neurosis? They say that when a man leaves a woman he begins to paint her black. Perhaps he wants to impugn the only real witness to his failures. After all, who would know them better? I was shocked, years later, to learn that Mirra was speaking of me as "that bastard." Me! That was what she had been calling the Other Man when I first courted her!

Hell. I was no more bastard than she was bitch. We rarely quarreled. If there was anger between us it would be over some too strongly held political point of view. More often it would center on some opinion of a movie or the failure of an overambitious, muscle-bound choreography or when I teased her by blunting myself to her intense estheticism. Mirra would look at a painting and speak of its "all over arabesques." She had studied with a maestro who blocked out sections of Old Masters with colored chalks to end up with a very contemporary abstract painting. I had attended some of these demonstrations with Mirra. "Arabesques" were her religion.

Once I chose the wrong moment to scoff. "But I don't see any Arabs!" We were looking at a Piero della Francesco.

I thought Mirra would kick me in the balls, right there in the Frick mansion. I had to "make nice" as we used to say, to distract her with the story of how the anarchist Alexander Berkman had fired a revolver at old man Frick. He had another claim to fame.

"He was Emma Goldman's lover," I reminded her.

We had been to an Anarchist colony once and Mirra had liked it. An antique poet in a Santa Claus beard had read free verse about free love. It was Hippolyte Havel. He had been one of Emma Goldman's lovers, too.

"I did see the Arabs," I added and Mirra was placated.

I knew she wanted me to be quick and I enjoyed her sneaking admiration.

"Smart aleck!" Mirra said. "You're worse than *Ripley's Believe It or Not.*"

Mirra's eye for painting remained infallible, though she herself had stopped working. Her easel was in our bedroom. Tubes of Winsor & Newton, rows of Conte pencils were nicely lined up. Her brushes were stacked in the same Victorian chamberpot she had used in the whitewashed studio which had been invaded by Martians. Everything was too precariously neat. Only the faint smell of turpentine revealed occasional work.

Still, Mirra's taste was greatly respected by painters who were already on the threshold of fame. We saw Wim Shilling often. With Jonah we would get mellow with jazz, go down to the Jumble Shop on MacDougal Alley, and listen to Apollo Avakian's favorite story about the painter who was given a parrot that said, "Somebody's gonna get screwed tonight!" Avakian was Wim Shilling's only competition. Neither would go to see the other's work on the theory that a painter should paint as though he had never seen another painting before.

One night Apollo Avakian borrowed a fountain pen and drew Mirra's head on one of the big paper napkins. Mirra framed it. It's in the Whitney Museum now.

On Friday nights we attended Hans Hoffmann's lectures in his studio-school on Eighth Street. Once, during the question period, Apollo asked Hoffmann a half-hour question about "ancestors" which ended up with his saying he was the son of Moses! He was a great dissembler, a liar. He already claimed to be a cousin of Josef Stalin. And his name was not Apollo. Hoffmann listened patiently. Anybody who had seen Avakian's painting of himself as a small boy holding the hand of his immigrant mother knew he had genius. It is a large painting, stiffly posed, self-conscious as a passport picture but loaded with agonized intimacy. It is a page from the diary of a man who would, just eight years later, write on the wall, "Good-bye My Loveds" and hang himself.

That summer our whole crowd went to Provincetown. Wim Shilling was living with two women then. He brought them both. One of them made good money tying trout flies out of her cunt hairs for an eccentric millionaire. She was blonde but her bush looked like steel wool. I had a good look when we went skinny-dipping off the dunes of Truro. Wim was very modest. He had baggy trunks that came down to his knees. In these he would go to the surf, then throw them over his shoulder onto the beach, and jump into a wave. Mirra's skin could not take the sun. She came to the beach in a big straw hat and a long white robe. She looked better naked than any dame in Provincetown.

Nights we grilled ribs and wieners on great driftwood bonfires. There was wine and constant argument about leaving the figure to the Old Masters. Jonah worried about getting something across to the workers. He offered as a compromise between subject and abstraction John Heartfield's photomontage of a bleeding dove impaled on a bayonet.

"I am not a camera!" Mirra said. She wanted her arabesques.

It was a good vacation for Mirra. She began some flower studies, wondered if she should take a class with Hoffmann. But our two weeks were almost up.

Most of the people we saw had something to do with making art. In one of the Commercial Street bars, Mirra ran into a fellow who had something to do with selling it. Indeed, he looked and talked like a small merchant. He was almost as old as Mirra's father and I thought I saw in him a resemblance to Mr. Leopold. Both had a repertoire of jokes.

By an uncanny coincidence, he too was the father of a child delivered by a wife to whom menopause had supposedly come. She was there to tell us about the miracle.

"Pennies from heaven," she said.

You could see she was trying to hide how much it meant to her. She was a skinny thing, a chain-smoker. Her hair was steel gray, defiantly untouched.

Her first and only child. She was very happy about it. She lost no time telling us that papa was not. She had the sharp tongue of a neglected woman. She excused herself after one drink. She wanted to get back to the baby. She would never be lonely again.

"Before you go," the husband said, "listen to this. What famous American sculptor's name sounds like a fart in the bathtub?"

"Gutzon Borglum!"

Disasters, unless we think of a head-on crash between two Buicks on a highway, make no noise. No sirens, no state troopers, no ambulances. No more, in fact, than the chuckle after a raw joke. Gutzon Borglum! Carver of presidents on Mount Rushmore. I can never see pictures of those giant granite faces without a shiver of concealed despair.

Mirra asked if she could stay another week. She would take

Hoffmann's Provincetown class. I left her our checkbook and our car, kissed her goodbye, and took the bus back to the city. I didn't know why but I had a funny feeling in my gut. I couldn't put my finger on it. It was there and it was not there. Like the hole in a bagel.

And I knew nothing. I only knew how terrible it is to desire and not possess. Or think you possess and that her desire is yours and you would love each other more than you did yourselves. I thought I was "safe where none can do Treason to us except one of we two." But that is the pain of autobiography. You know how the story ends before it begins.

· 26 ·
"Cry, Cuckoo!"

I missed Mirra. Without her puttering around in her Madame Butterfly kimono our two-room apartment seemed to be an exhibit in a museum of contemporary living, deserted even by the occasional cockroach that makes a house a home. I did not feel like disturbing the nuptial bed with the perfectly placed African pillows on its batik spread. A portent? I stayed up late listening to Symphony Syd and slept on the living-room couch.

In a hypnagogic moment before dropping off, I saw all the girls I had ever had or wanted standing before me like suspects in a precinct lineup. They pretended not to know me. Anyhow, they were not allowed to speak. But Lucy, my Red bride, called out angrily, "When are you going to make me a fucking Communist?" They took her away, kicking and crying and cursing.

Coming home after work, down East Twenty-fourth Street, I never missed a good look at Bellevue. Mirra had only been away a couple of days and I was asking myself dumb questions like how do you know when you're crazy? I took to staying out with Charlie. By now, Magda had left him. At least she was not sharing his bed and board. There seemed to be an understanding that she would be coming back when she got her affair out of her system. Though she knew we were all in one room, the Hungarian Honeybunch was calling Charlie at the office. And he, poor schmuck, would cup the receiver with one hand and whisper desperately to her. When Charlie hung up he had a wad of splinters and a stub of copy pencil in his mouth.

I began to knock around with him. In and out of the office, we stayed half drunk half of the time. We would work late just to get into the publisher's liquor cabinet. In theory, the booze was there to oil up the union officers. Our publisher was a cheap bastard. Imagine Hymie Bronf, president of the Bakery Workers, drinking Four Roses! But Charlie and I did. We'd replace what we drank with ice water from the cooler. Did the publisher ever wonder why so many bottles were open and still full? He probably chose to let it ride. Here we were putting out labor papers and getting paid less than the Newspaper Guild scale. The difference was supposed to be a contribution to the cause. And we were doing a bang-up job catching up with the *Daily News*. We were only three million readers short.

Mirra came home and she was my wife but not the one I had known. As in those days in our courtship when she was inaccessible, I could feel her holding back. She was an honest person and some revelation was on the tip of her tongue. Some things are not true until they are said.

I think she wanted me to know. I had a troublesome awareness that there was love in her reluctance or inability to hide what she was doing. She did not want me to hate her for going behind my back.

I sensed it had something to do with Mirra's analysis, with finding her father and through him the mother in herself. I did not know, then, that these personae were supposed to be found in me as husband and in her as wife. Nor did I know that I was looking for them just as hard myself. Mirra and I were playing a game of Blindman's Buff and Mirra was It.

I cannot reconstruct from what clues I began to suspect that Mirra was involved with someone else. Nor was I, I still tell myself, quite sure how far it had gone. Charlie sent me on an assignment nearby and I came home early. Mirra turned up later, sadly tipsy. Her claustrophobia made her afraid to drink. She had already become a stranger.

"It's, it's . . ." That's as far as she got.

I was trying to be "civilized." But I brooded. I wondered who the man could be. And whether it had begun while Mirra was away. I thought of the jokester we had met, the Gutzon Borglum man. There was the eerie coincidence of his wife's unexpected motherhood, so much like Mirra's own mother's accident. Mirra had talked of the shock of picturing her parents having intercourse. I did not have the gall to confront her with this insult. It was aberrant, absurd for her to accept such attentions.

As far as the world knew, there was no rupture. We dragged each other around like marathon dancers at the end of the third week. *"Avec les visages si tristes, les derrières si gais."* It reached the point where we knew about each other only from what we overheard.

"Wazza matter, Mirraleh Shmirraleh? Aintcha got no smile for Diamond Lilly?" her modeling buddy asked.

"Like later," Mirra said and Lilly let it ride.

Lilly was absorbed in an affair with a Cuban landowner who had been married six times. Batista's gunmen were after him. The universe didn't revolve around our *tsores.*

We were in trouble in a way that was over my head. Mirra had gotten into something she wanted me to stop. But I was hurt and, like the toddler who bangs his head against the chair he thinks has bumped into him, I wanted to hurt her.

"You don't have a malicious bone in your body," Mirra had once said to me.

I was like everybody else now, guarded, paranoid, normal. We had reached the point where we no longer ate together. Rather, we did and we did not. Somehow Mirra would always be moving about, serving me at table like a too efficient waitress so that I didn't even have the excuse to ask, "Please pass the salt." Mirra herself seemed to be living on constant cups of coffee that she still made in what she called the New Orleans way, with a dash of chicory.

I was almost grateful that Mirra put out pillow and blanket on the sofa each night, a tacit agreement that it would be impossible to share the bed without explanations that would be painful and useless. The only way out was to forgive and forget. I did not know what I had to forgive and I found it impossible to forget. To tell the truth, I simply did not know what to do. I felt abysmally alone. I ran off to the world of others to whom you did as you would have done unto yourself.

Our print shop was at the edge of the Village. I grabbed an inky sample of *The Baker* and went to meet Charlie at a pushcart clam bar. With a Littleneck in one hand, Charlie looked at the full-page cut of FDR standing on the deck of that Atlantic Fleet destroyer, his cape blowing, the brim of his soft hat bent in the wind, the cigarette holder defiantly in his teeth. I had splurged on the engraving, a nice dropout with the words WE REMEMBER in 48-point Gothic bold. I thought Charlie was going to say, "It makes you want to believe in God!"

He didn't. We were tough newspapermen, one-day historians, Marxists, too. There were no heroes in history, only ineluctable forces, "combined and uneven development"—that sort of thing. Still, I had pulled out a couple of bathing girls from this issue. Out of respect. We had had a death in the family. We went to look for a wake.

We found a party in a Cornelia Street walkup that belonged to a girl who was a relative of Leon Trotsky. It was one of those Village apartments in which the bathtub is in the kitchen. Covered by a board, it became a bar with jugs of Dago red and slices of *salame cotto* from Bleecker Street. Charlie and I were getting plastered. The red wine was floating like an oil slick on a Homeric sea of the publisher's Four Roses. We were keening. FDR was dead.

Charlie was making the usual puns, giggling in his schoolboy way, but he was one of those people who can think two, three things at the same time. I'd seen him this way, talking on the phone to the publisher, chewing a pencil down to a stub which he would take, still talking, and change a word here or there on our yellow second sheets, holding up a correction for me to see, or showing me two fingers which meant I had to do two inches more. BAKERS BEREAVED.

You had to be a quick thinker to get Joe Blow off his political ass. I could see Charlie had something on his mind. Right now, FDR's body was coming up from Washington through Pennsylvania Station to Hyde Park.

"Allons!" Charlie whispered.

Charlie was so used to futile conspiracies, he made one out of this. I knew he meant we should go to see the funeral train.

We got down to some deep level of the station. It was very

quiet. Without the bustle of travelers, the long corridors looked like the inside of some pharaoh's pyramid. Some of New York's Finest were waving back a sad little crowd. The cops were all wearing white cotton gloves like Al Jolson when he sang "Mammy!" A curious minstrel show. The cops were all white. The mourners were all black. Charlie and I pulled out green passes that said PRESS. We didn't wear them in our hats. There were no three-alarm fires in the AFL. The cops pointed us in.

We traveled down another passage to the tracks. A few reporters were strung out down the cement platform like commuters waiting for the 7:15. Down the long tunnel you could see lights going red, yellow, green. The snake of coaches pulled in without breaking the quiet that crackled like that instant before one of *his* fireside chats when you were waiting for that burry squire's voice to hit the gothic panels of the Atwater-Kent. "My frrriends and fellow Amurrricans . . ."

It was a long train. All the Pullmans had names like Winnebago and Lake Pontchartrain. The last time I had been in one was coming back from Chapel Hill. FDR had just been elected. There was no light in any of the cars. Someplace in there were Eleanor, who hated war, and Jimmy, who lifted the Happy Warrior from his wheelchair to the microphone. His Pop would not need him anymore. He was in the last car, one without seats, its windows uncurtained, in an oaken box covered by the Stars and Stripes. A soldier, a sailor, a marine, and an airman stood stiffly at each corner of the bier. Had they been standing at attention all the way from Washington?

Charlie and I stood at attention, too, sobering, deeply moved to be a part of the final dignity of the President of this unusual time when we had come of age. The train rested there a few minutes. Then it was backed out. It was going some special way to Hyde Park. What I remember is the absolute silence. No calling out. No flashbulbs. Only the muffled sobs from that little band who had come to take him "over Jordan."

Charlie and I were cold sober, gunning the Plymouth across Thirty-third Street. It was a lively little car, could easily have made California, faster than the Joad family and no busted pistons or blowouts. I wanted to talk to Charlie about the Okies camping their jalopies along the Rio Grande. But I didn't. I dropped Charlie off. I would tell Mirra about the Okies. Somehow we had never talked much about those days. I thought now of Jim Howard, and Bonnie and Percy and Haysoos, of Nick in solitary on the day of the Hunger March. I even had a flash of Kiddy in her unbuttoned blue work shirt agitating Amateur Nite at the Empire Burlesque. There were all kinds of heroes in this world! At this instant, the Gestapo was tearing the fingernails from the hands of some trapped patriot. If I could hold on to the feelings I was having, I would change places with him.

I found a spot for the Plymouth in front of the livery stables. I could hear the nags snorting, kicking their stalls. "They shoot horses, don't they?" I felt like shit on a stick. I would wake Mirra. No, she would be awake, waiting, wondering, wanting. We would talk about FDR and find each other again.

I was almost running now. Our flat faced the street. There was a light in the window. Mirra was up. I took the stairs with the Yale key in my hand. I turned it. I tiptoed in. Why? I was paying the rent, wasn't I?

On the wall of the tiny foyer hung an Early American mirror in a turned frame. Its silver backing had peeled in patches. I looked at myself and saw a leper's face. Where my nose used to be there was a ragged hole. Mirra was crazy about these Colonial things. In Morristown, she had found a high-backed wing chair that hid you from the rest of the room when you sat in it. "George Washington whacked off here," I used to say. In the same barn Mirra had found a narrow spindle stand. It stood under the mirror holding a cobalt-blue vase, a reproduction she had swiped from the WPA American Arts Project. I never looked at it without thinking of my father fresh off the boat, shoveling sand in those South Jersey pits from which its blue glass came. Mirra had fixed flowers in it to look like a pastel by Odilon Redon. He was her favorite. The dying flowers gave off a bitter hospital smell.

There was something sinister about the silence. I should have been hearing Mirra turning the pages of *Italian Painters of the Renaissance* or coughing from too many Chesterfields piling up in the milk-glass ashtray shaped like an open hand. This was the quiet of a forbidden thrill. Or the minute before a crime. And then I heard a hissing like the rubbing of nylon between the thighs of a lazy girl. And then I heard a kind of growling. I thought of a burglar. He might be hurting Mirra. I had an old golf club in the closet. Could I bring myself to swing it, crack the carapace, sink the Spalding iron, like Raskolnikov's axe, into the mean brain?

The room was in shadows. The only light came through the

green shade of one of Mirra's converted kerosene lamps. But I saw her clearly enough. Mirra and not Mirra. Mirra and less than Mirra. Half of her, cut at the waist by the high arms of George Washington's chair. Her skirt moved on her haunches, rippled like the feathers on a chicken pecking at its lice. The points of her alligator shoes were buried in the rug, their heels pointed out like spurs at two shoeless feet whose toes were twitching absurdly in clocked black socks. The rest of her was hidden in the place from where the growling came, *ahhrrrgh,* hidden from herself, from Mr. and Mrs. Leopold, from Karen Horney, from the Art Students League, from Martha Graham, *ahhrrrgh,* from Louis Armstrong and his Hot Five, from Berg-dorf-Goodman, from Margaret Sanger, *ahhrrrgh,* from *La Pasionaria,* from Bernard Berenson, from Orson Welles, *ahhrrrgh,* from little Willie-Wilhelmina, from the Luftwaffe, from Billie Holiday, from Fiorello La Guardia, from Nicholas Vincent Gardenia, from the American Federation of Labor, from Piero della Francesco, from the Warner Bros., from the principal of Avon Avenue School, from sea to shining sea, from the bottom of my heart, from this day forward, from each according to his ability, from Tinker to Evers to Chance, from the halls of Montezuma . . .

From Twenty-fourth Street to Twenty-eighth, I was running through the streets like a victim of locomotor ataxia, running without will, ashamed and crazy. I rang Charlie's bell. I was leaving myself on the doorstep of the Hebrew Home for the Horned.

· 27 ·
Hymn to Hymen

One day Mirra and I were skittering around at thirty-two frames per second like Edna Purviance and Charlie Chaplin, she in her bloomers, dusting off our Home Sweet Home and me coming in with my empty lunch pail to an innocent kiss and a nice meal of shoelaces. *Slow dissolve and iris effect.*

That scene ends up on the cutting-room floor. The next I know, I'm tossing on a folding cot in Charlie's kitchen, hearing him—the talkies have been invented—huffing and puffing on his own bed of nails. He is running in his sleep. Either he is trying to catch up with his Hunzy Bunzy or he's being chased by a hairless bagel. He's moaning something that sounds like "Bronf! Bronf!" He's suffering in Esperanto. I know the language. It's okay, Charlie Boy! I'm dancing on a dime, myself. And giving a nickel change.

I got word that Mirra wanted me to see her analyst. I thought it was not allowed. Actually, it wasn't. Your analyst was supposed to be yours alone. The sons of Siggy were ruling the roost. No orthodox analyst saw husband and wife or even mother and child. That was "external reality." All that counted was interior fantasy. "Verking trough ze transferenz, *ja?*"

I never dreamed that ten years later I would be doing my bit to undo this orthodoxy, doing it the hard way, treating couples, even whole families, in the same room. They say you become an analyst to cure yourself. Did I become one to find out why I was flying off, feet first, like the upside-down bridegroom in a painting by Chagall?

I went to see Mirra's doctor. He was a refugee and he got my name wrong. But he had my number. "There are times," he told me, "when a man must bang his fist on ze table." Charlie should have gone with me.

The two of us went on pretending we were characters out of *The Front Page*. Trouble was, we were not hard-boiled and neither of us looked good in hats. Charlie was still coaching his runaway wife from the sidelines. If her boyfriend looked cross-eyed at her, she called in the middle of the night and kept him on the wire for an hour. I couldn't believe my ears. The guy was teaching the cheater how to cheat! Mirra would never pull anything like that. I knew from different people that she wanted me back. They wondered why we were apart. I'd die before I'd tell anybody why.

Misery loves company. The two cuckolds began to call up every girl they knew and a few they didn't know. They could not quit while they were ahead. Eventually, using as a procurer a friend of Charlie's who worked on *PM*, we got to know a crowd of girls who were all stenotypists. We folded up the Murphy bed and became a halfway house for the unattached. The stenos traveled in a covey and came to our parties in threes and fours. They made good money, brought their own liquor, sandwiches, and potato salad. They didn't seem to mind that they didn't have men of their own. There was a war going on and they were a forgiving lot, toughened by days in court documenting malfeasance and mayhem. They were bored taking down the endless words of others on their little machines. They liked Charlie's puns and his recording of Furtwängler's *Tristan*. By the time he got to the *"Liebestodt"* there wasn't a dry cunt in the house. That's how Hitler got Eva Braun in the mood.

And that's how I met Rosa Luxemburg. Not the real Red Rosa, the one who is credited with the "glass of water" theory of sex—you know, if you're thirsty, you drink. Her parents were old-time Lefties and that's how they had named her. She was an intense little thing who spent half of her life in Madison Square Garden as an usher for rallies to open up a Second Front. Or a Third. She could not wait to get to Russia. Instead, she dated Sovietsky sailors when one of their freighters came to port. Her fervor intrigued me. And something else.

She was fascinated by circumcision. The subject came up one night and I was drunk enough to fill Rosa Lu—as she called herself—with tales of Jewish *mohels* who bit off the foreskin. I may even have introduced the idea of clitoridectomy as a parallel and, for spice, those South Sea Islanders who implanted pebbles around the glans to make themselves permanent "French ticklers." From things she said, it suddenly struck me that running around with those Russkies as she did, Rosa Lu had never seen an unhooded specimen. Boytchik was ready to volunteer.

I'd call Rosa Lu and, every time, get her kid sister who was spending the night in the city. Rosa Lu was probably at the Garden giving a standing ovation to Earl Browder. The sister was named Ottie.

"You'll never guess my real name!"

I tried Faith, Hope, Charity.

"Give up? Give up?"

Her name was Octobra after the month of the Russian Revolution which had really kicked off in November. What a family!

We had a good time on the phone. The kid had an inviting, open laugh. There were touching little ploys like "You don't know me but I know you!" One thing led to another and one night Ottie said right out, "How about *me* instead?"

And why not? *Potchemu nyet?*

So, one night after a dozen Littlenecks, I broke away from Charlie—or he broke away from me—went to a pay phone, and got Ottie. Some instinct told her to meet me in the lobby of her sister's fifth-floor walkup over a midtown tuxedo rental. Looking back on Octobra's single-minded pragmatism, I see that she wanted to be on her own ground. She may have been staying over at her older sibling's, but she would make her own way into the psychosexual world.

Octobra was about eighteen and fresh as a McIntosh apple. She was as enthusiastic about her first Martini as she was about modern dance, which she took from Doris Humphrey. She seemed more Midwestern than mid-Manhattan. She vibrated absolute health. Everything her fanatic sister was saving for the Socialist millennium, Octobra was ready to spend right now. Her sister was studying Russian to be able to read Lenin's *What Is to Be Done?* Octobra had already answered the question.

"Let's do it!"

"What?"

"This! This for which I was made!"

The combination of Left Wing poet, heterodox Comrade, and sorrowing married man was more appealing to Ottie than I knew. Much as Ella had led me easily across the equator between innocence and manhood, Ottie was taking me over the same invisible line to her womanhood. She brought the subject up. It was her belief that virginity stood in the way if you were in love. You might hold it against the fellow. Or he might think he owed you something. Ottie wanted to be unencumbered of bourgeois baggage.

"Maybe I'm nayv,"—that's the way she said it—"but it's not something you give or take. I mean if you're honest with yourself, the two individuals are doing it willingly."

I liked that "two individuals." That's what we were. We were sitting face to face in a booth. I took Ottie's hand. She squeezed mine.

"Would you?"

Without the slightest trace of embarrassment, she was leading me to a point in her own future she had already chosen and planned. "I have seen the Future and it screws!"

We might have liquidated Ottie's maidenhood right then and there. But neither of us had a place to go. We could not risk the return of Rosa Lu with a Russian sailor in tow. And I was a displaced person with a strange bedfellow. What would I do about Charlie? Ours was not a truly proletarian milieu where the primal scene was old hat and the gang bang a ritual of growing up. Privacy is the opium of the middle class. I could hardly honor—or dishonor—Octobra on the cot in Charlie's kitchen with him snoring a chorus from *Götterdämmerung*. The kitchen part was okay. What better place to test the "drink of water" theory? I would get away from work tomorrow and we would meet at Charlie's during the day. Not a word was said about our purpose. Octobra had already led me down the primrose path.

I had to ask Charlie to send me out on some spurious assignment. To see what had happened to the hole in the bagel? I told him only I was going to use the apartment. A wink is as good as a nod to a blind horse! Charlie was a born conspirator. But the cause had to be good. I could see him sitting around the samovar with the Decembrists drawing a map of the Tsar's route with the stub of a chewed-up Eberhard-Faber #2. He told me where I could find some fresh towels.

Did I meet Octobra in some sad cafe with the jukebox playing "My Old Flame"? Did I ply her with Martinis? If I did, they were more for me than for her. I wasn't too sure Ottie had the right man for the job. My Boytchik had never been utilitarian. He was more spoiled prince than workman. And this time he would be safetied. He was not used to that. I had stopped in the corner drugstore.

"Rameses, please!" Like buying your first pack of cigarettes.

Octobra danced into the room where Magda had been queen.

"Oooo, it's like a museum," she said.

All those knickknacks, those porcelain sheep with pink bows around their throats as though they had already been slit, those lace-edged plates for *Schlagzahne* and itsy-bitsy teacups big enough for gnomes, were just as Magda had left them. Charlie's greatest concern when we had a party was that something of hers would be broken. What Octobra and I were going to break could not be mended with Magic Glue.

Ottie laughed when she saw my cot in the kitchen all neatly made up as best I knew how.

"I'm just a vagabond lover . . ." I sort of sang, trying it on for size.

"No," Ottie said, "you're the doctor. We're going to play doctor."

She was taking off her clothes and tossing them into the

sink. She was smaller without them. Her titties were like two
scoops of strawberry ice cream. Against the white of the refrigerator, the stove, and the enameled cupboards she looked
like a snow maiden. Her flesh glowed like the face of a kid out
sledding. But stretched out on the cot she looked like Minnie the
Moocher on her wedding day.

I took her in my arms and she kissed me. Her sharp, little
teeth were fuzzy. She stuck her tongue out and I tasted but-
terscotch. I was licking a lollypop. The rest of her came in seven
delicious flavors. Ottie's skin was stretched tight as a drum on
her frame. Sonny Greer could have brushed "In My Solitude" on
her tootie. My hands avoided only the place where Boytchik was
going to hurt her. I was saving that, to soothe, to prepare her.
Ottie was pressing her virginity against me. She knew everything
that went on down there not inside-out but outside-in. She
pulled me to her and spread her dancer's legs until she looked as
if she had four arms.

"Do the fuck!" she whispered.

I still had my clothes on. I was the doctor, wasn't I? I ran for
a towel. Ottie raised herself like an acrobat and it was under her.
I was prepared for a bucket of blood.

Between her legs now, pushing out from a sparrow-colored
wisp, I could see the creased fig. It was opening to the sun. I
squeezed it and it spurted juice. Sea and Sardinia and Frieda von
R. and Lorenzo coughing up blood and imagery!

I opened the sex. Ottie's clitoris, poking out of its glans,
looked like the tiniest starter in an Add-a-Pearl necklace. The
labia were ruby red, tight to the introitus. My finger pushed
aside the little sentinel and went in. It was stopped by a rubber
door that yielded and pushed back. I pressed. It went in to the
joint and stopped, caught in a vise of contracting membrane.

Ottie had a tough hymen. I hoped it would not need something sharper than a prick to slit it. It was not likely that a
healthy kid like Ottie would have vaginismus. That would take a
Mack truck or three years on Dr. Bang Your Fist's couch to bust
open. The great Dr. Dickinson used to employ a lot of fatherly
sweet talk and glass test tubes in graduated sizes to spread these
neurotic nicks.

Naturally, I did not know any of this then, knew less probably than the boys in the YMCA locker room. I knew neither
myth nor truth. I had only my ignorance and my beheaded
schmeckele going for me.

"Is it ready?" Ottie asked.

"Almost!"

With all that white in that kitchen it was a little like an operating room.

"Speculum, nurse! Number-three probe!"

I tried my thumb. It went in easily, came away covered with the shiny stuff a caterpillar trails on a leaf. I saw no blood. Boytchik wanted to have a look. I poked his head into that jungle place.

"It's big!" Ottie said. She was surprised, not afraid.

I pushed. He pushed, I pushed again. He pushed again. Four downs later, we were over the line of scrimmage.

Ottie was too new at this game to do more than receive me. Her dancer's muscles held her arched. Her hands were on the cot palms down like mine, which were holding me high above her, leaving the instrument of incision free to draw cleanly against the small wound. Boytchik was behaving as though he had gone to medical school. He liked the job. Dr. Kronkheit.

I wish I could tell you about ecstasies. But it was all easy and jolly, although both of us got serious when the little murder had to be done. I finished and fell on Ottie, my gasping mouth against her hair on the pillow.

"Does it hurt?" Maybe I wanted it to.

"The opposite!" she said happily. "It's just what I thought."

Ottie's gratitude was just what I needed. She had chosen me. I was not Tom, Dick, or Harry. But I was too wounded for courtship. Not being lovers, we had no script to read. We were just looking at each other, smugly, I suppose. Together we checked the towel I had spread under her where we would be joined. There were a few red drops. Hardly anything to show the drunken peasants outside our window to prove that the groom was not getting secondhand goods.

We dallied awhile and then, just to prove a point, did it again.

Ottie was happy. She had taken care of the future. Maybe, for her, life would be filled with sensible, bright moments. I wasn't going to tell her her troubles were just beginning. I was feeling good myself. I was trotting around the bases like the utility outfielder brought up from the minors who homers his first time at bat in the Polo Grounds. I was batting .1000.

Octobra went off to be a counselor at a summer camp. I didn't see her again for many years until, by chance, we met at a

Free Soviet Jewry benefit. Rosa Lu had gone to Russia after the war, married a Party man, and disappeared.

Times change. I was a more "important" person now, and so was Ottie. Married to a physicist. She had not changed. Her hair was gray, but she had not put on a pound. You could see that her biology was still bouncy. That optimistic cunt would never grow old. Out of it had come another physicist—nuclear, Ottie was worried about that—and a mathematician and an ethnic dancer.

Octobra read my admiration. Unless she has told her husband, we have kept our secret until now.

"Does it hurt?"

"Oh no! The opposite!"

· 28 ·

Appointment in Samara

What can I say, without prevarication, about that callow time when I no longer had the excuse of rage to explain my denials of remorse?

Emissaries came from Mirra and I turned them away. What would I have done if she had come herself?

My father offered money. "If you *shmear,* you ride!" The Russian Jews got to ride on the railroad by bribing the conductor.

Mr. Leopold brought an olive branch in a cigar box. "Forgive thy neighbor and it will all come out in the wash!" His El Producto went out. He stopped calling me son.

Charlie fuddled himself with cheap sherry and listened for hours to *Parsifal.* If Christ could rise, why couldn't he?

It was Easter in Berchtesgaden and April in Paris and June in January and I was dancing with tears in my eyes.

That's putting a soft light on it. I was no good to myself or anybody else. But there is an angel for every blade of grass. And for every bum. So Laurie was sent down to me.

I was too sloppy for a crackup. Laurie had already had hers. With me there were always two possibilities. Laurie was too brainy to play around with the conclusions she drew from her own behavior. A one-sided affair with a professor had landed her, praecox, in the hospital. It was a quick thing, truly a breakdown. It would never happen again. She came out of it vulnerable but resilient.

Laurie was smarter and braver than I in dealing with the world. I rummaged around in a pushcart of things unsaid. Laurie had a prodigious fluency. If you put your ear against the belly of a goat, they say, you can hear the milk coursing down to its udder. When you got close to her, Laurie's racing intelligence made such a sound. In those days she was a little ashamed of her intellect. And sometimes her mind took more upon itself than she wanted. Like a two-faced friend, one part stayed alert, ready to mock the other's slightest mischance. Polarization is still her favorite word. When you hear her on the *Dick Cavett Show* she still speaks in question marks and exclamation points.

"You see? You see?"

After Vassar and some small-town reporting, Laurie was working for a liberal wire service. We doctored her stories and used them in *The Baker* without a by-line. I met her just after she had bluffed her way past the goons at an AFL conclave and gotten an interview with senile William Green. And *Harper's* had published one of her investigative pieces. It was a scoop of sorts and it was not her last. Laurie already had one foot in the door to important places. And what was strange, she looked so guileless. Just walked in with that Phi Beta Kappa kisser and found out how the milk got in the coconut!

Laurie became a well-known person. I think that is all it is safe for me to say. She is a public figure now, used by one side against the other in the family wars of the intellectual Mafia. I would not want to blow her cover.

Not that Laurie would give a damn! The last time I saw her in the flesh—that was one war later, this time a war even I did not want to be in—she grabbed me by the arm and paraded me from one beard to another.

"Dwight! I want you to meet my first lover! Lionel! My first lover!"

It was almost true. Someplace in the shuffle, Laurie had lost the evil professor who had been *numero uno*.

Standing there in a designer dress that cost more than both of us used to make in a month laboring in the vineyards of Labor, her manicured hand around a small sea of bourbon lapping over the tiny icebergs you get from caterers, herself rolling a bit with the waves the stuff was making inside her, could Laurie remember that far back? I did.

We were in Pete's Tavern, just sitting there side by side in a booth, keeping our hands to ourselves. Laurie was polarizing something, giving me a lot of "You see? You see?" One minute, I had no idea of interfering with her person. The next, I turned and kissed her on the cheek right on that dimple that made her look more innocent than she was. She stopped polarizing. I put my mouth to her ear and Laurie jumped.

"That gives me the jimjams," she said, hugging herself and laughing.

Things happened fast. Before we knew it, we were in a cab and riding uptown, and I don't think she took her mouth away from mine except to look for the key that her roommate had hidden under the doormat. Laurie was wonderfully eager. She kissed with the desperation of inexperience but with immediate heat. Laurie didn't wait for me to make a move; she boldly took my hand and led it inside the neck of her dress and into her bra. Her booby surprised me. It was round and hard as a baseball, just the right size for a game of catch.

Laurie was full of surprises. My other hand was between her legs before I knew I was putting it there. I found my fingers mowing through a plentiful bush toward an unknown bourne. It is forty years now, and I have not forgotten the shock of my encounter with another white man in that unmapped jungle.

"Dr. Livingstone, I presume?"

Dr. Livingstone, Dr. Jekyll, Dr. Kronkheit, and Dr. Kildare! It stood there like a cigar-store Indian, erect, throbbing, pressing forward out of a hooded pink glans, a clitoris as palpable as the tip of your pinkie. I was handling it as a child might a trapped mouse. But even this scared caress was bringing Laurie on.

Her breath came quicker. And now she began to sing a song that reminded me of girls jumping rope on Avon Avenue. "One, two, three a-lary, I spy Mistress Mary sitting on a bumble-ary. And a-one, and a-two, and a-three . . ." She held me tight in one endless kiss while the music quickened. And it didn't stop. "And a-four, and a-five, and a-six . . ." Her climax came rolling. A repeater.

I tried to pull myself away, to reach and free both of us to meet naked at our place of gender. But it was too late. I was tossed by a wave that swept from some South Sea Island in myself. I drowned. Laurie locked both her hands in mine and carried them to the place of her own drowning. "And a-seven, and a-eight . . ."

We lay there, mouth to mouth. With my last breath I resuscitated her. Like Adam. Or was it the Creator personally who had blown life into Eve? And her lungs filled and she returned my life to me and we were born and rocking in a cradle made by our own hands. We were mother and child and child and mother. One was crying and the other was saying "Hushabye!"

"I'm sorry. I'm sorry. . . ."

Laurie's spasms were rubbing her tears along my cheek. She was gasping. As a child she had been asthmatic. And now when she thought she was getting more than she gave, her breath would fly from her and leave her with a choking dismay.

"No, no, no . . ." I put my mouth to her. The air around us smelled of cut hay. I held it there until apology was forgotten. I took it away just long enough to say, "Next time!"

"Golly!" Laurie said.

I got back to Charlie's walking like a kid with a load in his diapers.

Charlie was curled up into a ball, only his face stuck out of the sheets. He looked frightened. I tiptoed into the bathroom and rinsed out my shorts. Naked—I had no pajamas, a homeless waif—I went into the kitchen, opened my cot, and fell into the place where I could help Charlie fight off the bagel from outer space.

"Next time" crept up on Labor's lovers. I usually held my liquor well. I had studied the subject at two universities. One night, misery and chemistry caught up with me. I had been boozing all day with Charlie. I had not eaten. Arriving at Laurie's from the Hebrew Home for the Horned—I only kept my clothes there now—I almost fell out of the cab. Laurie paid the driver and helped me to her door. I couldn't make the stairs. I would manage one step and fall on my knees. Laurie pulled and carried me to the Castro convertible. I fell on it, unable to move. Laurie got my shoes off.

Maybe it was this act of servitude that touched off some

atavism in me. Part infant, part bully, I wanted Laurie to be nurse, to be my slave.

"C'mere!" I ordered. "C'mere, tootsie!" I had never behaved this way before. I was playing out a whorehouse fantasy. I pawed her brutally. I opened my fly.

"What about *them?*" Laurie whispered.

She had a roommate, a tight-assed schemer who worked for the CIO and was having an affair with her boss. She had the bedroom. He had to sneak past us when he went home to his wife. Let Mr. Big Shot come through and see the Beast with Two Backs!

"I don't give a shit!"

I got Laurie by the hair, shoved her face against the stub of my Boytchik. He was as drunk as I was. Hemiplegic. The passion—it was more a release of restraints—was all in my head. I was falling into the polymorphous. I held Laurie hard. She might have escaped. But like the drunkard's wife who cries helplessness to the world, she became my accomplice. He, that ridiculous *mensch,* was too small to take in her mouth. She kissed him. Kissed him like a mother who, overcome by maternity, will nip at her baby's bottom.

"Mmm, mmm! I could eat you up!"

Boytchik came out of his coma. He was against Laurie's palate now, a cannibal food. I still had Laurie by the nape of her neck. And seeing how Cupid finds the strength to lift the sot, raise him from the floor of degradation, wipe the reeking froth from his muttering mouth, I met him halfway. I brought Laurie to her knees and lay myself over her haunches. I lifted her skirt. I was so deep into her that I lost my gender. I became breasted, blind Tiresias dragging his mammae on the ground, crying out with two mouths how the child shall make the mother big and undo the order of creation.

And even as I spurted from my genital she, having now within herself the two organs, became woman-man and called out the hurt of being so undone and let forth a golden stream that was her way of spurting, too.

Like the tortured bed-wetter, Laurie had spilled over. That perineal valve that she held shut with her counted climaxes— "And a-four, and a-five, and a-six . . ."—had given way, opened and let go.

"You see? You see?"

Laurie covered her face. Her shame drew me to her. I was not oblivious of the connection to the infantile in her not-so-rare dysfunction. I saw the universal mother, my own, pointing the manchild off the curb, aiming it for him, encouraging. "Pishee, pishee, pishee!"

I cannot say I was indifferent to the times when Laurie "lost control." And now that the secret was out, we prepared a rubber sheet against those occasions that gave her the greatest release.

My boozing had its uses for both of us. Through the buzzing of my hangover, next morning, I heard Laurie recite: "Blisse, last night drunk, did kisse his mother's knee. Where will he kisse, next drunk, conjecture ye." She had done honors in the Cavalier poets. She would have made the perfect alcoholic's wife.

In autobiographical sketches, Laurie makes much of herself as an adolescent ugly duckling. Don't you believe it! Unless, as it happens so often, she is still comparing herself to the prettiest girl in the class. And who looks good in the high school year-book? When you see her picture in the paper, Laurie sometimes looks like a Hadassah lady who needs a few sessions at Slenderella. When I held her, back then, she made a small, precious package. She would curl up with her elliptical tushy snuggled into the pit of my stomach—flat then—and my groin would press against slim thighs and the length of my Boytchik would rest between her buns like a Nathan's hot dog waiting for the mustard and relish. And the breasts of the Laurie Golden I knew were girlish, reaching out to be cupped. They had not yet been bared in the many causes that have earned Laurie her fame.

We were content with each other. Sunday was our best day. We spent a lot of time in bed nursing my hangovers and reading the *Times*. Laurie coddled me. "Good morrow to the day so fair; good morning Sir to you; Good morrow to my own torn hair bedabbled with the dew."

In the afternoon we would eat a blue plate at some greasy spoon and see a *triste* French film starring Raimu's belly or Jean Gabin's cap. I was ashamed to tell Laurie of a phobia I had to fight each time we squeezed through to the center of the Thalia's aisle: I imagined that in the dark I would find myself sitting next to Mirra. I was constantly apprehensive about encountering her. It was not hard to avoid the galleries, museums, and dance recitals where she might be. The metropolis is really a beehive of separate little *barrios*. And away from our typewriters, Laurie and I were often captives at long meetings where the tail of Lenin's ideology wagged the dog of reality. Still, even in a city of millions, I might find myself standing next to Mirra on the curb waiting for the light to turn green. I watched for her out of the corner of my eye. It seemed to me that if we looked just once at each other, we could only embrace and, without words, walk back arm in arm under the canopy held above us by four close-shaven uncles looking ridiculous wearing hats in the house. The world is a wedding, no? You can see it would be too awful to say it is a divorce.

I was still married but Laurie and I were behaving as though we were free. She spoke of taking me to Texas to meet her family. She apologized for this reversion to conformity. "It's just this thing, you see?" They would approve of me. Were we not both wayward children of merchants? Laurie's grandfather had walked into the Panhandle with a pack on his back. Needles, thread, dry goods. Now the Goldens owned a department store. They were the only Jews in the country club. We would not be poor. Laurie would write "pieces." I would follow my muse.

I did meet her kid brother. He came through New York in his shiny new lieutenant's uniform. Phil Golden had his army pay to burn. We took him to Nick's in the Village. Jimmy McPartland sang "I Wish I Could Shimmy Like My Sister Kate." The lieutenant was happy. Laurie was happy. I was almost happy. I wanted to take them to George's Bar down the street. Billie Holiday sometimes came there for a drink between sets at Cafe Society. I dreaded meeting Mirra. George's had been one of our favorite places. I was not to see Mirra for the rest of her life. I had an appointment in Samara.

Christmas came. Or was it New Year's Eve? Certainly it was one of those holidays when all of us must face the problem of pretending to be happier than we are. The publisher broke out the Four Roses. He even sprang for a platter of deli. Laurie and the kids from her service came. We got sozzled, dodged the usual half-wild shipping clerks throwing up between cars and screaming at the boss's world, and made our way to a party at the Newspaper Guild.

And there, standing at the bar with a glass of ginger ale in her hand, was Kiddy. We were married a few months later.

· V ·

Hello, Heartache

· 29 ·

The Pastrami Playhouse

But first both of us had to get unmarried. Kiddy's husband was overseas with the USO. It was a hectic evening when he came back and got his Dear John letter in person. I waited in the street below like a private eye tailing a suspect. Did Kiddy have a signal, raised shade, a blinking light? "Two if by land, and one if by sea!" She did not keep me waiting long.

"It was awful!" Kiddy's eyes were red.

Her ex was a nice enough guy, devoted to Kiddy in his own way, which included other devotions here and there. He became a Hollywood big shot. "Stick with me," he would tell Kiddy, "and you'll be wearing diamonds!" Diamonds! Pfui!

My farewell from Laurie I hear as a Puccini aria, softer, softer, until the only thing you hear is the coughing in the audience. My little bird mended her broken wing and flew again. Higher! Higher!

And Mirra? How did we dissolve our marriage without once meeting face to face? It was arranged. Lilly Curtis swore before Judge O'Reilly or O'Malley or O'Brien that she had heard me, very distinctly and more than once, say I wanted a flock of brats for whom I would buy balloons and lollypops. Ah, but between the sheets, it was another story! I always wore rubbers, Lilly testified. And just to make triply sure, I only cohabited when my spouse had her monthlies.

The bandaged eyes of Justice opened wide. By the City of New York, County of New York, State of New York, by the tonsure of Cardinal Spellman and the beard of the Rabbi of

Lubitschov we were annulled. We had never broken a BLT at Schrafft's, never SRO'd on three legs to see Martha Graham lament, never fallen, curled into a 6 and a 9, on the hard boards of a paint-spattered floor. We were expunged. As Walter Winchell used to write, we were pffft!

The first time I had been married in a language I did not know. The second time I thought I understood every word. A broad-minded Unitarian minister urged Kiddy and yours truly to "cleave to each other." Later, when things got rough I would crack, "Are you sure he didn't say we should cleave each other?" But that was in another country.

Kiddy and I moved into a one-room flat in a Forty-seventh-Street brownstone that's part of the lobby of a skyscraper now. The prior tenant had painted one wall green with a white lattice-work hung with lilac blobs. It was like living in an Italian restaurant. I began to write verse again on the kitchen table in front of this false al fresco wall.

I was chosen for that year's annual of new American writing. I was in pretty good company, some famous now, some pushing up daisies, some, like me, keeping alive with an occasional poem in the *Times*. One critic wrote, "He grinds his gears but he gets there." Was that because so many of my lines had been rehearsed on the cracked leather cushions of the Chrysler 77 on my uncle's used-car lot? For Kiddy I was still the unbroken sixteen-year-old poet. She was proud of me. She typed my poems and kept a 3 × 5 card file of my acceptances and rejections.

Politically I was still an anti-Fascist. But there weren't any Fascists. Where had they gone? I was obsessed by images of the extermination camps. I wrote an *Elegy at a Mass Grave* and it was set to music and sung by the choir of a Methodist university. I was beginning to find out who I was.

> Dark, dark a world I cannot see.
> My kinsman's wounds must be my eyes;
> And open them to for me.

Kiddy still carried within herself the fervent hope for a people's theater which had marched into the wings when the curtain fell on the Federal Theater of the good old Depression days. Her allegiance shifted to Stanislavsky. She worked at an acting school run by an expatriate Muscovite actress who called her husband Mamoussia, little mother.

"Mamoussia, tea please for Kiddy's poet!"

Mamoussia read *Pravda* and *Izvestia* every day. He told Kiddy there was anti-Semitism in Russia, that Jews were again without passports, *bezpassportniki*. Kiddy herself was still redder than the rose. But her petals were being shaken. There were stories of labor camps in Siberia. Kiddy was sure it was all an invention of the *World-Telegram*.

Kiddy fought the bourgeois life on whose edge we lived from my earnings at various occupations that had to do with the printed word. This is no *Bildungsroman* so I will skirt over the jobs I had and the careers I attempted. Like a trained bear, I danced in the courtyards of taverns where *muzhiks* jollied by vodka threw kopecks at me, aiming at the soft parts exposed when I got up on all fours and imitated a man. Some dangled honeyed cakes under my nose. But I was always muzzled and the cakes were tied to a long stick.

That's how I got to be associate producer of the Pastrami Playhouse. Of course, that was not its name. Nor did I actually attain such an exalted title. I was, as the joke goes, the only one who would associate with the producer.

Characteristically, my new occupation chose me. I had been a shoestring publisher of art books. Perversely, I made them cheap rather than expensive. For four years I was borrowing from Peter to pay Paul and from Paul to pay Peter. One day I told Paul to pay Peter and Peter to pay Paul and leave me out of it. I went gracefully bankrupt.

Waiting for the bailiff, I made an adaptation of a French play famous on the stages of Europe but never done here. I took it to the big agency where, I noticed, even the receptionist had a genuine eighteenth-century desk. The nice lesbian lady in charge of successes *d'estime* asked me, in passing, whether I knew somebody who had a good knowledge of literature for a radio show that was looking for a story editor. The wolf was at my door. Kiddy was big with child. I swallowed twice and asked, "How about me?" The nice lesbian lady leveled with me, urged me not to take the job. The producer was a tyrant. I would not last two weeks. And so on. P.S.: I got the job. On the night of the first show my son was born. I lasted until he could walk and talk. Luckily, he did both things early.

Barney Banner had been the boy genius of radio. In Hollywood, he had written and directed several movies which had
landed on *Variety*'s list of Box Office Champions. Now he was
back to revive a radio show he had done in the days before television. The sponsor wanted to try it again. We were to be radio
drama's last gasp. The show was done live before an audience in
an old Broadway theater. Music was supplied by a twenty-one-
piece orchestra. Each week we presented a Hollywood star.
Barney knew them all. He had given them their start.

"I told Kirk Douglas to curl his hair," Barney boasted.

Barney Banner produced, directed, wrote, and hosted the
aural spectacle. Our office was in the advertising agency that had
the sponsor's huge account. We were *not* selling pastrami. Our
staff consisted of Rosie, a Bronxy secretary who took down in
shorthand Barney's freewheeling half-hour versions of screen-
plays from M-G-M, Paramount, Universal, Warner Bros. We had
a gofer who brought Barney his cigars and the afternoon stock-
market reports. I had a little desk next to Barney's. The gofer
had to stand or lean against the wall. We were not allowed to go
out for lunch. Barney bought us pastrami sandwiches. The gofer
got them from the Stage Delicatessen, always with mustard, half
dills and Dr. Brown's Cel-Ray Tonic.

Barney, who pocketed most of the show's budget, sometimes
turned from the ready-made movie scripts to less costly plays
and even public-domain novels I found for him. Though he
rarely worked more than a day or two ahead of show time, he
would get very serious with me about "staying ahead."

"We should always have five, maybe six, properties in the
can!"

I had them. But Barney resisted anything that had not been
tried out on a double-feature bill in a drive-in. His immediate
reaction to my suggestions would be, "You're murdering me!"
Or a sarcastic "Me neither!" But he would not forget. Barney
would suddenly "see" next week's star in some play I had ver-
bally digested for him.

"Sexy Rexy! He's British! *An Inspector Calls*. Schmuck! Why
didn't he send a telegram?"

Barney never read the plays or books he was adapting. He
would start cold.

"Music: up and under."

Once Barney said that, the rest was inevitable. He would

glance a few pages ahead and cannily get the characters moving through the plot of the piece. After all, he only had a half hour to get boy to meet girl, lose girl, and find girl.

"Music: up and out." A sly look at me. He has done it again. *"Pastrami Playhouse theme. The End."*

For Barney, I was part courtier, part Greek slave. Within the limits of his paranoia, he trusted me. He knew I had no show-business ambitions. I had achieved my ambition to be like everybody else. I had a two-bedroom apartment on the West Side near Needle Park, I had a job that paid the rent, I had a son. I may have been happier at other times of my life, but I could not tell you when.

Jay had been a long time in the making. "And the poor have children." We tried and we tried. When the dot on Kiddy's graph bumped up, we tried. Kiddy's tubes were blown; we tried. I stood up to be counted in a sticky test tube. We tried again. Until one single little *neshumah* wiggled up the dark alley, tipped his hat at the speakeasy door, and said, "Acey sent me!" They let him in.

Kiddy was hanging onto a strap in the rush-hour subway when her waters broke. The contractions came fast. We bounced along the cobblestones down Tenth Avenue to French Hospital where Babe Ruth had said good-bye to his pinstripes. I held my hand on Kiddy's belly. I did not want whoever it was to be born in a Yellow Cab. The kid was two months early as it was.

Nurses wheeled Kiddy away to be prepped. I waited, three, four hours. I was all alone, filling a chromium ashtray that swallowed my butts into a trapdoor. Was I the only guy in that hospital having a baby? I did enough *couvade* for triplets. At eleven, the obstetrician came down. Oh, these professionals! A new soul comes into the world and he says, "Everything is fine!"

I made telephone calls. Our son was a real surprise. We didn't have a crib or booties or bottles. I should have sent to the Newark Department of Public Welfare for a layette.

Mothering came hard to Kiddy. During the months of infancy she was tense, trying to go by the book, uncertain and anxious. One morning, after nursing the baby through a bad night of colic, she panicked. She begged me not to go to work. But it was broadcast day, holier than Yom Kippur for Barney Banner. It was preceded by a read-through with the star. I really had nothing to do during these rehearsals but be there for Barney to look at triumphantly when one of his lines went over big. Or murderously when one laid an egg.

"You!" Barney would hiss.

It wasn't my line. It wasn't even Barney's. It had been written by a hack on the M-G-M lot. The most I ever would permit myself would be a shrug of the shoulders. Barney could read shoulders. That's what I was getting paid for.

"Don't go!" Kiddy pleaded. "Stay with me!"

I walked out of the door.

"Don't go! Don't go!" Kiddy called from the window. "Don't leave me alone!"

I kept walking. I was afraid of the boy genius with the golden Patek-Phillipe watch, the golden Dunhill lighter, the golden tongue.

What were we doing that week? *Sunset Boulevard* with Gloria Swanson in person? Kiddy should have plugged me—bang! bang! bang!—the way Gloria plugged William Holden when he walked out on her. I would have rolled belly-up in the silent screen star's swimming pool and Erich Von Stroheim would have given me the last rites. But Kiddy did not have a gun. She did have a long memory.

That night and every Thursday night, B.B. would come out on the stage in his monkey suit, introduce the star and the cast, leave them huddled around the mike, dash into the control room, light a cigar, and we would be ON THE AIR.

In the booth, B.B. would conduct the script like Andre Kostelanetz, nodding at *diminuendos*, tossing his head and shaking his curls for the *fortissimo* murders of literature. During the commercial, he held his hand up. You've seen the maestro wait like this for silence in Carnegie Hall. It came down on cue. *Allegro vivace* for wisecracks. *Andante cantabile* for tears. "*Music: up and under.*"

We were, off and on, the top show in radio. When the Nielsen rating showed us number one, Barney would be impossibly *chutzpahdik*. He would take the rating up to the head of the agency and always come back with a hot tip on an oil stock.

"Rosie, get me Lieberman the *goniff*."

Rosie would dial. Barney would put his feet up on the desk and shake his French cuffs to show his links, two golden *B*'s as big as a headline in the *Daily News*, light a cigar—his hands were free, he had one of those gadgets that holds the receiver to your ear—look at us in descending order of importance, me first, then Rosie, then the gofer, and say, "What a coinkydink!"

It is a mistake to appraise a man by what is lowest in him. Barney had his decent side. This was the era of *Red Channels*. Barney would hire blacklisted actors for inconspicuous parts. He pretended he did not have the infamous book in the drawer of his desk. He also gave bit parts to down-and-out Hollywood clowns and stooges who could look funny and do make-believe sneezes, hiccups, and burps. Barney wrote them into his scripts. He believed in laughs. When we went on the air the gofer had to keep an accurate count of how many the show got.

One recalls the anecdotes. It would be too difficult to capture the anodyne hours of waiting on meaningless, batty cruelties.

"Stop! You're driving me normal!"

I don't think Barney knew how degrading his megalomania was to us and to himself. Did I deserve a medal for spending two years under the bombardment of his half dill pickles? Or should I have had my sword broken, brass buttons ripped off my uniform, for opening the gate to the besieger, traitor to my misdirected self?

My emancipation from Barney Banner came in an unexpected way. Abraham Lincoln had freed the slaves; my nodule set me free. I had come up with a growth on my thyroid gland the size of a golf ball. If I had but one life to give, I was not going to give it to the Pastrami Playhouse.

From a Dixie cup, I gulped a millionth part of radioactive iodine. Isotopes were new then. They were supposed to go to the thyroid gland and stay there to be counted. I stood in front of a Geiger gadget that croaked like Aristophanes' frogs. Was the tissue hot or cold? The clicks were inconclusive. My fate was in the hands of the gods. Actually, it was in the hands of somebody's son the doctor to get a scalpel around a drifting pinpoint of malignancy.

· 30 ·
The Sisters of "Anna O."

My room at Mount Sinai was, for some reason, in the maternity wing. That was not inappropriate. I was expecting, if all went well, to come out with a new life. How different it would be, I did not suspect.

I went into the hospital on a Sunday afternoon. It was like checking into a motel. I wasn't sick. Kiddy and I sat around talking about Jay, our son, who had just spoken his first word. We could not decide whether he was saying "Car key!" or "Kaki!"

"No," I said, "it's got to be car key. That's in his culture. Kaki is what primitives say. He would be saying BM."

"But *we* don't have a car," Kiddy said.

This kind of talk avoided mentioning that I was about to have my throat cut from ear to ear.

A big Swede came in with a Gillette razor and a basin of suds. He looked like the mad barber of Fleet Street.

A shave? I wasn't going to a party. Kiddy had to leave. She stood in the doorway and gave me a look worthy of Joan Crawford at her best. I was either going up with the Lafayette Escadrille or down to the sea in ships. She was more afraid than I was.

"I got shayff you now," the Swede said.

"But," I said, "my operation is up here on my neck!" I was that innocent.

"Oh no, my dear sir," the orderly said, "you going to hayff a pressure bandage here 'nd here 'nd here." And he moved the hand with the lathered brush around his neck and under his arms and around his chest down to some place where you can find my *pupik.*

That Swede left me hairless as a transvestite.

In the morning, they gave me something that made me feel like three Martinis before breakfast, dumped me on a wagon, and rolled me down the corridor. I saw nothing but the green ceiling and Kiddy's face over me. It was like Frank Borzage's famous tracking shot in *A Farewell to Arms.*

They slapped a mask on me and everything started to go around and around. I was in Chapel Hill, passing out from too much corn whiskey. I woke up feeling as if a trolley car had run over my gizzard. From the neck up, I looked like The Invisible Man.

But my head was still on my shoulders. And so I took it back to Columbia to which I had commuted from Newark ten years before, while courting Mirra. Rodin's *Thinker* was still sitting there in front of Philosophy Hall. He was having a good long think.

I had been interested in psychoanalysis but thought it was a work open only to people who do not faint at the sight of blood. Quite by accident, I learned that I could become what is condescendingly called a lay analyst. I studied with one of the first of these, a former pupil of Freud who had sought in vain the hand of Anna, the Old Man's father-fixated daughter. Arriving in New York one step ahead of the SS, stripped of all but his famous masochism, he had been rebuffed by the nabobs of the American psyche. He started an Institute for off-horses like me.

I did my own three hundred hours of obligatory analysis. It had its moments. Asserting myself, I learned, was one of my unresolved problems. I was thirty-six years old. I did not know, it seems, whether I was a man or a boy.

Having come lately and accidentally to it, I was a maverick in my new profession. I had little in common with its ambitions for presidencies and executive committees, with the incessant examination of the other fellow's unconscious motives. Too many of my peers were Philistines, I was convinced, who read nothing but Rorschach blots. I was shocked to learn that a classmate had never heard of T. S. Eliot. This *yenta* had a thriving practice, though, doing "chicken soup" therapy.

Of course, she carried out to the letter the dictum put forth in a course called Managing Your Practice which said, "The patient must pay, even if he has to go out and steal!" I had trouble handling cash. Deep down, I believed with Havelock Ellis that money had no place in a work that should be done for love. Kiddy applauded when I compromised on my fees, charging less than others to keep the illusion that I stood outside the circle of greed. But when she herself consulted a therapist—there were several but none seemed able to reach her—she berated me for not knowing my own worth. She wanted me to hike my price.

"Who is *he?*" she railed. "Compared to you he's a nobody!"

I gave the illusion of being a somebody. I lectured, wrote articles, appeared on TV, but the patients who came to me were most often atonal musicians, failed graduate students, crazy painters who masturbated into their oils, writers who wrote all night and slept all day. The rich came to me by accident and did not stay. Did I have an unconscious wish to fail? Or was this failure my success?

Nourished by my family, I needed and wanted little more. I was inspired occasionally to verse, gentler now, dedicated to the small events of our son's growing up. We lived near Columbia University. I wrote how I had "wheeled my son in his Rolls-Royce pram/There where I had flunked a midterm exam."

Still, like a journeyman relief pitcher, I saved my share of interpersonal ball games. As God willed it, I specialized in marital problems. Of others, at first, and, eventually, of my own. In the Yellow Pages of those days, you could find, under "Marriage," The Listening Rabbi. I, too, became a hired ear. Eight hours each day except on the two Sabbaths, people no worse off than myself begged for the bread of my love. I gave them the stone of my ears. Naturally, they resented that I took money for these favors. An exception was an old whore. She took it for granted that business is business. She paid me as she was paid and we were quits.

I began to hear a new *Decameron.* My Boccaccios were housewives. Their city was besieged by a pestilence whose name was loneliness. And its medicine was sex. These were the modern sisters of "Anna O.," the first psychoanalytic patient who scared the pants off Breuer by getting hysterically knocked up. Or that other one whose arm, hanging over the back of a chair while she attended a sick father, had frozen into paralysis. She had let herself think of it in an incestuous embrace. Fifty years after *Studies in Hysteria,* it was accepted that every little girl wanted to sleep with her Daddy. The inhibitions of the turn of the century had become transformed into a tireless search for the Right Person.

Many were, of course, chained to the Wrong Person.

There was the madman who cut the sleeves from all of her dresses. And the transvestite who wore her garter belt. And the miser who kept her without a cent. And the sadist who made her crawl on all fours and bark "Bow wow!" Yet, if you asked why they stayed with the Wrong Person, the answer like a line from Tin Pan Alley was always, "But I love him!"

Or would, at least until Mr. Right came along. Would he ever? Until then I had to do. Warning: Do Not Accept Substitutes! "Sometimes a cigar is only a cigar!" Freud said. He smoked twenty Sumatras a day. And she got one, battery-operated, that went buzzz, buzzz, and testing, counted fifty climaxes. Another experimented. A bobby pin was removed from her uterus. Another made a salad, a cucumber in her pussy and a carrot up her ass. One got her breast into her mouth. Another, more limber, bent herself into autocunnilingus. The schizophrenic lover of another drank champagne from her vagina. Cordon rouge. Another went to an orgy and was bored. She was not with the Right Person.

Hitching their skirts, showing a bit of thigh, they talked wistfully of the Right Person. They exhuded intimations. It was understood that I took the hint. Sartre says someplace that "we yield our bodies to everyone, even beyond the realm of sexual relations, by looking, by touching." He should have added by listening.

I could defend myself against the red-hot mommas. Their sexuality was so external, rehearsed with everyone, and, as they eventually admitted, fraudulent. It was the mousy little things whispering behind seven veils of inhibition who were dangerous. They came to me as a sexual Lourdes. They would give to me, only to me, the dismembered body and soul which only I could join. The others did not count. The lewdness had been in their bodies, not in their minds.

Day after day, my ears were besieged by adulteries. I was utterly monogamous. "When I lust after a strange woman," the Yiddish poet said, "I turn to my wife. For who is stranger to me than my wife?"

I had contempt for my colleagues who broke the faith of transference.

"First you shake hands with the patient," Freud had written to Ferenczi, "then you let her sit on your lap. And then?"

And then? Hah!

Did I despise the backsliders more when my own discipline against temptation faltered? My narrowest escape from the clutches of countertransference came, of all times, on Yom Kippur, the Day of Atonement, when out of principle, I saw no patients. My office was part of my apartment with a separate

entrance of its own. Its bell rang. And there she was, the last
person in the ecumenical world I wanted to see on this day. She
was a minister's wife, so maybe Yom Kippur did not count. I was
sure I had canceled. Mrs. X. was often off in her own invert's
private world which she guarded with shocking hostility. She was
one of those who said, "I don't want to talk to you and I don't
have to!"

So why did she come? On Yom Kippur, yet!

Mrs. X. was one of the mousy ones. When her face was
flushed with that mixture of rage, suppressed sexuality, and pain
of which she refused to speak, she was pretty in a damp, just-
out-of-the-bath way. She seemed to be saying, "I was all naked
but you didn't see!" She wore starched little frocks that closed
high to a string of cultured pearls. Mrs. X. hid everything, including her desperate need of me. Warding off therapy, she hit
out at me by being openly, deliberately anti-Semitic.

"The bus was full of smelly Jewish ladies in mink coats!"

Mrs. X. insisted on using the couch. I did not want her
there. Clinical indications were to keep her sitting up and in the
here and now. What could I do? She told me she could not stand
to look at my face.

"Your nose is Jewish!"

She would say these things and draw in her shoulders as
though expecting a blow. Bad things had happened to the little
girl called Mrs. X. growing up in a Methodist manse.

And it was this one who was racked on my couch telling me
how much she hated my modern furniture, my vulgar diplomas,
and my Jewish lithographs. One was a rare Chagall. Mrs. X. had
smelled it out. With her, I had to call on every supervisory and
control session I had ever had.

I had defenses against attacks upon my person. But against
my prints! One—a gouache, actually—had been given to us by
Wim Shilling when Mirra and I were married. One to each of us.
Wimpy, as we called him then, was famous now. I sometimes
thought of selling the gouache, expunging that way the last visible link to my broken troth.

Fifteen minutes have passed and Mrs. X. has not made a
sound. She is repudiating me. I do not exist. She has hated me
out of existence. My patient's face is on fire with rancor. This is a
kind of sex for her. I must play this out. Therapist, from the
Greek *theraps,* servant. Until Mrs. X. fires me, I am her silent
butler.

"Why should I fall in love with my therapist and all that? Who do you think you are? I've had better offers!"

"And why should I pay you? You should pay me!"

I decide to join her resistance to the truth of our relationship.

"How much?"

"You would have to take me to a motel!"

This is a new wrinkle. Trying to turn me into a John.

"Do you know a cheap motel? I don't want to spend too much." Rub it in. She must fight me because I am taking away her dirty secret.

"I'm not coming here anymore!"

She wants me to beg. She cannot be left without some power. She twists on the couch. Her dress goes above her knee. She pulls it down as though she is Susannah watched by the Elders. And curiously, this pathetic game of hide-and-seek is seductive. Our combat is intimate. I am wrestling with my own imagination. Mrs. X. knows it.

"I won't have to look at your horrible pictures!"

I tug nervously at the lobe of my listening ear.

"Or your nose, your konk!"

My konk? What the hell is that? I control my rising anger. Or should I? That may be a mistake, letting her go too far. But another part of me does not debate, rises unbidden like a raised fist. Nose = penis. I'll konk her! I am shocked at the powerful erection which overtakes me. If I could not in conscience strike back at Mrs. X., my Boytchik was ready to defend the honor of the Jews.

"If you prick me, do I not bleed?" he was yelling.

And he stood tall as Shylock in the dock.

"Turn around," I wanted to cry out. "You don't want to look at my konk? Then look at this. I'll motel you, but nobody's going to pay anybody. We'll be equals, grownups. Bad girl is big girl now? Okay, then, act your age."

Suddenly I felt good, off the hook of countertransference. I was laughing inside. The playing-out of my banging rage took the blood out of Boytchik and we both settled down. He cooled off, still fat as a Hygrade salami. The doctor was safe from transgression. But he knew he was on the right track. Reverse psychology, that's what Mrs. X. needed. Paradigmatic strategy, it was being called now.

How cornered, how desperate and frightened Mrs. X. must be! All that psychic thrashing about. And that Jew-baiting! He did not die on the Cross for that shit! That was not good for anybody. I would "join" Mrs. X. as those who worked with disturbed adolescents did. Crowd her. Parrot her. "Jews smell, don't they? Chagall is crazy. He draws people upside down. Colonial furniture is better. Jews are interested only in money. And sex. Don't forget sex. Morning, noon, and night. Sex! Sex! Sex!"

Mrs. X.'s hour was up and more. The temptress was at the door, batting her baby-blue eyes. But no good-bye.

She knows the rules. Twenty-four hours' notice and we are quits. But she will come, week after week, bringing her awful love-hate like homework, until she graduates from Siggy's school, oral, anal, genital, and goes out to have a "love affair with the world." If she did not, she would be locked in the closet of her neurosis for the rest of her life. "The Lord is my shepherd. He maketh me lie down in the closet. . . . ."

I locked mine against the patients of the world. It was Yom Kippur, wasn't it? I was feeling very Jewish. *"Boruch atah adonay, melech ho aylum* . . . Blessed be Thou, O Lord our God, King of the Universe, for Thou hast made the fruit of the vine." I remembered that from Passover.

There was no Manischewitz handy, so I knocked back a couple of shots of Canadian Club, taking them straight as my Grandpa Avrom used to do. I became a patriarch under my very eyes. I didn't have a moustache or a silver comb, but I wiped my lips and made a grunt to show *them* who was boss around here!

I remembered that at sunset on the Day of Atonement, you were supposed to cast your sins upon the waters. The mighty Hudson flowed beneath my window. There was a raised walk along it where Jay used to tricycle. Mike, the Irish elevator man, took me down. Harry, the Jewish one, was observing the high holiday.

I walked through Riverside Park. Mrs. X. was right. Jewish ladies coming from temple were wearing mink coats. Their husbands wore hats. Their sons wore white yarmulkes embroidered with Stars of David. It occurred to me that Jay had not been Bar Mitzvahed.

For that, for getting a hard-on during a session and for a hundred other culpabilities, I went to the river's edge and threw my sins, mentally, out among the grotesque offal of condoms drifting out to sea, the great *Yom,* and into the mouth of Leviathan spinning the world with his evil tail.

· 31 ·
The Father Hen

All analysts, Freudian or not, take their vacations in August. This was when the Old Man had gone to the mountains and once, on his famous *Italienische Reise,* to Rome where he had discovered the agoraphobia he could not cure. If you can't get your act together by August, you have to come back after Labor Day. Your appointment is already down in your doctor's Week-at-a-Glance.

Jay was about ten when we began to go to the tax-deductible international congresses of Siggy's heirs. Our first voyage began in bombed-out Cologne where only the cathedral was not new and neon and all the street cleaners looked like stormtroopers. I tried to recover the abandoned German of Clinton High and Chapel Hill. *"Frisch weht der Wind die Heimat zu/Wo eilest du mein Irisch Kind . . ."*

We rented a Ford Taunus to be dropped off in Paris and headed south for a swing through Italy and around the Ligurian Riviera to Provence and Arles—"Next week the ear!"—and up the Route Nationale 7 to the Left Bank where I had a date with the Lost Generation.

It was on the Autobahn some place near Heidelberg—he riding with his head poked out of the sunroof—that Jay's Brooklyn Dodgers cap blew off and away forever. It was on the Autobahn, too, that we saw those signs that asked: "Have you gone wrong? *Falsch gegangen?*" They gave you a second chance to get off before you ended up in Auschwitz.

And it was on this trip that we first saw Venice. We had arrived for a *festa* of incredible fireworks. We watched from the steps of the Redentore Church built by Palladio to mark the city's salvation from plague. Even Kiddy did not dream that she would one day be living right next door.

Ten more years would pass before we exiled ourselves. By that time, Kiddy and I were picking quarrels as monkeys pick lice from each other's hair. *Falsch gegangen?* Where did we go wrong?

Between us there were now too many touchy subjects. "If you are not with me, you are against me." Even when I thought we were on the same side, we were not.

"You've changed. God, how you've changed!"

Changed? What the fuck! I hadn't changed a thing except my underwear. Kiddy, too. She wears those black things like Sophia Loren, a lift here and there. But she doesn't really need it. No getting around it. She was a beauty. Is now. Her skin still glows with that Post-Impressionist pink and her good legs, always ready for the Lindy Hop, taper into her thighs, softer now, weighted a little like a Maillol, her girlish mons just touched with fuzz to show where it is, her wisp still the color of a new penny. She should take a sample from down there to her hairdresser, Carlo di Roma. After being shaved to deliver our only child, the little mound of Kiddy's sex was never fully covered again. One, just one *bambino*. Salpingogram. Thermometer. Now! Now! In a river of gism, one swimmer, breaststroke with tiny fingernails . . .

Kiddy loved Jay so much she had no room left in herself for occasional displeasure with him. She oscillated between adulation and masochistic repudiation. I knew something about this process. Luckily, Jay was an even-tempered kid to whom things came easily. It seemed to me he understood his parents' needs better than they did. Before his adolescence, I can't recall too many times that he rocked the boat. I usually protected him.

"You hover over him like a father hen."

"Mother hen."

"*I'm* his mother."

In our home, you needed a scorecard to tell the players. But a blind man could see Kiddy was "moving toward, against, and away" from all of us who were not giving her the kind of confirmation she thought she deserved. She collected injustices, too, often like the girl in the fairy tale who is under an evil spell. Kiddy was desperate for love and it did not help that I was professional now and thought in terms of etiology and dynamics of personality. Everybody's but my own. In Freudian circles, they were talking about "womb envy." Is that what I had?

Jump cut—as they say in Hollywood. In the austere little auditorium of MOMA, Vernon and Irene Castle danced the Bunny Hug; Pavlova's wings broke the air for the last time; the Swan died. Joan Crawford did the Charleston for Saturday's children in party hats. Bojangles tapped with Shirley Temple. Martha Graham beat her breast. The Lindy Hop, the Shag, the Suzy-Q. On film, we have danced our way into our own time.

"Weren't those old shots marvelous?" Kiddy asked our only child. "And the Big Band era?"

He was accustomed to answering questions that should have been addressed to me.

Mom and Dad and Jay moved up the raked steps. From above, an expensively suited matron who looked like the president of the League of Women Voters was coming toward me. Was she a former patient? I belonged to the school that did not use that word, nor did I often employ the couch. Still, these vertical encounters were awkward.

"Mike Majority!"

No analysand this. She has called me by a name not many know, one of several pseudonyms I once used on the populist newspaper I dropped out of college to run. Mike Bolshevik, it meant.

"Sally?" I hesitated. It had been, after all, twenty years, give or take a missed menstrual cycle, since I had seen her.

Sally didn't hesitate. I remembered her being that way, always direct and without airs. She supplied her married name. I introduced her to Kiddy and Jay and she presented her husband, much taller than Sally, a kind of Abe Lincoln before the beard.

"What a nice surprise!"

Sally's voice recalled my past to me as a soldier is reminded of an old wound on a rainy day. Not even Kiddy knows more than a few nostalgic yarns of those times. My buried devotion to the Movement is—without her knowing it—the sticking point of our conflict about what she calls politics. Kiddy may be right when she says I have changed. The *Movimiento* had been my big truth. And, as far as I was concerned, it had been, without argument, betrayed. I believed now only in dissidence.

"You haven't changed a bit." Not to Sally.

I had and I had not. It was a left-handed compliment which I returned.

"You too."

We walked out into the corridor of Expressionist posters. *Metropolis, M, Die Blaue Engel.* I lit Sally's cigarette. And Sally, as she talked through the smoke, waved the present away with one hand. *Special effects by Slavko Vorkapich.*

We are in bed, each resting on an elbow, her short legs with those javelin thrower's thighs bent into mine like a Pompeian couple made stone. Her tickling mons presses against my emptied scrotum. Sally reaches over for the jelly-jar ashtray, her breast massages my shoulder. We are just returning from the solitude of two bodies made one, getting our minds back from nullity. It is, as Proust said, the beginning of the world with only the two of us alive.

"I like this part best of all," Sally always said.

Did she still? She was looking awfully efficient, a bit of a ball-breaker. At the university, she had the figure and style of what my mother used to call a *balabusteh,* the housewife competent in all departments. But where once Sally had looked older than her twenty years, she now looked younger than her forty. She had grown nicely into the severe suit and fluffy blouse.

"If you don't look after yourself, who will?"

That's what she had said to me. And in giving herself to me, she had been looking after herself. Technically, she was not a virgin. But her experience with a man she was supposed to marry had been weird. He was older than Sally, an accountant. Getting married was in his budget and he was ready to settle down. He gave Sally an engagement ring.

"A solitaire, a karat and a half."

The fellow seemed normal. After all, he was a CPA. He was very clean and he wanted Sally to be very clean, too. He explained to her the categories of cleanliness. There was, for example, foot category. If your feet touched the floor you must not put them on the sheets. There was also hand category, what your hand could or could not touch if it touched something else. He would only touch Sally through her panties. He did not want her to touch him. That was penis category. He masturbated until he was hard, making Sally watch and say all the dirty words she knew. Then he put on two condoms, closed his eyes, and took her virginity. Sally thought perhaps she was inexperienced and naive. When he told her that his mother still scrubbed his back and dried him after a bath, she gave back the solitaire and ran.

With me, Sally went to bed freely, without fuss or flattery. The only restriction she placed on our intimacy was that it be private—there were always those two empty brass beds beside us—and that I get her back to the dorm early. She thought Albuquerque was spooky.

"They roll the streets up at night," she said. "And those John Wayne *shaygetzes* give me the *kein ahora*." It was nice to have a girl friend who could talk about drugstore cowboys giving you the evil eye.

So Jim Howard saw more movies in those few weeks than he'd ever seen in his whole life. I gave him money, this pesky kid brother, to make himself scarce. The Organizer liked Westerns. His retellings in a mixture of Marxism and put-on hillbilly wonderment, were worth the price of the show and a pint of whiskey to boot. Somehow, the bad guys—whether they knew it or not—were always on the side of the Revolution.

The first time, Sally and I were too carried away to undress. We necked until neither of us had any shame, then managed a rude coupling that committed us, at least, to intimacy. The next time, flushed and ready, Sally held back just long enough to ask me to put a pot of water to boil on our kerosene stove.

"I'll want to douche," she said. "Penis category, you know!"

Naked, Sally looked very young. She had a practical body with a high, hard bosom and a strong muscle of belly. When I was with her, I often thought of Ella. Does one ever forget that first kindness? But Sally did not have Ella's savannahs of skin, or line of gab. Sally did not parade herself. She jumped under the covers quickly, fell naturally into the female supine position. Her knees made a tent into which I crept like the Sheik of Araby.

Sally was always moist and open. Our thrusts at each other would grow rapid and we would come always, more or less, together. No wild blue-movie lip synch, just that arching and reaching and Sally saying to herself, to me, to the whole world, "Oh, good! Oh, good!"

Sally talked a lot about anthropology. If she could only do fieldwork! That was her dream. To be like Clyde Kluckhohn! We loved that name. He had studied Navajo toilet training. They let the kids make *kaka* wherever they wanted.

"Can you picture the streets of Milwaukee?" Sally would ask.

I invented the slogan, "Curb your child!" We sometimes said

this to each other, a private joke.

All this came back to me as we stood there before a poster that showed Marlene Dietrich in a top hat and Emil Jannings drooling over her plump thighs. I had an urge to say, "Clyde Kluckhohn! Curb your child!" But there were too many husbands and wives around.

Sally wanted to know what I did for a living. I was almost ashamed to say. But she was impressed, as people were more likely to be in those days. She made a half-mocking little "Ooooh!" I was glad she was not like those innocents at parties who tell you, "I bet you're seeing right through me!"

I mentioned my paperback, *Varieties of Sexual Behavior*. And Sally said, "You?" rather archly and I wondered what Kiddy and Abraham Lincoln thought.

"I'm still in early childhood," she said smartly. She taught preschoolers. "I guess that's where I belong. And your poems?"

She hadn't forgotten. I used to read them to her sometimes in that postcoital glow in which anything sounds better than it is.

It was a good time for me to be asked. I was awaiting, just then, a decision from an editor who had written me, "I want to read your poems again. I like them. But I can't make up my mind whether they are too funny to be sad or too sad to be funny."

"Is that bad? It's two for the price of one." Sally was a Yiddishe mama, knew a bargain when she saw one.

She remembered Jim Howard. "He used to call me Sis. Imagine."

"And your friend? The good-looking Italian boy? Still out there?"

Yes, Nick is out there. "O lost, and by the wind grieved, ghost come back again." Way out there and forever, in the little cemetery of Placitas, at the edge of Albuquerque, where we ate the hottest chili cakes wrapped in dough like Haman's hats, and the men of *La Liga* slapped us on the back to give us back our tongues. Yes, not far from the concrete irrigation canal, the Big Ditch where we waited, pitchfork raised, for the silver streak of trout, always missing, the prongs stabbing into the soft silt, the *compañeros* laughing at our city ways and showing us their own fish shimmying on the tines. And the brown, burned grass and some blue flowers I can't name climbing the stone slab that bears the flower of his name.

And so I told Sally what had happened to Nick Gardenia.

He did marry Consuela, the local girl who had defied everybody to go with him. He had been teaching, finishing a doctorate in esthetics, writing on some meanings of time. Had he known he had so little left?

The circumstances of Nick's death were so absurd, I had to tell them quickly. Nick needed to have a tooth pulled. He could not face it, asked for anesthesia. What sort of losing one's soul will save it forever? They put the mask over his face. Nick went under. He never came up.

"Oh, my God!" Sally shivered like a believer on whom God has turned His back.

I could not tell Sally or anybody else that I had not yet accepted the fact that Nick would not rise again as he had done so many times after the small oblivions of Booth's High and Dry.

We stood in that silence that comes when we refuse to say what everybody says and yet know nothing else to say.

But Sally was a *balabusteh*. She pulled herself back into the tasks of the day. They were eating at Sardi's and taking in the out-of-towner's show. They had to run.

"We're picking up our middle one."

I envied people who spoke so casually of "my middle one" or "my ten-year-old," as though they had a whole department store of posterity.

Jay had still been in diapers when, without any trying, Kiddy had become pregnant again. It did not go well. She stained, was ordered to stay on her back. But only Sophia Loren can stay in bed for nine months. The same rubber-gloved hand that had lifted our son into the light sent this new seedling into the dark. Kiddy had a curettage. She had wanted a little girl who would turn into a big girl, another Sarah Bernhardt, a Duse, a firebrand, Madame Kollontai in a long run on Broadway. Kiddy grieved. She, at least, had me to blame. I could not blame her uterus for not holding on to that miraculous speck that would become a little girl. Only once did I cry out, "Would she not have been my daughter, too? Didn't I lose a child, too?" Me, the father hen who would keep little half-chick under his wing even if the sky fell down!

Sally gave me her hand. Touching her sent a startling thrill through me. I used to kiss that hand sometimes, putting my lips along the palmist's life line, holding them there until their warmth reached Sally and she would take that hand and put it

against one breast, trying to put the exact center of the kiss
against her nipple.

Sally looked too composed to remember things like that.
And then she had turned for a good look, first at Jay and then
up at me. She was examining Jay, I thought, in a special way,
studying him like an aunt who is getting ready to ask, "Now,
whom does he resemble?"

"You know," Sally said, "I have a son who's going to be old
enough to vote this year."

Old enough to vote!

I was still no better at arithmetic than I had been at Avon
Avenue School. I couldn't do fractions. But I could add and sub-
tract to the time I was holding Sally's tidy ass in my hands and
shooting sticky darts at her cervix. "*I* have a son." she had said,
as though he were hers alone, no part of Honest Abe.

When we had been together, I had never given a thought to
contraception. Sally would ask me to close my eyes. First she
would put on her slip, then hop across the old ballroom and lave
her Mary Jane in the same tin tub in which the Organizer
washed his long johns, winter and summer. True, with Sally I
had never noticed the characteristic odor of spermicide and
sudation that goes with a diaphragm. There were many things I
had never noticed. I hadn't really known exactly what douching
did, but I assumed that a young lady so competent and collected
as Sally would know what she was doing.

After our trysts, we would stand in the light of the Palmas
Bar and wait for the bus to make its turn around Spanishtown
plaza. I would squeeze Sally's hand and say: *Mi corazon!* Sally
hadn't exactly been my heart. But I'd known enough to say
something romantic. I hadn't known enough to wear a condom.

Am I a phantom parent? Does Jay have a brother in Milwaukee? He would like that; he wouldn't be alone anymore.
Someday, perhaps, I will tell him. I would never tell Kiddy,
though. She is still grieving for what she is sure had been "a little
girl." I bite my tongue and let the lost child be hers alone. Like
Sally's son who is old enough to vote. Republican or Democrat?

But I have Jay. My small son, who takes in The Museum of
Modern Art and Ebbetts Field with the same bright curiosity,
looks up at me. He has pitcher ears. My heart jumps with love.
People say we are too close.

We will stay that way. He will keep that gentle innocence,

this side of the *nebbish*, Prince Myshkin in Berkeley, hard only in holding on to principle, going up against the riot squad with only his hair for a helmet.

And he will look at me this way, years later, when I am bereft, up to my ears in clay feet, almost a lush.

"Dad," he will say, "you smell like one of those bars on Seventh Avenue. The Blarney Stone."

And his precise naming of a soggy corned-beef-and-cabbage-shot-of-Four-Roses-for-fifty-cents kind of place makes me pull him to me, right there on the street. He will push me off, lightly, laughing himself.

And he will put me, lovingly, into his first novel—a garrulous, tippling, world-weary psychoanalyst named Dr. Pepper.

· 32 ·
The Key to Paradise

"Everybody's family seems happy except one's own!"

Nobody asked me about mine. I did not have the distance of Tolstoy's observation to comfort me. By profession I was a scavenger in the detritus of many marriages. Each working day, I poked into urine-stained mattresses looking for lost wedding rings; turned over piles of dented pots on the chance of finding the lost rent money; wandered among stacks of practically never worn shoes, the Sunday clothes of dead men finally discarded by ambivalent widows; kicked at sentimental objects, teddy bears, pillows that brought greetings from Atlantic City and exposed artifacts, whirling douches, polyurethane breasts, dildoes. This vast dump, like the one under the Pulaski Skyway that goes to my hometown, smoldered, broke into flame on windy nights when the sparks of Eros blew across the cattail swamps.

Kiddy and I lived at its edge. We had the Eames chair, the Saarinen table, the Barcelona bench, but ours had become a rag-and-bone house. Everything shiny, unused as in a museum. Purpose over, an empty nest.

The Bluebird of Happiness—who was really a freckle-faced boy with large ears and dreaming eyes—had hopped from the twig of nursery school, tried his first songs in the grades, his wings on Park Avenue dates ("Dress British! Think Yiddish!"), and flown away into a cloud of marijuana smoke and mace.

Jay had taken himself three thousand miles away to an experimental college that was so small it had only a mininuclear reactor buried near its soccer field. This was supposed to be "a community of scholars" and run by them. But its black students—all three of them—had asked for their own thing, and suddenly Trustees came out of the woodwork and academe had split like the atom.

We visited the campus, arriving in the evening, and found a Che Guevara banner hanging from Jay's window and a note on his dormitory door saying he was at an SDS meeting in the chapel. We found a hairy crowd there listening to Mark Rudd, who was fielding questions like Willie Mays, shoestring and over the shoulder. The question period was cut short for a mock wedding that had been scheduled by the opposing faction. They came in with candles and Gregorian chant. The Weatherpeople left.

A kid wearing a pair of mechanic's overalls from Wheels & Deals, Elk Grove, California, came toward us. His pants were too short and you could see he was not wearing socks inside his chukka boots. He had grown a sort of beard. Over the pocket where there should have been a pair of pliers the name George had been stitched in red.

But he couldn't fool me. It was Jay, all right. He'd let his mother kiss him. I'd slapped him on the hand, giving skin, and said, "What's shakin', my man?"

"The whole world, Dad!"

Including his parents.

Kiddy and I were, by that time, living among the shards of our own early history. I would find her rummaging through a shoe box of old snapshots. There she would find us on our honeymoon under a Miami Beach palm tree, me in my Humphrey Bogart period, she in Lauren Bagel bathing suit made out of what looked like a spiderweb of string.

But mainly the snaps were of our Jay—in his crib, taking his first steps, in his costume as Dick Deadeye in *HMS Pinafore,* and, suddenly, with a moustache and hair down to his shoulders, looking like the mad monk Rasputin.

After a year Jay had left that Halloween campus, but stayed in California to live the alternative life. He was not quite a Weatherman, but he was very serious about changing his world, as I had been, and Kiddy still was, about ours.

When Nixon had come to New York and the SDS, driven from the Waldorf, took to trashing Saks Fifth Avenue, Kiddy had been there, grabbing a cop's nightstick, screaming, "Don't hit him! He's my son!" Her real son was a continent away testing his head against the billies of Berkeley's Blue Meanies.

I admired her. But . . .

"But me no buts! I hope they broke every window in your favorite store!"

There were no buts in Kiddy's religion. I bought my shoes at Saks—they were the only ones who carried 12A. Still, when we went there, Kiddy could not resist looking for a Pucci on the clearance rack.

"White wine is poison for the Red soldier!" I dragged out a Bolshevik slogan.

"Some soldier!" Kiddy answered.

That reminded Kiddy of Jay and the Draft.

"No son of mine is going to Viet Nam!" She said it as though his father were George Babbitt.

I held my tongue, geared myself to seeing Jay in jail or exile. I pictured the kid, not the cause.

"What's happened to you?" Kiddy railed.

Against me there was directed an unrelenting appeal to be what I used to be. Kiddy was a great sentimentalist, a dangerous one.

"You don't remember. You've changed so!"

I remembered too damn well. I would happily have turned back the clock, knew just where I would have pointed its hands. There was that moment of truth when I had been asked to go to Spain with the International Brigade to be in what became the last war of hope. The best I could do now was hang, like Harold Lloyd, on the giant hands of a skyscraper clock, trying comically to pull myself back before I fell—splat!—into the void of lost enthusiasm.

Kiddy and I were riding in those Luna Park electric cars, striking sparks from a steel saucer, bumping each other, making mock accidents, and pretending that the cruel hickies we made— mainly around the heart—did not hurt.

Kiddy was becoming increasingly restive. She hid her disappointments about her acting career under a righteous repudiation of Broadway and its people. As always, there was a grain of truth in her denunciations.

"Would you rather be a hit in a shit? Or a shit in a hit?"

Kiddy wanted fame but on her own unyielding terms. Laurie Golden was one of the few people who had met her tests. She had risen not on the shoulders of others but on a wave of social history. Her politics, if not perfect, were good enough. We were watching Laurie on the *Dick Cavett Show.*

"Your little bird . . ."

I felt Kiddy looking at me. A quarter of a century and she still gives me that look!

"Are you sorry?"

I had felt this coming. About Laurie, Kiddy was Chekhovian, played a what-might-have-been game. She was using a small, coy voice that drove me into myself. I'd be damned if I would answer. Not that I was sorry. If anything, I believed that the Laurie of today and the world she lived in was not for me. But Kiddy and I had been having problems. I was ashamed that I should, indeed, at this moment be thinking—or at least feeling something—along the lines that Kiddy thought I was thinking.

"Call her up!" Kiddy was saying over the soundtrack of my memories. "She's divorced."

The television was off. Laurie had broken up into electronic blips.

"Well, are you sorry? You didn't answer."

Laurie was out there someplace in the dark. Kiddy and I were left in the light of her third degree.

"For crying out loud!"

I suppose she wanted me to take her in my arms and tell her I had never had any regrets. I could have said that without telling a lie. I could have said truly that I had never, up to this minute, been sorry. It always happened this way. When I had to propitiate, I became stubborn. Nor had it occurred to me that Kiddy could ever be sorry she had given up her returning soldier for me. Her former husband was running one of Hollywood's big talent agencies. "Stick with me and you'll be wearing diamonds!" Kiddy did not want diamonds. She wanted love, or something by that name which would bind the bleeding ends of her ambivalent being-in-the-world.

"All the other girls are jealous of you!"

Kiddy's mother had told her this so many times, she had become all those other girls. Kiddy was jealous of everything she felt she did not have. She contradicted the Gemara which says, "A woman is jealous only of another woman's thigh." With the illogic of the sentimentalist, she had pushed aside the plain chronology that I had lain with Laurie before I had lain with her, had given up what I had known with Laurie for what I had not known with her.

"Some people think I'm not so bad. In fact, they think I'm great."

Touch someone and you hurt someone!

"Whozzat?"

Her demons had spoken and mine were answering. I gave the obligatory response to a double bind. It would have been insulting to pretend indifference and it was painful for me to ask.

"So and So!"

So and So outdid Laurie as a Well-known Person.

Kiddy's confession had embarrassed us both. We went to bed. Usually, Kiddy waited for me to approach her. I knew that Kiddy would want me tonight, proof she had won me from my Well-known Person and that she had chosen me over hers. Suddenly I was hornier than the Pope's tomcat. I wasn't sorry about a goddamn thing.

But tomorrow is another day. And tomorrow. And tomorrow.

I was uneasy with Kiddy's demand for a blank check on which any sum of love would be written. Who cared if it bounced? My new role as healer of minds did not help. I could not close my eyes to Kiddy's insatiability. I knew it sometimes went beyond handling. And Kiddy suspected this.

"I can see what you're thinking."

"Kiddy . . ."

"Don't Kiddy me. You're not my therapist."

I wasn't. And there were no rules and regulations to keep me from taking her in my arms, holding her even if she pushed me away. But the bell to my office would ring. My first patient of the day, a surgeon whose wife had just become a Christian Scientist, would arrive. I would swallow the last of the Zabar's coffee filtered in the Chemex and go in to hear more of man's small-time inhumanity to man.

I was beginning to feel pretty much like that "beast of burden" to which Freud compares himself in a letter to Havelock Ellis. I saw myself as the milkman's horse of my childhood, waiting in the shafts for the next bag of oats and the next kick in the ribs.

Kiddy and I bickered. To outsiders it seemed to be over nothing, but we knew it was about everything. To them it sounded like crying over spilled milk, but we knew the stuff was blood. They took each of us aside separately, urged tolerance of the intolerable, including our failed gods.

"You and your Solzhenitsyn!" His revelations about the Gulag Archipelago tortured Kiddy.

"Go, go watch your Johnny Carson!" My anodynes tortured her.

"You're dying and you don't know it!" Cassandra's clairvoyance tortured her most of all. Neither of us knew how close to the truth her angry words had hit.

Kiddy seemed already to be in mourning. Something had been lost. Something had to be found. But what? But how? But where?

And then, as though a scenarist had been holding this plot twist up his sleeve, Kiddy had a windfall. The backwash of a Broadway hit put some money in our bank. One reality consideration was removed. Take the money and run! We would quit the rat race. Venice, that never-never land we both loved, would be the perfect place to go. Had not Le Corbusier called it the city of the future? It was a wild idea. Kiddy pressed it hard.

"Your neurosis will destroy us all!"

"Why don't you just say yes and see how fast my neurosis goes away?"

Kiddy's courage shamed me. In this bind of cowardly indecision, I turned mean, I scapegoated.

"You would be unhappy in Paradise," I said when I was cornered.

"That's right, call the men in the white coats. Go ahead and call them!"

I dreaded this end to reason from which there was no place to hide. We would fall into a pattern of searing silences, sleep in the same bed without exchanging a word. This would go on for days until some *deus ex machina*—a letter from Jay, the obituary of a friend or someone we both admired, the shared horror at seeing, on a TV screen, the running torch of a napalmed child, an antiwar protest march when we marched side by side, an extra drink that flooded our leaky dikes—would throw us back into conjugal contact.

One gets tired even of unhappiness. As some people live from hand to mouth, Kiddy and I lived from embrace to embrace. In their soft aftermath, I let her speak of Venice, perhaps led her on. I knew that we should be in another place, any place, where I did not have to watch the gates of Paradise closing in my face.

· 33 ·
Topless in Gaza

One day, I came home from the clinic where I supervised therapists-in-training and found a note from Kiddy. "There is no longer a might-have-been," it said. "Given my vulnerability and your temperament, the might-have-been could not have been. Could it? I have gone away. This is all I can say now."

Her note was perfectly placed on the page, each line justified as though poured from a Linotype, written in the flowing hand that had won the writer her penmanship prize at Clinton High. There was no salutation. And I knew why. Each word counted too much. The casual Dear or My Dear might be taken as an insult. Anything more intimate would be ambiguous, might be read as a weakening of resolve.

That plaintive "Could it?" turned me inside out. If I agreed, reconciliation would be doomed. If I protested, I would have to make some move to show how the might-have-been could still be. I looked for the answer in the bottom of a glass. I began to drink, knocking back one shot after another. My heart was pounding, missing on its cylinders like a jalopy with a bent piston.

My first impulse was to find Kiddy and bring her back. I thought of the friends with whom she might have sought shelter. Should I phone them? What would I say? There would be questions I could not face. And what if Kiddy had already changed her mind? I was convinced that she would come back as soon as the circle of her desperation came around again to where it began in our confused love and need for each other. She might call. It happened sometimes that a rash act steadied her.

The phone did not ring. I was getting drunk. I carried my glass from room to room like a man looking for misplaced keys that are in his hand all the time. Anger and pity hammered me, setting up a great din through which I heard Kiddy crying my name, calling for help. I began to answer her, the words almost out of my mouth before I realized I was talking to myself. This is how it happens, I thought, how you go crazy. And I remembered with great shame that the last words I had spoken to Kiddy had been, "You're crazy! And you're driving me crazy!"

I had to do something that would immediately take me away from the life I had spoiled. I wanted to be someplace where there were no childhood sweethearts. I knew where that was. I took a cab down Broadway, stopped the driver at a topless bar. The last time I had been at the Metropole, down-on-their-luck jazzmen had been faking their way through Dixieland. Now, four girls with glittering stars pasted on their nipples were bumping around in front of a mirrored runway in back of the long bar. They were young, with pretty faces and bodies good enough to get this job. Why weren't they all married to psychoanalysts?

Maybe I was missing something. I wasn't seeing too good. I was eyeless in Gaza. The dancers had dollar bills tucked into their G-strings. If you offered one, a girl would dance in front of you, for you alone, bending back and shaking her coo in your kisser. The mirror that showed her buttocks harden as she rolled her jelly, showed me the face of a sap. I lasted through one CC on the rocks before shame and disgust drove me out.

It was still light in the street—the long summer dusk of Manhattan, the asphalt cooling, the air etherized for dark entertainments. I was sobering but I did not want to go home. Kiddy would not be there. Without her, I would not know when to go to bed or when to wake up, what shirt to wear, whether to eat or what. I would not shave. I would go into mourning, the Orthodox way, sitting *shiva* on an orange crate, my sleeve ritually rent, all mirrors draped or turned to the wall. I would face the east and rock. "*V'yiskadal, v'yiskaddash . . .*" I knew only these opening words. I did not know what they meant. The Hebrew religion was a father-son thing. I was not sure you were permitted to say Kaddish for a woman, for your own wife. Women were unclean. *Oi!* I would leave the world and learn how to pray. I would scotch-tape a sign to my office door: Closed on Account of Confusion in the Family. Or, maybe: Patient, Heal Thyself!

I found myself in front of a big adult bookstore and peep-show, really more of an emporium, a department store of sex. The window showed an assortment of torpedo-shaped vibrators. Among them a waxy replica of the real thing, engorged, a facsimile even to some blue, swollen veins, looked old-fashioned and false. Its tip pointed to a book I had lately been offered in the lurid mail that came sometimes to members of the Society for the Scientific Study of Sex. It was an anthology of *Your Old-Time Favorite Little Dirty Comic Books.* The collage on the cover had Mutt and Jeff with their pants down, Maggie hitting Jiggs with a rolling pin while he is in *flagrante* with the maid, and Tillie the Toiler taking dictation while giving head.

This was a pointed time to find Tillie, that hot, googly-eyed porno steno. I had a great desire to look again on those India-ink office orgies by which the Badger Street gang had been instructed in vice.

"Hey! Shtuppeninnatush!"

"G'wan! Yuhmuddascallinyeh!"

How old were we? Nine? Ten? Tillie was my real childhood sweetheart.

I went in, passing a sign that said "Be 18 or Be Gone." The sex shop was long and narrow. In front of each of some fifty peep machines along its walls, there was a man bent like a scientist looking for a Nobel Prize. As soon as one finished, another took his place. Quarters falling into slots made the room sound like a blacksmith's shop. After looking, the men pretended they had seen nothing at all. They went to the changer for more quarters. They looked angry. Misogyny was eating them up.

I went to the books and magazines on whose covers every prick, cunt, asshole, and stuffed mouth was covered by a black square. No payee, no peekee! Originally the dirty comics had been the size of a boy's hand, easy to hide in the pocket of your first pair of long pants. This new compendium was oblong and an inch thick. I picked it up. I wanted to see Tillie sitting on the edge of her desk, chewing Spearmint and puffing up her shingle while the office boy buried his head in her twat. But the book was sealed, hot-wrapped in cellophane. It cost six dollars, which used to be a month's rent. For this I had grown up and become a man?

I staggered out. A hophead whore in hot pants bumped me and asked, "Going out?" It frightened me that in a single hour of bachelorhood she had already recognized me as a John. I turned from the girl, pretended she had made a mistake. She hadn't. Misery loves company. I could be turned. I was a trick like everyone else in pants.

The chippy moved from me to a gibbering, toothless grandfather. She bargained with him. And they went off, she walking in front of him, he calling amorous nonsense at her back. She was ashamed of her customer. And I was ashamed that I did not have his manic honesty.

"I'm gonna bite yer tomato!" the old guy was calling out.

The girl was wearing a halter. Between her thin back and adolescent legs the red satin shorts she wore were pulled into her tootie. It did look like a Jersey tomato. And I saw with horror that there were many little hematomas on her arms and thighs. Someone was beating the shit out of her. She was about the same age Kiddy was when we had had our first date.

I was sober now, sick with my peculiar, private pox. I cabbed home. The driver was a young Israeli who thought he was too good to be pushing a hack. He said he had been a tankist in the Six Day War. Now he was going to become a psychiatrist. I gave him an outrageous tip.

I saw Kiddy's valise as soon as I came in the door. My heart jumped.

"Kiddy! Kiddy!"

I was happier than a lost child in the police station. I wanted to hold her in my arms and tell her that, but she had locked herself in the bedroom. I heard her, between heaving sobs, call out with the voice of a Dybbuk, "Mama, mama, take me with you. I can't stand it any more."

"Kiddy! Kiddy!"

I pounded at the door as though I were resuscitating an arrested heart.

But the heart that had stopped was my own.

· 34 ·
Intensive Care

I woke up the next morning on the couch in my waiting room where one divorcing couple usually sat looking away from each other and hating the classical music from WQXR which was always on to drown out the recriminations of another divorcing couple inside, having their last licks while I refereed the bout.

Whomp! The Gestapo—or maybe it was the deputy sheriffs in Gallup, New Mexico—had me down and were lacing me across the shoulder blades with some kind of long billy club. Whomp! Each time it came down it felt as if the world had caved in and I had come out through the other side of the pile and ended up in the same place.

I was fully dressed—shoes, suit, necktie. I'd slept in my clothes. I remembered that I'd been drinking. Some trouble with Kiddy. I was in the doghouse.

Whomp! Getting kicked in the balls was what it was like. "Foul! Foul!" Except it felt as if my balls were hanging from my throat and were the size of grapefruit and each time—whomp! —it was $E = MC^2$.

I stood up. The room tilted but I didn't pass out. I sat down. Sitting or standing, it made no difference. I was clubbing myself black and blue, from the inside out, with every breath. I did not know what was hurting me this way but I was angry at it, so angry I thought I could fight it off. I was sure it had something to do with Kiddy and I wanted to fight her, too. Stand on my own two feet. Get rid of both of them. They weren't giving me a chance, coming at me out of left field, the shit hitting the fan when you're just minding your own beeswax and wouldn't harm a fly.

Where was Kiddy? Of all the unforgivable things we had to forgive each other, this distance between us at the instant of my infarct stayed as a secret Mason-Dixon line, on one side forgiveness, on the other revenge. But if Kiddy had broken my heart, she could also mend it. I began the short walk to her in the nuptial chamber from which I had been barred. The weight on my chest was so heavy I was bent over like Lon Chaney in *The Hunchback of Notre Dame*. Kiddy wasn't sleeping. She was wearing a black nightgown, and sick as I was, I realized she had been waiting for me to come to her. Though we'd been married for twenty years, she pulled the covers over her breasts. She was looking at me with the fear and longing of a spinster school-teacher meeting the deflowerer of her dreams.

"Something bad is happening," I said. "Get a doctor."

Those were the first words I had spoken to her in days, but at once I saw on her face that she would give her life to save my own.

But you never do get a doctor—you get his Service. Kiddy kept trying. She didn't want to lose her childhood sweetheart. I took her hand and we were back in Flamingotown, for better and for worse, in Blue Cross and Blue Shield, until the Liberty Mutual Assurance Company did us part.

Kiddy remembered a refugee doctor around the corner. It was eight in the morning but he told us to come immediately. Kiddy pulled off the nightgown and stepped into some jeans. I saw how her breasts still fell outward, round and pink. I wasn't dead yet.

The doctor was wearing a short-sleeved sport shirt that didn't cover his concentration-camp number. He took one look at me and gave me a shot of morphine from a syringe that was big enough to dope all the horses in the sixth race at Aqueduct.

"You are a lucky fellow," the good doctor said.

It seemed that the odds on making it to his office without fibrillating had been five to one.

"A real lucky fellow," the doctor said again.

And seeing that tattoo on his arm, I thought that maybe I was.

In the Checker cab to the hospital, Kiddy sat with her arm around me and begged the cabby to make time. He was an old-timer and he did.

"Mark my words," the hackie said, "you'll dance yet at your children's wedding." His grammar was lousy but his heart was in the right place.

I ended up in Intensive Care. For three days the monitor's skittering blip became the most important part of me. It bounced up and down like the little white ball over the words on the screen during a sing-along at Fox's Cameo Theater on Belmont Avenue in Newark. I was waiting to find out if Pearl White had fallen into the Grand Canyon last Saturday.

When they finally wheeled me back to my room and I was alone and alert for the first time, I shuffled out of bed and walked the few feet to the bathroom. I went peepee standing up, holding Boytchik familiarly in my hand. Then I shaved, dolled myself up. Nobody had told me I shouldn't because half my heart was shot. When the doctor discovered what I had done, he raised holy hell. "You're committing suicide!" he yelled. I hadn't realized that, for the moment, I was a living corpse.

"Dad?" Jay was calling from Berkeley. "Dad?"

In that one word was all the love a man would ever need. That little question mark carried all the grammar of existence.

"I'm okay, Jay. Just relaxin' at the Camarillo."

Jay laughed. Camarillo was the hospital in California where "Mezz" Mezzrow and later Charlie Parker had gone to get their heads straight.

"Dad, you're nuts!" Jay said, and everything became copacetic.

My father came. "Smoking! Inhaling! Blowing through your nose like a chimney!" I was fifteen again, just starting to shave, caught with a pack of Camels I had taken from the pocket of the old man's other suit. When nobody was looking, I had myself a good, long cry.

But I continued to be a bad boy, sneaking out of bed. "Pishee, pishee!" I was not going to be a baby again. I convinced the doctor that, in my particular psychological case, it would be more strain on me to be bedpanned. He sent up a mobile potty I never used.

But I could not escape a flirty Puerto Rican nurse's aide who washed my privates a little too deftly. She was about forty, fleshy and brash. She was tawny and her heft showed like a shadow through her nylon uniform. When she bent, I could see two coconuts in the cups of a black bra. She was like the nun in the classic porno film who comes to an assignation in her wimple but on stiletto heels, and gives head.

"Lookee, lookee," my burlesque nurse said as my little rascal stirred. "Don' worry. Joo gon' use him pretty soon now." I was willing.

I blushed so hard I broke into a rash from the neck down. There was no other explanation. My prick was flaming. The Hot Tamale powdered it with cornstarch, getting her tropical fingers under the scrotum, lifting my blistered cock to the light. Her hand felt like a butterfly wing.

"Oi, oi, oi," she was always saying, "joo got it bad." She dandled the itchy member. "My boyfren', he's circonsize. It's more healthy. And joo know . . ." She actually rolled her eyes and smacked her lips.

Ah yes, I would have other duties to perform in another bed. Would I be able? The veteran call girl who was my patient specialized in old men who came to her regularly once a month. Her great worry was that one of them would die during whatever weird act they paid her to perform.

I dreaded the thought of being an invalid. Six weeks in a Johnny coat was enough. The doctor told me to take some time off. I used the needs of my patients as an excuse to get right back to work. And only then did I realize how useful I had been to them. The Gentiles had prayed for me. The Jews swore they would never go to anybody else. The bitterest of them, a girl whose mother had committed suicide when she was born, who had always accused me of seeing the world through rose-colored glasses, now felt I had suffered enough to see things her way. "You're living in my world now," she said.

I did not realize it showed. Sitting with my patients, listening, listening, keeping rein on the transference, I sometimes had to hold myself steady in the saddle of the Eames chair. A sudden kick or flip-flop of the tired ticker put everything in the life-is-too-short department. It did not matter whether I was receiving love or hate. And I no longer had the patience to neutralize the boredom of stubborn neurotic reiterations. So much of this work depended on a balance between objectivity and vulnerability that carried with it no secret wish for gratification.

Kiddy now pressed the idea of Venice as a way of saving my life. Was I killing myself, as she claimed? I had never paid attention to my body; I didn't think I could do much about it now. Not even for Jay, who rebuked me. "The head! Always the head!" I could see this was his way of telling me to stick around.

I had to get away from New York and its fifty-minute hours. I suddenly dreaded the possibility of keeling over on the Seventh Avenue subway or of being found in the street like a broken package waiting for the Sanitation Department to call off its strike and haul me away.

In Venice, they will get you to the *ospedale* by gondola in a pinch, two gondoliers stroking the lagoon without a splash, racing as they would for a false silver trophy to hang in the bar of the Juventus football club. And if they lose the race, well, the gondola is already painted black and will be banked with carnations and roses and white-throated lilies and they will take you right to the little, tumble-down Jewish *cimitero* on the Lido and put you next to the Finzis from *The Garden of the Finzi-Contini*.

We booked passage on the old *Cristoforo Colombo*—cabin accommodations for us and first class for our Skye terrier in the kennel up in the ship's smokestack. On the day of our departure, the crew went on strike, Italian style, for twenty-four hours. Moored to the Fifty-second Street pier, we used our cabin as a hotel, went into town for an O'Neal hamburger, and spent our last night at Lincoln Center seeing *The Merchant of You Know Where*.

> Thou know'st that all my fortunes are at sea;
> Neither have I money, nor commodity
> To raise a present sum: therefor go forth;
> Try what my credit can in Venice do.

· VI ·
Sinking in Venice

· 35 ·
May Day and Other Days

"It's May Day today," Kiddy was saying. *"Primo Maggio!"*

"Yeah, all day," I said. "You marchin'?"

Since coming to Venice I had begun to talk like a Manhattan cabby, hanging on to America through lingo. Being away from home—exiled?—was Americanizing me. I was buying the Paris *Herald Tribune* just to look at the standings in the leagues. Reggie Jackson was mashing a lot of 'taters and Oakland was winning again.

"Why don't we speak Italian to each other?" Kiddy said. "It's the only way to learn."

"Or get yourself a local tootsie, like they say."

"Good idea," she said, not meaning it at all.

I did not want to talk Italian. I did not know how and I had too many things to say.

"You're making up for all the years of listening to others," Kiddy said. "You don't listen to anybody now."

High time! I thought but did not say.

Suddenly, as though on cue, we heard the *"Internationale"* being played by a big brass band. "Arise, ye prisoners of starvation. . . ." It was loud enough to get the sleepiest proletarian to rise and shine. That was no tinhorn band playing. From the sound of it we could have been in Red Square with all those intercontinental ballistic missiles trundling by the Politburo.

We ran to the window and threw open the shutters every Venetian keeps closed against bad vapors and second-story men. The music was coming from a baby buggy rigged up with speakers. A gray-haired man with the big hands of a stonemason was pushing the music in front of him as if it were a new grandchild. There was a turntable, I guessed, run by batteries. *Giradisco.* That was an Italian word I knew. The record playing was some kind of collection of songs of the people. I wondered if I would hear "Hallelujah, I'm a Bum!"

Our flat was on the corner of two small canals joined by a cast-iron bridge you would not find in any guidebook. I loved it. It reminded me of something you would find along the Lackawanna right-of-way crossing the Passaic. William Carlos Williams country. "Let me teach you, my townspeople, how to make a funeral . . ." Or make a parade. Coming over the *ponte* was a ragtag troop of companions—not comrades, that word had been sullied by Mussolini. In front of the kiosk that sold Motta ice cream, potato chips, and Coke, three or four activists were hawking the Communist newspaper. They carried the Word over their shoulders in cloth sacks stamped *L'Unita.* In their hands they held bunches of red carnations which they were giving to everybody whether they bought the paper or not. Kids in shorts and soccer shirts took the flowers by the stems and marched around in a circle holding them like flags. Oh, we were going to like Venice!

We muzzled our pooch—that was the law in Venice—and followed the music along the canal, up and down bridges and by the paving stones of the *fondamenta* into the Alley of the Nobles and to a sign that said *Sezione Che Guevara, PCI.* Pay chee eee. It was dark and cool inside. Fellows were drinking wine. They saw us and invited us in. *"Prego! Prego!"* First they admired the dog who was unique in Venice, saying *"Che bella!"* How beautiful! Only they said it *"Kay bayo!"* in Veneziano. "Masculine or bitch?" "And how is she called?" On her papers she was Petite Mite de la Termitière, but I called her Girlie. *Ragazza* in Italian. The companions thought that was *carina,* cute.

At once we were drinking the white wine called Tocai and talking to Roberto who was the *Segretario* and knew some English. There was a blackboard in the room with numbers on it. The Section was raising money for a new meeting hall. I pulled out a bill, not even looking, and Roberto began to write out receipts that were also raffle tickets. He gave me ten because they were only printed up in donations of a thousand lire. Everybody was impressed, including me. But it was only money.

By their standards, I suppose we were rich. They had no way of knowing we didn't have a pot to piss in or a window to throw it out. Kiddy and I had stopped thinking about things like that. "Seize the day!" We had sublet a flat in a new condominium built around a restored palace and a walled garden. The tenants were mainly well-heeled Milanese who had bought the apartments to use for weekends.

We were on the Giudecca, a long sandbar between the lagoon and the other islands of Venice. The Giudeccans were working people and some said they were a bad element. It was true that when a kid got picked up for breaking and entering he was likely to be from one of the squatter families who had taken over an abandoned convent behind us. Our ritzy joint was patrolled at night by a *portiere* who carried a gun. Our landlord was said to be the Pope.

The Giudeccans were a people apart. They were living in a kind of village where everybody had grown up with everybody else. Grandmothers called each other by the nicknames they had had in kindergarten. *"Ciao, Titi!" "Ciao, Nini!"* They were all very authentic. It was only three or four minutes by free ferry to the other side of the canal, that other place the Giudeccini called Venice.

Some people said Giudecca was where the first Jews of Venice had lived. But the word for Jew in Italian is *Ebreo*. There is no evidence of a synagogue. On old maps the sandbar is called Zuecca. I found out these things from my new friends—stonemasons, gondoliers, ex-footballers, printers. They called me *Dottore* and Kiddy *Professoressa* and forgave us for living in the Pope's condominium because we were *innocente* and American.

I had always worked and at many things. Now I was not allowed to work. I had just received a diploma from Washington that said I was officially disabled. *Totalmente.* Kiddy thought I should write a book. I came up with an idea for a canine cookbook, recipes for dog and master. We would try them out on Petite Mite and ourselves. I wasn't serious and I found out that it had already been done. I didn't need my name on another book. I would have been happier to write a decent sonnet.

Then we met Raymonda. She had lived in Venice for a long time, on a widow's budget now, but before always *prima classa*, the Gritti, the Danieli, and before that the Georges Cinq in Paris, the Madrid Ritz, Cuernavaca, Central Park South.

"Bread cast upon the waters," she said, "And, boy, have I cast!"

Raymonda was a painter. Like Mirra, she had studied at the League and then with Siquieros in Mexico. She painted generously, big canvases of seagulls against a hot orange sky that was the same color as the flames from the burn-off at the refineries where the sun set over the Serenissima.

Raymonda gave me some jars of poster color and sheets of brown wrapping paper.

"Just let yourself go," she told me. "Splash."

I did. I had caught onto something from watching Mirra in her studio, and in my head I had a microfiche of many museums. "Always paint what you can't paint," Braque had said. I was always in that position. By working hard and not being afraid, I began to come up with images that "stayed on the picture plane" and in the mind. I began by painting the laundry, the underwear of Adam and Eve, the baby socks of Cain and Abel, the black bras of Lilith, which hung on the lines of a Mussolini tenement I saw out of my window.

"These things are not for the eyes of everybody," an old maestro said.

And then Duke Ellington died. Nobody's passing, public or private, not even FDR's, had moved me like this. I was a long way from the A train but I rode it up to Harlem. I wanted to do something for the Duke. Across the top of a canvas I stretched the ebonies and ivories of a piano keyboard and then the burnt sienna gams of a high-kicking Cotton Club chorine.

It was good enough to exhibit. That's what the same maestro said. He spoke of its *semplicitá* and its *candore*. I did not know enough to be a fake. His own work in pierced shapes of rusting iron was, like the man himself, unremittingly severe. People were surprised when he offered me a wall in his next show.

These first months in Italy had turned me on. I was bursting with ideas and Venice was a good place to carry them out. For my show, I decided to do a portfolio of portraits accompanied by verse. I called it *May Day!* The exclamation mark meaning privately *M'aidez!* My SOS had been answered.

Pablo Neruda died just as the colonels seized Chile. I did him in a fisherman's cap and holding some flowers. "It happens that I am tired of being a man," he had written. *"Sucede que me canso de ser hombre . . ."*

And I did the late Pope Paul as a schoolboy against a background of his own handwriting from a penmanship exercise. *"Io amo, io amo, io amo . . ."*

I did Jay wearing an Oakland A's cap and called it *Christ in California.*

Kiddy got a new dress from Roberta di Camerino who had a little outlet place here that the Jewish ladies knew about. Roberta was one of their success stories. I had a neighboring bar bring in drinks and little sandwiches—that was the least I could do to repay the maestro—and we had an opening that reminded me of the Belasco Room over Sardi's but without the agony of waiting for the review in the *Times.*

I was admitted to a circle of painters, vaguely Surrealist, who showed together. Ten years older than Gauguin when he ran from the bank and his family, I had become a painter.

I worked furiously. Ten times a day, I called Kiddy to see what was on my easel. When it came together, I could not believe my own eyes.

"I've seen it," she would say. She had and she had not. Acrylics dry fast and the work would be transformed. Sometimes it would be completely new.

"I've got my own work," Kiddy began to protest.

Kiddy had come here as an ardent feminist. Her consciousness did not need to be raised. The Italian feminists were more political, more solidly rooted in the *donne* of all classes than their sisters in New York. Kiddy personalized, brought the banners of their street demonstrations into the kitchen, the parlor, the bath. She spoke often of "all men." All men were this, all men were that. She seemed to be separating herself from me. If women were "the slaves of slaves," Kiddy was going to be a boss.

Kiddy had become interested in the Ghetto, wanted to revive its moribund museum which had some great things, Renaissance menorahs and such, if you could see them. Money had to be raised. The Venetian Jews were giving theirs to Israel. They had good reason. Two hundred of them had never returned from the death camps. Kiddy and I went to a service at the synagogue at which their names were read out: Bassani, Anna; Bassani, Benno; Bassani, Arone . . ."

I went to artist hangouts now, when I was not painting away in the spare bedroom, busier than a one-armed paperhanger. My tape deck was always on. I had recorded a lot of stuff in New

York and carried the Sony across the Atlantic in my hand. I needed my daily fix of what the hip deejays were beginning to call Black Classical Music. I did not mind hearing Billie Holiday sing "I Cover the Waterfront" twice. Or thrice. Kiddy would call out to me to change the tune. I would put my brush in my mouth and grab another cassette. My favorites were beginning to look like a Kool-Aid paint job on a '59 Chevy hot rod. I managed to get some paint on the canvas, too.

Raymonda marveled. "Where did you get that sense of placement?"

I stuck my faces a little off center but somehow smack in the canvas. They *looked* at you. That was my thing, to get them looking at you and saying, "See any green?" It took me some time to realize that I had studied all this when I used to put my bathing beauties or the gold-toothed face of Hymie Bronf, the president of the bagel makers, into the columns of *The Baker*.

Kiddy was always urging me to study. "Why do you think they have schools? Actors have to learn technique. So do painters, I'm sure."

I could have told her I had studied with Mirra Leopold. We never spoke of her. In fact, Jay had discovered only by accident that both his parents had been married before. We had not intentionally kept it from him. It simply had never come up.

I knew that I had arrived at whatever art I had by finally throwing off the burden of shame. I had gotten here by my years, by secret ways that could not be taught.

Dinah Washington sang, "When I get myself together, I'll be a mean old so-and-so!"

I was getting myself together and it was throwing Kiddy. I didn't know how badly.

I painted hours at a stretch, sometimes forgetting to eat. Ironic, that I who had been on a treadmill had jumped off and landed on my feet. I was finding a new way to live. Kiddy was living on the credit she got for giving me the shove. The passage from Herald Square to San Marco had turned out to be harder for her. My new weight had shifted the balance of our neurotic interaction. Kiddy was caught in a bind. It was for my own good, wasn't it? Ambivalence was getting the better of her.

I usually painted from a swipe file of clippings from magazines. I looked for certain kinds of off-guard grimaces in the *papparazzi* photos. This did not fit Kiddy's notion of the artist.

"Why don't you create something of your own?"

"Francis Bacon does it. Ben Shahn did it."

"Stop comparing yourself," Kiddy would say. "Don't be such a genius."

I knew what a genius was. Wim Shilling was a genius. If Titian had painted with his penis, I painted with my *pupik*. I dug it out of myself like lint from a belly button.

"You're becoming a character," Kiddy said, "a fifty-year-old hippy."

It was not all that easy to be one. I had not fully learned that life is to be lived, not to prepare to live. I was trying. Because I was in a hurry I may have tried too hard. I did not tell Kiddy of the times during the night when I would be thrown out of sleep by something that felt like the kick of a mule inside my chest. My pump went one, two, three, four, five, six, and then . . . "Come on, baby! Come seven! Papa needs a new pair of shoes!" I may have been playing against the house with loaded dice but I was on a good roll.

The acrylics were splashing when Kiddy stormed in and, without asking, shut off the Sony. She had never done anything like that. Cutting off the blues was like cutting the cord to your own telephone. In Emergency Dial 911.

I painted awhile in awful silence, then walked out of the house.

· 36 ·
Life Class

I ran into Jeffries in front of the bar at the Giudecca ferry crossing.

"*Ciao,* old bean!"

Jeffries was the only person in the world who called me old. But he was very Brish and the Brish are allowed to call you anything they like as long as they show their Players-stained, crooked teeth. Didja ever see a Brisher—outside of the Prince of Wales—who had good teeth?

"Prende qualcosa?" "Take a little something?" was the Venetian equivalent of "Have a cuppa?"

We went in and I bought Jeffries a "baby." That's what they call a shot of whiskey here. A baby. Like that, in English.

"What's shakin', man?" I said. The more Brish Jeffries got, the higher uptown in Harlem I moved. Sugar Hill. Hotel Theresa where Fidel waved the live chickens at the *Daily News* photographers.

One Haig and Haig led to another. I didn't like Scotch. I had my usual double "corrected" coffee, two shots of brandy in a thimbleful of espresso. It was funny. I felt honored to be buying this kid drinks. He was a "real" painter. What the hell was I? A searcher of physiognomies, I guess.

"I'm having a life class today," Jeffries said. "Why don't you come? The model's all paid."

I knew other models Jeffries had who were not paid. He looked something like a young Francis Bacon but his forte was a kind of *Playboy* bunny dressed in feathers and real glass spangles he glued onto their hides. Stuff for hotel lobbies. They sold well enough for Jeffries to live in borderline bohemian style. He had a studio big as Grand Central Station. Every Saturday night was party night. Jeffries supplied a *pasta e fagole* and you brought the wine or anything else. The first time Kiddy and I came, we brought cream cheese and lox, *salmone affumicato,* just for New York's sake. It disappeared before you could say Enrico Berlinguer.

Once a year, Jeffries gave life classes for a London prep school which offered a Venetian "experience." I needed time to think over the offer. It excited and frightened me in about equal parts.

"Do you good," Jeffries was saying. "You've got a bleeding museum in your head."

I had my Rapidograph in my pocket. Its point was so fine you could draw a line as thin as a cunt hair. I had never had a chance to try it on the real thing.

When I saw how young my fellow students were, I felt like a dirty old man. They all had giant sketch pads, charcoal sticks, and smudgers. They were set to make a single literal study of the kind I could never do. My strategy was to make many quick sketches and hope for the best.

The model's name was Paola. I knew her slightly from the bar next to the Academy of Fine Arts. She was about nineteen. When she undressed her parts were startling, heavier, more defined and fleshy than I had expected. She was not nude—she was naked. I had read Lord Clark on the difference. The studio was cold. The girl's body turned as blue as the acrobat's woman in Picasso's *La Vie*.

Jeffries suggested difficult poses, I thought. Because Paola was being paid, he was laying it on with a heavy hand. Paola was not professional and everything she did so obediently came through as an awkward, erotic compliance. Paola's labia showed purple as she twisted and lifted. Jeffries even got her on all fours. She reminded me of the girl in the chicken feathers in *La Dolce Vita*. She was wearing a heart-shaped locket and when her breasts fell forward, it swung between them like a bell.

I drew very rapidly. The scratch of my pen was the only sound in the room. I was working in line, shading in the hairy places with a few squiggles. Like many girls from the south, Paola did not shave under the arms. I indicated that, tickling her with India ink. And between her legs, too. I stylized her face, focused on the eyes looking out from a helmet of curly sheep's hair. I always tried to get the eyes to reflect an awareness of being seen. That made them look alive.

Jeffries called a rest. Paola put on a kind of duffle coat that came just to her mons. She pressed her legs together and blew on her hands. I was touched. It could have been her first life class, too. The English were indifferent, showing their charcoals to each other, saying inconsequential broad-A'd things that sounded like a Pinter play. The boys all seemed to be called Cyril and the girls all looked like Mrs. Astor's pet horse.

I lit a cigarette and saw Paola looking at me, wanting one but not ready to ask.

"*Fuma?*" I offered her a Marlboro. They were the most popular cigarettte in Italy.

"*Grazie.*" Paola's voice was hoarse with laryngitis.

When she bent to my light, the duffle coat opened. Paola pulled it to her with one hand. She had probably grown up sharing a bedroom with brothers, possibly her parents. The difference in our ages suggested incest.

"*Freddo,*" she said. When a Sicilian girl says it's cold, you can believe it.

"*Non che riscaldamento,*" I said. The Italian word for heat sounds like cold—coldwater-flat-*tenemento.* There was a ceramic stove in the room but too far away from Paola to do her any good. I was wearing a flannel Pendleton and over it a Columbia sweatshirt with my Alma Mater's motto, *In Vino Veritas* or some such.

"*Parla bene Italiano,*" Paola said timidly. It is customary to flatter the foreigner even when he is murdering your language.

"*Bruto, bruto,*" I said. Badly, brutally. *L'art brut,* that's what I was making of this goose-pimpled kid, a men's-room *graffito.*

The recess ended. Jeffries put Paola into a kind of odalisque pose, on one elbow, one leg over the other, making a shadow V at her sex. I did a dozen drawings on the Delacroix principle that if a man jumps from a window he should be drawn before he hits the ground. It was harder now to separate the girl from her lines. I was paying much more attention to her face. The eyes looked at you, indolent and ready.

Time ran out. Paola pulled on a kind of lavender leotard. She stepped into cork platform shoes before she hooked her bra. I turned away. She had that pathetic look Fellini gets into backstage scenes of small vaudevilles.

I watched her leave. My eyes which had put her parts on paper saw her now, in those absurd shoes, as provocative and available. She would go with you, not for money but for a little praise and a pizza.

Jeffries, looking over my shoulder, had been impressed by the vigor of my drawings. "Keep it going, old bean," he had said. He wanted me at the next class. There would be a new model. He mentioned a French woman who had modeled at the Beaux Arts.

"This one's a klutz," Jeffries said.

I laughed. Jeffries was a hipster. He would prefer a professional. Paola's amateur *verismo* had gotten to me.

The fog began to roll in as I walked home, the famous Venetian *nebbia* that comes on in minutes and hides the city from itself and makes people forget who they are. And I was already not myself. *The dirty old man goes to life class* . . . Life class? That was a curious name for it. *Scuola di nuda* the Italians call it, school of the nude. School of hard knockers. *Paola. Crayola.* Rhymes were running through my head. *His eyes become two pencils . . . More naked in her bra and purple pantyhose/Than in those ravished minutes that she froze.* Ravished? I knew enough about what comes unbidden, washes up from roiling sea of words not to deny the impact, the depth charge of this naked girl.

What would it be like with Paola? There were plenty of old geezers around with young chicks on their arms. Look at Picasso! Look at Pablo Casals! Look at Tommy Manville! I had seen couples like that in my office. The man was usually a dress manufacturer and the girl would be one of his models for whom he had left a White Plains wife and family. The complaint would be that she was not interested in sex. "I get more out of a hand job," one guy said. And the ex-model crossed her nifty legs and said, "So . . ."

What could I do for these vulgarians? What could I do for myself? Kiddy was pushing me in their direction, the "find 'em, fuck 'em, and fool 'em" world.

"You only stay with me because you're afraid to be by yourself," Kiddy had begun to say.

I told her that she was working on a self-fulfilling prophecy, making me do what she was afraid I was going to do. She was right about my not wanting to be by myself. Let's say I tried it, not with a kid like Paola, but with some divorcée or young Venetian widow. There were some around who made eyes at me. What would we talk about?

"Didja ever hear of Herbie Hoover the Engineer? Didja ever see a family of Okies on Route 66 in a Model-T Ford with two flat tires? Didja ever neck all night on the beach at Belmar, New Jersey? Didja know Delmore Schwartz went there? No, of course not. Didja ever see Leopold Stokowski and Deanna Durbin in *One Hundred Fingers and a Girl*? Didja cock today? Didja ever have a pastrami sandwich on rye with dill pickle and Dr. Brown's Cel-Ray Tonic? Didja ever pledge allegiance to the flag and to the Republic for which it stands? Didja? Wontcha? Wouldja? Couldja?"

Kiddy was waiting for me, worried because I'd been gone so long. I told her about Jeffries' life class.

"How did it go?" Kiddy asked.

"Okay," I said. I could have told her a poem-full.

She wanted to hear more. But I did not know how far I could go with the truth. I saw now that my new courage rocked the boat of our established dependencies. I had not realized before that Kiddy could be daunted, and so easily.

"Let me see."

She opened the sketchbook. I looked over her shoulder and saw my own gropings, a grotesque foot, a dwarfed torso on ostrich legs. And then came a drawing that caught Paola in all her expectant nakedness. My eye had really been looking.

And Kiddy was looking pretty hard, too, first at Paola's heavy young breasts, and then up at me and at Paola's little cave hidden by a blueberry bush and up at me and at Paola's waiting eyes and at mine and I felt a surge of loving closeness for Kiddy. It rose in me like the kick of alcohol, bootleg Booth's High and Dry in my first speakeasy with Nick, White Mule, calvados in a bistro near Notre Dame.

"Kiddy," I wanted to tell her, "what's left of it could be the best time of our lives. *Miracolo!* We're young again!"

It was not true. Paola was young. And my wife was looking at that sacred heart I had placed between the model's juicy nipples. I had indicated them as petals of flowers.

"Slightly Matisse," I said.

"Why do you always say it's like somebody else?" Kiddy said with a little more steam than I liked.

"Because," I said.

We were right back to square one.

· 37 ·

Walking the Dog

And we stayed that way until Kiddy scrammed, took a powder, shuffled off to the University of the Estranged and left me, as the fellow said, between a rock and a hard place. The days were bad enough but the nights were like being in one of those sensory deprivation tanks in a psych lab.

Days, at least, I can hang around the gallery-workshop of Luciano who printed the serigraphs for my first show. Luciano will "take a little something" with me at any hour. And there's a chance of running into some painters who come in to touch up a negative or check on a color. They accept me as one of them, tell me my work has candor, that I must show in Milano. I am too sophisticated for the shopkeepers here who buy only for investment. This is good medicine for me. Better than the Negronis I drink with Rinaldi who always paints the same blue-eyed girl sitting in front of a mirror so you can see her tits and her ass at the same time. You find her in every hotel room in Venice. Rinaldi is a fan of mine. He warns me not to learn any tricks lest I become like him a big whore, a *grossa putana*. Rinaldi makes a lot of money and loses it at the Casino. He is a great ladies' man. Reminds me of my Uncle Phil.

"C'mon, girlie," I say to the pooch.

"I love you madly," she says like Duke Ellington.

"Me, too, sshweetheart," I say to her like Humphrey Bogart and look around to see if anyone has heard me.

No one will. I am alone, deserted by that two-legged sweetheart who has been my wife for thirty years. Running away from home is getting to be a habit with Kiddy. Right now, I don't even have her telephone number.

The bells of the Church of the Redeemer, almost next door, are ringing the hour as I come out of our little alley onto the broad Giudecca Canal where the freighters come and go from the inferno of the refineries on the mainland. *Otto, nove, dieci, undici* . . . Eleven bells, bedtime.

Eleven is late in this hardworking quarter just four minutes by waterbus but a world away from the Gritti and Harry's Bar. By seven tomorrow morning, the paving blocks of the embankment will clatter with the clogs and spiked heels of Botticelli girls in Wrangler jeans dancing their asses into our one factory. They make cheap watches. When their mothers made bomb parts there during the war, the Nazis painted a yellow line around the area and shot at children who crossed it chasing a ball.

Green wooden shutters have sealed each house like a fort. Except for a faraway drunken song and the screams of oestrous cats making more blind kittens to be drowned, there is only the sound of the canal slapping against its stone banks. The moon is up and the water is high tonight. It splashes over the *fondamenta*, washing the marble steps of the Church of the Redeemer, sunken, green with barnacles. No Doge has trod here since Venice was divorced from the sea. Each wave leaves a littoral of orange crates and polyurethane sculpture. The dog ducks around the wake. I think she thinks she's at the beach on Martha's Vineyard.

"C'mon, girlie, do your stuff."

The terrier has her favorite corner in the angle of the plague-promised church where some grass pushes through the cracks in the paving stones. It's where the Franciscans in their brown robes walk to their dormitory. They don't mind. Stepping into a pile is considered to be good luck. When the dog makes her last circle and squats, she turns to me for approval. She has done her duty.

"Good girlie!"

She is eleven years old, my *cagna,* my bitch. She looks at me, turning her head and cocking one ear as though to say, "What's up?" It's a good thing Clara Bow bangs cover her eyes because you couldn't look at them without breaking up.

"Walkin' the Dog." Eddie Lang had a good solo on that. With Bix and Tram? Or Joe Venuti? What did it mean? Something dirty, of course. Why do we call it dirty when, baby, it feels so good? "Let Me Play with Your Poodle." The blues. Best American music. But killed a lot of guys making it. "What did Bix die of?" "Everything!"

"Maestro!"

Coming toward me is the big plainclothes cop of Giudecca making his last tour. We usually pass the time of night when I walk the pooch. He calls me Maestro because he knows I have begun to paint. The Italians are great on titles. So, though he's just an ordinary town cop, not even a tough *carabiniere,* I call him Brigadier. Sometimes I call him Commander and he calls me Professor.

"*Ciao, Comandante!*"

"*Carissimo Professore!*"

I get a kick out of hearing a cop call me "Dearest." The dog is licking the flatfoot's brass knuckles. He must speak to her, too.

"*Ciao, bella!*" he says to her.

And, wanting to talk to someone, I tell the cop again how big he is, how he could play guard for the Dallas Cowboys. Because a million lire isn't much, I have to tell him he will be paid *milliardi,* billions.

"*Si, si,* you could play professional!"

Big Boy likes this kind of talk. He has the bashful boy's laugh of a huge man. They say he was a Fascist. Who wasn't? The current government is Center-Right, and it is the time of

the referendum on abortion and the whole town is plastered
with posters. You had to vote no if you wanted to keep the new,
good law and yes if you wanted to throw it out.

VOTA NO! VOTA NO!

All those nos remind the cop of Kiddy. Kiddy is still fighting
City Hall. She debates with Big Boy.

"And the *Signora* is good?"

Bene, molto bene, benissimo. Big Boy knows there is something
unkosher about her being away. The whole island knows it.

"A woman very modern, *feminista*."

You just said a mouthful, Big Boy.

VOTA NO! VOTA NO!

All the pretty girls on the Communist posters saying "No!"
when they really meant "Yes!" Big Boy shakes his head. What is
the world coming to! Personally, he is voting yes. No *aborto* for
him.

"It is against God," he says piously.

"I pray you not to forget." My pal tells me again that I must
let him know at once if I have any trouble. He doesn't mean
the kind of trouble I am having right now. He salutes me.
"Comandi!" I have only to command him and he does not care
who they are, he will break their balls, *rompe coglioni.*

"Thank you infinitely, Brigadier!" But nobody is bothering
me but myself, and my balls have already been romped.

The honorary brigadier goes off into the *nebbia,* the famous
Venetian autumn fog that makes me think of Dr. Jekyll and Mr.
Hyde, of Jack the Ripper and Sherlock Holmes. *The Case of the
Missing Feminist, Or: Who Put the Pinprick in Tillie Peshkovitz's Pess-
ary?*

"Elementary, my dear Watson! The woman left her wedding
ring next to her tube of KY jelly and a tax-free bottle of Femme
by Rochas."

I get Petite Mite pointed in the right direction. I have to tug
at her leash. She does not want to go home any more than I do.
But there's nothing left outside.

I drag myself up the marble steps of my *casa.* Everything is
marble here. The steps are too high and slippery for the low-
slung dog. She has arthritis. I have to go down and give her a
push from behind. None of us is getting any younger.

"I grow old, I grow old. Shall I wear my trousers rolled and
part my bare behind?"

I climb into the queen-size bed, big enough for two people

to sleep without touching each other—*matrimoniale,* the Italians properly call it—and listen to jazz from Yugoslavia. The only word I understand is *saxaphona.* But I know it's John Coltrane and I listen hard to "Naima" and "My Favorite Things" until they sign off with the first chords of the "Internationale." Da dee da dee . . . Da dee da dee . . . Just those four chords. *"Arise ye pris . . . Arise ye pris . . ."* Like an unfinished poem, like the unfinished Revolution. Like my marriage. Or maybe it is finished.

This uncertainty tortures me. I am the ass between two bales of hay. Or is it between two tufts of pubic hair? It's getting harder for me to joke my way out of this glitch. I am slipping, slipping. The only thing I can hang onto—I'm as bad as Kiddy—is the past.

Radio Capodistria is still signaling. Out of the hum of dead air it comes, over and over. *"Arise ye pris . . . Arise ye pris . . ."*

The terrier is snoozing on Kiddy's pillow and I've got the empty-bed blues. And I get to thinking of Kiddy's soft places, more familiar now than when her pleated skirt flew in the air showing her "Sis! Boom! Ahhh!" to the whole grandstand when she was cheerleader at Clinton High.

"I'm nobody's sweetheart, now!"

The ol' Redhead! Flamingo! Titian Typhoon! I miss her as keenly as a part of myself. The best part, because Kiddy is my history before I became ashamed of my own triviality.

· 38 ·

The *Americanina*

"But tomorrow," as the gondoliers say, "he's another day!"

It was a perfect day, a great Saturday morning for the human race, including the Jews. I stopped at the first musty bar next to the church and had an espresso corrected with brandy. The owner poured generously. He knows I drink the coffee for the booze.

"Tutto okay, *Professore?"*

These people don't miss a trick.

"Tutto okey-dokey." I brushed off the barman's concern. *"Cosi si dice in Brookelino."*

"Hokey-dokey," he repeated. He had relatives in Brooklyn.

I was a great joker. And I was ready for another correction but I didn't want to make a *bruta figura.* That is the important thing, to make a good figure.

I crossed to the other side of the canal and under the Accademia Bridge I had a brandy without coffee. It was going to be one of those days. This old Buick needed a ring job. It was guzzling oil. The brandy was called OP, for *Ora Pila.* Oral pill? If Mirra had had the pill back in '38 would I be here now?

I made my way to Luciano's gallery, in the San Vio *sestiere,* rolling a little. Venice is a raft floating on thousands of trees brought from Dalmatia and driven into the mud of the Riva Alta, high bank, Rialto now.

Luciano and the apprentice were running the squeegee over Rinaldi's latest print, the usual nude with the usual exaggerated ass. They were doing the blue now for her startled eyes and the mirror into which she is admiring herself the way Rinaldi wanted you to admire her. He was making his normally unprintable comments on the *putana's* anatomy when this indubitable American girl-woman wearing miner's boots and the usual Levi's, with two bouncers under an Oakland Raiders T-shirt, came in, asking the way to Peggy Guggenheim's loaded *palazzo.*

"Where, *prego, il* Museum *di* Guggenheimer?

She seemed to have Peggy's joint mixed up with Old Guckenheimer, a cheap American rye. Italian gallantry would translate anything she said any way she said it.

The *Americanina* made an immediate impression on Rinaldi, who said something obscene in a dialect only older Venetian whores understand. I thought he was saying he saw the thigh of a plump chicken and would like a bite *a la cacciatora.*

I spoke good New Jersey *Inglese* and came to the rescue. Yes, Peggy Guggenheim's was around the corner. "But here, under your nose, are beautiful things no one else will see. Here, for instance, are a hundred nudes of the same girl by the great Rinaldi."

I introduced Rinaldi and he kissed her hand. Her name was

Rosemarie and Italy was absolutely *fantastico,* a gas. So we went across the alley to Adolfo's bar. Rinaldi came, drank a *bianco,* and munched chocolate kisses.

"*Ciocolattini?*" I asked him. "Why chocolates with wine?"

Rinaldi said he had an assignation with a titled lady, very noble, but an inexhaustible *putana.*

"I must eat chocolates for the energy."

And Rinaldi fluffed up the carnation in the buttonhole of his white suit and left us.

Rosemarie had been in Milan for a year doing PR and "hanging out." And now she was going home to El Ay but absolutely had to see Peggy Guggenheim's and the Giotto chapel in Padua if it was the last thing.

Adolfo was putting himself out for Rosemarie. He even brought a tray of midget ice cubes. "Please, lady, take ice." And I was telling him he must get an ice machine and I would teach him to make American drinks just like Harry's Bar and all the tourists going to Peggy Guggenheim around the bend would stop here to refresh. We would put tables outside and have waitresses in very short skirts.

"Carhops," Rosemarie said. And she would do the PR.

"Where will my friends go?" Adolfo wouldn't hear of it. "I will have money in the bank but I will be truly poor."

It was a shame to leave Adolfo. Adolfo is a sweetheart. But we went down the *calle* and saw Miss Guggenheim herself standing there on her stork legs in bright red Ferragamos, waiting on the little bridge with her two Shih Tzus, for the tourists to come out of her own house. I said hello to her. We had met. But you could see she didn't remember. She's got her own troubles. Including the little room in her museum set aside for daughter Pegeen's naif watercolors. What greater pain than to outlive one's own child?

We made a pause at a table outside Beppe's across from the Gritti and the Hemingway suite. Beppe served us himself. Beppe was a kid waiter when Hemingway used to drink at the old Ciro's. He wanted the writer's portrait. So I had done him an acrylic of Papa, bearded and apoplectic. Beppe brought us his special gondolier's champagne, a bubbly wine mixed with aperitif. I was making a *bella figura* with Rosemarie. Rosemarie was doing fine. She had the proverbial hollow leg.

She also had a roving eye. One of those young sharpies with

his shirt open to the top button of his fly and a bishop's cross hanging from a chain on his curly-haired chest, came over.

"Don't I meet you in Lido, miss? In Jesolo, miss? In Cortina, yes?" All that stale shit.

He wouldn't go away. I remembered that Beppe's was the hangout for the classy young whores of Venice. When I first saw them I thought they were all *contessas.*

"*Va fan culo!*" I said, tough as a Mafia soldier. "Up your asshole!" I said it properly now, with the right accent and inflexion, not the way we used to say it on Avon Avenue when we were as innocent of the language as we were of the act.

I didn't think Mr. Italia expected anything like this from me. How tough brandy and a girl on your arm talk! I didn't expect it myself. But I had the key to this city. You get it with a dollar account at the Banco Nazionale del Lavoro. The pimp didn't have one. Nor was he a *Professore.*

"If you didn't have gray hair," he said to me in Italian, "I would throw you in the canal."

"*Prova!*" I said, which means "Try it!" I had gondolier friends at the crossing by the Gritti, which was the nearest water.

Rosemarie caught on. She put her hand on my shoulder and the pimp went back to his table of whores who looked like a double-page spread from the Italian edition of *Vogue.*

Did I have gray hair? My New York driver's license still said: Color of hair—Blk; Color of eyes—Brn.

I guess I thought I was old Doctor Hemingstein himself. I was not of that generation but I was lost. Up shit creek without a paddle with Kiddy at the University of the Estranged. I'd had only one phone call from her.

"Do you have anything to say to me?" Each word was pulled from the guts of a piano fixed for some aleatoric piece by John Cage, sound, silence, sound, silence. What the hell do you say after thirty years of coffee, bagels, and the *New York Times* for breakfast? Maybe it was thirty-one years. One of Kiddy's big grievances is that I always forget our anniversary. And her birthday. And a zillion things I forget and remember and forget.

And I let myself forget my scruples and pushed open Harry's swinging door for Rosemarie, and the sun lit up bottles and leather and shiny wood. Ruggiero, the head bartender, gave us his diplomat's smile. If he had any questions about why the woman I was with was not my wife, he was not asking them with his eyes. The only time I ever saw Ruggiero lose his cool was when a dozen Yugoslavs came into the bar and ordered milk all around.

"Two Jolly Rogers, Doctor?" Here I was Doctor.

We also ate some of those marvelous triangles of chicken and mayonnaise they put right under your nose so you think it's the free lunch but it isn't. And after the OP, the gondolier's champagne, and a couple of Rogerses, Rosemarie was saying, "You can't beat this with a stick."

I was beginning to think so, too.

I remembered that I had to walk the dog. Rosemarie had never been on Giudecca. "Come up and see my etchings," I said.

"Fantastico," Rosemarie said.

We took the Number Five, touched at San Giorgio, and got off at Redentore. Petite Mite de la Termitière was stretched out on top of the stairs waiting, as she had been for two weeks now, for the lady who combed her bangs and called her Dolly as in "Dahling!" The pooch was nice to Rosemarie, too. "If you want a friend, get a dog."

The three of us staggered down the *rio* to look at the palace of the late Queen of Yugoslavia. Petite Mite did her duty on the royal premises. I had to grab Rosemarie from falling into the canal. We raised a few eyebrows but I no longer cared that Rosemarie was doing the Watusi around me.

"Italia fantastico!" she was telling the natives.

In front of the Redentore Church, we ran into Roberto, the secretary of the Communist Party. He was taking a *passeggiata* with his wife and kid. I told Rosemarie who he was.

"No shit!" she said. She had never seen a real-live Communist.

Roberto was giving me the bad eye, the Politburo look.

"O Companion Roberto, don't look at me that way! We're on the same team. We're just playing in different ballparks."

"Ciao, Compagno!" I said to him, making us Comrades again, like it or not.

"Goodbye to you, Miss!" Roberto said to Rosemarie. And to his son, he said, *"Dai la signorina un bacio."*

But the little boy did not want to give Rosemarie a kiss. He was an exception.

I had trouble getting Rosemarie back to the house. She did not have the experience of the wine drunkards who handle the marble edge of the *fondamenta* like tightrope walkers.

I led Rosemarie by the hand into the nuptial bedchamber with its unmade *matrimoniale*. She barely made it. When she pulled the Oakland Raiders shirt over her head, I saw a pair of breasts flat and round with dark-brown nipples surrounded by mounds of corrugation that looked like shiners. Rosemarie pulled off her boots and fell against the wall.

"Jesus, Joseph, and Mary!"

There was no panic in her drunkenness, no concern about being at the will of a man stranger to her by less than a day. I guess she had my number. Rosemarie rolled her Levi's down. Now her panties came off. She had a triangular mons that ran across the bottom of her belly to the tops of her legs. She was surprisingly broad-hipped. That didn't show in clothes. Rose-marie's face was so lively it directed all your attention to itself. Right now she looked like an overdeveloped high-school girl getting undressed for gym.

She fell on the bed and curled up like a fetus, this woman-girl, half my age. I moved against her, put my arms around her. She was still conscious enough to say, "Please, no. I don't want to!" And then she passed out.

I had just enough juice feeding from the Con Edison of the old Superego to hear her loud and clear. Whatever rein the situation gave me to do with or without her assent, a tight bit at the mouth of memory pulled me up short.

I stared at that back with its short valley down her spine running into two hills of plump. Rosemarie was, as we boys say, all ass. The Willendorf Woman. I felt only a tingle of engorgement. Remarkably, she was not as desirable as the Ol' Redhead. There wasn't time to go into the whys and wherefores. But Kiddy was giving the interloper in her bed a good twenty years and winning hands down.

I placed Boytchik close to the divide of those two mounds of avoirdupois. There he rested, beyond desire, beyond frenzy, content as an opium smoker after two pipes.

· 39 ·
The White Ship

We woke up with huge hangovers. Rosemarie knew that I had not harmed whatever part of herself she still held inviolate. She gave me a big whiskey kiss. We were as naked as jaybirds but we might as well have been dressed by Pierre Cardin.

"You're a nice guy!"

Nice guy, my eye! The leopard doesn't change his spots. They turn gray. His hide goes bald in patches and is scarred by the claws of tougher, honcho cats. His teeth rot. He wears a bridge. His canines are so loose, his Italian dentist calls them ballerinas. But he still thinks he's King of the Jungle. But it's a constitutional monarchy, now. One man, one vote.

"Don't be ashamed of it," Rosemarie said.

I made *caffe latte* for us. With it I took my usual pharmacy of pills. I added a five-grain Valium. My heart was going like a bop drummer, in and out and around the beat. Rosemarie was game for Padua. My *tristezza* didn't want company. But I had promised to show Rosemarie the Giottos and Donatello's big horse.

We hopped the Circolare to Piazzale Roma and got a bus that pulled across the causeway and through the industrial plants in the Port of Venice that always reminded me of what you see from the Pulaski Skyway that takes you to the place where I was born.

The bus stopped right in front of the Church of the Hermits. But I needed a pick-me-up. Rosemarie was not averse. I took her to the Cafe Hildebrandt. I knew they made Alexanders there. I had shown some prints in a gallery down the street. There was a poster of my show still in the window. That was a nice surprise.

The bartender remembered me and took the poster down for me to autograph. His name was Egoberto. I wrote: "*A mio caro amico Egoberto.*" Every bartender is my *caro amico*. When I held out some toilet-paper lire notes, he refused my money.

"You've got it made, fella!" Rosemarie was impressed.

We had one Alexander and then we drank the brandy called OP.

"Oral Pill," I translated for Rosemarie.

"Ask him if he's got any IUD," she said brightly.

I took Rosemarie back to the Eremitani. She put a handkerchief on her head. The Church doesn't care how drunk you are as long as you are dressed properly. We looked at the Mantegna fragments. Padua had been plastered by our Air Force. Luckily the Giotto frescoes just a ball field away had not been hit. We looked at the panels of Christ's *Via*. They were like a big comic strip. The first "human" paintings in the West.

We went past the university to the Great Hall of the Council and walked under Donatello's giant stallion. His balls were big enough to fire from a cannon.

We crossed the Piazza delle Erbe, the market square, and bought roasted chestnuts. We ate them looking into a window of bridal dresses, using up our supply of platitudes about marriage.

"No question about it," Rosemarie said at one point, "they're either made in heaven or they're nowhere."

It was time for her to go. I put her on a *rapido* for Rome. All her worldly goods were in a pack on her back. Rosemarie found a seat, lowered the window, and waved.

"Chow mein!" she called out, cute and tough.

I waited until the train pulled out. It was like an Italian movie we used to see at the New Yorker Theater on Eighty-eighth Street and Broadway. Now I was in it. Vittorio Gas Man and Gina Lowerthebritches.

I rode back from *terra firma* that ended at the big Municipal Garage. The Numero Cinque took me around the unpretty backside of the Serenissima, full of rusting tramp steamers, silos painted with extremist slogans.

I was sitting in the open rear of the *vaporetto*. Throughout this itinerary, a couple of sixteen-year-olds held each other in one kiss. They were lost to the world. Both of them were wearing jeans. The boy's hair was longer than the girl's. Unisex, but not quite. When they pulled apart for a moment, I saw that the girl was wearing a T-shirt that said MAKE LOVE NOT WAR in English. Two adolescent points pushed out the peace symbol. The kid didn't have too much equipment for either activity. They started young over here. They were still at it when I got off the boat. I used to kiss Kiddy that way in her hallway. You clutched until your arm fell asleep.

There was a letter from America pushed through the slot marked *Lettere*. It was from my old friend Julie, the Mad Fiddler. I hadn't heard from him in years. I pinched it in my fingers as though it were a Fourth of July cherry bomb with a sizzling fuse.

Petite Mite was waiting for me at the top of the stairs. She sat there all day now that Kiddy was away. She barked at me. I deserved it.

"Okay, girlie," I said and put my finger in her mouth. She held it in her teeth but did not bite. "Wanna biscuit?"

The pooch ran around in circles. I needed a biscuit myself. I went to the medicine cabinet and put a sublingual nitro under my tongue. The pooch was nipping at me.

"Momento," I said through my teeth. The nitro was waking up my mouth. I only took it because there wasn't anything else that gave such an illusion of doing yourself some good. I needed a drink but I didn't think it was recommended to chase nitroglycerine with Canadian Club. I slit the envelope open with my palette knife.

Mirra is dead! Cancer of the breast. Dying with dignity, I am told, at her easel until the last. Oh my God! Beautiful Mirra who modeled at the League. Fastidious Mirra! Julie wrote that she wore a little Renaissance cap to hide that her hair was gone, sheared by chemotherapy. Mirra! I worshiped you! Mirra! My bride! And before, in the studio we whitewashed together, you usually so careful about the diaphragm and jelly. What do they do with that unformed thing that is a child? What do they do with the severed orb? Which of those two rising beauties did they take? The left which you showed me reached slightly lower than its twin? That breast might have nursed our child. Mirra! Everything was my fault. Forgive me! Let me explain. No, I don't want to explain. I explained too much. I should have banged my fist on the table and said, "No questions! I am your husband. This is the way it will be because I say this is the way it will be!" We will go to your studio and crank up the old Victrola and I will kiss you, stopping only to put on the Pathé record of Django Reinhardt, may he rest in peace! And kisses interrupted, then Frankie Newton, may he rest in peace! And Louis, may he rest in peace! And Velma Middleton, may she rest in peace! And Edward Kennedy "Duke" Ellington, may he rest in peace! The whole world is spinning around, nice and slow, 78rpm cranked by me, nothing in this world but this Tin Pan, low-down, funeral song.

I don't know how long I sat there staring at an empty canvas, sized, locked in the easel, ready to be defiled by the likes of me, crazy old dilettante. And Mirra dead. I wanted to dig a hole and crawl in with her.

I went out on the terrace. I was nursing a Canadian Club on the rocks. I swallowed the last of my drink, sucking the whiskey from the ice. Dusk was falling on our sandbar. Off the Lido side of the lagoon, the big Fiat sign went on. The boat from the island of the mad was making its last trip. On the Giudecca Canal, I watched a white ship flying the hammer-and-sickle being pulled easily by two tugs. One was called *Strenuus*. The other one was called *Fortuus*. The ship's name was *Odessa*. Odessa where the sailors of the *Potemkin* revolted, maggots in their meat, Eisenstein showing them in closest closeup. That incandescent Edison's invention; first put His Master's Voice into a box, then Eyes and Ears of the World. "Up, periscope! Up Evil Eye!"

If Kiddy's mother had stayed in Odessa, I thought, no Kiddy for me, ending up in that mountain of corpses filling the ravine of Babi Yar. And my own mother not too far away. *Einsatzgruppen*. A frightened face in a photograph of frightened faces. And no Jay for us, the flame of life curled in a wisp of smoke from the oven of Treblinka.

That did it. I went to the phone and gave *Centralino* Kiddy's number very carefully, spelling her name in code. There is no *k* in Italian. The phone rang. I waited for Kiddy's actressy voice.

My heart was outside my skin now, I could see it as much as feel it. Suddenly, everything was very clear. I had been sick. And I knew why. I was sick of being ashamed of myself. Sick of all calculations and miscalculations—a whole journal of miscalculations. Sick of annulments. Sick of separations. Sick of all shitty meanness. I want to make up for it all! Join the human race, love everybody. Keep them all with me in one big tent like a sheik before they found oil. Like Grandpa Avrom, all in one ferocious tribe eating "a nice piece of fruit" out of my hand! Everybody! My half-blind Mama who still wants to run the American Jewish Congress. And Pop who was happier in Russia in his tsarist schoolboy cap. And my kid sister who thought I was great even when I zipped her head into the cover of my tennis racket.

"Quiet on the set! Camera! Action!" *Sweethearts*—A Vitaphone Production—Take 1. *Fade in*. Mirra shorn of her flame-colored hair, clipped like a French collaborationist whore. *Fade out.* Laurie dragging me drunk up the stairs. *Fade in, pan up.* To Fanny scrubbing, singing, showing her holy twat. *Dissolve.* Kiddy in her cigarette-girl short skirt running from the Cossacks on Union Square, crying out, "Don't hit him! He's my son!" *Lap dissolve.* Jim Howard, the Old Sky Pilot, marrying Gypsy to the Wrath of God. *Wipe lap dissolve. Fade in.* Jay taking his first baby steps. *Fade out.* Nick with his wicked smile and those moony Abruzzi eyes, waving a fifth of Booth's High & Dry. *Dissolve. Optical.* Now, now, showing Gale Storm in her girdle, her silk thighs hissing, and me, seventeen, eighteen, nineteen, worshiping, blundering, innocent, gauche, gifted, happy, crazy, gunning a zippy roadster right through a montage of pages flying from a calendar, on, on, into my incompleted life.